Dear Reader,

The editors at Harlequin and Silhouette are thrilled to be able to bring you a brand-new featured author program beginning in 2005! Signature Select aims to single out outstanding stories, contemporary themes and oft-requested classics by some of your favorite series authors and present them to you in a variety of formats bound by truly striking covers.

We plan to provide several different types of reading experiences in the new Signature Select program. The Spotlight books will offer a single "big read" by a talented series author, the Collections will present three novellas on a selected theme in one volume, the Sagas will contain sprawling, sometimes multigenerational family tales (often related to a favorite family first introduced in series) and the Miniseries will feature requested, previously published books, with two or, occasionally, three complete stories in one volume. The Signature Select program will offer one book in each of these categories per month, and fans of limited continuity series will also find these continuing stories under the Signature Select umbrella.

In addition, these volumes will bring you bonus features...different in every single book! You may learn more about the author in an extended interview, more about the setting or inspiration for the book, more about subjects related to the theme and, often, a bonus short read will be included.

Watch for new stories from Janelle Denison, Donna Kauffman, Leslie Kelly, Marie Ferrarella, Suzanne Forster, Stephanie Bond, Christine Rimmer and scores more of the brightest talents in romance fiction!

We have an exciting year ahead!

Warm wishes for happy reading,

Marsha Zinberg

Marsha Zinberg
Executive Editor
The Signature Select Program

SPOTLIGHT

JOANNA WAYNE

The Gentleman's Club

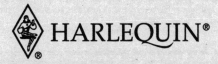

HARLEQUIN®

TORONTO • NEW YORK • LONDON
AMSTERDAM • PARIS • SYDNEY • HAMBURG
STOCKHOLM • ATHENS • TOKYO • MILAN • MADRID
PRAGUE • WARSAW • BUDAPEST • AUCKLAND

ISBN 0-373-83651-1

THE GENTLEMAN'S CLUB

This edition published by arrangement with Harlequin Books S.A.

® and TM are trademarks of the publisher. Trademarks indicated with ® are registered in the United States Patent and Trademark Office, the Canadian Trade Marks Office and in other countries.

www.eHarlequin.com

Printed in U.S.A.

Dear Reader,

New Orleans has always had a special mystique that intrigues everyone who visits this fascinating city nestled in a crescent of the Mississippi River. Writers from Tennessee Williams to Anne Rice have found the city's unique blend of Old South, voodoo and sultry sensuality the perfect setting for their works, as have many writers in all fiction genres. Romance and romantic-suspense writers are certainly no exception to this draw, and over the past ten years, I have set many of my stories in this area. When I first got the idea for *The Gentleman's Club*, I knew that the story and the French Quarter were a perfect fit.

The Gentleman's Club is a story of men posing as gentlemen though their hearts are black and their deeds are incredibly evil. But it is also a story of a man and woman who are willing to fight for what they believe in no matter the cost to their personal lives. More, it is a sensual story of passion and falling in love in the midst of danger; and a mystery with lots of twists and turns and the type of emotional wallop I like to deliver.

I love to hear from readers. Please visit my Web site at joannawayne.com. You can write me at joanna@joannawayne.com or Joanna Wayne, P.O. Box 265, Montgomery, TX 77356. Include an SASE to receive an autographed bookplate.

Happy reading!

Joanna Wayne

PROLOGUE

"ONE, TWO, buckle my shoe. Three, four, shut the door." The little girl shivered as she chanted the words, her shaky voice filling the dingy bedroom. "Five, six, pick up sticks."

She was too big to cry. Mommy said so. She closed her eyes tightly, as if that could shut out the loud voices that shook the house like stomping monsters.

"Seven, eight, lay them straight." She slid from the bed and scooted her bottom across the rug, her limp dolly hugged against her chest, the wiry doll hair tangled in her trembling fingers. She didn't stop until she reached the back corner of the room.

"Don't be afraid, baby," she crooned to the lifeless doll. "My mommy will be all right. She will." A tear pushed from her eye and slid down her cheek. She brushed it away with the sleeve of her flannel pajamas.

The high-pitched voice from beyond the door broke into sobs, and the little girl buried her head in her arms and rocked back and forth. She was sucking her thumb like a big baby, but she didn't care—not now. "Mary had a little lamb."

Suddenly, a noise like thunder cracked through the house, and the door to her room shook as if it had been struck with a giant fist. She huddled in a tight ball, quiet now, the words to the nursery rhyme swallowed up by her fear.

She cowered in the dark corner, clutching the doll and waiting for her mommy to take her in her arms and tuck her back into bed. But the door didn't open, and the house stayed silent.

"Mommy?"

Still clinging to her doll, she pushed herself to her feet and crept toward the closed door. She wrapped her shaking fingers around the cold roundness of the doorknob and twisted. The door didn't budge.

It couldn't. It was stopped by the dead weight of a woman who'd never answer to Mommy again.

CHAPTER ONE

IT WAS a quarter to eight when Rachel Powers slipped her key from the lock and stopped to stare at the brass nameplate that gleamed from the center of her office door. Rachel Powers, Attorney at Law. Taking a tissue from her handbag, she gave the *Attorney* a quick swish. She hated smudges on her one bit of identity in a building where she bobbed just above the bottom of the seniority pool.

She breathed in the odors as she stepped through the heavy wooden door. The rich fragrance of leather, the subtle scent of vanilla from the half-used bag of flavored coffee she kept stashed away in the top drawer of her file cabinet, traces of perfumes and musky aftershaves left by clients and colleagues.

Early morning was her favorite time in the office. It was stately, judicious, the way she'd imagined a law office would be when she'd been struggling to get her degree and pass the bar. Before she went to work for a firm where the bottom line defined justice.

If you can't stand the heat, look somewhere else for employment. That had been Phillip Castile's advice the day he'd interviewed her for the position she'd finally landed. Welcome to the law firm of Williams, Williams and Castile.

Rachel slipped her arms from the raw-silk jacket of her forest-green suit and draped it over the back of her chair. The suit was her most expensive piece of clothing and her favorite. It brought out her skin coloring and the lighter locks of her short auburn hair.

Mostly she liked it because it wasn't gray or navy or black, the colors the firm requested their young attorneys wear. But forest green was as far as she dared push the limit.

She pulled the file for Ballin Industries then settled at her desk to pore over the research the firm's most efficient law clerk had compiled yesterday. *Chaos* was the first word that came to mind. Ralph Ballin was in his seventies, and he hadn't changed his accounting methods since Lyndon Johnson had been in the White House.

The attorneys for the new and friendlier U.S. Treasury Department were surely counting on a field day with his antique methods of record-keeping. But at least with Ballin it was inability to adjust to new technology and not greed that had led to his intimate relationship with the lawyers of the IRS.

"Already at it. What did you do, sleep here last night?"

Rachel highlighted a couple of figures she wanted to return to, then glanced up to find Ted Boyd standing in her doorway. He looked great as always, suave and boyishly handsome and more rested than she ever was these days. "I sleep here every night," she said. "Didn't you know?"

"I believe it."

"What brings you in so early?" she asked.

"A case review that Williams Senior wants by noon. Tell me again why I thought being an attorney was better than working in my dad's used furniture store."

"It gives you a better pickup line with babes in the bars."

Ted snapped his fingers. "How could I forget?"

"I'd love to chat with you," she said, looking back to the

case file, "but I have a meeting with the IRS at ten, and I need to know what I'm dealing with when I talk to them."

"Who's the IRS attorney?"

"Mark Effring."

"Then you better have your shit together. He treats every tax dollar as if it were food being yanked from the mouths of his own kids."

"So I've heard." More reason she didn't have time to waste. She walked over to close her door as soon as Ted walked away, but his voice regained her attention.

"Are you looking for someone?"

"Yes. I'm here to see Rachel Powers."

The voice was female, tentative, almost as if the woman was unsure she had the name right or that she was in the right place. Rachel kept the door open a crack so that she could hear the conversation.

"Is this business or personal?" Ted asked.

"Business."

"Do you have an appointment?"

"Yes I do."

A blatant lie. Rachel had no appointments scheduled until her 10:00 a.m. visit with the IRS attorney. She peeked through the door, hoping to get a glimpse of the visitor without being seen.

The woman was standing near where the corridor split off from the reception area. Her back was to Rachel, but still Rachel was pretty sure she didn't know her.

She was in heels—a couple of inches higher than anything in Rachel's closet—and a pair of hip-hugging designer jeans that fit low enough below the waist that they revealed a wide border of perfectly tanned flesh between them and a silky, long-sleeved blouse. She did not fit the image of their usual corporate clients.

Ted would have come to that same conclusion by now and would probably have already checked her credentials and ushered her out the door if he hadn't been so busy ogling her breasts. Even from here, it was pretty evident by the slant of his eyes and the way he was leaning over the woman that he was checking her out.

The woman backed up a couple of steps. "I don't have a lot of time," she said. "I really need to see Ms. Powers *now.*"

Spunky—or else desperate. At any rate something in her voice got to Rachel. She knew she should let Ted take care of this, reminded herself of that fact even as she opened her mouth and did the unthinkable.

"Oh, there you are," she called. "I didn't expect you quite this early."

Ted shot Rachel a look that indicated he thought she'd lost her last shred of sanity. The woman muttered a low thanks and marched into Rachel's office.

Rachel motioned her to take a seat, but didn't take one herself. Instead she leaned against the backside of her desk and continued her assessment of the woman and the situation.

She was midtwenties at the most, probably younger, though there was a hint of hardness in her delicate features. Great body. Long silky hair the color of the pale-yellow roses her Aunt Gladys used to grow. Her eyes were lost behind a pair of oversize, dark sunglasses that didn't hide the purplish flesh stretching over her left cheek. Someone had worked her over recently.

"I appreciate you seeing me," the woman said.

"Why did you lie about having an appointment?"

"I would have made an appointment—if there had been time."

"If we're going to talk, I need to know your name."

"Tess Shepherd. Ms. Tess Shepherd."

"I was about to have a cup of coffee," Rachel said. "Will you join me?"

"Coffee would be swell."

Rachel went to the coffeepot and filled two china cups.

"How do you take it?"

"Black."

She handed Tess the cup and took a satisfying sip of her own. It was her first of the morning. "Now, what is it you think I can do for you, Ms. Shepherd?"

"I need you to represent me in a custody battle," Tess said.

Now she knew the woman was in the wrong place. "How did you get my name?"

"From a friend. You come highly recommended."

"I appreciate that, but I'm afraid your friend gave you bad advice. This is a corporate firm and we don't deal with domestic issues."

"I'm not looking for charity. I can pay."

"It's not a matter of money."

Finally, the woman pulled the sunglasses from her face and met Rachel's gaze. As Rachel had expected, the tissue surrounding the eye was even more bruised than the cheek.

"Look, as far as I'm concerned, a lawyer is a lawyer. I've heard you're the best, and I need the best because I'm up against a wealthy, arrogant son of a bitch who thinks he can walk over me now the way he did five years ago. I don't intend to let that happen."

The rich, arrogant bastard description got Rachel's attention. She'd met more than her share of those since coming to work for WW&C.

"Is this rich son of a bitch the biological father?"

"Exactly. He thinks he can just walk up and take my sons from me, the way he takes everything else he wants. But he's

not going to get away with it. Not this time. I'll kill him before I let him have them. I swear I will."

Rachel used a calm voice, trying to defuse the woman's
anger. "I'm sure killing is not the best option. Why don't you
tell me a little more about the situation?"

"The situation is Logan McCain."

The name evoked an instant image, but surely they were
not thinking of the same man. "This wouldn't be Logan Mc-
Cain of McCain Construction?"

"McCain Construction. McCain Development. McCain
Towers. McCain take what we want and screw everybody
else. I'm sure you've heard of him."

More than heard of him. Rachel had met Logan briefly a
couple of weeks ago. He'd sat across the table from her at one
of the charity events members of WW&C were expected to
attend. She remembered the evening well. Logan McCain
was the reason.

Hard to buy that he was fighting this woman in a custody
battle. Yet here she was. Angry. Bruised. And asking for help.
But if there was any question before of Rachel's being able
to help her, it was off the table now. The McCain family was
not only wealthy, they were politically connected and socially prominent. There was no way in heaven or hell WW&C
would let Rachel touch this case.

But if Tess really was the mother of Logan McCain's sons,
someone would take the case. An attorney looking to make a
name for himself—or herself.

"Tell me about your relationship with Logan McCain."

"There never was a relationship. I was just a convenient
distraction."

"How long ago did this distraction take place?" Impulsively, Rachel reached over and flicked on the small recorder at the back of her desk.

"Five years ago. August 17, 2000. Danny and Davy are four."

"Twins?" Rachel asked, just to be sure she had this straight.

"Yes, twins." Tess took a slow sip of the coffee and stared into the cup.

"Has Mr. McCain provided financial support for the children?"

"No way," Tess answered, looking up. "Not a penny. I sell my soul to the devil on a regular basis, and I can afford to give them anything they need. I wasn't good enough for Logan McCain five years ago, so my sons wouldn't be good enough for the haughty jerk now."

"How did you meet Mr. McCain?"

"In a bar on St. Charles Avenue. I was out with some of my friends from school. Logan came around and started hitting on me."

"By school, you mean college?"

"High school. It was my eighteenth birthday. We were celebrating."

At least she'd been legal. She wondered if Logan had known that—or if he'd cared. "So you left the bar with Logan McCain?"

"Yeah. I know now it was stupid, but I didn't know shit about men then. He had a cool car, and he told me I was beautiful. I fell for his lines. Like I said, I was young and stupid."

"Where did you go when you left the bar?"

"We parked awhile, out by the lake. We started kissing, and things just got out of hand. You know how it is when your hormones are pumping."

"Did you ask him to stop?"

"As a matter of fact, I did. I started crying and told him to let me out of the car. He held me down."

"So you're saying he raped you?"

"I don't want to press charges against him at this late date. I just don't want the bastard getting his hands on my sons."

Rachel tried to listen objectively, lawyer-fashion, but all kinds of scenarios were running rampant through her mind and none of them made Logan McCain look like a gentleman. But she also knew that Tess Shepherd could be lying.

"Go on. You had intercourse with Mr. McCain and became pregnant. What was his reaction to that news?"

"There was no reaction. How could I tell him? You don't think he gave me his real name? He knew my name and number, but he never called again. He didn't want me, but now he wants my sons. And he has the money to hire any lawyer he wants. That's why I need you to represent me."

"So you never told Logan McCain that you were pregnant?"

"The boys were eighteen months old before I even found out who he was. I saw a picture of him in the society pages. He was escorting some debutante to her ball. Friggin' big shot. Wait, I can tell you exactly when that was, too. I have the date right here in my notes."

"Do you always keep such good records?"

"Always have. Now I even keep a duplicate copy of everything I do, and I mean names, places and dates." She thumbed through a small notebook. "Here it is, October 22, 2002."

She *was* precise. "Why didn't you call him then?"

"So he could take them away from us like he wants to do now?"

"From *us?*"

"My stepmother and me. She takes care of the boys while I work."

"Do you live with her and your father?"

"My father died while I was pregnant with the boys. Cancer. Never even got to see his grandsons."

"And you're positive Logan McCain is the father?"

"Oh, I'm sure, okay. He was the first guy I ever went all the way with, the only one until after the boys were born."

"If you didn't tell Logan McCain you gave birth to his sons, how did he obtain that information?"

"I'd love to know that myself. All I know is he found out…and now he's demanding I give them up or he'll take me to court and prove I'm an unfit mother."

"Would he have grounds to do that?"

"No, but he probably thinks he could just because I'm a dancer at the Fruits of Passion. That's a gentleman's club in the French Quarter. It's a classy place. There's no shame in working there."

Rachel studied Tess's expressions as she talked. She was usually good at reading the faces of clients. Sometimes it was the eyes, sometimes a nervous twitch or a catch in the voice when they veered from the truth. But Tess was hard to read. Maybe it was the bruises and the fact that her cheek and eye were swollen.

Still, Rachel was pretty sure Tess was leaving out a few pertinent facts. "Out of the blue, after almost five years of seemingly not knowing you existed, Logan McCain appeared and asked for custody of his sons. Was this at your house, on the street, at work?"

"Not *his* sons. *My* sons."

"Did Logan come to your house?"

"First he sent his personal lawyer. Mr. Artie Fonteneaux. What a creep that guy is. I know that date, as well. I can look it up if you need it."

"No need." Artie Fonteneaux. Rachel had heard of him. He had a reputation for being savvy and persuasive and was known for his piranha-like attacks on the opposition.

"Logan didn't show up until I told Fonteneaux what he could do with his orders," Tess continued. "Then Mr. Mighty showed up in person and mad as hell."

Rachel leaned over and ran a finger lightly over Tess's bruised cheek. "Did Logan do this?"

Tess stared into space without answering.

"You have to be honest with me, Tess, if you expect me to help you. Did Logan do this?" she repeated, her voice sharper than she'd intended.

Again, Tess looked away, this time studying her hands as they slid back and forth on the armrests. "Don't worry about the bruises. They're nothing. I got them while working out at the health club. One of the machines swung back and hit me in the face."

Rachel didn't buy that for a minute. "Being rich doesn't mean Logan's beyond the law or that he has the right to beat up women." Rachel waited until Tess lifted her eyes and met her gaze before she asked again. "Is he the one who used you for a punching bag?"

"I didn't come here about that. I came to hire you to help me keep my sons. Are you going to take my case or not?"

"I can't take your case, Tess, but I can recommend someone who knows a lot more about this sort of thing than I do."

"Is she an attorney?"

"No. She runs a center for abused women, and she's familiar with several attorneys. I'm sure she can hook you up with one who'll handle your case reasonably and competently." Rachel rounded her desk and retrieved one of her friend Karen's cards from the top drawer.

She handed the card to Tess. "I want you to call this woman, and I'm sure she'll be able to help you."

Tess took one look at the card for the Abused Women's Center, then stood and set her coffee cup back on the desk so soundly that the dark liquid spilled over the top and pooled onto the polished wood.

"Keep your phone number. My friend was wrong. I don't need your help. I can take care of this myself."

"No, wait, Tess. You can't fight this by…"

Her pleas were interrupted by the ringing of her phone. Rachel started to ignore it but thought better of it. Obviously the call hadn't gone through the receptionist, so whoever was calling had her extension. "Excuse me a minute, Tess." She picked up the receiver. "Hello."

"Just checking to see if you need me to get rid of your visitor," Ted offered.

"It's under control."

"Okay, just remember that I offered when Mark Effring is wiping up the floor with you."

"I'll remember." By the time Rachel hung up the phone, Tess was already out the door.

Exasperated and annoyed, Rachel went back to the file. She tried to regain her focus, but even with the prospect of facing Mark Effring staring her in the face, she couldn't totally put Tess Shepherd out of her mind.

She scribbled Logan McCain's name on a sheet of paper and tossed it in her to-do basket. She had no idea why except that she was almost certain that Tess's visit was going to come back to haunt her.

CHAPTER TWO

LOGAN MCCAIN stood outside the crumbling brick building on the edge of the French Quarter and stared at the flashing neon lights. Fruits of Passion: A Gentleman's Club.

The black-and-white sign hanging lopsidedly on the inside of the door said Closed. It was only 9:00 a.m., too early for even the party-hardy tourists to seek out the fruits just yet.

Logan walked over and peered through the glass. Two men were inside, propped against a wooden bar that stretched the length of a side wall. A cigarette dangled from the mouth of the hulk. The average-size guy was drinking from an oversize coffee mug and reading the newspaper.

Knotting his right hand into a fist, Logan banged on the door. The guy looked up from his newspaper, glared at Logan and pointed at the closed sign. Logan banged again. Finally the man sauntered in his direction, fumbled with the lock, then jerked the door open.

"We're closed," he barked, tapping a short, grizzled finger on the sign.

"This is a business call," Logan snapped, pushing his way inside the door. "I'm here to see Craig Graves."

The guy scratched his whiskered chin and stared at Logan, clearly not impressed that he knew the name of the owner of the establishment. "Mr. Graves is out of town."

"Who's in charge when he's away?"

"Me. Name's Elton Pierce. I'm the manager. So what is it you need?"

The man couldn't manage a spitting contest, Logan decided. Still, he might have the information Logan was after. "I need to see one of the dancers."

"Oh, that kind of business." The man's eyes lit up and a lecherous smile revealed a row of very white teeth that seemed at odds with the rest of him. "We open at eleven. Come back then and we'll show you all the action you can handle."

Logan walked past him and peeked through an open door and into a large, open room that smelled of stale cigarette smoke and staler sex. Lines of tables surrounded a circular stage, chairs upside down on top of them. No one else was in sight. Too bad.

The man pushed in front of him. "You don't hear any better than you read. I said we open at eleven."

Logan stepped back into the bar area. "I'm not here to check out your action. And I'm not impressed with your wisecracks. I want the address of Tess Shepherd."

"Yeah, well, we all got wants."

Logan caught movement from the corner of his eye and realized that the hulk had taken a few steps in their direction. Up close, he looked even bigger, his biceps rippling with muscle and tattoos that crawled beneath the rolled-up sleeves of a white T-shirt.

No way Logan could take him, and he wasn't stupid enough to try. He reached into the front pocket of his trousers and pulled out a monogrammed money clip. Slowly and deliberately, he peeled off two hundred-dollar bills.

The self-proclaimed manager merely grunted. "We don't run a dating service. If you want to see one of the dancers, show up and catch her in the act. If she wants to see you again, she'll be the one to tell you where to find her."

"Then Tess Shepherd does work here?"

"I never said that," the man snarled, his lips clenched into tight lines.

Logan wrapped the bills back into the clip. "I'll be back," he said, then turned and flashed a smile at the bruiser in the back corner. "Count on it."

Agitation bordered on silent fury as Logan strode out the door and back into the sunlight. Bourbon Street was coming to life. Residents out for morning strolls. A bag lady dressed in black, pushing a rickety grocery cart full of cans. A group of early-rising tourists carrying clear plastic cups of spicy bloody Marys, sploshing the red liquid onto the sidewalk as they laughed their way toward the day's fun.

Logan hurried past them, his usual quick gait even faster today. He had a meeting at ten with the bank officers who were handling the financing for the new condominium complex he had going up in the old Smithy warehouse, and then lunch with the building contractor.

Damn! He didn't have time for this. Tess Shepherd couldn't just disappear, not even in a city the size of New Orleans. He'd found her once; he'd find her again. His hands knotted into fists as frustration hammered against his temples.

A hand on his arm tugged him to a stop. He spun around and stared into the dark eyes of a striking young woman. Long ebony hair spilled over her shoulders and set off a flawless complexion. She was petite, but shapely. The kind of woman who'd make any man look twice.

"Are you looking for Tess Shepherd?"

"Yeah. Do you know where she is?"

"Yes."

"Where?"

"First we come to an agreement."

Logan pulled out his money clip and started to remove one of the hundred-dollar bills.

She waved him off. "I don't want your handouts."

"Then what *do* you want?"

"A promise that you'll never mention to Tess that you've talked to me. In fact, never mention it to anyone under any circumstances."

"Fine. Where can I find Tess?"

She pressed a folded slip of paper and a key into his hand. "You can find her here. And don't forget your promise."

"Who are…" Logan didn't get a chance to finish his question. The woman ducked behind a passerby and disappeared inside an open doorway.

Adrenaline pumping, Logan shoved the note into the pocket of his suit coat and headed in the direction of the printed address. He'd tried to be reasonable. Now it was time for a showdown that was almost five years overdue.

SATURDAY DAWNED gray and gloomy, another sunless weekend. Rachel padded across the thick beige carpet from her bedroom to her kitchen. She wasn't complaining. No need for sunshine when she'd have to spend most of her weekend cooped up in her windowless office finding a way to keep the IRS from sending Ballin into bankruptcy.

She started the coffee, then walked to the door of her condo and stuck her head and hand out into the hall for the morning paper. At least on Saturdays, she took time to make coffee at home and to linger over her bagel and cream cheese while she read the *Times Picayune* from cover to cover.

Her highlight of the week. Talk about exciting.

The coffee had begun to drip by the time she got back to the kitchen. Rachel sniffed. Brewing coffee had to be one of the top ten smells of the world.

She could see the list now, popping up on Letterman's *Late Show.* Chocolate cookies baking in the oven. Fresh pine at Christmas. Honeysuckle. The smell of Logan McCain when he'd leaned over her that night at the charity dinner to whisper in her ear.

Gorgeous. Sexy. Sophisticated. And possibly with a penchant for one-night stands and beating up women.

The dripping ceased, and Rachel filled her pottery mug to the top with the chicory-laden brew. Tess Shepherd and Logan McCain. Strange bedfellows, or maybe not so strange after all. Five years ago, Tess wouldn't have had the rough edge. She'd have been innocent and excited about her birthday. Logan would have been out of college by then and used to having any woman he wanted. A one-night fling with a woman hours past jail-bait status wasn't a shocker.

But the charming and very charismatic Logan McCain raping or physically abusing a woman in any way was tough to buy. Still, stranger things had happened, and frequently did in the Big Easy.

The piercing ring of the phone snapped her from her thoughts. She checked the ID. She was safe. It was her best friend and not her new and very nosy neighbor.

"You sound terrible," Karen said after they'd exchanged hellos. "Did I wake you?"

"No. Just haven't finished that first cup of coffee yet."

"Grab your morning paper. I'll wait."

"I've already got the paper. What's so interesting?"

"It's the woman you were asking me about—the one who came into your office yesterday with the bruises."

"Tess Shepherd. What about her?"

"Your instincts were right on target. She was in big trouble."

"Was?"

"Was. Section A, page 7, near the bottom."

Rachel scanned the paper until she found the photograph and the brief article.

Tess Shepherd, a dancer at the Fruits of Passion, was found strangled and beaten to death in her French Quarter apartment. The nude body was found by a friend just after 4:00 p.m. Shepherd had apparently been dead for several hours.

Tess. Murdered. The picture seemed alive, staring accusingly at Rachel. "I'll call you back."

"Are you okay?"

"I've been better," Rachel admitted.

She read the brief article again then stared at the photograph. It wasn't recent. Tess's hair was darker in the picture, long and straight, and her smile was sans bruises.

Rachel sipped the coffee but didn't taste it. Her mind went back to the night when she'd met Logan McCain. She didn't recall the specific charity or why Mr. Williams, Sr., had insisted she attend that particular function.

So why was every detail about Logan McCain etched in her brain? The muted stripe in the three-piece suit, the way his eyes had danced in the light, dark and mischievous, and too damned sexy for anyone to ignore him.

No longer hungry, Rachel forgot the bagel and headed to her bedroom. She had absolutely no facts to back it up, but her gut feeling was that Logan was tied to Tess's murder.

Thirty minutes later, Rachel was showered and dressed in

a pair of tan slacks and a yellow silk blouse. Dark suits weren't required on Saturdays. The doorbell rang as she rummaged in her handbag for her keys. It was probably her neighbor. The woman had way too much time on her hands.

Rachel swung open the door, but it was not her neighbor but Logan McCain who pushed into her space. He planted his right foot on her side of the threshold, blocking any chance to slam the door in his arrogant, unsmiling face.

CHAPTER THREE

RACHEL STARED at Logan as visions of a murdered Tess crept across her mind. Her gaze settled on his hands as if she expected to see blood dripping from them. But, of course, they were clean, smooth, the hands of a gentleman, except that a scratch ran the length of one finger, a jagged red pattern spoiling the perfectly tanned flesh.

"I know I shouldn't have stopped by without calling first," he said, "but this is urgent."

His gall was incredible. "What do you want, Logan?"

"To talk to you about Tess Shepherd."

"What about her?"

"Are you actually representing her in a custody battle?"

"How dare you ask me that at a time like this?"

"I just think that if you are, you should know the whole story."

Meaning his version of the story, no doubt. "I don't represent dead people, Logan."

"Dead? What are you talking about?"

If this was some kind of act to convince her of his innocence, it wasn't working. "You surely know that Tess was murdered yesterday."

His eyes darkened, and his face twisted in an unreadable scowl. "Son of a bitch."

"Your grief is touching."

He stared past Rachel as if she weren't standing there. The strain was showing now, plowing furrows into his forehead and giving new definition to the muscles in his neck.

"I didn't know. I wouldn't have barged in on you like this if I had—or maybe I would have."

She tried to push the door shut.

Logan didn't budge. "I'd still like to talk to you."

"I suggest you see your own lawyer and that you follow his counsel."

"I'm not interested in counsel. I'm interested in Danny and Davy."

"Then you've come to the wrong person."

"I can only imagine what Tess said about me, but cut me some slack here, will you? I need to locate the boys."

Locate them and take possession as if they were property or material goods and not two youngsters who'd likely just been hit with the news that their mother was gone forever. The realization of that struck a new nerve, and Rachel felt as if some giant fist had dropped from the clouds and crashed into her chest.

"I don't know what you want from me, Logan, but it's not going to happen. So do us both a favor and leave before I have to call security."

"I'm sorry Tess's dead. Really sorry. But can't you just listen for a few seconds?"

She retrieved her cell phone from her handbag and started to punch in the number.

Logan grabbed her wrist and held it so that she couldn't finish. "You saw Tess yesterday, Rachel. You had to see the bruises. I don't know what the hell she was into that got her killed, but there are two little boys out there that she may have dragged into the same mess. All I'm trying to do is make sure they're safe."

Damn him. How dare he try to twist this so that she had to help him in order to protect innocent children. "How do you know I saw Tess? Were you having her followed?"

"She told me she'd hired you to fight me in the custody battle."

"When did she tell you that?"

"Yesterday. I saw her after she'd been to your office."

That admission surprised her.

"Did Tess tell you where the grandmother had taken the boys?" he asked.

"I'm not free to discuss any of what Tess told me in confidence."

"You said yourself, you can't represent a dead woman." He took a deep breath and let it out slowly. "Look, let's both settle down. I'm sure we can get this straightened out if we talk calmly."

"You can have three minutes," she said. "Talk as calmly as you want, but talk fast."

"Be reasonable. Ask me in. This matter is too important to discuss in a doorway under the pressure of a stopwatch."

Rachel hesitated. She did need to calm down and try to think more professionally. Her gut feeling was that Logan couldn't be trusted, but she was basing all of that on the testimony of an exotic dancer she hadn't met before yesterday. Besides, if he'd come here to hurt her, he could have forced his way inside any time he wanted.

"Okay. You can come in," she said, "but only for a few minutes."

Reluctantly, she stepped back and he walked past her into the high-ceilinged foyer. She struggled for a firm, calm voice. "Exactly what is it you want from me, Logan?"

"I need to know where to find the boys."

"Didn't they live in the French Quarter apartment with Tess?"

"No. They'd lived with their grandmother on the Westbank. I drove by the house this morning hoping to talk their grandmother into letting me visit with them. I knocked, but no one answered. The next-door neighbor was out cutting his yard. He walked over and told me they'd moved out three days ago in the middle of the night."

Tess hadn't said a word about that to her, and if Logan was leveling with her, she could understand why he'd be worried. "I wasn't aware they'd moved. I don't have a clue where they might have gone."

He muttered a curse under his breath. "Sorry. This is just so frustrating."

"I'm sure the police will locate them."

"Then you have a lot more faith in the New Orleans Police Department than I do. But even if they find them, they'll just release them back to their grandmother."

"Makes sense to me. Their grandmother has been their caretaker. They know and trust her. I think they should be with her at a time like this."

"Their mother was murdered. And before that, someone had beat the crap out of her. Now the grandmother has moved out of their home in the middle of the night. Does that sound like a safe and stable environment for two four-year-olds to you?"

His point was valid. Still… "I'm not qualified to make that judgment."

He shook his head. "I know this probably looks bad, but I'm not the problem here. Everything I've done or tried to do was in the best interest of the boys."

"Like legally ripping them from the only family they've ever known?"

"If it came to that. I tried to reason with Tess."

"And when she didn't listen to reason?"

He leaned back and threw his arms in the air. "Okay, I threatened her. What did you expect, that I'd sit back and do nothing? How could I be certain that whoever was physically abusing Tess wouldn't turn on them."

"You threatened to kill her?"

"No. Hell, no!" He fisted his hands over and over again, before shoving them into his pockets. "I threatened to abduct the twins, and right now I wish the hell I had. Then at least I'd know where they are."

Logan was convincing. And standing here beside him, close enough to touch, it was almost impossible to believe he could have hit Tess, much less murdered her. Not that he couldn't have easily overpowered her. He was a little over six feet tall and hard-bodied. His thick, dark hair was stylishly cut, though long enough that one errant lock fell onto his forehead. He looked every bit the part of a gentleman, sophisticated and classically handsome.

But looks could be deceiving. Only facts could be trusted. It was a lesson every lawyer learned early on.

"I want the boys in my custody so that I can make sure they're safe, Rachel. Surely you can understand that."

"Then do what you have to."

"I plan to, but you could be a big help."

"I don't see how."

"Go to the police and vouch that I'm their biological father. That way they'll be a lot more likely to place the boys in my care."

"You don't need my testimony. A simple DNA test will prove parentage."

"Blood tests take time. And who knows what could happen to the boys while we're waiting around for that. Or where their grandmother might run off to with them."

"I'm sorry. I can't interfere in this." Not when she didn't know who to believe.

Rachel opened the door. Logan had been here long enough. This time he left, but instead of grabbing her coat and rushing to the office, she leaned against the wall and fought the sickening image that filled her mind. Two small boys who would never again feel their mother's arms around them or feel the touch of her lips when she kissed them goodnight.

THE HEAT was already stifling as Logan crawled behind the wheel of his car, the temperature as crappy as the turn his life had taken over the last few weeks.

He gunned the engine and pulled out from the parking space and into the nearly deserted street. Impulsively, he steered the car toward the Quarter. The words Tess had hurled at him yesterday knocked around inside his head, grating against his raw nerves the way her fingernails had scratched his arm and brought blood to his finger.

You'll never get your hands on my sons. They're gone, and you will never find them.

The high-pitched wail in his head evolved into a blaring horn, and Logan threw on his brakes just before he was broadsided by a city bus. Damn! He'd run right through a red light.

Paying more attention to traffic, he made his way to St Ann, slowing as he drove past the apartment where he'd pleaded his case with Tess yesterday. He parked a half block away and walked back to the black iron gate that opened into the courtyard and the private stairwell that led to the second- and third-floor apartments.

The gate was ajar, the broken latch hanging loose, just as

it had been yesterday. He hesitated, then ducked into the stairwell. He wasn't sure what he was looking for other than some lead to finding Danny and Davy.

The second-floor landing was dark, but light enough so Logan could see the bright orange tape strung over the door. The smart thing would be to turn around and leave. Start messing with cops and judges and the bureaucratic tape could get sticky and tangled. Better to have the boys in his possession before the legal hassles began.

But the information Logan needed could be just beyond the orange tape. A scribbled note. A name. A phone number. An address. And as long as he replaced the crime scene tape, who would know? Logan stuck his right hand into his pocket and let his fingers tighten around the key the dark-haired woman had given him.

He'd just fitted it into the lock and eased the door open when he heard the crash of splintering wood. He stepped back, but not before he'd been spotted.

"What the hell are you doing here?"

Logan looked up and into the glazed eyes of the big bruiser he'd seen at the strip club yesterday. The man was towering over him, some kind of book clutched in his meaty hand. Past him, inside what had been a neat living area only yesterday, was the kind of havoc usually caused by hurricanes or wrecking crews. Furniture was overturned, cushions from the couch strewn across the floor and the bookshelves raked clean, their contents dumped to the floor.

"I asked you a question. You got business here?"

"No, I just heard you were throwing a party." Logan stared again at the book in the man's hand. It was the size of a notebook, but covered in some kind of flowered fabric. More like a journal than a book. Could be just what Logan was after, but why would the bouncer from the strip club have come here for it? Unless…

Unless a million things. Who knew what Tess had been into before the murder? "Actually I came after that book you're holding."

"Ain't that too bad?"

No way was Logan going to take it away from the big guy with force. And threats or reasoning were probably a waste of breath. "I say we make a deal," Logan said. "Be a good time for you to leave town, what with you being a major suspect in the murder."

"You're crazy. I didn't kill Tess."

"That's not what I heard on the news just now," Logan lied. "If you're innocent, somebody must be framing you. I got five hundred dollars on me. Get you a long way from here."

For a second, Logan thought the man might hand over the book. But something fired in his eyes, and it was as if he went mad in a manner of heartbeats. Before Logan could duck, the guy slammed a fist into the right side of his head, knocking him against the wall with enough force that Logan thought his skull might have split wide open. He grabbed the handrail at the top of the landing, trying desperately to keep his balance.

He held on as long as he could before his fingers slipped from the smooth, worn wood. The stairs started twirling like the intake of exhaust fan and he was sucked into them, headfirst.

DETECTIVE HOAGIE MORRISON stared at the pictures of the department's latest victim. Tess Shepherd. Age twenty-two. Would have turned twenty-three next week. Exotic dancer for Fruits of Passion. Discovered nude and battered to the point it had taken dental records to give a positive ID.

Just what New Orleans needed to top off one of the hottest summers on record. You'd think even killers would take a break from the relentless heat and humidity and cool off in somebody's pool. But no. Murders were up by ten percent, keeping them all working long, thankless hours.

Griffin Paulson leaned over Hoagie's shoulder to examine the name and photo of the corpse. "I heard Tess Shepherd was murdered. I've seen her in the club before. She was one of their hottest."

"Know any reason why someone would want her dead?"

"No. Did she have a record?"

"Not even a misdemeanor."

"What about the autopsy? Any drugs in her system?"

"Clean as a whistle. Could have run in the Olympics."

"I'd say crime of passion. Boyfriend or husband got jealous cause she was getting too cozy with one of the guys sticking bucks in her silk thongs and went nuts."

Hoagie nodded, thinking Paulson was probably right, though he didn't have a lead on a boyfriend. "Whoever worked her over meant business."

"Any semen?"

"No. No immediate signs of recent intercourse, but CSI is still looking at the evidence."

"Could be dealing with someone like that psycho they arrested over in Slidell last year. The one that went crazy and thought an alien from outer space had taken over his wife's body. Now there was a lunatic for you."

"This victim didn't have a husband. She has two kids, though."

Paulson groaned and walked to the front of Hoagie's desk where he straddled a chair. Dressed in street clothes, he looked more like a street hood than a cop, but he was older than he looked. And he worked the Quarter beat, which is why Hoagie had asked him to come and chat with him today.

"Rough to see your momma die like that," Paulson said. "Saw a lot of that growing up in the hood. The one thing that could drop the toughest to their knees. How old are the kids?"

"Twin boys," Hoagie said, picking up the Shepherd file and scanning it. "Age four."

"They got other family?"

"A step-grandmother. That's about all I've been able to get out of the victim's co-workers. They say that Tess lived with the grandmother and the boys on the Westbank. None seemed to know about the apartment in the Quarter she'd moved into last week."

"The one where she was killed?"

Hoagie nodded. "Or at least where the body was found."

"So what's Craig Graves's take on this? He runs a tight ship. He'd likely know if one of his dancers was in some kind of trouble."

"He's out of town. Supposed to return today. You know him?"

"I've met him on several occasions. It's my job to know who's running the businesses on my beat. The club's high-class. Far as I can tell, they play by the rules. But I'll keep my eyes and ears open on the street. If I hear anything, I'll let you know."

"Yeah, do that. You know you might make a good homicide detective one day."

"I'd make a good one now if they gave me a chance. I'm up on the latest forensics info and CSI procedures. What else is there to know?"

A lot. Being a detective was about more than measured calculations, forensics and statistics. It was about seeing things that everyone else missed; it was about hunches.

Hoagie had a hunch that this case was about more than a jealous boyfriend going into a rage. He didn't know how much more, but he felt the dread mixing with a kind of uneasy anticipation. God, he loved to solve a tough case.

LOGAN LIFTED his head, cringed from a quick stab of pain at the base of his skull and spat out a mouthful of blood. Reality sank in slowly as he pulled himself to a half-standing position. The stab of pain turned to a steady grinding, as if something was making mince of his brain.

His legs were still shaky, but he managed to stagger to the top of the stairs and through the open door. For a second, he expected to hear Tess's voice, but the smear of bloodstain on the floor was a sickening reminder that he wouldn't. Tess was dead. The boys had disappeared.

The sensation hit again, the same unnerving barrage of emotions that had attacked the day he knew for certain the boys were McCains. Impossible to define. Too unresolved to understand even when he was totally lucid—which he wasn't now.

He kicked through the rubble and walked to the bedroom. More of the same chaos. Mattress torn off the bed. Drawers emptied. He wondered if the rabid bouncer had done all of this, or if someone else had beaten him to it. At any rate, the bouncer apparently had found what he came for.

Logan swayed, then grabbed hold of the bedpost for support. One blow to the head, and he was still reeling. A man like the bruiser could have made short work of Tess. She wouldn't have had a prayer against him. But why would he? Attacking the dancers for some kind of employee infractions couldn't be standard operating procedures for a fancy club like Fruits of Passion.

But someone had murdered Tess and wrecked her apartment.

It might not be important at all, but Logan would love to know what was in that flowered book the bruiser had left with.

A new barrage of sharp pains cut through Logan's temples like ice picks as he headed back to ground level. Raising a hand to the left side of his head, his fingers inched across a knot the size of a tennis ball.

Curses rocked though his brain, riding the crests of pain. He pushed through the door and into the sunlight. And there was the bruiser again. Only this time he was the one flat on his back. Blood pooled behind his head and his bulbous eyes stared blankly into the morning haze. His hands were open—and empty.

Logan fell to his knees and tried to roll the dead weight of the man's body over so that he could search beneath the layers of fat and muscle for the journal. Nausea hit him full-force and he swallowed fast, trying to keep from being sick.

"Stand up and keep your hands in front of you."

Logan rocked back on his heels and looked up and down the barrel of a gun pointed at his head. Then he threw up, all over the dead body of the bruiser. It was the only thing that had happened right all morning.

CHAPTER FOUR

"THIS IS NOT what it seems."

"Never is." Hoagie kept his finger on the trigger as he tried to assimilate the scene. One guy was dead from a bullet wound to the back of the head, apparently fired at close range. No gun in sight. The other guy was retching, pale as a ghost and with an ugly knot protruding from his left temple. Aside from the knot, he looked vaguely familiar.

"I'd suggest you start talking," Hoagie said, "though you have the right to remain silent."

"I'm aware of my rights."

"Good. Put your hands against the side of the building and spread your legs."

Hoagie patted him down. No sign of a weapon. "I need to see some ID."

"It's in my wallet, back right pocket."

Hoagie removed it and located the driver's license. Logan McCain. The name jumped out at Hoagie like a striking rattler. The address was St. Charles Avenue. *The* Logan McCain. His family practically owned the city. No wonder he'd looked familiar.

Damn. There was no way in hell this could be good.

IT WAS two hours later when Logan, Artie Fonteneaux at his side, walked out of Tulane University Hospital. They'd wanted to admit him for observation, but he'd refused. He could recover from a mild concussion at home in his own bed—when he got there. Right now he had bigger headaches to deal with.

Detective Morrison had been a lot more accommodating once Logan had identified himself, but that didn't mean he believed his explanation of how he happened to be bending over the dead hulk. Logan had to hand it to the detective, though. He'd kept a poker face when Logan had told him he was the father of Tess's missing sons.

But the secret was out now and it was only a matter of time until the media got hold of the story. They'd twist it and turn it every way but loose, and no doubt they'd lace the coverage with insinuations that he had something to do with Tess's death and maybe the bruiser's, as well.

Artie opened the passenger door on his silver BMW. "You never make things easy, Logan."

"Everyone has a talent."

"Including me, though I'm guessing you don't see it that way."

"I've never questioned your counsel."

"You haven't been listening to it lately, either."

Logan fastened his seat belt while Artie rounded the car and climbed behind the wheel.

"I thought we'd agreed that I would handle the situation with Tess Shepherd," Artie said, gunning the engine and backing out of the numbered space in the parking garage.

"All I did was talk to her."

"That's not letting me handle it."

"I thought she might be reasonable. I made a mistake."

"More than one, but going back to that apartment after

she'd been killed was the biggest. I can't even imagine what you were thinking."

"Doesn't seem that far a stretch to me. I was looking for some clue as to where Tess had sent the boys. With her murdered, she sure as hell wasn't going to tell me."

"Instead you run into some guy who slams your skull against the wall before taking a bullet himself."

"He wasn't just some guy. He worked at Fruits of Passion."

Artie's eyebrows shot up. "Did Morrison tell you that?"

"No, I told him. I ran into the bruiser there yesterday."

"You were at Fruits of Passion yesterday? This is getting worse by the second. I suppose you informed Detective Morrison of that, as well."

"Yeah."

"You know damn well you shouldn't talk to a cop without a lawyer present."

"I would have told him the same if you'd been there. I don't have any reason to lie. Besides, better he hear it from me. He would have found out anyway."

Artie groaned. "You are a total idiot."

Logan gingerly traced the knot on his head with the tips of his fingers. Still tender, but the stabbing pain had eased. "Did I mention to you that the crime-scene apartment was totally trashed?"

"No surprise. I'm sure Tess fought back. She was a hellcat, that one. I could tell that just from talking to her."

"I'm talking about more than just some furniture overturned in a struggle. Someone had taken the place apart, dumped the drawers and shelves, that sort of thing."

"Probably a doper who knew the place was empty and was looking for something to unload for quick cash. The Quarter's crawling with scum like that."

"Ones stupid enough to cross crime-scene tape?"

"Addicts aren't known for their brilliance."

Could be, but Logan couldn't shake the flowered journal from his foggy mind. The bruiser had it. Then he was murdered and it was gone. Logan hadn't mentioned the journal to the cops or to Artie. He wasn't sure why.

"I think the break-in was tied to the murder," Logan said, as much to himself as to Artie.

"That's possible. Tess Shepherd was a stripper and could have been on drugs herself. She could have been mixed up in anything. The important thing is that you stay clear of it from this point on."

"Aren't you forgetting something?"

Artie swerved to miss a car that cut too closely in front of him. "Like what?"

"The boys are still missing."

"I'm not forgetting, but the situation has changed, Logan. This is a criminal case now, and I have to insist that you leave the investigation and finding the boys up to the police. I'm certain your father is going to agree with me on this."

"The decision is mine to make. Not yours and not Dad's."

The light turned green, but instead of hitting the gas, Artie turned and stared at Logan. "I suggest you rethink that or else hire a new layer. A defense attorney, because if you keep screwing up like you've been doing, you'll be on trial for murder one."

Murder. Strange how the word had come alive over the last few hours, developed the arms of an octopus that reached out and entangled—and formed a stench that seemed to be attacking the lining of Logan's esophagus.

But he wasn't backing down. "Nothing personal, but I have to do this my way, Artie. You can come along for the ride— or not."

Artie didn't answer, but then Logan hadn't expected him to. Not until he talked to Logan's dad. Artie was a powerful, hard-nosed attorney who liked the way his bread was buttered, and was smart enough not to cross the man who provided the spread. He was Harris McCain's man all the way.

But with or without Artie, Logan was sure he would be having another talk with Detective Morrison very soon. The detective would make certain of that.

CRAIG GRAVES stood in the back of the building, the one man not turned on by the gyrating bodies of beautiful young women, all seminude and all with the power to tease and excite a man as he'd likely never be turned on by his wife or conventional lover.

But Craig had seen it day and night for the last ten months. Even near-naked dancing ladies became old hat after a while. Ten months ago, this had seemed the dream job, the good life right here for the taking. It was fast becoming the biggest headache of his life.

Pieces of the toothpick he was chewing broke off in his mouth, and he spat them to the tiled floor. The action didn't match the elegance of his expensive three-piece suit or the high-class tone of the establishment. He'd have to watch that. In this business, image was everything. That and the quality of the women he brought to his tabletops.

He sputtered a string of curses when he looked up and saw Detective Hoagie Morrison swaggering through the door. He recognized him from the description his go-to man Elton Pierce had given him. Not that Craig wouldn't have guessed Morrison was a cop just by the swagger.

The visit from the detective wasn't a surprise, but it was one more blow to a day that had gone from bad to worse since Graves had wakened to the news that Hank Matthews had had his brains blown out. Murder made everybody nervous, especially his dancers. And this was their second murder in two days.

The detective wasn't the type of man who went unnoticed. He wasn't particularly tall, but he had that bad-boy look about him that women seemed to like these days. He had on a white dress shirt, but opened at the neck with the sleeves rolled up to near the elbows. No more than in his early forties, Graves guessed, but his dark hair was already salted with a scattering of gray. And the five-o'clock shadow on his chin was prominent, though it was only half-past three.

Graves watched Morrison for a few minutes, then went over and introduced himself. "You must be Detective Morrison."

"Have we met before?"

"No, but word gets around." He extended a hand. "I wish I could say it was nice to see you, but under the circumstances, it would be a heartless lie."

Morrison looked around the room, his gaze scanning the action. "I take it you've heard about Hank Matthews."

"I heard. Why don't we step into my office? Most of the ladies don't know yet, and I hate to get them upset while they're dancing."

"The show must go on?"

"No. I'm just concerned for their emotions. They're still reeling from Tess's murder. I'm sure you realized that last night when you talked to them."

"It's hard to lose a friend to a senseless murder."

"Yes, and I've lost two in two days." Graves opened the door to his office and ushered Morrison in, already dreading the barrage of questions that was sure to follow. He seldom drank hard liquor, but he'd love a stiff drink now. He'd forego the temptation. He didn't dare risk doing anything that would dull his senses and make him let down his guard.

"Could I get you something, detective? A mixed drink? Coffee? Water?"

"No. I'm good."

Graves took the leather chair behind his desk. Morrison didn't sit, merely rested his palms on the back of a chair. Graves figured he thought standing gave him some kind of edge the same way Graves figured sitting behind the massive leather desk gave him the illusion of power. It was all a game.

"When was the last time you saw Hank Matthews?" Morrison drawled, his tone as relaxed as if they were discussing the weather.

"Last night. He was my bouncer on the late shift. He usually came on about eight o'clock and worked until closing."

"What time is closing?"

"Somewhere around four. This morning, it was exactly four-ten when the last party of patrons left. I remember looking at my watch as I locked the door."

"I'd heard you were out of town."

"I was. My plane got in at nine-thirty. I drove straight to the club."

"Guess we just missed each other."

"So I heard."

"Was there any trouble at the club last night?"

"Nothing unusual," Craig said. "Around midnight Hank had to usher a couple of guys out who'd had too much to drink and started grabbing the dancers while they were performing. Out-of-town businessmen here on convention. They left without putting up much of a fuss."

"Do you know of any reason someone would have wanted Hank dead?"

"No, but then I really don't know anything about his personal life."

"Yet you referred to him a minute ago as a friend."

"We were, when he was on the job. He was a good man. Worked the hours I asked without complaining and always showed up when he was supposed to. That's a lot in this business."

"How long had he worked for you?"

"Ten months. He hired on when I opened the club."

"And you never heard him mention any personal problems?"

"No. I got the idea he didn't have a lot going on in his life, but other than that, he seemed content enough."

"What about girlfriends—or boyfriends?"

"He wasn't gay, if that's what you're asking. I don't think he was involved with anyone, though. He had a habit of stopping by here during the day and just hanging out or doing odd jobs that needed doing."

"Ever hear him mention problems with family, neighbors, friends, that sort of thing?"

"Not that I recall. He didn't talk that much about himself."

"Did he get along with the other employees?"

"I haven't noticed any problems. He was protective of the dancers. They appreciated his attitude. This will hit them hard."

"Were Tess and Hank involved?"

"Romantically?"

"In any way?"

"Not that I know of. He walked her home occasionally when she worked late, the same way he did several of the dancers. Four o'clock's not always the best time for a lady to be strolling in the Quarter alone."

"Not the best time for anyone to be strolling the Quarter

alone." Morrison leaned forward, still resting his palms on the back of the chair. "Did Hank have gambling problems?"

"Couldn't tell you."

"A drug problem?"

"Not on my time. If he did them on his, he didn't do enough that it affected his work."

Morrison left the chair and walked over to a window overlooking a courtyard that belonged to the tenants of a Royal Street antique shop that backed on the club. There was nothing much to see other than some potted plants that could use a little water and a couple of iron benches, but Morrison was scrutinizing it as if he thought the answers to his questions might be hiding in the sunbaked scene.

Finally, he turned back to Graves. "You ever heard of Logan McCain?"

"I know who he is."

"Is he one of your customers?"

He threw the question out nonchalantly, but Graves felt the increase of tension, as tangible as if someone had turned up the heat in the small office. "He's never come in as a customer, at least not that I know of."

"What about to see one of the dancers?"

"Not that I'm aware of. I don't know everyone who comes and goes, of course."

"Of course. Just thought you might have seen him in here." Morrison rocked back on his heels, then propped a hand on the window facing, leaning against it.

"Did you ever meet Tess's stepmother?"

"Not that I recall. I seldom meet the families of my dancers. Some don't want their families to know how they make a living. A lot of them aren't from around here."

"Tess Shepherd was."

Craig picked up a pen and turned it over and over between his fingers like a miniature baton while he tried to read the detective. He got nowhere.

"Tess and her stepmother had lived together in the same house for six years," Morrison said. "Tess moved out a week ago. Her stepmother and the boys left a few nights later. None of the old neighbors know where they went."

Craig looked away, avoiding the burning intensity of Morrison's stare. "I don't know anything about that. All I have is whatever address she wrote down on her information sheet when she applied for the job."

"That's too bad, Mr. Graves. Really too bad that no one around here knows anything about Tess Shepherd or Hank Matthews. Be worse if uniformed cops start crawling all over this place like roaches on molded bread. Might make your customers nervous or run them off altogether."

"Might." The room grew hotter, and the sweat pooled into a sticky wetness beneath Craig's armpits. "I've told you all I know, detective. The Fruits of Passion is a legitimate, law-abiding club. You'd best look elsewhere for clues to your murders."

"I plan to look everywhere, Mr. Graves." Morrison left the window and walked to the office door. "That's the thing about me," he said, stopping with his hand on the doorknob. "I'm just too damn stubborn to rest until I get my man—or woman."

Craig stayed in his chair and didn't respond to Morrison's cocky pantomime of pointing and shooting a gun as he walked away. Someone's ass would roll over these two murders, but it wouldn't be his. He was far too smart for that. And he had his ace carefully tucked away but ready to play at a moment's notice.

THE DAY had been extremely unproductive for Rachel. Ballin's tax records were laid out in front of her in neat orderly fashion. She'd been through them meticulously, making notes on every inconsistency, but it was Tess Shepherd that claimed her mind. Tess and Logan McCain.

Yesterday morning Tess had been in this very office, angry, determined…bruised. By dinnertime she'd been beaten to death.

Finally giving up on any pretense of interest in Ballin's problems, Rachel reached across her desk and flicked on the recorder. Tess's voice filled the room and Rachel pictured her in the chair where she'd sat yesterday.

Resentment was the word that stuck in Rachel's mind. But that had changed when Rachel had asked her about the bruises. Until the subject of the bruises came up, everything had been Logan's fault. But the mention of the bruises had seemed to throw her. She'd become evasive and made up that story about getting hurt at the gym.

Rachel switched off the recording, then stood and massaged the tight muscles at the back of her neck. There were murders in New Orleans every weekend. Drive-by shootings. Bar brawls turned deadly. Drug deals gone bad. Domestic violence. They were so frequent, it barely registered anymore when Rachel heard of them on the morning news or read about them in the *Times Picayune*.

If Tess Shepherd hadn't walked through her door yesterday morning, her murder would be another of those events that only grazed Rachel's consciousness level. Now Rachel seemed consumed by the death—and the possibility that Logan McCain was connected to it.

He looked like a gentleman and was very convincing in the concerned father role. But Rachel knew from listening to Karen talk about her work at the center for abused women that some men had two faces. Men who were respected by their friends and colleagues but whose controls were faulty and twisted. Men who flew into rages. Men who hammered in the faces of their wives. Men who beat women to death.

Logan McCain could be one of those men.

Rachel dropped back to her chair. She was overreacting, going against all her attorney training. There was no real evidence against Logan, and she had to keep an open mind. She didn't, however, have to cooperate with him. Wherever the boys were, they were surely with their grandmother and safe.

Unless… Unless Tess really had been caught up in something that would impact her family.

Rachel reached for one of Ballin's folders. This was police business. She hadn't actually been Tess's attorney. This didn't concern her.

But her shaky fingers fumbled with the stiff manila, and the folder slipped through her fingers. She grabbed for it as it fell and knocked her coffee cup off the table in the process. The few drops of brew left in the cup splattered like brown rain over the carpet and the loose sheets of figures. She slipped from her chair and knelt to pick them up.

"Are you okay, Rachel?"

The voice startled her. She hadn't heard Mr. Castile come in, but he'd obviously heard her. She looked up to find him in the doorway, looking impeccable as always in a light-blue sport coat and a pair of navy slacks. She had no idea how old he was, though the office gossip mill put him near sixty. He could have passed for years younger, probably because he kept himself in great physical condition and wore the aura of authority and wealth so well.

"I'm fine," she said, grabbing a tissue to dab at spots of moisture on the rescued papers. "I accidentally knocked a coffee cup and a folder from my desk but there's no serious harm done."

He walked to her desk and watched as she slid the papers back inside the folder. "So it's the Ballin case that brought you in today. How are you coming with that?"

"I've found a few loopholes and I've been able to justify most, but not all, of the inconsistencies that the IRS questioned. I think we can get them to settle for thirty thousand dollars in additional taxes."

"What was the original assessment?"

"Eighty thousand."

"Then Ralph Ballin should be pleased with thirty."

Castile lingered, and she knew he'd stopped in for something other than to investigate the clatter. He was not one to spend a lot of time in idle dialogue with junior staff members, especially if he ran in to pick up something on the weekend.

"Mr. Ballin called me yesterday afternoon," Castile said.

"To complain?"

"On the contrary. He wanted to commend you for your efficient manner of handling the case."

"Thank you for letting me know."

"It's always a pleasure to share the comments of satisfied clients."

She wasn't sure she bought that since he'd never shared a positive comment before, and this sudden surge of affability made her uneasy.

"You have a lot of potential with our firm, Rachel. Not only do you work hard, but you've exhibited consistent good judgment."

"Thank you. I'm glad you're pleased with my work."

"We expect hard work, good judgment and loyalty from our employees." He moved to the front of her desk and locked his gaze with hers. "We serve a very select clientele, Rachel, and propriety is an essential component of everything we undertake at WW&C."

Castile's tone had changed, and in a matter of seconds he'd gone from compliments to what almost seemed a threat. "I understand completely, Mr. Castile."

"Then I can trust you not to take on any cases, pro bono or otherwise, that aren't appropriate for our firm?"

He was clear as a freshly washed window now. Somehow he'd heard about her visit yesterday from Tess Shepherd. Ted Boyd and his big mouth. She doubted he'd mentioned it to Mr. Castile, but he'd mentioned it to someone and the news had obviously made its way to the top.

Mr. Castile would be a lot more upset if he knew that the woman in question had been murdered.

"You don't have to worry about me, Mr. Castile. I'm well aware of the importance of propriety to WW&C."

"That's good to know. I think you'll go far with us, Rachel. In fact, I'm quite sure of it."

Rachel watched him walk away and wished she felt less as if she'd just sold out Tess Shepherd. Not that she had any intention of getting involved in Tess's murder investigation. All she had were a few suspicions with no facts to back them up.

She spread her notes on Ballin's case in front of her and tried to focus, but her thoughts jumped from Castile to Tess to Logan, making work all but impossible. Frustrated, she decided to call it a day.

She straightened her desk the way she always did before leaving the office. The need for neatness drilled into her by Aunt Gladys was so deeply instilled it approached compulsion. One of Rachel's many shortcomings.

Good old Aunt Gladys. She had her faults the same as

everyone else, but she'd been the relative to the rescue when Rachel's parents had died. She'd supplied care, love and tons of admonition. Number one: be successful, and make your parents proud.

Rachel walked to the file cabinet to put away the folders she'd been working with, then stopped in front of the photo of her parents that held a spot of honor on top of her laden bookshelves. "Are you proud?" she whispered. "Are you looking down from a lofty position atop a fluffy cloud and thinking how great it is that I landed a position with one of the most successful and most respected corporate law firms in the state? Or are you a crumbling mass of dust six feet under the ground?"

Aunt Gladys would be appalled at that last question—if she was still her old self. She wasn't. A stroke fifteen months ago had left her with some brain damage. Now there were days on end when she didn't even recognize Rachel.

Rachel's cell phone rang, breaking into her glum mood. She picked it up and checked the caller ID. Unavailable. She hesitated as the persistent ring continued. If this were another attempt by Logan McCain to harangue her for information, she'd as soon avoid it.

The phone quit ringing. She breathed a sigh of relief as she grabbed her handbag and briefcase. The relief was short-lived. The ringing started again, and this time she gave up and answered.

"Hello."

"Listen and listen good."

The voice was muffled to the point Rachel couldn't tell if it were male or female. "Who is this?"

"Forget what Tess Shepherd told you."

"Who is this?" she demanded again.

"Forget you ever saw Tess Shepherd."

The caller broke the connection, and Rachel stood in the middle of her office, holding the phone and trying to make sense of the call. Was Logan behind this? Could it be that he was actually threatening her?

The possibilities swirled in her head, making her dizzy and sick at her stomach as she left the office and took the elevator down to the parking garage.

Propriety. That's what it took to progress or even to stay on staff at WW&C. She couldn't let the phone call get to her, couldn't let the threat push her into fighting back and taking on a battle that wasn't hers.

Yet when she started the car, she found herself driving toward the French Quarter and the Fruits of Passion, the only link she had to Tess Shepherd other than Logan McCain.

CHAPTER FIVE

RACHEL STOOD in the middle of Bourbon Street and stared at the flashing neon sign designed to lure customers into the Fruits of Passion. The club was sandwiched between a T-shirt shop and a hole in the wall that specialized in frozen drinks to go, but the entryway had been dressed up to indicate that it was far more sophisticated than its neighbors.

Rachel had never been in a strip club in her life though she had seen male strippers perform at bachelorette parties, and she had seen clubs like this one portrayed in movies and TV shows.

She watched as a group of guys who looked to be in their teens or early twenties approached the club and walked inside. They were back on the streets in minutes, likely turned away after ID checks. Several other groups of guys walked in and didn't come out. Business appeared to be brisk for a Saturday afternoon in the middle of summer.

I've sold my soul to the devil on a regular basis.... Tess's words echoed in Rachel's mind to the background music of a street sax player and the calliope from a paddle boat on the nearby river.

She should have asked what she meant by that. Dancing in a gentleman's club might not be everyone's choice of a way to make a living, but it wasn't as if Tess had been sold into sexual slavery. No one had forced her to choose this lifestyle, and if she hadn't liked it, she could have quit at any time.

More likely, she hadn't been referring to her job as an exotic dancer. She could have been into drugs or prostitution or who knew what other aspect of life in the underbelly of the city. If she'd gotten mixed up with a domineering pimp or a supplier, then the words would ring a lot truer.

Rachel's cell phone rang and her chest tightened as she checked out the caller ID. This time it was Karen. She welcomed the distraction.

IT WAS a quarter to seven when Detective Morrison rang the doorbell of the mansion on St. Charles Avenue. The place was hidden in the shadows of huge spreading oaks, some of which were over a hundred years old. At least that's what Hoagie had read in the newspaper a few weeks ago. The ancient oaks were being relentlessly attacked by Formosan termites.

The house looked as if it might be, as well. Seemed more like a home for a young Frankenstein than for a mover and shaker like Logan McCain, but then old money had a way of capturing its young.

Hoagie had done his homework this afternoon. Logan's great-great grandfather had made his fortune in sugar cane. The following generations had multiplied the wealth with extremely profitable and sometimes questionable real estate developments, frequently evoking sharp protests for their part in destroying Louisiana's fast-disappearing wetlands.

They were definitely not environmentalists, but they were major contributors to the local cultural scene and charitable organizations. A mixed bag. Society money grabbers with a semi-conscience. Not that any of that mattered to Hoagie. His only interest was in his case.

The little evidence that he had in either murder was tied to Logan, but he'd have to go easy with this. He couldn't even think of officially linking Logan to the crimes without solid and substantial evidence. Who said money didn't talk?

Then again, Logan wouldn't be the first McCain to get sideways of the law. His brother had beat him to it.

He was about to ring the bell again when the door swung open.

"Good evening, detective."

Logan himself. That was a surprise. Hoagie had expected a house like this to have a uniformed servant perform the task.

"Be better if it was ten degrees cooler. How's the head?"

"Aching." He ushered Hoagie inside, where it was probably a good twenty degrees cooler. Logan was dressed in a pair of white shorts and a yellow polo shirt. His hair was mussed and he looked tired, as if he might have just come from a round of tennis or golf. But the bulge on the side of his head was still prominent.

"I appreciate your talking to me tonight. I wasn't sure you'd be up to it."

Logan touched his fingers to the protruding knot. "It seemed better not to put it off."

Definitely better for Hoagie. He followed Logan into a high-ceilinged room off the side of the marble foyer. The room was filled with couches, chairs, tables and a grand piano. The furniture was probably priceless, though it didn't look a lot different than the kind Hoagie's mother had discarded as junk when his grandparents had died.

"Nice house," Hoagie said, though the truth was the old Gothic structure gave him the creeps.

"The house has potential," Logan said, "but it needs work. I inherited it from my grandmother last year, but haven't had the time to do anything with it except create a functional study. Actually, why don't we talk there? It will be more comfortable."

Now this was more like it, Hoagie decided, following Logan into the kind of room he would have wanted if he had a bank account the size of Logan's. Two chairs and a massive couch were brown leather. Another chair was overstuffed and upholstered in a striped pattern that matched the oversize ottoman. There was a fireplace on one wall, a big-screen TV on the other. A huge basket of newspapers and magazines sat near the hearth, and a bookshelf loaded with hardcover and paperback books lined a wall opposite a huge desk.

And it looked as if it would be just him and Hoagie for this little chat. He'd expected a team of attorneys, sitting in a semicircle and watching him like wildcats ready to spring the moment he asked any kind of question that they felt might violate their client's rights.

Hoagie took one of the leather chairs. Logan took the other, leaving them face to face, separated by a few feet of space and the ottoman.

"I guess restoring a house like this would take quite a bit of time," Hoagie said.

"Yes," Logan agreed. "But I know you didn't come here to discuss the family manor so we may as well get down to business. You have a killer to catch. I need to find my sons."

That pretty much laid the issues out front and center, and made it clear that Logan had his own game plan. "The boys aren't officially listed as missing persons at this point," Hoagie said, deciding it best to get that detail straight.

"Does that mean you know where they are?"

"No."

"Then official or not, they're missing."

"There's another problem here, Mr. McCain. The only

proof we have that you're the father of the boys is your say on it. None of Miss Shepherd's friends or acquaintances seem to be aware of that fact. I guess you have DNA testing to prove your claim."

Logan hesitated, just enough to stir Hoagie's suspicious nature.

"The boys bear a strong McCain family resemblance. Tess told me I was the father. I believed her."

"You're a mighty trusting guy. Me, I'd want proof of a thing like that."

"Guess we're different that way. I suggest you talk to Rachel Powers, detective. If you ask her about it directly, I'm sure she'll substantiate my claim."

Hoagie pulled out a small notebook and scribbled the name on a sheet of clean, white paper. "Any idea where I'd find this Rachel Powers?"

"She's an attorney with the law firm of Williams, Williams and Castile. Tess wanted Miss Powers to represent her in a custody hearing."

"And how do you know this?"

"Because I saw Tess Friday morning, and she told me."

Hoagie almost dropped the pen as Logan let that zinger fly. Logan, on the other hand, didn't blink a eye. "I should remind you, Logan… Is it okay to call you Logan?"

"Call me whatever you're comfortable with."

Hoagie nodded. "I should remind you that whatever you say could be used against you in a court of law. Are you certain you don't want a lawyer present for the rest of our talk?"

"Quite sure. I have no problems with telling you what I know about the victim. That's the only thing I plan to discuss."

"Fair enough. Why don't you tell me exactly when and how you found out that you were the father of Miss Shepherd's children?"

"I received an anonymous phone tip two weeks ago saying that Tess Shepherd was the mother of four-year-old twin boys and that I was the father."

"Did the caller say why he or she was telling you this?"

"She feared the boys were in danger."

The story sounded about as solid as melted butter to Hoagie, but then he seldom took anything he heard from a suspect at face value.

On the other hand, the boys' mother was dead and they and their grandmother seemed to have disappeared.

Forty minutes later, Hoagie had heard enough to know that either Logan was a very convincing liar or else he had nothing to do with Tess's prior beatings or the one that had left her dead. Nor did he have any solid evidence against him in Hank Matthews's murder. Logan hadn't had a weapon on him when Hoagie had found him standing over the body, and none had been found in the courtyard.

But there was that one little element that stunk up the story. A man of Logan's wealth and position did not take an anonymous phone caller's word that he was the biological father of kids he'd never seen before, born to a mother he'd had a one-night stand with almost five years ago.

Yet it was clear that Logan was desperate to find the boys. As far as Hoagie was concerned, that meant only one thing. Logan knew more than he was saying. That bothered Hoagie. It bothered him a whole lot.

The possibility of kids in danger always did.

THE ROOM was thick with a pulsating sexuality that seeped into Rachel's consciousness and made her extremely uncomfortable. She tried to find somewhere to fix her gaze besides on the dancers who were making moves she didn't think her hips could execute and waitresses with star-studded pasties over the tips of their nipples. After meeting Karen for a bite to eat, she'd persuaded her reluctant friend to accompany her to the gentleman's club to get a handle on the situation with Tess.

"There's a table in the back," Karen said, all but yelling to be heard above the din of music and voices.

"I'll follow you."

"In that case, I'm going back out the door."

"Don't wimp out on me now." Rachel placed her palms between Karen's shoulder blades and nudged her toward the empty table.

A guy pulled a chair into their path. "I got two seats right here. Savin' 'em just for you."

"Sorry. My sweetie and I like to sit alone," Karen quipped, brushing past him and the chair.

"You nut. Before you know it everybody in here will think we're gay."

"Duh… So should I just announce that you're here to stick your nose into an ugly murder case where you have absolutely no business?"

Rachel had no comeback for that. She slid into one of the chairs and finally got the nerve to look up and take in her surroundings. The dim lighting came primarily from a series of gaudy glass chandeliers and a few lamps covered in red silk like the one that sat on their table. A large half-moon-shape stage, that also served as a bar for those with front-row seats, covered the entire front wall of the spacious room.

Most of the front row of seats was taken up by what appeared to be a bachelor party or a group of college guys out for a night of stuffing dollar bills into the G-strings or garters of nearly nude dancers. The rest of the clientele was also primarily male, but there were a couple of groups that appeared to be couples out for a night of riotous entertainment.

Karen leaned toward Rachel as one of the dancers stopped at the table next to theirs to do a few gyrations and collect her tips. "I've never seen that outfit at the local department store. Do you suppose it comes in an extra large?"

"Couldn't say. I'm not looking above the boots."

"The boots *are* the outfit, except for a little scrap of lace covering her uh-huh."

"Judging from the leering drools of the guys, they like the lace—or the uh-huh."

A waitress showed up to take their drink order. They both ordered cosmopolitans and Rachel sank back into her chair and into thoughts of Tess Shepherd. She imagined her on the stage, her long hair flowing, her hips gyrating to the throbbing beat of the music, her sexuality flashing like the neon sign outside the building.

She had danced and collected tips and cared for two preschoolers until someone had decided her life was dispensable.

The waitress brought their drinks, and Rachel took a long sip as she tried to decide what she was really doing in this place. If she expected some kind of knowledge breakthrough on who'd killed Tess, it wasn't happening.

"Let's finish our drinks and go," she said, as another woman joined the group on stage.

"Wait a minute," Karen said. "I know that dark-haired dancer."

"You know her. How?"

"She stopped by the center one day about six months ago to pick up a friend."

"You have a good memory."

"Who could forget a woman who looks like that? I hated her on sight."

Karen was kidding, but the dancer was striking. A size two

with at least C-cup breasts. A complexion that looked like porcelain. And long, shiny hair as black as night. The men were crowding around her, eager to slip folded bills into the garter that rode close to her lace-covered crotch.

"Her friend was a woman I once tried to help."

"And couldn't? Did she walk back into an abusive situation?" Rachel asked.

"And didn't walk out again. Her nude, bloodied body was found by trash collectors two nights later in a Bourbon Street alleyway."

Rachel wrapped her hands around the drink glass and took an unladylike gulp. All the talk and thoughts of death were getting to her—so much so she nearly knocked over her glass when she felt a firm touch on her shoulder. She recovered, turned and found herself staring into the dark piercing eyes of Logan McCain.

"I thought that was you," Logan said. "What are you doing here?"

"I… We're…" Damn him. There was no reason for his presence to fluster her. "I could ask you that same question, Logan."

He pulled out the chair in spite of her response and settled in beside her. The lights were dim, but not so low that she didn't notice a large hematoma on the side of his head. She was certain it hadn't been there that morning.

She turned to Karen. "See if you can get the check while I'm in the ladies' room. I've seen enough."

Karen shot her a quizzical look, but didn't argue. Logan was not so accommodating. She was aware of his footsteps behind her as she marched toward the back of the room.

He grabbed her arm just as she reached the restroom door. "We need to talk, Rachel."

"I can't think of any reason why."

"Well let me give you a couple. I don't know why you're getting involved in Tess's murder, but this club is no place for you to be hanging out. Mess with the wrong people and you could wind up as dead as Tess."

"Is that a threat?"

"A threat?" He finally let go of her arm and threw up his hands. "Hard as this may be for you to believe, I was trying to protect you. Tess's death was more than a fight between screwed-up lovers. The bouncer from Fruits of Passion was killed on the stairs to Tess's apartment this afternoon."

"How do you know that?"

"It doesn't matter how I know. I know."

Logan didn't have any physical hold on her now, but her legs were so shaky she feared they might fold and drop her to her knees at any second. She stared past Logan to a well-dressed man striding toward them.

"Is this man giving you any trouble?"

Logan turned and stared at the man, answering before she had a chance to figure out what the response should be.

"No, I'm not the one giving her trouble." He turned back to Rachel for the briefest of seconds, but his gaze burned into hers. "Remember what I said."

Then he turned and strode away.

"I'm sorry," the man said. "Let me send you a drink on the house to make up for his poor manners. Unfortunately, some men don't know how to treat a lady."

"You're right. But the drink won't be necessary. My friend and I were about to leave anyway."

"I hope you've enjoyed yourself."

Enjoyment had never crossed her mind. "Everything's cool," she said and dismissed him with a wave before finally ducking into the bathroom. Everything was cool—except for Tess Shepherd—and the fact that death, danger and Logan McCain seemed to be taking over her life.

CATHY SHEPHERD stood outside the open door to the boys' bedroom, listening to the soft, steady sounds of their breathing as they slept. Danny had cried to go home tonight. And once Danny had started crying, Davy had joined in.

She was thankful that they hadn't asked for their mother yet, not that they were used to having her around all that much or that they ever seemed to care if she was there or not. But she had been their mother, and Cathy would have to tell them one day that Tess was dead. Not yet, though. Being on the run was enough for them to deal with now.

And running was the only way to stay alive. Cathy knew that instinctively, though she didn't know who they were running from. She'd tried to get it out of Tess when she'd called in the middle of the night and told her to take the boys and disappear. But all Tess had said was that the boys were in danger. Cathy hadn't run far at first, only to a motel on Airline Highway. She'd planned to wait it out until things blew over.

But things hadn't blown over. Tess had been murdered. Now Cathy was all that stood between the boys and a killer. And she didn't even own a gun.

CHAPTER SIX

LOGAN'S OFFICE was on the tenth floor of McCain Towers. The huge picture window faced the Mississippi River and gave him a clear view of the bridge that linked the east and west banks of the city.

He stood in front of the window now, watching the Algiers Ferry as it docked near Spanish Plaza. Just beyond it, people were lined up along the Riverwalk to board a cruise ship bound for somewhere in the Caribbean. And in the middle of the muddy waterway, a couple of tugboats guided a huge barge toward one of the warehouses west of town. A typical Monday morning, but not for him.

The hematoma was barely noticeable this morning, and the headache that had nagged him all day yesterday had disappeared, but the rest of his life was careening out of control. Artie Fonteneaux had phoned Logan's father in Europe and filled him in on all the latest happenings, and Harris McCain had cut his trip short by days. He'd no doubt come bounding into Logan's office any minute, raising hell six ways to Sunday about Logan's involvement in what was now a murder case involving the mother of grandchildren he'd never met and showed no interest in meeting.

Worse, there was still no word on the whereabouts of Davy and Danny. As far as the police were concerned, they were not officially missing. Not that Logan had any intention of leaving this in the hands of the police.

He'd gotten practically nowhere trying to glean information from the employees of Fruits of Passion. About the only thing of value he'd learned was that the dark-haired beauty who'd slipped him the number of Tess's apartment worked as a dancer at the club. He'd gotten just a glimpse of her Saturday night after Tess and her friend had left. Apparently she'd spotted him, as well. She'd disappeared after that, and hadn't resurfaced.

But he'd been more successful yesterday. He'd finally gotten one of Tess's former Gretna neighbors to talk. She'd given him a description of Cathy Shepherd and a picture of Cathy and Tess with the boys that had been taken at a neighborhood Christmas party this past December. It wasn't much, but it was a start.

As for Rachel Powers, he didn't begin to understand her. She wasn't willing to help him protect two innocent boys, yet she'd insinuated herself right in the middle of the danger by showing up at the Fruits of Passion. He'd been tempted to pick her up, throw her over his shoulder and carry her out of that place. Of course if he had, she'd probably have slapped a lawsuit on him.

The intercom on his desk buzzed. He punched the speaker button.

"A Mr. Pellegrin is here to see you."

"Great. Send him in."

Logan made a quick assessment of the PI as he walked through the door. Probably midforties, but already with thinning hair the color of burned toast and a seriously receding hairline. Tall and lanky, unruly brows, a long, skinny nose and slightly sagging shoulders. Nothing in his looks to suggest he was the best PI in the area for locating missing persons, but his reputation indicated otherwise.

"Pete Pellegrin," he said, extending a hand.

"Logan McCain. Nice to meet you, Mr. Pellegrin."

After the handshake, Pete scanned the office, taking in his surroundings the way you'd expect a good investigator to do.

"Nice view. But then I guess it would be if your name is on the building."

"It gives me a few perks." And that was enough small talk. "I understand you have an impressive track record in locating missing persons."

"I miss a few, but only when the client decides they're not worth the cost of the hunt before I find them."

"I won't be giving up the search."

"Then I'm your man. From what you said on the phone, I'm guessing this is a case of custody kidnapping."

"More or less. I don't have legal custody—at least not yet, but no one seems to know where the children are except that they are likely with their step-grandmother."

"Where's the mother?"

"She was murdered on Friday."

Pellegrin's eyes showed their first spark of real interest. "Who killed her?"

Logan motioned to a large leather chair in front of his desk. "Why don't you have a seat, and I'll fill you in on everything I know?"

Logan spent the next half hour supplying the basics. It bothered him that the PI made so few notes, but the guy might have a crackerjack memory. He'd give him the benefit of the doubt—at least for now.

"It's very important that I find the boys quickly," he said, stressing his words to make his point. "Find the boys within ten days, and I'll throw in a five-thousand-dollar bonus."

Pellegrin nodded. "That would raise the priority level a bit. Tell you what. Why don't we go for double or nothing? If I find them within five days, make the bonus ten thousand dollars. If it takes me longer than that, you keep the bonus money."

Cocky and sure of himself—qualities Logan admired in a man. "Do you usually see results that quickly?"

"All depends."

"On what?"

"On how much head start they have. How badly they want to stay hidden. How much cash they have on them. Whether or not they're still in the States."

"That's a lot of variables."

"Yeah, but those things don't usually play into this kind of case. Most novices don't have the slightest idea how to cover their tracks. They leave a paper trail so blazing it might as well be paved in neon lights."

Logan took a business card from the leather holder on his desk and slipped it into a brown envelope which already held copies of the original photo he had of the boys and the one he'd gotten from the neighbor. It also held the thousand dollars in advance salary and expense money they'd agreed on. "If you have any news or questions, call me at my cellular number," he said, standing and extending the envelope to Pellegrin. "Any time, day or night."

"Gottcha. Have they had the funeral yet for Miss Shepherd?"

"No. It's this afternoon, a graveside service. The details of the funeral were in this morning's paper, though there was no obituary."

"Morning paper, huh? I'll check that out and make sure I'm among the bereaved."

"Why waste the time?"

"A funeral can be a great source for leads. You never know what family members will talk when emotions are running high."

"The only family I'm aware of is the missing step-grand-mother and the boys."

"Someone must have paid for the funeral," Pete said. "Any idea who?"

"No."

"Maybe the stepmother," Pellegrin said, standing and running a hand deep into the front pocket of his trousers to rattle his keys. "There's always a possibility that she'll show up at the funeral. Might even be ready to talk terms with you now that she's become the sole caretaker of two preschoolers."

"I'm certainly not counting on that."

"You can rest easy, though. I'll track Cathy Shepherd and the boys down in no time. Women and kids are always the easiest to find, except for one case I had where the mother was an ex-cop. She knew all the tricks. But I don't expect anything like that this time."

"Good." And if Pete Pellegrin located the boys within five days, it would be well worth the bonus money.

As long as they were alive.

Logan swallowed past a choking lump in his throat as Pellegrin left, then rushed through a half dozen important phone calls he had to return, hoping to get out of the office before his father came in. He didn't make it. Good old dad bounded through the door unannounced, his nostrils flaring like a mad bull.

"I hope you have a damn good plan for handling this, Logan."

"Welcome back, Dad. Good to see you, too."

"I THINK that covers everything, Mr. Ballin. Just remember to let me do most of the talking tomorrow when we meet with the IRS attorney."

"I'll try, but I don't like the idea of some young whipper-snapper putting the squeeze on me just because he's got a little government clout."

"I'm afraid Mark Effring has more than a little clout, but you'll do fine."

"Not if he starts hitting me with a bunch of questions involving my accounts. I can't regurgitate figures the way I once could."

"You have me for that."

"You sure that won't just piss him off more? I mean, you know how men are. They hate to get bested by a woman."

"The IRS hates to get bested by anyone, but they have some very good female attorneys themselves. Besides, we're not trying to put anything over' on them. We just need them to be reasonable."

"I'm seventy-four years old. About the only reasonable thing I remember the government doing is kicking butt in the Second World War."

"This won't be quite that big a deal," she said, smiling. Ralph Ballin was what Rachel's aunt would have called a corker. Dapper, spry and thin as a rail, he would have passed for a man twenty years younger were it not for the deep ruts that cut through his forehead and cheeks and the shaky timbre to his voice.

"Tell my wife it's not that big a deal. She's going around like a crazy woman, worrying they're going to cart me off to jail."

"Trust me, you are not going to jail. Assure your wife of that. All you need to do is get a good night's sleep, have a nice breakfast and show up here at 10:00 a.m. tomorrow morning. Everything is under control."

She left the conference room with Ballin and walked him to the elevator. If all her clients were as nice as him, her job wouldn't be half bad.

Half bad?

What a way to think of this position when landing it had made her the envy of half the graduating class in law school and put Aunt Gladys into orbit. She'd singsonged her favorite mantra for days.

Your parents would have been so proud of you, Rachel. So very proud.

Was that what Logan was looking for? Children to make him proud, to carry on the family name and add even more treasure to the family vaults?

Whatever he wanted, it was no longer any of her concern. She'd called the police department yesterday and given a statement to one of the officers. Now she needed to concentrate on her job.

The receptionist stopped her as she passed her desk. "There's someone waiting in your office, Rachel."

"I don't have an appointment scheduled for another half hour."

"I know, but he's from the NOPD. He said he needs to talk to you. It sounds serious."

Serious as murder. Her muscles had tightened to taut cords by the time she reached her door and faced her guest. He was dressed in blue slacks and a white shirt, open at the neck with the sleeves rolled up to his elbows. He was nice-looking, but intimidating. It was the eyes, she decided. Piercing and a tad accusing, even though he was smiling.

"Rachel Powers," she said, extending a hand.

"Detective Hoagie Morrison with the New Orleans Police Department. Homicide."

Once he'd dropped her hand, she stepped behind her desk. "How can I help you, detective?"

"I'm here about the statement you gave to one of the officers concerning the Tess Shepherd murder case. I hope you don't mind my just stopping by."

She did. More importantly Williams, Williams and Castile would mind her being questioned by a detective inside the sacred walls of the firm. The only thing that might save her from getting reprimanded was that he was wearing street clothes instead of a uniform and there was no obvious revolver at his waist.

"When I left the information, I specifically requested that I not be contacted at work," she said. "I left my home and my cellular phone numbers."

"I'm sorry. I guess I missed that part of the statement."

She doubted that. He didn't look like a man who missed much of anything.

"I really don't have time to talk to you right now. I have an appointment scheduled in thirty minutes."

"Believe me, I understand. You've got appointments. I've got a murderer to catch. We're both busy, so I'll make this as quick as possible."

And when he put it like that, his business did sound more pressing than hers. Besides, he was already here. The damage, if there was any, had been done. "A half hour," she said. "I can't keep my client waiting."

She dropped to her leather swivel chair. He took the same chair Tess had sat in Friday—when she was still alive.

And then the questions began. At first the detective was low-key, friendly, making the questioning seem more a formality than anything else. But when she mentioned what Tess had said about the pregnancy with the boys being the result of rape, his mood and questioning intensified to the point Rachel felt as if she were on the witness stand being questioned by a hostile defense attorney.

"I don't have any reason not to be totally honest with you,

detective. I don't actually know the victim or Logan so I certainly couldn't have any motive for being dishonest."

"I'm just trying to make sure I have the facts right. You mentioned in your statement that you'd had an unexpected visit from Logan McCain."

"Yes. On Saturday morning."

She filled him in on all the details of that visit and the anonymous phone call on Saturday afternoon, then finally about running into Logan at the Fruits of Passion on Saturday night.

"So, about that phone call you got warning you not to get involved, do you think the caller could have been Mr. McCain?"

"If I said yes, I'd only be guessing. As I told you, the voice was disguised to the point that I couldn't tell if it was a male or a female. I believe the caller must have used some kind of device that made the words sound as if the caller had a mouth full of rocks."

"You must not have taken the caller seriously."

"On the contrary. I took the call very seriously."

"But still you made a visit to the club where Tess had worked before she was killed?"

"I explained that to you a minute ago. I'd hoped I'd get a better handle on all of this if I saw where Tess worked."

"I'm not sure I know what you mean by that."

And neither did she now. "I was upset. One day Tess is in my office, bruised and desperate and asking for help I couldn't give her. The next day I find out she's been murdered. I've never had anything like that happen before. I guess I just needed some kind of closure on who Tess Shepherd really was."

"But she wasn't actually a client of yours?"

"Right." She glanced at her watch. Her secretary would have buzzed her if her client had arrived, but Rachel had had more than enough of Detective Hoagie Morrison. "I've told you everything I know, and I have an appointment to keep."

He nodded, then ran the eraser end of his pencil down the margin of his notes before making eye contact. "Just one more quick question. Are you certain that Miss Shepherd denied that Logan McCain was the one who'd left the bruises on her face?"

"Yes, but she denied anyone had hit her, just as I told you. She said a piece of equipment at the gym where she worked out had swung back and slammed into her face."

"And she never mentioned where her stepmother had taken the boys?"

"No. At the time, I didn't know they were missing."

"I'm not sure *missing* is the right word. Could be their grandmother just took them somewhere so they wouldn't see their mother all bruised like that. Depending on where they are now, she may not even know about the murder. At any rate, if you think of anything else I'd appreciate a call."

"Of course."

The detective tapped his pencil on his notes one last time, then pushed himself from the chair. "If you get any more threatening calls, I'd like to know that, too."

"You don't think I'm actually in any kind of danger, do you? It's not as if I know anything that could identify the killer."

He grimaced. "The killer may not know that."

Great. Now instead of feeling relieved that the detective was leaving, she felt as if someone had just torn the lid from a giant black box and was about to squash her inside it and lock it shut.

Now that the detective had pointed it out, why wouldn't the killer assume she knew something? Logan had. The detective still did. It was evident in the way he was questioning her. They all knew she'd talked to Tess the day before she died, and they all thought Tess had told her something that had to do with the murder. They couldn't be more wrong.

But the next time Ted Boyd was escorting someone out the door, she'd keep her mouth shut even if it was Publisher's Clearing House delivering her a check.

LOGAN STOOD beneath an oak tree several yards from the small white tent that sheltered the mourners and the gray coffin from the blazing sun. Pete Pellegrin was among the guests, as he'd said he would be. Logan had considered joining the group, as well, but decided against it since he was pretty sure he'd be recognized and unwelcome.

He'd been run out of the gentleman's club Saturday night for what the bouncer had called harassing the dancers. Actually he'd been as much a gentleman as anyone else in the room, except that his propositions had probably been more decent as he'd slipped his twenties into their garters. Big tips for information. None took him up on his offer.

An acorn fell from the tree, hit his shoulder and bounced to the ground beside him. He ground it into the dirt with the toe of his shoe and stepped back so that he was deeper in the shadows. The temperature was hovering right at the hundred-degree mark, and sweat was already pooling under his arms and wetting the back of his shirt.

It had been cold the last time he'd watched while someone was lowered into the ground. And wet. Incredibly wet, the aftermath of a hurricane that had come crashing ashore just west of Bay St. Louis.

That time the body had been reduced to ashes resting in a brass urn. At least most of the ashes were in the urn. He'd taken what amounted to a couple of handfuls with him and tossed one into the middle of Lake Pontchartrain and the other into the splintered remains of the tree house where his brother had tried to teach him about risk and courage.

"Climb higher. You can't see anything from down there."
"I can see enough."
"You're a scaredy-cat."
"I'm not scared. I just don't like climbing."
"You don't have to like it. You just do it. We've got to go to the top."
"Why?"
"'Cause we just do, that's why."
"If you fall, you'll break your leg or something."
"If I fall, it'll probably kill me, but I'm not going to fall."
"Aren't you scared even a little?"
"Naw. I'm never scared. Not of nothin'. That's for sissies and big, fat cowards."

LOGAN TOOK a handkerchief from his pocket and wiped a stream of perspiration from his brow. Josh hadn't been afraid. He was dead all the same. And now…

Now Logan had best focus on what he had to do. He forced the memories into the background as the priest left the front of the group and began offering private words of comfort.

There were less than a dozen people in attendance, all but three of them female. He couldn't see their faces from his observation spot, but from what he could tell most of the women were young, about Tess's age with the same kind of slim, lithe body. A couple of them were hugging each other now. Most were dabbing at their eyes. All seemed sad, but none appeared to be overcome with grief, and none looked anything like

Cathy Shepherd. That ruled out Pellegrin's suspicion that she might actually show up for the burial, unless of course she was hovering behind a tree in the distance as he was.

Pellegrin was standing near the coffin, head down, as if having a final moment with an old friend while he was no doubt eavesdropping on the quiet conversations around him. The other two men stepped away from the group, finally turning so that Logan got a better look at their faces.

Logan was pretty sure that the one in the light-blue suit was the strip club's owner, Craig Graves. He'd never met him, but he'd found a picture of him while doing a Google search on the Internet last night. It had been part of an article in a local magazine about the Fruits of Passion and its charismatic owner.

The other guy was the so-called manager he'd talked to in the Fruits of Passion Friday morning. He looked different cleaned up, but it was the same guy. Mid-forties probably. Thinning hair, puffy folds drooping over his eyelids and skin that looked like it had been left out in the sun to dry.

The group began to break up. They started back to their cars in twos and threes, all except two blond women who were still standing near the coffin. Logan shifted and tried to shrug off a wave of sadness. He wondered what Tess had really been like. Had she been excited when the boys were born? Had she thought back on the night they'd been conceived with any kind of tenderness? Or had it all been regret and resentment as it had seemed when he'd talked to her?

Now she was about to be buried, and neither her stepmother or her sons were there to grieve or say their goodbyes. No matter what he thought of her mothering skills, she didn't deserve this. No one did.

He started back to his car, ready to clear out of here. And then he spotted her—the woman with the long, black hair—

walking alone, head down. A full head shorter than the other women, she hadn't been visible when they were clustered together, but it was her. Logan picked up his pace and cut across the cemetery. He was only a few yards behind her when she turned and saw him.

"Wait. I'd like to talk to you."

She darted to a red car parked a few steps away and climbed inside before he could reach her. She looked back at him through the side window. Her eyes were red and swollen as if she'd been crying, but the look on her face was pure panic. A second later, she sped away.

IT WAS eight o'clock when Rachel grabbed her briefcase and started to the parking garage. The whir of the cleaning crew's vacuum cleaner and the clatter of trash cans being emptied were the only sounds she heard as she locked the door to WW&C behind her. The near-empty building didn't usually bother her, but tonight she felt incredibly alone as she walked the deserted hallway and waited for the elevator.

It was almost as if she were grieving for Tess, but Rachel knew the feeling wasn't that selfless. It was too intimately linked to the longing that had tormented her all her life.

The psychologist she'd seen in her teenage years had said she missed the concept of a mother more than an actual person and that many children who lost a parent either through death or divorce experienced that same nebulous emptiness.

Tess's sons would know that pain no matter what kind of future they had. Even if they ended up with Logan and he turned out to be as wonderful a caretaker as her Aunt Gladys had been, they'd always wonder about and miss their mother.

The elevator door clanged open, and Tess stepped into the dimly lit parking garage. There were only a few cars still here, and hers was in sight even though it was parked four rows away. She hurried toward it, unlocking the door by remote and watching as the back lights blinked at the command.

She'd already swung open the door and had one foot inside when she noticed the small brown bag sitting on the hood. It was scrunched at the top as if it held someone's leftovers from lunch. But then it could be anything. She'd check before she tossed it into the trash can on her way out.

Nothing to get alarmed about, but still she felt uneasy as she climbed out of the car and reached for the bag. Impulsively, she looked around for the night watchman. No sign of him, but the elevator doors clanged open behind her and a man she'd seen several times before stepped out, briefcase in hand. He smiled and waved and she waved back, feeling much more confident now that someone else who worked in the building was in sight.

She picked up the sack. It weighed no more than a few ounces. Her first guess at the contents were probably correct, but just in case it was something more valuable, she opened it and peeked inside.

It wasn't food, but a scrap of material. She pulled it out, then went weak. It was small boy's shirt. The front was stained with what appeared to be blood. A small scrap of white paper fell from the folds and drifted to the floor. Grasping the shirt between her thumb and index finger, she stooped, picked up the slip of paper and read the words printed on it in red ink.

Keep silent or Tess's sons will never be heard from again.

She stared at the note as her insides twisted into cramping knots. What in hell's name had she been dragged into?

"Are you all right?"

She jumped at the sound of the voice and almost lost her

balance. She leaned against the car for support as the man from the elevator approached her.

"I didn't mean to frighten you. I just saw you stooping by your car and thought you might need help."

"No." She stuffed the note and the shirt back into the bag. "I just… I dropped…something."

"Are you sure you're okay? You look a little shaky."

"I'm fine," she said. "Just tired. Too many late hours, I guess."

"Tell me about it. My wife complains all the time at the hours I keep, but you gotta make a living."

She nodded, then got into the car.

"Take care," he said, closing her door for her before he stepped away.

She shifted into Reverse and backed out of her space. The man was still standing in the same spot and watching her, probably thinking she was some kind of nut. But he was the least of her worries.

Keep silent.

"I don't know anything to tell, you murderous lunatic."

But the note was not the most chilling part of the warning. The blood-stained shirt was the real horror. Did it mean that the killer had the twins? Had they been abducted? If so, Logan might have been right all along. Tess could very well have been involved in something that had put his sons in danger.

She reached across the seat and unzipped her briefcase. She located the detective's card in the side pocket where she'd put it. Her fingers traced its sharp border, but instead of pulling it out, she chose the card behind it, the one Logan had given her.

The blood-stained shirt might well belong to one of his sons. He should be the first to know.

CHAPTER SEVEN

CRAIG GRAVES wanted to see her in his office. Cheri Trosclair shivered and hugged herself, running her hands up and down her bare arms as she let the worst possible scenarios play in her mind.

He'd seen Logan McCain call out to her at the grave site and had realized that was not their first encounter. Logan had broken his promise and told Craig she'd talked to him about Tess. Or worse, Logan had told Detective Morrison and he had come to Craig.

"Hey, how about a lap dance, sweetie?"

A middle-aged guy in a blue suit stepped in front of her and tried to stuff a dollar bill in the white garter that circled her thigh. She dodged him and kept walking. She had to get a story together. She was good at lying. She could do this. No matter what Craig had heard, she could pull it off.

Play it cool. That was the main thing. There was always the chance this was routine business and she was panicking over nothing. Maybe one of the customers had complained about her. She'd certainly been less than enthusiastic this afternoon, and nothing got Craig riled quicker than a dissatisfied customer. Well, almost nothing.

Her bravado sank as she tapped on the door.

"Come in."

She stepped inside. The only light in the room came from the window and the dusky glow of a day that was almost over. It took a few seconds for her pupils to adjust to the drastic change from the stage lights. When it did, she stepped closer to the desk. Craig sat behind it, his arms folded across the leather pad.

"It hasn't been a good day, has it, Cheri?"

Dread knotted in her stomach and balled in her throat. "The funeral was tough," she said, the one safe comment she could think of.

"For all of us, but especially for you. I know you were close to Tess and her sons."

She'd adored the boys. And this is where it had gotten her. "We spent some time together."

"I didn't think you were coming in tonight," he said. "I suggested you take the night off."

"I didn't want to be home alone after the funeral."

He nodded as if he understood. "It's hard to believe Tess and Hank are really dead."

"That's what the other dancers keep saying."

"I plan to talk to them, too," he said. "I started with you because I knew you and Tess were friends, but I want you all to know that we're a family here. We've had two deaths, but we'll hang together and get through this."

The breath that had caught in her lungs like tiny ice crystals melted in a rush of relief. He didn't know. She was safe—for now.

"That said, there are a few things we should talk about."

"What kinds of things?" She eased into the chair in front of his desk. The tweedy fabric felt rough and tingly on the bare flesh of her thighs. She should have taken time to pull on one of the silk robes from the changing room.

"I think you should take a few days off."

"I'm fine, really. Today was hard, but I can handle it."

"I know, but the job is demanding. The men expect a good time. If you're feeling low, it's hard to keep it from showing."

"What about Friday night? You still need me for that party, don't you?"

"All Elite parties have been cancelled until further notice."

Cancelled. She hadn't expected that. Craig might feel bad for Tess and Hank, but he would never cancel the Elite affairs out of respect for the dead. He was worried. Or else the guests were worried.

"Does that mean that private engagements are cancelled, as well?"

"Those will be handled as before, but there is one other thing." He stood and walked to the front of his desk. "Did Tess tell you that she'd seen an attorney?"

"No, but I knew she was considering seeing one about a custody case."

"I wasn't aware there was a problem with that."

"The twins' biological father has decided he wants the boys. Tess didn't want to give them up."

"Not a particularly good decision on her part as it turns out. Who's the father?"

Cheri hesitated, but Craig would find out anyway. Better she get credit for supplying the information. "Logan McCain."

"Well, that explains a few things. Are you sure that the custody hearing is all Tess talked about with the attorney?"

"I would assume so. Tess never mentioned that she planned to discuss anything else with an attorney."

He picked up a brown envelope from the corner of his desk. "This is a little something extra to make up for the tips you'll be missing while you're off."

"I appreciate that."

"Look inside," he instructed, handing her the envelope. "I think you'll find it a very generous bonus."

She slipped the tip of a perfectly manicured fingernail beneath the seal and ripped it open. The envelope was stuffed with hundred-dollar bills. A payoff, but for what? Did he suspect she knew what Tess had been planning?

"This is too much."

"I don't think so. Neither do your friends. It's a thank-you for being the type of employee we can depend on to handle this situation and Detective Morrison."

Craig stepped behind her chair and rested his hands on her shoulders. For a second she flashed back fifteen years, and it was her stepfather's fingers pressing into her flesh.

"I don't want you to mention our discussion about Tess and Logan McCain with anyone else, Cheri. Can I depend on that?"

"Of course."

"And if McCain tries to talk to you, walk away. In fact, if you even see him in this club, alert me immediately. You do understand the importance of that, don't you?"

Our little secret. Your mother doesn't need to know. You do understand, don't you, Cheri?

"I understand, Mr. Graves."

"Good." He stepped away and opened the door. "Call if you hear from the detective again. I like to keep tabs on what he's up to."

"I will, but he talked to me last night. I don't see any reason why he'd question me again."

"Who knows what reasons the detective has for anything he's doing. I'm beginning to think he's getting his kicks out of hanging around the club."

She breathed a lot easier leaving his office than when she'd gone in. But she doubted this was the end of it. Trouble was like an avalanche. Once it got started, it roared down the mountain and buried everything in it's path.

Tess and Hank were the first two to go. Cheri did not plan to be victim number three.

RACHEL CALLED Logan the minute she got home, then spent the next half hour vacillating between wondering if she'd made a mistake and being certain that she had. Detective Morrison would not like it that she'd bypassed him. Worse, she was suffering an extreme guilt attack, feeling as if she'd turned against Tess.

She started a pot of coffee. Logan would probably want something stronger after what she had to tell him, but coffee was like soul food to her. Not only the taste, but the aroma and the feel of the warm cup in her hands. And tonight she needed all the steadying powers she could get.

She still didn't trust Logan, but the pat little conclusions she'd jumped to when Tess was in her office Friday morning were too naive to hold water in light of the latest frightening development.

She started to make herself a sandwich, then decided her stomach could never handle it, not as long as that blood-stained shirt was in her house, taunting her with all its terrifying implications.

The piercing ring of the doorbell startled her, causing the coffee mug she's just taken from the shelf to slip from her fingers and shatter on the ceramic tile floor. She raked the pieces aside with her foot, but didn't bother to pick them up. That could wait.

"I got here as fast as I could," Logan said, sweeping through the door the second she'd opened it. "What's up?"

She took a deep breath, then swallowed hard. "I think you may have been right about the boys. I think they could be in danger."

He looked at her questioningly. "What is it? What have you heard?"

"There was a package on the hood of my car tonight when I started home. A brown paper sack."

"Go on."

She walked to the table, picked up the bag and handed it to him. "I wish I didn't have to show you this, Logan, but I…"

He didn't wait for her to finish the statement before he reached inside and pulled out the shirt. He stared at it for a second, then held the small shirt next to his broad chest.

"Son of a bitch! What kind of sick bastard would want to hurt a couple of innocent kids?"

"There was a note with it. All it said was keep silent or Tess's sons will never be heard from again."

"Keep silent about what?"

"I don't have a clue. The only thing Tess told me was that you were the father of her sons, and that's common knowledge now. Except…"

"Go on."

"She said you raped her the night she got pregnant, but that she didn't want to press charges."

"That's a damn lie."

"I'm just telling you what she said."

"I suppose you told that to Morrison, as well."

"He asked what Tess said when she came to my office. I told him the truth."

"Have you told anyone about the shirt?"

"Not yet," she admitted. "I thought you should know first since this is obviously about your sons. Yours and Tess's."

"I appreciate that. I'd like to see the note."

"Okay, but look at it through the plastic bag I put it in. With any luck, Detective Morrison can get fingerprints from it. He might be able to get them from the shirt, as well, and he can run a DNA test on the stain."

"If he bothers."

"Why are you so negative about him?"

"He's a cop." He studied the note.

"This is the second warning I've gotten," she said, when he finally returned the note to her. "The first was a phone call Saturday afternoon from someone disguising their voice. All the caller said then was that I should stay out of things. I did tell the detective about that."

"Hard to stay out of it if the lunatic keeps pulling you into it." Logan raked his hands through his hair as if the motion could clear his mind. "Are you sure Tess didn't say anything to indicate what she was mixed up in? Drugs? Prostitution? Blackmail? Any reason at all for someone to kill her?"

"She only talked about you and the boys. I thought you might know more."

He locked his gaze with hers. His dark eyes were piercing, yet troubled. "I know she let some guy beat the crap out of her. I know one of her friends thought the boys needed to be taken away from her."

"What friend?"

He shook his head. "The contact was anonymous."

Anonymous contacts, disguised phone calls, scribbled threats left on her car. This was becoming more convoluted by the second, And more sinister. And here she was talking about it with the man she'd originally thought guilty of murder and feeling almost as if she were in league with him.

"What will you do now, Logan?"

"I won't give up. That's for sure. And I'm not taking the blood on the shirt to mean anything at all, certainly not that the boys are…"

He skipped over the word *dead,* but it hung there between them as tangible as the shirt.

"It could be a scare tactic," he said.

"If it was, it worked," Rachel admitted.

He shrugged. "I never meant to drag you into this."

"You didn't, but since you're here, I think we should talk."

"I'll talk all you want, but I don't see how going over and over the same thing is going to help at this point."

"It might help me understand what I'm dealing with. I have a fresh pot of coffee. Would you like a cup? Or there's wine, might even be a beer in the fridge."

"What are you having?"

"Coffee."

"Sounds good. I'll go with that." He followed her into the kitchen, watching while she pulled mugs from the shelf and filled them with the brew.

"Cream or sugar?"

"Straight."

He took his cup and walked to the kitchen table, standing and holding out a chair for her until she joined him. The manners of a gentleman, but that didn't necessarily mean he was one.

"When did you actually find out about the twins?" she asked.

"I received a letter with a picture of Danny and Davy. That was…sixteen days ago to be exact. The note said they were my sons and that they were in danger."

"Is that all it said?"

"No. It had Tess's full name and the address of the house she supposedly lived in with her stepmother and sons on the

Westbank. The note said I had picked her up at a bar almost five years ago and impregnated her."

"You must have remembered that."

He shook his head, but made no excuses. Apparently one-nighters were frequent enough with him five years ago that they didn't register. She wondered if that were still the case.

"You surely aren't seeking custody based on an anonymous note."

"No. I thought the picture was a doctored version of one of my brother and I at that age. I figured it was a scam to get money."

"What changed your mind?"

"I drove over to Gretna and hung around until I saw the boys outside with their grandmother."

"And that's all it took to convince you they were yours?"

"There's no doubt they're McCains."

"So you went to see Tess?"

"No, I talked to our family lawyer, Artie Fonteneaux. His advice was to let him handle everything, so I let him make the first contact. Tess tossed him out. So I paid her a visit."

"I take it she was not glad to see you."

"She did the hysterical routine, started yelling about how I had treated her five years ago. I couldn't even get her to discuss the boys. When I went back the second time to tell her that I was going to petition the courts for custody and would need DNA testing done on the boys, her stepmother said she'd moved out."

"Did you try to see her at the club?"

"Not that day. I didn't know where she worked. I left for London that night on an urgent business trip. Artie tracked down her place of employment while I was away. I got back to town on Thursday night and made a visit to the club on Friday morning. You know the rest of the story, or at least as much as I know." He exhaled slowly. "I never thought it would end like this."

Only it hadn't ended. The boys and their grandmother were missing. Tess's murder was unsolved. The killer was still roaming the streets and making threats.

Rachel sipped her coffee but there were no comforting effects tonight. This was too bizarre to be credible. Yet, the shirt was real. The note was real. And a real body had been buried today.

Logan picked up the shirt again, this time holding it toward the light and studying it for several minutes. "I don't think this is blood," he said. "It's too thick."

"I hope you're right."

"Even if it's not blood, the situation is frightening. You can't take that threat you got tonight lightly."

"I'm not taking any of this lightly. I'll make sure the deadbolt is on every time I'm in the apartment."

"You should get a security guard to walk you to your car at night."

"I will if I leave late."

"Have you considered a bodyguard? My company's used them before when we had foreign dignitaries in town. It's no trouble to arrange one."

"On my salary? I can't even afford a Boy Scout."

"I can hire one for you."

She thought about it for a minute, but the idea of being watched made the situation scarier. "I appreciate the offer, but no thanks."

"If you change your mind, you have my number."

She hoped that nothing was going to happen to make her change her mind.

"I'd like to take the shirt with me and get it thoroughly analyzed."

So that's why he was being so accommodating. "I'm sorry, Logan. I called you first because I thought you should know of the danger to your sons, but I can't withhold evidence from the police."

"I don't guess there's anything I can say that would persuade you differently?"

"Afraid not."

"You don't really trust me, do you, Rachel?"

"I don't really know you, Logan."

He carried his coffee cup to the sink. "You're sure you won't change your mind about the shirt?"

She shook her head.

"Then I guess I should be going."

She followed him to the door and opened it. He extended a hand, but when she offered hers, he merely held it while his thumb massaged the back of her hand. The effect was unsettling, and she could easily see why a young and innocent Tess could have been totally seduced by him. She pulled away.

"You've nothing to fear from me, Rachel."

"I'm not afraid of you."

"Good. Take care, and be careful. Be very, very careful."

She closed the door behind him, then leaned against it, shaken, but not sure if the strange sensations skidding around her nervous system were from some ridiculous, misplaced attraction or the seriousness of his tone when he'd warned her to be careful.

If it was the first, she'd find a way to shake it. There was no way she would let herself become involved with him, at least not until she knew who'd killed Tess Shepherd.

No possible way.

HOAGIE MORRISON was waiting in the back room of a family-owned restaurant and bar in the Faubourg Marigny neighborhood when Griffin Paulson sauntered in and took a seat next to him. It was a great place to eat, not only for the food but because they kept Hoagie's hours. You could have dinner until eleven. But he was eating early tonight. It was just past nine.

The owner stuck his head in once Griffin took his seat. "What can I get you two?"

"Got any of those red beans and rice left I saw on the specials board?" Hoagie asked.

"You bet," Billy said. "How about you?" he asked, aiming his stare at Griffin.

"I'll take a burger with grilled onions. Lots of onions. And some French fries."

"And a couple of cold beers to wash it down?"

"Not for me," Hoagie said. He could use one, but if he got started, he'd probably want a six-pack after the week he'd had. And he wasn't ready to call it a night just yet. He might just wander back down to the Fruits of Passion.

"I'll take a draft," Griffin said. "Cold as you got it."

"Coming up."

"I figured you'd have Logan McCain behind bars by now," Griffin said, once Billy was out of hearing distance.

"If it were only that easy. So tell me you dug up a lead for me among your friends in low places."

"Not anything concrete, but I found a little tidbit I thought you might be interested in."

"Hit me with it."

"Both Logan McCain and Rachel Powers were in the Fruits of Passion last Saturday night sitting at the same table. I thought you might find that interesting since Rachel said Tess didn't give you any information that would incriminate Logan."

Hoagie didn't bother to tell Griffin that he'd already heard all of that from Rachel, but it was nice to know he was actually keeping up with what was going on at the gentleman's club. "You're convinced Logan's the perp, aren't you?"

"He's the only one with a motive," Griffin replied.

"I need more than that to arrest a McCain."

"The McCains have had their trouble with the law."

"Guess you're talking about Joshua McCain."

Griffin nodded. "Yeah."

"He never had a felony record."

"'Cause his old man paid off the right people."

"What do you know about Elton Pierce?" Hoagie asked.

"He helps Craig out at the club. I'm not clear what his job responsibilities are, but he's around there most every night. Why do you ask?"

"I ran some checks on him. He spent some time in jail a few years back for petty theft, but he's also had a couple of arrests on possession, bad checks, illegal gambling—that sort of thing."

"How long ago was that?"

"Jail time was twelve years ago. His record's been clean since, but I just thought you might have heard something about him on the streets."

"Not a thing. Guess he's reformed," Griffin remarked.

"Maybe. Maybe not."

"You got any reason to think he'd kill one of the club's dancers and the bouncer?"

"Just keeping all my options open," Hoagie said.

"Go ahead, but I got a croaker says when all is said and done, Logan McCain will be breaking up rock at Angola."

Billy had just brought out the food when Hoagie's cell phone started vibrating. He checked the ID. Rachel Powers. That was the last person he'd expected to hear from tonight.

HE WALKED by the Fruits of Passion with his wife. He didn't even glance that way, but still he felt a tightening in his groin. It had only been three weeks since he'd been to one of the Elite soirees, yet he was already going crazy with the need to fulfill his sexual cravings again.

"Fruits of Passion: A Gentleman's Club." His wife read the sign and chuckled. "Gentleman. I just bet." She linked her arm with his. "Have you ever been in a place like that?"

He looked at her as if she'd lost her mind. "Can you even imagine me in a joint like that?"

She couldn't, of course, and that was the beauty of it. And that was why it was imperative they not let anyone destroy what they'd created. Not Tess Shepherd. Not Hank Matthews.

And not Rachel Powers.

The games had to go on at any cost.

CHAPTER EIGHT

KAREN WAS usually so caught up in her work at the center that she could barely think of anything else. But ever since she'd talked to Rachel last night and learned of the latest threat, she couldn't get her friend off her mind. Karen was used to dealing with violence on a day-to-day basis, and she got plenty of threats of her own from guys who didn't want her counseling their partners to get out of an abusive relationship.

But this was different. Nothing fitted together, and there was no clear picture of where the danger lay. As far as Karen was concerned, Rachel's continued involvement with Logan McCain wasn't in Rachel's best interest. It was ludicrous to call him instead of the police last night, but she sincerely hoped it wasn't that Rachel was falling for the man.

Wow! She'd never expected to hear herself say that. For years she'd been pushing Rachel the other way to no avail. Any time a relationship started to click for her, Rachel backed away like a crawfish on speed.

But she could see the attraction. The guy was classically handsome and wore the scent of money well. With money came power, and power was the greatest aphrodisiac of all.

Money could make a guy look like a gentleman. It didn't make him one. But Karen had to admit that based on her one encounter with Logan, he hadn't seemed like someone who'd punch a woman.

Charm her pants off during a one-night stand? Yeah. He was probably capable of that. But not knock her around—and definitely not murder the mother of his sons. But then Karen had been wrong about at least one man before.

Unfortunately, she hadn't found that out until after she'd married the jerk. He'd slugged her once—hard enough that she'd lost two teeth and needed ten stitches to close a cut under her left eye.

That had been all it had taken for Karen to toss everything of his out the window of their second-floor apartment. Even his beloved CD equipment. She'd made her point. He didn't contest the divorce or bother her again.

She'd quit her job as office manager for a contractor and gone out and raised money to open the Center for Abused Women, the one good thing that had come from her marriage. Well, that and the jewelry she'd hocked to buy food while she was getting her new project started.

Karen pulled a chart on the woman who'd just checked into the center for the third time in as many months. Sandra Peterson. Her boyfriend was a traveling salesman. At work, he was affable and imperturbable and a dynamite salesman. With her, he was jealous and possessive and could turn violent at the slightest provocation.

Sandra had also been the name of the woman who'd been killed by her boyfriend last winter. Beaten to death just days after the dancer Karen had seen at the gentleman's club the other night had picked her up at the center to take her home.

Sandra Valencia.

Impulsively Karen pulled her file. Age twenty-three. Single. No place of employment listed. No emergency phone number listed. No address listed. Karen flipped through the counseling notes to some newspaper articles that had been clipped and included in the file.

Karen skimmed the articles, then stopped reading as one line jumped from the page as if it had been written in flashing neon. And suddenly her fear for Rachel leaped to a whole new level.

RACHEL SIPPED iced tea while she waited for Karen to arrive. The lunch invitation had been a surprise. Actually more like a shock. Karen never took time for lunch. But she had been insistent today, and fortunately Rachel didn't have an appointment until two.

The restaurant was Italian, a small family-owned establishment on Magazine Street, the kind with red-checkered tablecloths and dripping wax candles. The smell of garlic dominated a pungent mix of odors that went well with the Italian opera music coming through the speakers and the clatter of dishes.

As in so many restaurants in New Orleans, the health-food fad had not made a significant impact here. The Big Easy with its fried seafood, gumbos, po'boys and fat-hearty meat dishes was probably the heart-attack capital of the world.

A waiter passed, carrying a tray with two plates heaped with pasta and gigantic meatballs, all topped with a thick red sauce. For the first time in days, Rachel experienced a genuine hunger attack.

She'd missed dinner last night and had had only a piece of buttered toast with her coffee this morning. When the waiter set a basket of hot garlic bread on the table, she dove in.

She was still savoring the first bite when Karen came rushing in, only five minutes late—a record for her. She was wearing jeans and a yellow T-shirt that showed off her tan and her ample breasts.

Karen was a good fifty pounds overweight, but she never seemed to notice and neither did anyone else. She was smart, caring and fun. What were a few extra pounds compared to qualities like that?

She dropped her overstuffed black handbag and a manila folder into one of the empty chairs at their table for four and took the chair opposite Rachel's. "You look good."

"Then lack of sleep and living a nightmare must become me."

"I think it's more that the dark circles under your eyes go with the charcoal suit."

"You have such a way with words."

The waiter came and took their order, a garden salad and a chicken marsala for Rachel, a dressed meatball po'boy for Karen.

"So am I going to hear what this emergency luncheon is all about now or do I have to wait until after we eat?"

"I didn't say it was an emergency."

"That didn't answer my question."

"It might go better after lunch."

"I'll take my chances...spill."

Karen grimaced. "It has to do with the woman I told you about the other day. You know, the one who was killed by her abusive boyfriend."

"What about her?"

"I checked out her file. And are you ready for this?"

"Probably not."

"Then get ready. Her last place of employment was the Fruits of Passion."

Rachel's spirits plunged again, not that they'd been high to begin with. "Great working environment, huh?"

Karen picked up the manila folder and set it on the table between them as the waiter appeared with her glass of tea. Rachel turned the folder so that she could read the name on the tab. "Sandra Valencia."

"That was the name we knew her by. Apparently it was fake."

Rachel pulled the first article from the folder. The accompanying black-and-white photo was of a very attractive young woman who looked to be in her early twenties. She read the article slowly, letting the words sink in. Sandra Valencia's nude and beaten body had been found in a back alley in the French Quarter.

"Very similar to the way Tess was found," Rachel said, feeling a few pangs that had nothing to do with hunger.

"Keep reading. There's more."

Rachel picked up the next article. Victim's boyfriend kills himself over murder. The details were skimpy, but the bottom line was that Sandra Valencia's boyfriend had shot and killed himself after writing a suicide note saying he couldn't go on living knowing he'd killed the woman he loved in a fit of rage.

"Too bad he didn't kill himself first," Rachel said.

"If he killed himself at all."

Rachel slipped the articles back in the folder. "Why would he write a note admitting the crime if he wasn't guilty?"

"Maybe he didn't write the note. Maybe it wasn't suicide."

Rachel ran her finger over the outside of her tea glass, smearing the drops of condensation. "You said yourself her boyfriend beat her up on a regular basis."

"That's what she told us, but then everything else she said was a lie, so why would we assume that's the truth? It might have been someone else she was afraid of. She could have come to the center to hide out. And even if she did have an abusive lover, that doesn't mean he killed her."

"You're jumping to a lot of conclusions. This is not like you."

"But my conclusions make sense. The man who actually killed her could still be on the loose. He could have killed again."

JOANNA WAYNE   101

Rachel shuddered. "You've got to stop watching *CSI*."

"Don't talk such blasphemy." Karen's facial expression contradicted her attempt at humor. "Think about it," she continued. "Tess had bruises. Sandra had bruises. They both worked at the Fruits of Passion. They both were found beaten and nude."

Rachel *was* thinking about it, and it was making her blood run cold. "Do you really think some perverted madman is targeting dancers at that particular club? Someone so vile and cunning that he killed the boyfriend to make it look as if he was the culprit?"

"Stranger things have happened. It could be an employee, or maybe even a customer. Maybe he becomes obsessed with a dancer, then kills them when they refuse to go out with him."

"Why would he kill Hank? Surely he wasn't obsessed with him."

"No, but with obsession comes jealousy. Maybe Hank had a thing for Tess, too. He could have been friendly with Tess or even dating her. Oh, I know…"

Rachel shuddered. "I don't think I want to hear this."

"What if the killer was planning to leave another suicide note with Hank's body," Karen continued, ignoring Rachel's comment. "He might have gotten interrupted before he could plant it, maybe by Logan."

The scenario played in Rachel's mind. It was positively sickening, but it was all coincidence. "Surely the guy wasn't stupid enough to think the cops would buy a second murder/suicide in the same small work population, especially within months of each other."

"I didn't say he was a smart madman."

"But smart enough to set someone else up for the crimes. No. I know you love a good mystery, but you're off base this time. Your theory is downright weird."

"No more bizarre than leaving a bloody kid's shirt on your car."

"Stained shirt. I'm not even certain the stain was blood. And if you're trying to freak me out even more, it's working."

"You should be freaked out. So freaked out you quit making nice-nice with Logan McCain."

"Whoa. You can't be tying him into your theory of an obsessed multiple killer?"

"It's possible," Karen said.

"But extremely farfetched."

"Granted, but no matter who the killer is, he's a dangerous nut who believes you know something that could hurt him."

"He's wrong."

"Convince him, not me."

"I would, if I knew who he was."

"All I'm saying is you should stay out of the investigation and away from Logan McCain altogether. It's not your fight, and Tess probably wasn't leveling with you any more than Sandra was leveling with us."

"Tess told the truth about Logan being the father of her sons. At least Logan seems convinced that she did. And you don't need to worry. I am staying out of it."

"Visiting the Fruits of Passion is not staying out of it. Neither is inviting Logan McCain to your condo."

Karen was right as usual. She hadn't taken Tess Shepherd as a client and never would have. And she definitely didn't owe Logan anything. "You make a valid point, girlfriend."

"So does that mean you'll stay away from Logan McCain and that you won't go anywhere near that strip club?"

"I'm not sure I can make that promise."

Karen threw up her hands in exasperation. "It's Logan Mc-

Cain, isn't it? I don't know how he's done it, but that guy has gotten to you."

"It's not Logan."

"Then what? Face it, Rachel. You hide your face during scary movies. You are not one to piss off a madman deliberately."

She swallowed hard. She could never explain her real reason to Karen's satisfaction. She didn't fully understand it herself, but two young boys had lost their mother and now they were in danger—if they were still alive.

"It's just something I have to do."

The waiter returned with their food, but Rachel had totally lost her appetite.

"To drastically change the subject, isn't that Stone Littleton walking through the door?"

Rachel looked up just as the controversial producer and his entourage—that included such notables as a past mayor and a current state senator—stepped into the restaurant. "That's him."

"He's even better-looking in person than he is in those paparazzi shots that make *People* magazine."

"I told you he was good-looking," Rachel said. "Every female in the office drools whenever he comes in."

"I can't imagine anyone as hot as him hiring a law firm as stuffy as WW&C for anything."

"See what charcoal suits can get you."

Rachel picked at her lunch while Karen devoured hers. As far as she was concerned, Stone Littleton was just another reminder that she worked for the most prestigious firm in the city and that she'd be a fool to do anything to get her fired.

Mr. Castile had warned her. Propriety was all-important. That might even outweigh the threats as reason not to get involved in Tess's murder case.

But then there were the boys.

CRAIG GRAVES was sick and tired of Detective Hoagie Morrison. The guy had been in the club all afternoon, hanging around, questioning people and making the dancers nervous. That wasn't good for business.

He picked up the phone and punched in the private number of one of his biggest investors, a man with enough clout that he was supposed to take care of things like this.

"Hello."

"Craig," he said, identifying himself before he went on. "Something needs to be done about Detective Hoagie Morrison."

"What's wrong?"

"He's acting like this is the only murder the town's seen this year. He's bugging the hell out of the dancers. Got them so worked up they're jumping at their own shadows out there."

"You said you had everything under control."

"It's under control. He's not going to find a thing, but I don't like the guy harassing my dancers."

"It's best if we let this run its course. He'll snoop around awhile, but when he doesn't find anything, he'll move on."

"Let's hope that's sooner and not later."

"It will be. The homicide department is stretched to its limit. They don't have the manpower to keep up the heat on low-priority murders like these ones."

"He's not acting like these are low-priority."

"A dancer and a bouncer in a Bourbon Street club? Trust me. They're low-priority."

"Not if Logan McCain is officially named as a suspect."

"He won't be. His family has too much clout."

"Does that mean you're not going to do anything?"

"It means I'd rather not make an issue of this unless I have to. Talk to the dancers. Give them a bonus. Do whatever you need to do."

"Okay, but we're taking a risk with Morrison. Guy's into this case. I don't see him walking away."

"I'll take care of the situation if and when it becomes necessary."

"Best not wait too long."

PETE PELLEGRIN was glad he hadn't already spent the bonus money he'd originally figured was a sure thing. Twins seldom went unnoticed, especially kids as cute as these were. Strangers fawned over them, asked their ages, sometimes their names. And four-year-olds would have blurted out the answers to those questions before a grandma could stop them.

Pete had done enough legwork to find out that the only trips Cathy Shepherd had made in the last few years were to the beaches near Gulf Shores, Alabama, or to play the slots at casinos along the Mississippi Gulf Coast. He'd pretty much covered those areas and nobody remembered seeing her or the twins.

He was all the way to Fort Walton, Florida, now, hitting the restaurants and beach rental agencies. Hard to imagine that one little area could have so much rental property.

He pulled his Volkswagen into the drive of a real estate office whose sign advertised beach rentals. Time for another performance. A bell clanged as he pushed through the heavy glass door.

"Can I help you?"

The woman behind the counter was about his age, skinny, crooked teeth, but a nice smile. "I hope you can," he said. "I'm looking for my sister and her two grandsons. I know they're vacationing in this area, but I don't have the name of the place they're staying."

"What's her name?"

"Cathy Shepherd."

She typed something into the computer, scrolled a bit, then frowned. "I'm sorry. No Cathy Shepherd."

"She could have used her married name. She does sometimes, though she's been divorced from the jerk for years."

"What's the married name?"

"Hilliard. Hillian. Oh, God, I can't think right now. My niece, the boys' mother, was in a terrible car accident. She's hanging on, but barely. That's why I've got to find my sister. It's her only daughter."

"Oh, bless her heart. You're right. You've got to find her." She typed some more. "I don't find any names similar to that."

"Take a look at these pictures then, if you don't mind. I may have that name wrong."

The woman took one look and her hand flew to her mouth. "Oh, my goodness. She was in here a few hours ago. The boys were with her. She said her reservations had gotten messed up, and she was stuck with no place to stay. I tried to help her, but we don't have any vacancies."

"Did you suggest anywhere she might find a room?"

"No. Most every place around here is full this time of the year. It's high season. And there's some kind of national Boy Scout meeting going on this week. They've taken any extra rooms there might have been. I did tell her where she could get a check cashed, though. I would have cashed it for her, but we only take checks in payment. It's the policy."

"A big check?"

"Five hundred dollars. She said it was good, but I couldn't

risk it, especially since it wasn't local and it was a personal check, you know, not a payroll check or anything like that."

"A personal check?"

She nodded. "From a bank in the Cayman Islands. That made me a little nervous, too."

"I don't suppose you remember the name of the person who wrote it."

"As a matter of fact, I do."

LOGAN LEFT a city planning meeting where he'd been pleading for some zoning changes, and crossed the street to Mr. B's restaurant for a cup of coffee and a bowl of soup before the after-work crowd came in for drinks and dinner. He'd missed break-fast and lunch, and he was starting to get a killer headache. Not that food would necessarily relieve it, but it might help.

He'd gone through the motions of work today, but his mind had been consumed with the situation concerning Danny and Davy. The shirt left on Rachel's car might not belong to one of the boys. It could well be a scare tactic, just as he'd told Rachel.

But why the hell was it left on her car? What could she possibly know that made her such a risk to the psycho who was masterminding all of this? And how did Cathy Shepherd fit into the picture?

The questions plagued him as he went in and was seated by the hostess. The questions...and Rachel Powers.

He'd thought about her a lot since the night they'd met. She'd made quite an impression on him. Not just her looks, though she looked fine. Great body. Terrific legs. Nice hair, auburn and soft. Short, but he liked short hair on a woman. Most men didn't, but he always had. And then there were those gorgeous green eyes.

But it was her wit and intelligence that had really gotten to him. And her laugh. Not quiet and controlled the way most women he knew laughed, but genuine and bold. She seemed restrained most of the time, but not when she laughed.

He'd planned to call and ask her out, would have if he hadn't received the information about Davy and Danny. It was all unbelievable that she'd gotten dragged into this sordid hell. What were the chances that a young attorney for a corporate firm with the sterling reputation of WW&C would ever give an appointment to an exotic dancer looking for representation in a custody hearing? What was the chance a dancer from Bourbon Street could afford someone that expensive?

But somehow it had happened, and now Rachel was right in the middle of the mess, caught up in the danger. The lunatic knew where she worked and probably where she lived.

And he could be anyone. A stranger on the street that Rachel wouldn't notice until it was too late. That was the fear that had played in the back of his mind all day.

He shrugged out of his suit coat and draped it over the back of his chair, then pulled out his cell phone and made a call to his secretary. He listened as she gave him his messages. None from Detective Morrison, Pete Pellegrin, Rachel or anyone else connected to the murder case.

He broke the connection and dipped a spoon into the bowl of corn and crab chowder the waiter had set in front of him. The temperature outside wasn't conducive to hot soup, but he'd been in air-conditioned buildings all day, and soup could satisfy his hunger a lot quicker than a salad could.

He was half through with the soup when his cell phone vibrated. He checked the ID. Pete Pellegrin. A surge of adrenaline hit his bloodstream, though he was afraid to become too optimistic.

He didn't bother with a hello. "Have you located the boys?"

"No, but I think I'm close. And I have some interesting information for you. Some very interesting information."

CHAPTER NINE

LOGAN'S FRUSTRATION LEVEL shot to the limits. "You have to be mistaken."

"I don't think so, Mr. McCain. The woman I talked to said it was a personal check signed by Harris Benson McCain and drawn on a bank in the Cayman Islands. There's no way she could have pulled that name out of the blue."

He hadn't seen this coming. If this was true, his own father had a part in the disappearance of the boys and of putting them in harm's way. He was too furious to think clearly, but it was a damn good thing he wasn't in the office now. If he had been he might have strangled his father with his bare hands.

He listened to the rest of what Pellegrin had to say, then tossed some bills on the table without waiting for the check. He couldn't have finished if he'd wanted, not the way the soup he'd already eaten was pitching around in his stomach.

He hit the streets of the French Quarter, darting between and around pedestrians while old memories had a field day in his mind. His father manipulating, pushing, punishing, always in control of everything and everyone.

Everyone except Josh. They'd clashed at every turn, until the day his brother had slammed out of the house never to return again. And now this. It was incomprehensible. Loathsome. Disgusting. Perverted.

Logan walked aimlessly until, exhausted from his fury and the humid heat, he collapsed onto one of the steps along the Moonwalk. The river was only a few steps away, and tourists and locals milled about, some staring at him. Not that he gave a damn.

He glanced at his watch. It was after seven, and still the heat was relentless. His shirt was soaked with sweat. His tie swung haphazardly from a loose loop that was inches below his collar. His suit jacket was missing, probably left at the restaurant when he'd paid his bill and rushed out.

Logan propped his elbows on his knees and cradled his head in his hands. Finally, dizzy from a blinding headache, he stood and dusted the city's grime from the seat of his pants. He needed a painkiller. He needed a shower. He needed a stiff drink. And then he'd have a talk with his father.

His car was back at the parking garage near the restaurant. He started walking, slower this time, struggling to get his thoughts together. He wouldn't go off half-cocked and blow the confrontation. He'd call the shots this time.

He paused when he got to Bourbon Street and turned toward the Fruits of Passion. It was a block away, but he could see the glaring neon sign in front of the building. He wondered if the dark-haired woman was working tonight. Maybe he'd check that out later, too. He was pretty sure she wouldn't talk to him in the club, but if he could slip her a note, she might agree to meet him somewhere.

Up until tonight, he'd foolishly believed that people at the gentleman's club might be his only link to Danny and Davy. He'd never even suspected that his father had ever met Cathy Shepherd, much less given her money.

Logan turned away, and continued walking toward the parking garage where he'd left his car. He started across the street, then stopped dead in his tracks. Rachel Powers was a few feet away from him, walking the other way—toward the club. He crossed and ran to catch up with her.

"WHERE DO you think you're going?"

Rachel swung around. "Logan. Are you okay?"

"Not particularly."

"What happened? Were you mugged?"

"Not physically. Guess I look like shit."

She doubted he could ever look that bad, but he did look a lot worse for wear. "Did you get news about the boys?"

"Yeah. Guess you could say that."

"What did you hear?" It hurt to ask, and she dreaded to hear the answer.

"There's no word on their whereabouts."

Her heart steadied. She looked around. Bourbon Street was too crowded but she knew a bar around the corner where it was quieter. "Have a drink with me, Logan. You can talk about what's bothering you—or not."

"Yeah. A drink would be good."

She led the way, glad that he'd agreed, but feeling awkward. He needed a friend, not an acquaintance. But situations changed things, and this one had thrown them together and bound them in a way even friendship couldn't have. Besides, if he hadn't wanted to have a drink with her, he could have said no.

They found a corner in the back of the bar and sat in silence except for giving their order to the waiter. She didn't want to push, though she'd love to know what was wrong.

He downed his whiskey, then leaned in and propped his elbows on the table. "I wonder if orphans know how lucky they are."

The statement caught her off guard. For a second, she thought he was cruelly referring to his sons, but then they weren't orphans. They still had a father. His words cut into her all the same.

"You don't know what you're saying, Logan."

"Don't I?"

"No." She seldom mentioned her past, but this time the words wouldn't stay inside her. "I'm an orphan. I missed my parents every day of my life. I still do. There's no way you can call that lucky."

"I'm sorry. I wasn't aiming that at you."

"I guess your family is taking the boys' disappearance hard," she said, still unsure exactly what he was saying.

"My mother doesn't know about them. I'm not sure it would register with her if she did. My father has his own way of handling any crisis."

He gulped down the rest of his drink, then rocked the glass back and forth, making tinkling noises with his ice.

She waited to see if he'd say more. When he didn't, she brought up the subject that was troubling her. "Did you know that another dancer at the Fruits of Passion was murdered about six months ago the same way Tess was murdered?" The question got his attention fast and seemed to shake him from the strangling hold of his dark mood, at least temporarily.

"How did you find that out?"

She filled him in on what she knew.

"The plot thickens yet again." He motioned to a passing waiter to bring another drink. "I wonder if Detective Morrison even knows of Sandra's murder."

"Maybe he just doesn't think it relates since it was an open-and-shut case."

"Could be." He didn't look convinced.

"At least one of Sandra's friends still works at Fruits of Passion. Karen pointed her out to me when we were in the club Saturday night."

"Did you talk to her?"

"No. We only saw her for a second, and then she disappeared."

"What did she look like?"

"She was petite, pretty. She had the dark, exotic look of a Creole."

His eyes narrowed, but she clearly had his full attention now.

"Did your friend Karen know the dancer's name?"

"She couldn't remember it, but I'd like to talk to the woman. If she was a friend of both Tess and Sandra, she might know something."

Logan's face twisted into a scowl. "Why are you doing this, Rachel? Why are you putting yourself in danger when you only met Tess once, and even then she didn't level with you about who'd punched her lights out?"

"Tess sought my counsel."

"That's not why you're doing this and you know it."

"Then why do you think I'm doing it?"

"Because you feel the boys' disappearance was somehow your fault. It isn't." He reached across the table and put his hands over hers. A simple, unexpected touch, yet it had a strong effect on her. Maybe any man's comfort could have had the same effect at that point.

But it wasn't any man. It was Logan McCain. And her only connection to him was a murder case. She had to keep that in mind.

"I'll talk to the dark-haired dancer," he said, "but I don't want you near that strip club. Not tonight and not ever again. Promise me you'll stay away from there."

It was the second time that day she'd been asked to do that. Neither her reasons nor her answer had changed.

"You don't have to make me your responsibility, Logan. You have enough to worry about without taking me on."

"That's one way of looking at it. It's not the way I see it."

"How do you see it?"

"Knowing you're safe means I have one less thing to worry about."

Normally she'd take that attitude as chauvinistic. The events of the last few days had changed that, and it wasn't as if she wanted to put herself in the path of a killer. "I won't go there without letting you know first." That was the best offer she could make.

"I guess I'll have to settle for that. Now let's finish our drinks, and then I'll walk you to your car. I've got to take care of a little business tonight that can't wait."

FROM THE OUTSIDE, the sprawling mansion on Napoleon Street looked the same as it had when Logan was growing up. It rose three stories and stretched to the top of the giant oaks that surrounded it. The third-floor turret had been the play room, and he and Josh had spent endless hours on rainy summer afternoons designing elaborate structures with their motorized building sets or playing with their action figures and imagining themselves everything from architects to astronauts traveling the outer realms of space.

He'd never imagined himself a businessman. He'd never imagined Joshua dead.

Logan didn't bother to knock. He opened the door with his key and marched inside. The maid and butler would have retired to their own quarters in the guest house attached to the back of the main house. His mother would be in her room watching television or simply staring at the ceiling. His father would be in his study with his cigars and his brandy if he was home at all.

Logan hoped to hell he was home. He wasn't disappointed.

His father looked up from the investment magazine he was reading when Logan strode into the room. "You should knock before you just bust in like that. You startled me."

He crossed the room and stopped right in front of his father's chair. "Tell me about you and Cathy Shepherd. Fill me in on this great friendship the two of you have."

His father puffed up, the way he did in business meetings on the rare occasions when things didn't go his way.

"Don't storm in here accusing me of things you know nothing about."

"So straighten me out, Dad. Tell me why you're writing her checks so that she can steal your grandsons."

His father tapped the end of his cigar on the edge of the ashtray by his chair, then left it there. "I can explain the checks."

"I'm waiting."

"Pour yourself a drink, then sit down and we'll talk about this reasonably."

"Reasonably? I don't think you know the meaning of the word. But go ahead and explain the situation to me. I can listen just fine standing up."

"Suit yourself. I'm having another drink." He walked to the bar in the corner of the room and poured a few fingers of brandy from the crystal decanter. If he was upset at all, he didn't show it, which pissed off Logan that much more.

"This is not the way it looks, son. And you should be thanking me, not throwing a temper tantrum. Cathy Shepherd is a slut, just like her stepdaughter was. Only Cathy is also greedy and a two-bit crook."

"False piety doesn't become you, Dad. Just explain the check."

"It wasn't just one check, Logan. It was a series of checks paid over the last three years. Cathy Shepherd contacted me claiming the boys were your sons. I didn't believe her, of course. Trash like her are always trying to find a way to milk anyone who has a little wealth."

The fury rolled inside Logan, and it took all his control not to slide over the edge of reason. "Three years ago? You've known about the boys for three years and never said a word to me?"

"I didn't see any point in ruining your life by entangling you with the likes of Tess Shepherd."

"*My* life. Not yours. *Mine.* But you still don't get that, do you?"

"Are you going to let me finish, or just go on raving?"

"Oh, by all means, finish. I wouldn't want to miss a word of this."

"I knew the woman was lying."

"Then why did you let her blackmail you?"

"It was right after your mother got out of the hospital. She'd just had a complete emotional breakdown, thanks to your brother. I couldn't put her through this on top of everything else."

"Josh only did what you drove him to."

"Think what you want. Anyway I paid the woman to stay out of our lives. It was no big deal. I frequently spend five hundred dollars taking a business associate to dinner. And it's much cheaper than another emotional breakdown."

Logan collapsed into the chair he'd refused earlier as the incredibility of the situation ground in his gut. "Didn't it even occur to you to check and see if the boys were McCains, to see if they were your grandsons?"

"Don't get all holier than thou with me, Logan. What didn't occur to me was that you slept with harlots."

"If I'd slept with a dozen whores and had kids by all of them, it wouldn't be as bad as denying my own flesh and blood the way you did with Josh. And now the way you've done with two innocent boys."

"How dare you talk to me that way? If you want to be a McCain, then act like a McCain. And that doesn't include sleeping with and having children with sluts."

"If those boys die because you kept their identity a secret from me, I'll…" The words wouldn't come. But Logan couldn't take any more of this.

"I did what I had to do, and one day…"

Logan shook his head and started for the door.

"Don't walk away from me when I'm talking to you."

Logan kept walking. If he stopped, he might do or say something he'd regret the rest of his life, and he already had as much regret as he could handle.

CHERI HUNG UP the phone. Her reprieve was over. There would be a personal engagement tonight. Not surprisingly, her number-one john couldn't wait for his fix of kinky and perverted sex. The party for two would be in the club's penthouse apartment in the warehouse district since the private upstairs room of the club was off-limits for now. Detective Morrison had them all running scared.

You had to love the way one middle-aged cop was jerking some of the city's biggest hotshots around. At least she would have loved it if it weren't upping the risks for her.

Not that she'd ever make the kind of mistakes Tess had made. There were some things in life you just didn't do. Jump from an airplane without a parachute. Step in front of a speeding bus. Screw up with the powers who controlled the Fruits of Passion.

Craig Graves didn't fool her. He was as big an ass kisser as she was, and for the same reasons. It paid extremely well. She made more money than she'd ever dreamed of making. Drove a Mercedes. Wore Manolo Blahnik shoes. Carried a Marc Jacobs handbag. Had more than one Yves Saint Laurent dress in her closet.

The wages of sin were good—as long as she was young and desirable. And as long as she lived by the code. Break it, and she'd wind up like Tess. She hated what had happened and feared for Tess's sons. But she didn't dare interfere again—not if she wanted to keep on breathing.

She picked up the fashion magazines that were spread on the sofa and carried them back to the bedroom. She'd have to wash her hair and get a bikini wax. Everything about tonight had to be perfect. It was the way the game was played. Anything the guy needed to make his fantasies come true.

The odd thing was she didn't hate the job. There were rare times when she actually enjoyed it. Other nights…

No use to dwell on that. She belonged to the Fruits of Passion.

IT HAD BEEN two days since Pete Pellegrin had called with the news of the check Logan's father had paid to Cathy Shepherd. At the time, Pete had been optimistic that he'd know the whereabouts of Cathy and the boys in a matter of hours. Yet they were still missing, and Logan had no better handle on what they were running from.

In fact, he had no better handle on any part of the situation. Detective Morrison had ordered him not to leave town, but he hadn't brought Logan in for further questioning. And the detective had never released his name to the news media. He supposed he should be thankful for small favors.

He'd managed to avoid his father altogether for the last two days, not an easy feat since their offices were on the same floor of the McCain Building. At some point, they'd have to interact—the business required it. But Logan didn't know if he could make even a feeble attempt at civility as long as the boys were still missing.

The dark-haired dancer from the Fruits of Passion appeared to be missing, as well, or at least laying low since he hadn't been able to track her down. Logan had hired a young and very enthusiastic private investigator to stake out the club and let him know when she showed up for work. So far, no luck.

He felt guilty that he hadn't told Rachel that she was the one who'd given him Tess's address the day Tess had been killed. But he'd made a promise, and he never broke them without a very good reason. Besides, Rachel would have surely gone to Detective Morrison with the information, just as she had with the boy's shirt. There was still no information back on that— at least none that the detective had shared with Logan.

The intercom on his desk buzzed. He pushed the response button.

"Bob Sway is here. He doesn't have an appointment, but he says he's got some things that belonged to someone named Tess Shepherd and he thinks you might like to have them. That's all he'll tell me."

Logan had no idea who Bob Sway was, but if he had any connection to Tess, he definitely wanted to talk to him. "Send him in, and hold all my calls while he's here."

"What should I do about your ten o'clock appointment with the representative from Protection, Inc.?"

"Have him wait."

"Yes, sir."

The man introduced himself as the owner of the apartment where Tess had been killed and explained that he'd gotten Logan's name from Detective Hoagie Morrison. He was a short guy, no more than five-six, but he didn't suffer in the girth department. His paunchy stomach hung over his belt and his second chin pretty much covered his neck.

Logan was overly cautious these days, but the guy seemed genuine and friendly. "Have a seat," Logan said, hoping the guy had information as well as the small plastic grocery bag he was holding.

"No, thanks. I can't stay but a minute. I have a dentist's appointment at ten-thirty. I was just eager to get this stuff off my hands. I don't like dealing with murder cases. They make me nervous, you know what I mean?"

Logan nodded, which was all it took for the man to continue.

"The cops were in the apartment yesterday. They boxed up some stuff and carried it off. Not that there was a lot left after the neighborhood druggies came in and took what they wanted of Miss Shepherd's stuff."

"I thought the apartment was taped off."

"That yellow tape don't stop nobody. They heard she was dead, so they just came in and helped themselves to her belongings."

"Couldn't you have stopped them?"

"I didn't see any reason I should get involved. No use in my getting shot over things that weren't mine to begin with. Anyway, the cops took the tape down yesterday and turned the apartment back over to me. I cleaned it all afternoon and half the night."

"What's in the bag?" Logan asked, tiring of the man's long-windedness.

"A small box of stuff. Mostly photos of the boys and a few of their toys. That's why I thought you might like to have them."

He set the bag on the corner of Logan's desk.

"And that's all that's left?"

"Pretty much. Miss Shepherd didn't bring much with her when she moved in. I was watching from my window. I live on the third floor, right above the apartment I rented to her. That big guy that was killed, he helped her unload her car. Between them they didn't make more than five or six trips back and forth."

"Did you hear any strange noises coming from her apartment the day Miss Shepherd was killed?"

"No. Not that day. I heard plenty before that, though. I don't guess there's any reason I can't tell you about the fight, seeing as how you're the father of those boys. I told the detective. He didn't tell me it was confidential."

"What fight?"

"The one that took place right after Miss Shepherd moved in. Yelling. Foulest language I've ever heard come out of a woman's mouth. And banging noises, as if they were tearing the place apart. In the middle of the day. That's when I knew I'd rented to trash."

"What did you do?"

"I should have called the police right then and there. I came close, I can tell you that, especially since I knew she had those two boys there visiting with her, but I just beat on my floor with a broom handle and they got quiet. Next time I saw her, she was bruised up pretty bad."

"Did you say her sons were visiting?"

"I didn't know it was her sons at the time, but I saw her with them in the courtyard earlier that day and then I saw some woman come and get them after the fight."

"Then the boys didn't live there?"

"No. Place was hardly big enough for one."

"Were there other fights?"

"Not that I heard. It was pretty quiet after that. I was glad. I hated to ask her to move since she'd paid two months' rent in advance."

"She must have planned on staying for a while."

"She only paid that much 'cause I insisted on it. She said she couldn't give me references since she'd just moved to town. Another one of her lies. But she paid in cash. Just peeled hundred bills off a stack as if they were ones. I've had those hurly-girly dancers for tenants before, but they never had that kind of money."

"Guess some clubs pay better than others."

"More like it she was into something else. Turned out she didn't even give me her right name. It was almost as if she was hiding from somebody. If she was, I reckon he found her. I'm not glad of that, mind you. I hate to see a mother get killed, but she was into something."

"Did you see anyone else in her apartment during the time she lived there?"

"I didn't see anybody else the day of the fight, but the murdered guy was there a couple of other times. He usually came around late at night. Other than that, it was just Miss Shepherd. She seemed to be there most of the time. I don't think she was working, probably on account of the bruises. Ain't much place to hide bruises under them scanty outfits them strip dancers wear, you know what I mean."

"Miss Shepherd had a friend. A woman about her age, petite, long, black hair, very pretty. Did you ever see her in the apartment?"

"No. Detective Morrison asked me about that same

woman. I never saw her. I'd remember someone who looked like that. Actually I'd have noticed anyone coming or going if they'd been there when I was. I try to keep track of who's on my property."

"Probably a very good idea."

"Yeah. Should never have rented to Miss Shepherd. I had bad feelings about her from the very first. Anyway, I gotta go. I'm sorry about the boys' mother, but they might be better off. Like I said, no telling what she was mixed up in."

And Logan was no closer to finding out. He took a business card from the wooden holder and handed one to Bob Sway. "Thanks again for stopping by and bringing the photos. If you do happen to remember that someone else was there, I'd appreciate your giving me a call."

"I've told you everything I know." He glanced at the bag. "Not much there, but I'm glad to have it off my hands."

Off his hands and into Logan's. Too bad the boys weren't in his hands, as well. He waited until Bob Sway was out the door before rummaging through the bag. There was a red, heart-shaped box, the kind candy came in for Valentine's Day and two stuffed animals.

He pulled them out. A lion and a dalmatian, both showing signs of wear, which was probably why no one bothered to steal them. They wouldn't bring in enough money for even one fix.

But they must have had some sentimental value to Tess. Perhaps they'd been favorites of Danny and Davy, at least for a while. The boys might have snuggled them against their chests while they slept at night.

He wondered where they were sleeping now, if they were safe, if they were crying for their mother. If they had anyone or anything to cuddle with when they were afraid.

The buzzer on his desk went off again.

"The representative from Protection, Inc. is here to see you."

"Give me about two minutes to get my desk in order, then send him in."

He slid the stuffed animals back into the bag. He'd find the boys and he'd bring them home if it was the last thing he ever did.

CHAPTER TEN

RACHEL PULLED the file for her most pressing case. As usual, it carried a lot more work than clout. One of the companies they represented was revamping its contracts and wanted to make certain everything was legal and airtight.

Contracts were tricky business no matter how careful the wording, but she wanted to check the research very carefully to see if any cases with similar language had met with problems in the courts of Louisiana.

She settled into the recorded cases the law clerk had pulled for her, but three pages into the first long and boring court decision, she found herself thinking about Tess Shepherd again. Tess and Logan McCain.

The man was an enigma. He intrigued her...fascinated her...just plain messed with her mind. The first time she'd met him, he'd crawled right under her skin. He still did, but now the attraction was far more complex than it had been when it was just a flirtation with an attractive and very charismatic man.

Now her feelings for him were all mixed up with her concern for his sons, boys she'd never met, yet felt connected to. She couldn't think of them without remembering the nightmares and hearing the dreaded monsters march through her mind. It was all part of the sickening loss that had tormented her when she was a little girl. She'd thought she'd put it all behind her during the extensive counseling she'd gone through as a teenager, but apparently she'd just tucked it away in a dark corner of her mind.

Unable to concentrate on the contracts, she reached over and punched the replay button on her recorder. She'd listened to the tape of her interview with Tess several times, always convinced that there had to be something there to explain the murder. There never was.

She leaned forward, doodling on the legal pad in front of her while she listened. She played it all the way through, then rewound it and started over at the point where she had started questioning Tess about how she'd first realized that Logan McCain was her boys' father.

The boys were eighteen months old before I even found out who he was. I saw a picture of him in the society pages. He was escorting some debutante to her ball. Friggin' big shot. Wait, I can tell you exactly when that was, too. I have the date right here in my notes.

Do you always keep such good records?

Always have. Now I even keep a duplicate copy of everything I do, and I mean names, places and dates. Here it is, October 22, 2002.

Why didn't you call him then?

So he could take them away from us like he wants to do now? From us?

My stepmother and me. She takes care of the boys while I work.

"What are you listening to? That sounds like that woman who crashed her way into the office last week and then got murdered."

Rachel reached over and switched off the recorder as Ted

Boyd sauntered into the room. She hadn't realized she'd left the door open a crack, making it possible for anyone passing by to hear the tape.

"I was just checking some facts."

"On that woman?"

"No, I was skipping over that part to get to an interview with a legitimate client."

"Did you know she was murdered not long after she was in here? They had her picture in the paper this morning along with an article on the number of unsolved murders in the city. It's a jungle out there."

"So it seems." She hadn't seen the day's article, but she'd look it up.

"She looked better in person than she did in the picture, except for the bruises. The article said she was a stripper."

"She told me she was an exotic dancer."

"Same thing. Probably got killed by the guy who'd given her the shiner. Good thing you didn't get mixed up with her. But I wouldn't let Castile hear you replaying that interview. He's already jumped all over me today for not turning in enough billable hours."

"Is he here this afternoon?"

"Yeah, roaming the halls, checking on us."

"In that case you'd best get back to your billable hours before he finds you in here chatting with me."

"Don't you know it." Ted started to leave, but hesitated. "Say, what are doing Friday night?"

"Are you asking so you can laugh at my dateless condition or is this an invitation?"

"An invitation. My girlfriend has a cousin in town. She says he's got a great personality."

"Which translated means he's a look-alike for Frankenstein."

"But what if it turns out he's a look-alike for Brad Pitt?"

"Then I guess I'll have missed out."

"Aw, come on. As a favor."

"Not this time. I have plans for Friday night." Washing her hair or cutting her toenails unless…

"We have reservations at Emeril's."

He ducked out, and she went back to the note she'd just doodled. *A record of everything—in duplicate.*

Finally it hit her. That was it. Everything they wanted to know about Tess Shepherd's life was all written down somewhere. All they had to do was find her notebook or files or maybe a diary. If they did, they might very well discover who killed her and get a lead on finding the boys.

Excitement rocked around inside her as she punched in Logan's number. The records might not be easy to find, but they existed. She was certain of it.

THE LAST PLACE Rachel had expected to be tonight was sipping a fruity cabernet in a fragrant English garden with Logan. He'd been in a meeting when she'd called and hadn't gotten back to her until almost five. He'd suggested she meet him at his house to talk, and she'd agreed.

The house had intimidated her from the second she'd pulled into the driveway. But the garden was cozy and welcoming and far less stuffy than the century-old rooms with their antique furnishings and heavy drapes.

But neither the house nor the garden seemed to fit the man who sat beside her on the old wooden porch-style swing that hung from the huge branch of a majestic oak. This was from a more genteel era gone by. Logan was a modern-day mover and shaker.

He was direct and forceful, clearly used to being in charge.

But he didn't make her feel inferior or subordinate the way she felt when dealing when one of the head partners at work.

She sipped her wine as they settled into a gentle sway in the creaking swing. Logan laid his arm across the back of the swing, not touching, yet it hinted of a familiarity that didn't actually exist between them.

"You said you wanted to talk about the notes Tess brought to your office that day she asked you to represent her against me," he said.

"Not so much the notes themselves as the fact that she had detailed notations as to every date and event we discussed. She referred to her notes several times."

"Obviously she'd given the custody hearing a lot of thought, then."

"True, but she said she kept notes of everything, not just one set of notes, but two."

"You mean like a journal?"

"It could have been a diary or a journal, or just a notebook of facts to reinforce her memory."

"If that's the case, I think I know what happened to the notes."

"What?"

"I didn't mention it before, didn't even mention it to Detective Morrison, but when I ran into Hank Matthews right before he was killed, he was holding a fancy notebook with a flowered fabric cover. At the time I thought it resembled a journal. When I came to and found him dead, the journal was gone."

"So whoever killed Hank Matthews could well have taken a tell-all journal."

"That would be my guess," Logan said. "If there was a journal like that."

"The journal would have been one set of notes, but Tess emphasized that she kept duplicate copies of everything."

"So you think she may have copied the pages of the journal after she wrote them?"

"I think she did," Rachel said. "I guess the question now is where would she have kept the backup?"

"Her stepmother could have it," Logan said. "In which case we're back to square one."

"But we don't know that." And Rachel wasn't ready to give up on this just yet. "She said she didn't take chances, so I think she kept the records somewhere only she could get to them. Maybe in a secret hiding place in her apartment."

"The journal Hank Matthews had could have been in a secret hiding place. Her apartment had been totally trashed as if someone was looking for something."

"But he would have quit looking after finding the first journal, so the second set of notes could still be there."

"I doubt that," Logan said. "According to the landlord, there's nothing left in the house. What the police didn't take, burglars did."

"We have to at least look, Logan. Call Detective Morrison and see if he'll let us go inside the apartment."

"Oh, yeah. I'm sure he'd okay that. But actually I think the landlord might unlock the door for me. We're old friends now."

She sipped her wine while he told her about his surprise visit from Bob Sway, and all the while her mind was working overtime, trying to think of where in an old building in the French Quarter someone could hide a notebook or a folder of copied notes. There could be a million places.

Strict codes controlled every aspect of the buildings in the Quarter to preserve their historic authenticity and the character of the area. There had to be niches in the old brick, loose floorboards, maybe even safes built into the thick walls.

She'd heard of one building on Royal Street that had a secret passage where the owner had stored liquor during prohibition and another that had a secret door to a walk-in closet. When the new owner found it, it was full of rats that had clawed their way through the wood and a couple of skulls. She shuddered at the thought and wrapped her arms about her chest.

"I know you can't be cold," Logan said.

"No, I was just thinking of hiding places. I'd like to go with you if the landlord lets you check out the house."

"That's probably not a good idea."

"Two heads are better than one."

"More targets for the villains. You do remember that the last time I was in that building, I acquired a sizeable goose egg on the side of my head?"

"There's no reason to think that would happen again. Besides, I'm a woman and I'd be more likely to think the way Tess did. That could help. And this is my idea."

"I'll consider it."

That was more promising than she'd expected, so she'd let it ride for now. She tried to relax, but she was far too aware of Logan's presence not to be uptight. Odd that they'd be here in this idyllic setting sipping wine and talking of something so macabre as the notes of a murdered woman.

But it had been days now and even with Logan living with the strain of not knowing where his sons were or if they were safe, he had to eat and sleep and breathe.

"The police still don't have any word on the boys," he said, as if reading her mind. "Every trooper on the roads should have the license-plate number of Cathy's car and the description of her and the boys."

"Then it can't be long until they find them."

"I keep telling myself that."

She put her hand on his arm, an impulsive comforting gesture. Awareness shot through her, and she jerked it away too quickly.

Logan turned to face her. "What was that about?"

"Nothing, I just…"

"You're afraid to touch me?"

God, he was so direct. "I think…" What did she think? That she found him attractive and that frightened her. That the situation was too emotional to risk adding any kind of sexual tension to the mix. "I don't want to make you uncomfortable."

"I'm tense to the point of exploding, worried so much that I haven't slept more than three hours a night since Tess was murdered and I learned the boys were missing, so befuddled by what's going on that I feel as if my brain is scrambled. I don't think being uncomfortable is an issue right now. But for the record, having you touch my arm doesn't make me uncomfortable."

"I didn't exactly mean it that way. It's just that we don't know each other all that well. We've been pushed together due to the circumstances."

"I'm not sure I know anyone all that well, but if all we were about were the circumstances, I'd have had this conversation over the phone, not invited you over for dinner."

She hesitated, not wanting to start anything she wasn't ready for, yet not wanting to push him away. "And if I hadn't wanted to be here, I would have turned down your invitation."

The attraction issue was out in the open now. She was pretty sure he was no more ready to act on it than she was, but at least they wouldn't have to tiptoe around it. She finished her wine while sparrows chattered over her head and two squirrels scurried in and out of the roots of the ancient oak.

Logan swatted at a mosquito that had decided to feast on his right hand. "Time to go in. Once the mosquitoes sample, they don't quit. Probably time I should put the steaks on, anyway."

"Could we look through the things the landlord brought first—I mean if you don't mind my looking at them?"

"I've already been through all of it, but you're welcome to examine it. There's no journal or notes in there. It's mostly photos of the boys, a few odds and ends and a couple of toy animals."

"I'll just take a quick look. Or I can help you with dinner if you'd rather."

"No need. I stopped at the deli for a salad and bread, so there's really nothing to do but grill the steaks."

They walked in together, not touching, but side by side. He put a hand to the small of her back when they climbed the back steps to the veranda. They'd inched closer to some kind of relationship in the past few minutes. But it was steeped in murder, and she had little hope that a relationship that started that way could build any kind of lasting foundation.

RACHEL SETTLED in one of the straight-backed kitchen chairs. The first item she pulled from the bag was a receipt for groceries. Eggs, cheese, bread, orange juice, cereal. The next thing she touched was a hair scrunchy. She pulled it out and let it drop to the table, all of a sudden spooked that she was going through the belongings of dead woman.

Hesitant to even put her hand back into the bag, she dumped the contents onto the table. The toy dalmatian seemed to be staring at her with his big glass eyes. She picked him up and held him close, then hurriedly set him and the lion aside before they sent her sliding into a blue funk.

The next item was a heart-shaped box. Rachel opened it

carefully, then picked up the top photo. The two boys were standing with Tess, and she had an arm around each of them.

The old ache hit so hard Rachel had trouble breathing. But this wasn't about her; it was about Logan's sons. His and Tess's.

Tess had said they'd been conceived during a one-night stand and that making love to her had meant nothing to him. Rachel had bought that story easily enough in her office that morning, but now that she knew Logan, it was hard to imagine him making love to a woman he had no feelings for. Or maybe she was reading qualities into him that weren't there.

He walked over and set a bowl of salad on the other end of the table, away from where she'd set the stuffed animals. He'd changed into a pair of tan shorts and a short-sleeved knit shirt. The buttons on the neck placket were undone, revealing a sprinkling of dark hairs. His arms were muscled, not bulging like a body builder's, but firm.

Lean and hard, and incredibly virile. All that and sophisticated and rich. Almost too good to be true.

Rachel went back to the photos, thumbed through them until she reached the bottom of the stack. Beneath them were some nipple pasties that Rachel avoided touching, and a small brass key with the number 182 engraved into it.

She picked it up and placed it in the palm of her hand. Too small to be a house or car key. Could be a key to a piece of luggage—possibly one that held a copy of the writings in the journal that had been stolen. But if the luggage was stolen, any thief in the Quarter could have it.

She dropped the key in her pocket for safe keeping while she went through the rest of the items. More cash receipts, a couple of pens, some loose thumbtacks and paper clips and a comb. Nothing that helped in the slightest. Rachel fitted the items back into the plastic bag, then went looking for Logan. She found him out by the grill, cell phone at his ear.

"Did you find anything of interest?" he asked once he'd ended the phone conversation.

"A key, but I don't know what it's to." She pulled it out and handed it to him. After examining it, he gave it back to her so that he could take the steaks off the grill.

"That was Tess's landlord I was just talking to," he said, sliding the spatula beneath a filet. "He's rented the apartment Tess was murdered in, and the new tenant is taking possession tomorrow."

"Wow! That was a quick turnaround."

"The new tenant's Hank Matthew's replacement bouncer at the club. Keeping it all in the family, so to speak. But Bob Sway said we could come out tonight and take a look around if we wanted."

Evidently Logan had decided she could go with him tonight. That was both good and bad. She'd never been in a room where someone had been murdered. The thought of it was already giving her chills. It would be frightening enough if the killer was behind bars, but he was still out there somewhere, and she had the crazy feeling that he knew they were about to visit his killing turf.

CHAPTER ELEVEN

CATHY SHEPHERD buckled the boys into their seat belts, then moved the few groceries she'd bought into the passenger side of the front seat. Panicking the way she did and running away without enough money had been a big mistake. She could have sold Tess's slinky dresses on the street and had enough to live on for months.

She'd cashed the last of the checks from Mr. McCain. There was no way the rich old fart would continue paying her off when Logan and anyone else who was interested already knew that the sons of the dead Bourbon Street stripper were McCains.

Tess, dead. She still had trouble believing that though she'd known it was just a matter of time. The woman had shit for brains. Got that from her father.

"He's got my Tarzan."

"No, I don't."

"Do, too."

"Play with something else, Davy. We'll be home in a few minutes."

"Our real home?"

"Our vacation home." Some vacation.

"I want to go back to Gretna. I wanna play with my friends."

"Yeah, well, don't we all?"

"Can we get burgers?"

"We're having spaghetti and green beans for dinner."

"Not again," Danny protested.

"Yeah. Not again." Davy could never stand to be left out.

"You love spaghetti," she reminded them.

"But I wanna play on the slide."

"Not tonight."

"Borrring," Davy said, his favorite word since starting play school.

But he'd just have to be bored awhile longer until she could think what to do. There was no going back to Louisiana. She pulled into the parking lot where they were staying, an overpriced dump that was nowhere near the beach.

As always, she cruised the parking lot before she stopped, checking for anything that looked suspicious. She'd registered under a fake name and smeared the license plate and the back of the car with enough mud that you couldn't see the numbers, but that didn't mean she couldn't be found.

She slowed when they passed her room, then nearly ran into a parked SUV when she noticed that the curtain was open. Not much. Just a few inches. A few inches more than she ever left it.

She muttered a stream of curses. Most of what they had with them was in that room. The boys' pajamas. A few toys. Her makeup and a couple of changes of clothes.

Crazy! Why was she even thinking about that? She had to get out of here. Fast. She circled through the lot and pulled back into the street.

"Now where are we going?" Danny asked. "I'm hungry."

"We're going on an adventure."

"Yea! For burgers," Davy said, ever optimistic.

She didn't tell him differently. She pulled into the road and headed north. She'd already checked out the map and found routes that let her avoid Interstate highways just in case the cops had an APB out on them.

What she needed was money to get out of the country for a while. Mexico. Or one of the Central American countries. Maybe an island in the Caribbean. At least there she'd have a beach. But she'd need a lot of money for that.

She'd never be able to draw the money out of Tess's bank account. They'd be expecting that and watching for her, and even if she waited around, she doubted Tess had put her down as the beneficiary.

Cash. Cold, hard cash. There had to be a way to get it without...

Of course there was a way. The perfect solution. She should have thought of it in the first place.

THE GOOSEBUMPS STARTED the second Rachel set foot in the dimly lit and very narrow stairwell. Murder was such a heinous crime. Dark and demented, and Rachel could swear that evil remnants of the deed coated every breath of the hot, dank air.

Logan had bounded ahead, but he stopped and waited when he realized she wasn't right behind him.

"It's not too late for you to back out," he said, taking her hand and squeezing it.

She held on tightly. "I'll be okay once we get inside." That was probably a gross understatement, but she wasn't chickening out at this stage of the game.

"Good. Let's get this over with and done with."

"You don't think we'll find anything, do you?"

"Let's just say I have a wary optimism." He knocked on the door and waited. Bob Sway swung it open a second later. He was in a pair of navy cotton shorts and an undershirt that showed a lot more of his hairy chest than Rachel wanted to see.

"You're welcome to look around. I've gotten most of the junk out, but the floors and walls are still a mess. The new tenant offered to clean them. Guy was anxious to get the place. Good, cheap rentals like this are hard to find in the Quarter."

Cheap she could believe. The good part was evidently very subjective. She let her gaze roam the room while Logan got rid of the landlord.

"Let's start in the bedroom," she said, as soon as Bob Sway had left them alone.

"As good a starting place as any." Logan led the way into a small, cramped room barely big enough for the double bed and marred wooden dresser.

There were blood smears on the rug. She held on to the bedpost while a wave of queasiness passed, then wiped her hand on the front of her slacks and tried to focus. There was nothing on the bed but wooden slats, and she wondered if the mattress set had been removed because it was soaked in blood.

"Was this Tess's furniture?" she asked, hating that her voice was as shaky as her insides.

"No. She rented the apartment furnished, such as it is. According to the landlord, all she brought with her were a few boxes of clothes—and apparently the pictures of the boys."

"And the key." More evidence that whatever the key unlocked could be in this apartment. Rachel studied the room, hoping for some kind of revelation that would point her to possible hiding places. She opened the drawers to the dresser one by one, taking them all the way out as she did and setting them on the floor.

Logan pulled up one corner of the rug. A couple of two-

inch cockroaches raced out and under a crack in the base-
board. "Nothing suspicious under here. It's all covered in the
same cheap tile as the rest of the place."

Which eliminated the possibility of something hidden
under loose floorboards. The ceiling looked solid, too. And
above it, Bob Sway was probably listening to see if he could
figure out exactly what they were doing down there.

They both checked the closet. She dug around in the bottom while Logan rifled through the top shelves. The only
thing the search produced was more roaches. "I can't imagine that Tess actually lived in a place like this even for a week,
not when she supposedly had plenty of money."

"She had to be running scared," Logan said, "though I
can't imagine why she didn't run farther than this."

"But running from whom? If it was from someone at the
Fruits of Passion, why bother hiding by day if she went to
work every night?"

"She wasn't going to work that week."

"But evidently some people at the club knew where she
was living if someone there told you how to find her that
morning."

"Maybe only the people she trusted knew. I think I'll take
a look around the kitchen," Logan said. "We've pretty much
covered this room."

The temperature in the bedroom seemed to dip to freezing
the second he left her alone. The fear was so real it was pal-
pable, like a sheath of thin ice around her heart.

She swayed and grabbed the bedpost again, this time holding on to keep from falling. The fear was familiar. It was the
old paralyzing fear that had crept into her room every night
when she was little and then again when she'd hit adolescence.

Fear of loss. That's what the psychologist had said. But

why now? Why here in this place? Unless this was Tess's fear, reaching back from the grave.

Show me what you want us to know, Tess. Just show me, and I'll try to help.

But if Tess's ghost was present, it remained silent. Rachel's breathing slowly returned to normal, and she leaned back and stared at the slowly revolving blades of the ceiling fan Logan had switched on with the light.

The motor was encased in plastic, but there was a space between it and the ceiling. One last place to look. She pulled the chain that stopped the fan, then climbed on the railing of the bed, steadying herself with the bedpost.

Warily, she reached behind the motor and ran her hand along the surface of the plastic casing. Roach shy, she jumped back when she noticed something black on the bottom of the casing. It wasn't a roach or even a spider. But it was something. "Logan, can you come here a minute?"

He was there in an instant.

"Take a look at this."

Logan helped her down, then took her place on the bed railing. "I'll be damned. It's a tiny surveillance camera. Either our Mr. Bob Sway is a voyeuristic landlord, or else someone else was spying on Tess—or on someone who lived here before her."

"Why would they be…" Rachel stopped midsentence. The front door to the apartment had just creaked open and there were heavy footsteps heading their way.

Logan pushed her behind him. "Is that you, Mr. Sway?"

"No, it's just your friendly local police officer."

Detective Morrison. She breathed a sigh of relief, but Logan's grip on her arm tightened, and the muscles in his arm flexed.

Morrison stepped into the doorway. "Looking for something?"

Logan let go of Rachel's arm and she moved from behind him and took a step closer to Morrison. "Yes, and we found something," she said. "There's a camera embedded in the fan over the bed. At least it appears to be a camera."

Morrison stepped over to take a look, but didn't climb onto the railing as they had. He stared at it for a minute, then moved his gaze to Logan. "How'd you get in here?"

"Mr. Sway let us in. Do you have a problem with that?"

"I might."

Another roach ran out from the wall and scurried toward Morrison. He stamped on it without even seeming to look down. "I'd think you'd want to stay away from here, Mr. Mc-Cain, considering you've already come around here a couple of times too often."

"It was my idea to come here," Rachel said. "Not Logan's. I just had this hunch that we might find something to explain Tess's murder and help us find the boys."

"A hunch?"

"Lawyers have hunches, too."

"But you don't represent anyone involved in this case. Even if you were, collecting evidence is the responsibility of the police department. We're pretty good at it, but if we need your help, we'll let you know."

"Did your investigators find the hidden camera?" His facial expression told her that they hadn't.

"You and Logan are an interesting alignment," Morrison said. "You were approached by Tess to keep him from taking her sons. Yet here you are snooping around the crime scene together. Makes a cop wonder."

"While you're doing all that wondering," Logan snapped,

"you haven't managed to find a couple of missing boys and their grandmother, have you?"

"We're taking care of that."

"Yeah. The way you thoroughly searched this apartment and missed the camera."

"Why don't I stay around and watch while you two search," Morrison said. "See if I can learn a thing or two."

"Maybe another time," Logan said. "We're all through for the night."

"Then I'll just walk out with you."

Rachel hadn't been through, but if they didn't get out of here soon, Morrison was liable to cuff Logan and cart him off to jail. What with Logan's mistrust of the police and Morrison's disposition, the two of them were more combustible than Michael Moore at a Republican convention.

Logan put a hand between her shoulder blades and nudged her toward the door. Morrison moved aside just enough to let them pass, then followed them down the stairs and out into the courtyard.

"You know, if I were you, Miss Powers, I'd find company who wasn't a suspect in a murder case. Just a thought."

She kept walking, but Logan stopped at the iron gate and looked back. "If I were going to kill someone, Detective, it wouldn't be a defenseless woman. But if someone hurts those boys, I'll tear them apart with my bare hands. Then you'll have plenty of evidence to haul me in."

Rachel tugged him out the gate, glad to finally be off the property even though they were no closer to the truth than they had been. The key was still in her pocket. She wasn't through yet.

MORRISON WAS FURIOUS. The freakin' CSI team should have found that camera. *He* should have found it. And it made him madder than hell that Logan McCain had showed them up. Too bad he didn't have enough evidence to throw him in jail tonight, or at least to go after an arrest warrant.

But he didn't have the evidence. He didn't have squat on anybody. Worse, Logan was right. Despite his efforts to locate Cathy Shepherd, there hadn't been one confirmed sighting. They didn't even have a clue what state she was in.

If Hank Matthews hadn't been killed, Morrison would have had no trouble believing, as Paulson did, that this was a custody battle that had turned ugly. It had happened before. Just last fall Hoagie had worked a case where some guy had shot his wife and her boyfriend over a custody fight. He'd taken off with the kids. They'd found him two days later in Mississippi and he'd admitted everything.

But there was more than a custody battle going on here, which still didn't guarantee Logan McCain wasn't involved. He sure had a way of showing up in all the wrong places at all the wrong times.

Hoagie had thought Rachel Powers was way too smart to be suckered by a man like Logan. Smart, pretty and classy. Not to mention that he'd always had a weakness for auburn-haired babes.

You could have those women at the Fruits of Passion. Hoagie liked class, and Rachel Powers had it in spades. Then again, there was one dancer at the club who got his juices pumping. But Cheri Trosclair also set off lots of alarms in the suspicion department. She got too nervous when he questioned her, couldn't even look him in the eye.

So the questions remained unanswered. Who killed Tess Shepherd and Hank Matthews? And would they kill again if it would save their hide?

You bet your sweet ass they would—unless he apprehended them first.

RACHEL GOT very little rest after the field trip to Tess's old apartment. Her sleep was interrupted with bizarre nightmares of ghosts and monsters—and disturbing dreams of Logan that had seemed to linger long after she was awake.

And he'd stayed on her mind throughout the busy, hectic day at the office. It was totally unlike her. Usually, the more attractive she found a man, the more cautious she became. She was always the one who wanted to take things slow, to keep the sex on hold until they knew each other really well.

Sex. Where did that thought come from? The guy was dealing with missing sons. Who could expect him to get turned on and want to go at it with all he had on his mind?

When this was over, there would be plenty of time to see if the flirtation was going anywhere. She might not even like him once she got to know him.

Yeah, right. The same way she might not like orgasms or hot bubble baths on cold nights.

She looked up at a knock on her door. "Do you have a minute?"

"Or course, Mr. Castile." *All I'm doing is thinking about orgasms and bubble baths.*

He walked in and stopped at the edge of her desk, peering over to see what she was working on. Fortunately it was official, something most definitely billable.

"I've had some disturbing news, Rachel."

"What have you heard?"

"That you had a homicide detective visit you here at work."

She should have known he'd find out about that. Nothing got by the man. He probably rewarded the secretaries for squealing on the rest of them. She folded her hands and struck a professional pose. "I was visited briefly by Detective Morrison of the NOPD, but I've requested that in the future he not call on me at the office."

"So this is ongoing?"

"I'm not sure."

"Are you in some kind of trouble with the law?"

"No. It's nothing like that. A woman I'd met a few days ago was murdered. The detective hoped she might have told me something that would help him identify her killer."

"Evidently someone else is of that same opinion."

"I'm not sure what you mean."

"Detective Morrison has requested film from the surveillance cameras in the parking garage. He told the building superintendent that someone left a threatening note and package on the hood of your car."

"I wasn't aware of the request, but yes, there was a threat."

"I'm sorry to hear that. I've talked to security. They're going to increase manpower for the next few weeks, and I'd like you to have one of the guards walk you to your car until you're quite sure this situation is in hand."

The man surprised her. Perhaps he did have a heart, or more likely WW&C didn't want an employee to get attacked in the parking garage for fear it would make the news. Might not instill trust in their clients.

Mr. Castile adjusted his tie, though it didn't need it and ran a hand down the front of his expensive suit jacket. "I do hope you'll be careful, Rachel. Murder is an ugly business. When you're on the fast track to success, as we think you are, involvement in that sort of thing is not only dangerous, it can be detrimental to your career."

And now they were back to the bottom line. Don't make waves, make money. "I'll be very careful."

"I'm glad to hear that. And please, if there are any other

problems anywhere in the building, come to me first. Actually, I'd like you to keep me posted on whatever comes of this murder investigation."

"I'll do that, though, as I said, I'm not actually involved in the investigation." Lying never came easy for her, but it was easier with Castile than anyone else. Maybe it was because she always felt he was manipulating the conversation, saying one thing and meaning another.

He stayed a second more, asked about the file she was working on, then left. She tried to go back to work, but now the murder investigation had a firm hold of her mind. She read a couple more paragraphs, then walked over, closed the door tightly and played the tape of Tess's interview one more time.

LOGAN HADN'T SAID that he'd call, but still Rachel had expected that he would. It irritated her that she felt let down, and by seven she was antsy and couldn't concentrate on the data she was trying to review. It was Friday night, a full week since Tess had walked into her office and Rachel's calm and predictable world had been caught in a whirlwind of danger and confusion.

She cleaned off her desk and stuck the file she'd been working on in her briefcase just in case she decided to work tonight. Following Logan's suggestion and Mr. Castile's orders, she had the security guard walk her to her car. They made small talk as he did, with no mention of the reason why she suddenly needed the escort service.

She stopped at the deli on the way home, chose a chicken Caesar salad from the serving line, then decided to pick one up for her aunt, as well. Aunt Gladys would have eaten dinner a couple of hours earlier, but she used to love the deli's salads.

Maybe Rachel would catch her during one of her more lucid moments, and she'd actually recognize her and talk about people Rachel knew instead of the ones that lived only in her mind and distant past.

Even prior to the stroke, Rachel wouldn't have told Aunt Gladys about her adventures last night with Logan. Her aunt would have been shocked that Rachel had become entangled with a man involved in a murder case, even one as rich and socially prominent as Logan McCain.

But Rachel would have shared all the details about her conversation with Mr. Castile. Aunt Gladys had been quite taken with Phillip Castile; declared him a true Southern gentleman the first time she met him. Kiss her fingertips and she was putty in your hands. Of course the fact that he was successful and wealthy hadn't hurt.

Rachel suspected the reason her aunt was so impressed by anyone with money was because she'd had so little of it herself. She'd taught English and literature at a private girls' school for most of her life. The pay had been low, but Aunt Gladys had managed to support herself and Rachel on her meager salary and to save enough to pay Rachel's tuition all the way through law school.

You must make your parents proud. Her mantra had been preached with renewed fervor every time Rachel showed signs of slipping from her own commitment to be the top scholar in her class.

When Rachel was a little girl, she'd imagine her parents sitting on top of a cloud, leaning over the edge and looking down to see if she was making them proud. Later, she'd learned to hate the words and think of them as some kind of yardstick by which she'd always be measured and fall short.

But who knows? Maybe they were sitting up there now,

tapping their toes to some jazzy harp music and telling all the other angels how their daughter had landed a terrific position with the moneygrubbing firm of WW&C. Or lamenting that she was about to blow it over the death of a stripper.

Ten miles and twenty minutes later, Rachel checked in at the nurses' station and walked back to Aunt Gladys's room. She was in her rocking chair, watching a rerun of *Wheel of Fortune*. It was her favorite show, and no matter how confusing the rest of her conversation might be, she was lightning-quick with the right answers for the show's word puzzles.

"Want to buy a vowel?" Rachel asked teasingly, as she stepped inside the small room.

"Don't need one. It's peanut butter and jelly."

Rachel studied the puzzle. The only letters in place were the *p, b* and the *l*'s, but it did look as if Aunt Gladys was right.

"I don't know why they never serve peanut butter and jelly in this place."

"I don't have any peanut butter and jelly on me, but I brought you a chicken Caesar from Rodney's Deli. Are you hungry?"

"Indeed I am. We had tasteless red beans and rice for dinner. I'm quite certain the cooks haven't heard of spices."

They'd had this discussion before, so Rachel bypassed it and set one of the disposable containers of salad on the small table next to her aunt's chair. "And we have oatmeal raisin cookies for dessert."

"I think I shall have that first."

"Then I think I'll join you." When in Rome…or the Loving Care Nursing Home.

"How have you been, dear?"

"I'm great," Rachel lied.

"And how are things at work?"

"They're going very well. Mr. Castile seems to think I'm on the fast track to success."

"That's wonderful. Your mother had such dreams for you. She'd be so proud."

"Don't want to let down my mother."

Aunt Gladys took tiny nibbles of her cookie, chewing each tidbit thoroughly before taking another bite. "It's peanut butter and jelly," she said again as the contestant bought a vowel.

"You should go on the show," Rachel remarked. "You'd be the champ."

"I'd get stage fright and look like an imbecile."

They talked while they finished their cookies and started on their salad. It was one of those rare occasions when her aunt seemed totally tuned in. "Maybe we can go to lunch tomorrow. We can go to Commander's Palace and you can have the bread pudding soufflé you like so much."

Her aunt didn't respond. She just stared into space and poked at her salad with her fork. Rachel groaned. The moment of lucidity was slipping away fast.

"Estelle had dreams, you know?"

"I'm glad." Estelle, again. Rachel had no idea if she was a real person from her aunt's past, or an imaginary friend who'd moved into the clouds of confusion that roamed her mind.

"She should have left him," Aunt Gladys announced.

Her lips developed a slight tremor and her eyes took on a haunted expression that disturbed Rachel even more than her talk of Estelle.

Her aunt reached over and squeezed Rachel's hand as hard as she could with her thin fingers. "He's a dangerous man when he drinks."

"Estelle will be fine," Rachel whispered, trying to put her aunt's mind at ease.

"No. She died so young. So very young."

Rachel shuddered. Her aunt was talking out of her head, but the strange conversation was hitting too close to home. She forked the salad and forced herself to eat a few bites, though she'd lost her appetite entirely.

"I never liked him, you know?"

"You never liked who, Aunt Gladys?"

"Your husband. I told you not to marry him." Aunt Gladys pushed her salad away.

Rachel took it from the table, returned both containers to the bag they'd come in and tossed them in the wastebasket.

"I'm Rachel," she said, leaning over her aunt. "I'm your niece, Rachel. I have to go now, but I'll be back."

"Where are you going?"

"I'm going home."

Her aunt nodded as if she understood. Rachel had no idea if she did or not, but at least the haunted look had disappeared from her pale-green eyes.

Still Rachel was edgy as she drove home, and jittery as she parked and took the elevator up to her condo. She slid the key into the door and stepped inside, grateful to be home.

Her fingers were on the deadbolt, ready to push it in place, when a chill ran up her spine. Something didn't seem right.

A scent? That was it. A musky scent. Indistinct and unfamiliar. She scanned the area quickly. Everything was in place, yet she felt an overwhelming sensation that someone had been in her condo while she'd been out.

Or that they were here now.

CHAPTER TWELVE

RACHEL BACKED OUT of the apartment and pulled the door shut behind her. Something had definitely spooked her, yet nothing had been out of place. She took a few deep breaths, trying to decide if she should get someone from security and have them think she was some kind of nut for having them check an apartment where everything was just as she'd left it, or if she should just bite the bullet and barge in.

The elevator bell clanged behind her and she jerked around, hoping it would be someone who lived on her floor. Another human in the empty hall would probably go a long way toward dissolving her fears. And if it was the banker who lived down the hall, she might even ask him to wait while she checked the premises.

The elevator door opened and Logan stepped out. Her heart jumped. She wasn't sure if it was totally from relief or if it was partly that he was wearing a pair of running shorts that showed off powerful thighs and a muscle shirt that did great things for his pecs.

"You look upset," he said, hurrying toward her. "What's wrong?"

"Nothing. It's just that…" She hesitated, hating to sound so paranoid.

He propped his hand on the door and leaned over her. "You didn't get another threat, did you?"

"No." She might as well explain, or he'd think she was a nut anyway for standing out in the hallway staring at her door. "When I opened the door to my condo a second ago, I had this crazy feeling that someone had been in there—or might still be in there."

"Was something out of place?"

"No. Everything was just as I'd left it, and the door was locked. I'm sure it was just a case of nerves. The building is secure. You have to have the code or an electronic opener to get through the gate to the parking area or to come through the front door." She took a step backward. "So how did you get in?"

"I followed another car."

"There goes my feeling of security."

"Wait out here while I check it out."

"But if someone's in there?"

"I'll go easy on him."

She thought he was making light of her fears until she saw him ease the door open, then step inside and pick up a heavy crystal vase from the table in the small foyer. It wouldn't stop gunfire, but it could easily crack a skull.

She waited a few seconds, then went inside. She could hear Logan in the bedroom. She peeked in the kitchen. The newspaper was still on the counter where she'd left it. The knives were all safely stored in their wooden block.

The increased adrenaline flow had pretty much disintegrated by the time Logan joined her in the living area.

"You were supposed to wait outside," he said.

"I waited until it seemed safe."

"There's no one here now but us."

"Like I said, it was probably just a case of nerves."

"I can understand that," he said, "with all that's going on."

She'd almost have liked this better if he were teasing her about getting scared over nothing. She closed the front door and turned the deadbolt, checking it twice to make certain it caught. "Your timing was great, but I'm sure you didn't just come by to see if I was hovering in the hallway. So why are you here?"

"I tried to reach you for over an hour."

She glanced down at his running shorts, but averted her gaze quickly. "I didn't answer the phone, so you ran over here?"

"Not exactly. I had planned to go jogging, but when you didn't answer the phone, I gave up on that idea so I could check on you. Is that so surprising?"

Surprising—and endearing. She'd never had a man worry about her, and she had the crazy urge to throw herself into Logan's arms and hold on tight. Instead she went to her purse and took her phone from the outside pocket of her handbag. It was off.

"I guess with all that's been going on I forgot to charge my cell phone."

"See, more reason that I should worry about you. I don't like the idea of you living here alone."

"I'm not particularly keen on it myself tonight, but it's not as if I can run away and hide until this is over. I have to work. I have bills to pay."

"You can stay at my place for a while." He put a hand on her shoulder. "Seriously. There's plenty of room, and you won't be coming home to an empty condo at night."

No, she'd be coming home to a man she barely knew, one whose mere touch was making her heart race and her insides tingle. If the situation were different, if they weren't entangled in a murder case, if his sons weren't missing...

"It's out of the question, Logan."

"Then let me hire a bodyguard for you. I've already talked to someone with Protection, Inc. They can assign people to twelve-hour shifts so that someone is with you every second of the day, the same as being in protective custody."

She reeled at the thought, then dropped to the couch. "Williams, Williams and Castile would never tolerate that. I'd be fired in a New York minute."

He perched on the arm of the sofa. "Nothing in the Big Easy is done in a New York minute. But you don't have to use the guard twenty-four hours a day. He can meet you when you get off work at night and stay with you until you arrive at the office every morning."

"All because I got a little nervous tonight. That would be a touch of overkill, don't you think?"

"It's more than that you're getting nervous. It's all of this." He threw up his hands in exasperation, then stood and walked to the window. "It's not knowing what the hell this is all about."

"We have to talk to the dark-haired girl."

"That's another problem. There's something about her I should tell you."

"Not another surprise."

"A minor one."

Tess listened to the account of how the dark-haired dancer had slipped the note and the key to Tess's apartment into his hand the day Tess had been killed.

"Why didn't you tell me that the first time I mentioned her?"

"I'd promised her that I wouldn't tell anyone. And I didn't trust you not to go to Detective Morrison with the information."

"So why tell me now?"

"I know you better." He dropped to the sofa beside her.

"No matter what you promised, we have to talk to the dancer, Logan."

"I've tried to talk to her. I have someone staked out watching the club every hour that it's open. She hasn't shown up since the day of Tess's funeral."

"You don't think she's been murdered, too?"

"I don't know what I think anymore, other than that I'm sick and tired of waiting for things to happen. And here I am hitting you with my frustrations when you've already had a rough night. I don't know about you, but I could use a drink."

"I don't have any hard liquor, but there's wine in the pantry. Nothing too expensive. I'm no connoisseur."

He walked to the kitchen and chose a wine while she got the corkscrew and a couple of glasses. It seemed strange having him in her kitchen, pouring wine, making himself at home. She wondered what it would be like if she did move in with him.

Would they have dinner together at night? Would she slip into pajamas and cuddle up on the sofa with her work as she did most nights now? Would they touch? Kiss? Make love?

A slow burn crept inside her and sent scorching fingers to every erogenous part of her body. She shouldn't be thinking these things when her emotions were so raw they were practically bleeding.

Logan's had to be in worse shape. He was worrying about his sons. His and Tess's. Sons born of a one-night stand. She tried to shake the thought, but couldn't.

"Were there many women like Tess?"

He looked puzzled. "I'm not sure what you're asking."

"One-night stands. Did you do that often when you were younger?"

"Of course not."

Reluctantly, she let the subject drop. His past affairs were none of her business. They took their wine back to the sofa. They didn't talk anymore of Tess or even the boys. Instead they talked of music and movies and the work he planned to do on the house he'd inherited from his grandmother. It was as if they needed an hour of normalcy to regroup for a world gone mad.

They finished the bottle of wine and still Logan lingered until near midnight. Finally, he reached over and took her hand. "I have to fly to Chicago this weekend on business. I tried to get out of it, but there's some complications with a shopping center we're building, and I have to take care of it personally."

"Don't worry about me."

"Go with me."

"I can't."

"Why not?"

"I have work that I have to get out. You have work there. You can't take me on full-time."

"Then I guess I should be going," Logan said, "unless you'd like me to stay the night."

The offer was tempting, just as the one to go with him to Chicago was. But if they spent the night together, they'd make love, and she wasn't ready to take that step just yet. "I'll be fine by myself. I'll lock the deadbolt, and I'm on the fifth floor. No one will be coming through the windows."

"If that's what you want." He took his glass to the sink and rinsed the red residue from the bottom before setting it on the counter. "I don't want to push in to anything, but at least think about what I said tonight about moving in with me or letting me hire you a bodyguard."

"I'll think about it." She walked him to the door, and when he lingered, the moment became charged with a sexual energy that zinged along her every nerve ending. It was all she could do not to say she'd changed her mind and wanted him to stay.

He caught her hands in his. "If you need me, call me."

"I will."

"Those questions about Tess… I mean, if you're thinking that I'll expect something of you if you move in, you don't have to worry. If we have any kind of intimacy, it will be a mutual decision."

"You are a very straightforward man, Logan McCain."

"Comes from living in a house where manipulation was the norm. After awhile, you have to rebel."

"Logan McCain, rebel. Has a nice ring," she teased, struggling to keep the moment light.

It didn't work. He leaned in, and she knew he was going to kiss her. Her knees went weak, but she didn't back away.

The kiss was tentative at first, but when she kissed him back, he took her mouth hungrily. And once he did, there was no holding back. She forgot her inhibitions and lost herself in the thrill of him. Loved the taste of his lips, the feel of his tongue tangling with hers, the mingling of their breaths. When he pulled away, she ached for more.

"Put the deadbolt on," he whispered, touching a finger to her kiss-swollen lips. And then he was gone.

She closed the door and leaned against it for support. Like everything else in her life right now, her feelings for Logan were spinning out of control. And this was no time to let her hormones lure her into a mistake.

LOGAN WAS a few blocks from his house when he took the call from his young PI on stakeout at the Fruits of Passion. The dark-haired dancer had returned to work. Although he was dead tired from the weekend and the plane ride back, Logan rushed home, showered and changed in record time.

He considered calling Rachel, but decided against it. She'd

want to go with him, and he hated the thought of her being anywhere near Fruits of Passion. Whatever Tess had gotten mixed up in, it was almost surely connected to the gentleman's club.

The club was hopping. Almost every table was taken and there were four dancers on stage and several working the crowd, shaking their breasts in the faces of leering men who nursed expensive drinks in one hand and tucked dollar bills into garters with the other.

He walked through a haze of cigarette smoke and boisterous men before finding an empty table off to the left. A smiling waitress was at his elbow before he settled in. He ordered a vodka martini, extra dry with a twist, but it was only for show. He wanted his brain crystal-clear for this.

He took out his wallet and removed a couple of twenties and a few fives. He slid them under the edge of his napkin, fives on top, while he searched the room. The new bouncer was standing in the back corner, arms folded, watching the action. As big as Hank and meaner-looking. Logan wondered if the guy had been told to look for him and to report to his boss if and when Logan showed up.

Craig Graves wasn't in the room. Neither was his so-called manager, Elton Pierce. At least that much was in Logan's favor. One of the dancers sashayed over and strutted her stuff. He slid a couple of fives from his stack, leaving it so that the twenty peeked out.

She leaned over him, shook all she had, then dipped to the floor as if she were riding an invisible pole. When she stood up, he slipped one of the fives inside her garter. He was considering asking her about the dark-haired dancer when the woman in question stepped onto the stage.

She made a couple of moves, and every eye turned in her

direction. There was no question who was queen of the establishment. Her breasts weren't nearly as large as some of the other women, but they were perky and perfect, and when she did her moves, they seemed to come to life.

Logan watched, mesmerized by the way she controlled the audience and had them gasping and drooling at every new twist and turn. She never smiled. In fact, her face showed no emotion. It was as if her body was unconnected to the person who lived inside it, yet she still managed to control a roomful of highly charged men.

He waited while she did her stint on the stage. There were too many eyes on her now for him even to think of approaching her and hope to get any information from her. He'd have to wait until she was working the tables, picking up requests for lap dances and whatever tips the guys away from the stage wanted to slip her.

A lap dance. That would work. But not just any lap dance. He needed a completely private performance. He was sure they offered them at a high-priced club like this one. Possibly even had rooms that Detective Morrison didn't know about.

Finally, the dark-haired queen finished her stint on stage and made her way through the crowds. She was in the middle of the room when she looked his way. Her body went rigid for a fraction of a second, just long enough for him to know she'd seen him. He half expected her to disappear again, but this time he was ready for her. If she made an attempt to leave the room, he'd follow her if he had to knock down a dozen guys to do it.

He didn't want to get her into any kind of trouble, but the stakes had been raised with the blood-stained shirt. He had to find the boys, and she might be the only one who could help him.

She didn't flee. In fact she made her way steadily toward him. When she got to his table, she put a leg on the chair next to him and did a little dip and sway.

"I'd like a lap dance," he said. "Very private."

"You made a promise." Her voice was so soft, he could barely hear it and he was certain no one else could.

"I have to talk to you."

"You're making a mistake."

He made a production of tucking a twenty into her garter and raised his voice so everyone within ten feet could hear him. "I'll take a lap dance with you, sweet thing."

"You're in for a thrill, big boy. I'll meet you in the blue room just past the bar in ten minutes." This time she played the game. Now if she'd only talk.

He watched as she made her way back through eager clusters of men. When she reached the stage, he left enough money to pay his tab and headed for the blue room. He'd expected a crowd of men to be waiting, but evidently she'd sent him somewhere other than the usual gathering place. Of course it could just be another dodge.

A few seconds later she joined him, all business now, beautiful, mysterious and swaying. "Private sessions are forty-five dollars for five minutes. I'll do all the touching. You just sit back and enjoy. I'll make it worth your while if you're still interested."

Obviously they were in a room where what they said could be overheard. "Forty-five dollars. Damn. You better be good."

"I am as good as it gets."

He followed her down a narrow hallway. She knocked before entering a closed room. When no one answered, she opened the door and motioned him inside.

The room wasn't much more than a small cubicle. There was one chair, straight-backed, with a gold-colored terry covering and a lamp with a red shade to provide dim lighting. She shut the door behind them.

"Take a seat," she said, "and we can get started. Remember, I do all the touching. House rules."

He sat down and she leaned over him until her lips were a fraction of an inch from his right ear. "There's a two-way mirror. Whisper. And act like you're enjoying yourself."

She swung one leg across his and lowered herself onto his lap facing him. He figured that meant the mirror was behind her. No one could see her lips, and if he leaned way back in his chair and let his head drop behind him as if he were in ecstasy, no one would see or be able to read his.

This was the chance he'd been waiting for.

CHAPTER THIRTEEN

CHERI WENT THROUGH the motions, keeping most of her weight on her feet while she slid and slithered across Logan's lap. Any other time she could have thrown herself into her work with a man like Logan. He was gorgeous and had that demanding, tough edge that turned her on.

She wasn't turned on now, though. Fear was not an aphrodisiac. The consequences would be severe if either Craig or Elton came in and found her with Logan. But they weren't around, and she had to take her chances that they wouldn't return in the next few minutes.

"You have five minutes, Logan," she whispered. "That's all I can stay in this room with you without risking making someone suspicious."

"Then don't waste my time. Why was Tess murdered?"

"She was involved with some dangerous people." Cheri tangled her hands behind her neck so that her breasts were in his face while she moved her bottom in a circular motion that should have been affecting Logan a lot more than it was. The guy was either impotent or made of steel.

"That doesn't tell me why they killed her."

"She made them mad. I don't know how. She got away from them once, but they came back and found her."

"What people?"

"I don't know."

"You're lying."

"No. I tried to get her to tell me what she'd done and who was after her, but she wouldn't. She said she didn't want to put me in danger."

"Did it have something to do with Fruits of Passion?"

"I think she may have met them here."

"Met them or worked for them?"

"This is just a club, Logan. We dance. That's all. There's nothing dangerous about it."

"Then why was Hank killed?"

"He was crazy about Tess. He probably tried to save her. That's all I can figure out."

"Bullshit. She was already dead when he was murdered. Why did Tess's stepmother run with the boys?"

"I don't know."

"Don't lie." Logan wrapped his hands around her wrists. His fingers dug into her flesh and a hot ribbon of pain shot up the length of her arms.

"I told you not to touch me," she said. "If someone happens to walk into the observation room and finds you breaking the rules, I'll get chewed out, if not fired."

"Then start talking straight."

"I don't know why Cathy took the boys and ran. I suppose she was afraid that whoever killed Tess would come after them."

"That makes no sense. They'd have no reason to kill innocent children."

"I'm telling you all I know. I tried to help. I sent you the note telling you they were your sons."

"So that was you?"

"Yeah. And this is the thanks I'm getting. I even tried to get Tess to give you custody of the boys so you could keep them away from the trouble she was in. She wouldn't. She hated you for getting her pregnant."

"Hated me so much she'd put her sons in danger?"

"Don't ask me to explain Tess. I doubt anyone can. Just stay out of it, and tell Rachel Powers to do the same."

His body hardened, but she knew it had nothing to do with her. "Is Rachel in danger?" he demanded, this time letting his voice rise above a whisper.

"Shh."

"Is she in danger?"

"All I know is Tess was murdered, and I want to stay alive. That's why I'm begging you not to drag me into this. Don't come around here again. Please, just stay away."

"Give me a name. That's all I ask. Give me a name, and I won't bother you again."

"I would if I could. I tried to help you. You should have taken the boys when you had the chance." She stiffened and raised off his lap. "Your time is up. You have to go." She pulled away from him, and to her surprise, he didn't stop her. She moved slowly, sensually, not for Logan, but just in case someone was watching.

There was seldom anyone in the observation room unless she pushed the red button behind the chair signaling that she had an unruly customer and might need help, but she could never be sure.

She opened the door, turned the sign to indicate the room was available again, then stepped into the carpeted hallway. Another dancer and her customer were coming toward them.

Logan fell in step beside her, thankfully playing the game. "Is that all I get for the money?"

"Now don't tell me you didn't enjoy that?"

Once the dancer and the man ducked into one of the rooms, he leaned in close and whispered in her ear.

"What's your name?"

"Cheri."

"Your last name?"

"Trosclair. Now go."

"I will, but if I find out you're lying, you'll wish Tess's killers had gotten to you first."

He meant to scare her, but she knew he was bluffing. He could never be as totally heartless or demented as the men who'd arranged for Tess's death. No one could.

CHERI WISHED now she'd listened to Craig's advice and taken off for the whole week. But she'd been going stir-crazy lolling around the apartment by herself. She'd never liked being alone.

She stopped in the dressing room and peeled off the silky thong, kicking it out of the way so that she could reach the sundress she'd thrown over the hook in her private niche. Bending, she stepped into the dress, pulling the soft cotton over her hips and then her shoulders.

She never bothered with underwear, couldn't imagine why any woman did. Men loved it when the nipples puckered the fabric of a blouse or dress, and they became instantly aroused when they reached beneath a skirt and could feel bare, warm flesh.

Most women had lots of rules about what they could and couldn't do. Cheri had only two. Do what felt right—and stay alive. That's why she'd let Logan know he had sons that needed protection. She'd been worried about them and doing something about it had felt right. Lying to him tonight had fallen under rule number two.

Grabbing her handbag, she left the building through the back door, walking fast.

"Well, well, look who's here. I didn't know you were working tonight."

Cheri's pulse skyrocketed when she saw Griffin step from the shadows. "I wasn't supposed to work. I got bored."

"Bored? I thought you could satisfy all your own needs."

"Not always."

"You know it can be dangerous walking these streets at night."

"Maybe you should just walk me to my apartment."

"Sorry. I'm on duty, but you be careful. I hear a woman can get in real trouble in that alley just past the tattoo parlor."

"What kind of trouble?" She made her voice breathy and teasing.

"A man might take advantage of her. It could get really nasty."

She ran her hand between her thighs. She was so hot, she thought she might go orgasmic right here on the street. Those rich bastards she catered to thought they knew how to turn her on. But no one had ever turned her on the way Griffin Paulson did.

The bad thing was he knew it. That gave him the edge. Sometimes she had to beg for it. But tonight he was ready. She could see his erection straining against the crotch of his uniform. She ran her fingers across the handcuffs that swung from his waist. "I'll be very, very careful."

And then she left him, knowing he'd follow her to a dark little niche somewhere in the alleyway. And then he'd have his way with her. She could hardly wait.

"YOU MISSED a good time Friday night," Ted said, sticking his head in Rachel's office a little after one on Monday afternoon.

"What makes you think I didn't have a good time?"

"Did you?"

"As a matter of fact, I did."

"Don't suppose you want to entertain me with the details?"

"Not a chance."

Ted walked over to her coffeepot and filled the mug he'd brought in with him, then stopped to look over her shoulder. "Sexual Harassment Case Reviews. How do you draw these cases? Do you piss off the man upstairs? Or the three pious gentlemen down the hall with Williams, Williams and Castile engraved on their doorplates?"

"Could it possibly be that I'm the only one on staff capable of handling these delicate and complicated cases?"

"So that's how Castile suckered you in. Funny, you don't look that gullible."

Ted hung around, chatting while he finished his coffee, then poured himself another cup.

"I hate to be unsociable," she said, "but would you mind taking that cup of coffee you just freeloaded back to your office so I can get to work?"

"You know you're starting to sound more like Mr. Castile every day."

"Now that's scary."

She went back to her notes even before the door clicked shut. Not that she was in the mood for this. She'd had the old nightmare again last night; the one with stamping monsters that had tormented her so when she was growing up. Now she had the beginnings of a headache just back of her eyes.

Ted was right about her bad luck with getting tough cases, but as difficult as her workload was, it was the easiest thing in her life these days. Unfortunately, she didn't see that changing anytime soon and she didn't think either of Logan's suggestions would do the trick.

Move in with him or have a bodyguard as a shadow. She'd given both possibilities a lot of thought this past weekend.

But mostly she'd thought about the kiss. And Logan's sons. Thought about them until the kiss and the missing kids were entangled in her mind the way her whole relationship with Logan was embroiled with danger and confusion.

And here she was letting him and his sons consume her mind again instead of doing her job. Keep this up, and she'd be unemployed. The senior Mr. Williams insisted on as many billable hours as she could squeeze into a week and still manage to get the minimum amount of food and sleep to survive.

Her intercom buzzed. More interruptions. She punched the button.

"You have a phone call from Cathy Shepherd. Will you take it?"

Rachel's heart slammed against her rib cage. "Put her through."

She grabbed a legal pad and pen and took a deep breath. She had no idea how to handle this, except to play it by ear—and take very good notes.

"Rachel Powers, how may I help you?"

"You don't know me, but my stepdaughter came to see you last week. Tess Shepherd."

"Yes, I remember meeting with her."

"I don't know if you heard or not, but she was murdered that same day."

So Cathy was aware of the death. She wondered if the boys knew, too. "I'm sorry to hear that, Mrs. Shepherd. The boys must be taking this hard."

"They don't know it yet. But it's the boys I'm calling about."

"What about them?"

"I took them out of town. Rescued them I guess you'd say."

"Rescued them from whom?"

"I wish I knew. Tess told me before she was killed to take them and run if anything happened to her. I didn't ask questions. I just did what she said."

Only, Cathy had run before Tess was killed, so she obviously knew at least a little more than she was admitting. "Where are you?"

"I'd rather not say. It's hard for me to trust anyone, especially now. I'm almost sure someone is following us."

"Why do you think that?"

"I can't go into it now, but there have been signs. It's not just something I'm imagining."

"You should talk to the police, or to the boys' father. You don't have to fight this battle alone."

"I don't trust the police any more than Tess did. And I definitely don't trust Logan McCain."

Rachel tried to think of something that would get through to the woman. "Logan seems very concerned about his sons."

"You may believe that, but I'm not convinced. Anyway, I don't want his help."

"What do you want from me?"

"Money. Not charity, just a loan to tide me over until I can claim the balance in Tess's bank account. I'll pay you back every penny as soon as I can."

"How much money are you talking about?"

"Fifty thousand should take care of us until the police have Tess's killer behind bars and it's safe for me to bring the boys back to New Orleans."

Fifty thousand. She obviously wasn't planning on returning anytime soon. "How would I get the money to you if I don't know where you are?"

"You can wire it."

"I'd still need somewhere to wire it to."

"I could call you later and let you know where and when. All you'd have to do is set up the transfer and we can do it all in a matter of minutes."

Tess tried to think. There were probably questions she should be asking. Things Logan was going to ask her. "Before I send money, I'd like to speak to the boys."

"Sure. Hold on. They're in the bathtub. I didn't want them to hear our conversation, but I'll let them say hello to you."

Rachel's hand tightened on the receiver.

"Say hello to Miss Rachel, Davy."

"I don't know her. I don't want to talk."

"You have to at least say hello."

"Why do I hafta? Make Danny do it."

"You have to because I said so. Now say hello. She's going to send us a present."

"Dinosaurs?"

"Something even better than dinosaurs. Now say hello."

"Hello."

"Hi, Davy."

"What kind of present you gonna send me?"

"What would you like?"

"I like dinosaurs. I got some really swell ones for my birthday. From Mr. Hank."

Rachel made a mental note of the fact that the boys had known the murdered bouncer by his first name. "Are you having a nice vacation?"

"Nope. It's a long way to the beach."

"Not too far I hope. Florida has nice beaches?" She was fishing, but lots of people in Louisiana vacationed on Florida beaches.

"Alabama has beaches, too, but my gramma won't take us there."

Cathy took the phone again. "That's enough talk."

But Rachel could hear water splashing in the background and the chatter of two young boys. They could be anywhere. In any town, in any state, except maybe not in Alabama.

"Make up your mind," Cathy said. "Are you going to help us or not? If you can't come up with the whole fifty thousand, even ten thousand would help."

Rachel weighed the decision, but it really wasn't a decision at all. "I'll help."

"Good. I can call you back about three to make the transfer. Is that too soon?"

"Three should work fine. Call me on my cell. Sometimes it's hard to get through on the office phones." She gave Cathy the number slowly and then repeated it so there would be no mistake.

"It's important that you don't talk to anyone else about this, Miss Powers. Not the police. Not Logan McCain. Not anyone. It has to be our secret. For the boys' sake. Possibly for their lives."

"I understand."

"Good, 'cause I don't want to take chances with the boys' lives." And then the connection was broken.

Rachel pushed up her sleeve and checked her watch. Thirty-three minutes after one o'clock. Standing, she grabbed her notes and crammed them into her briefcase. Whatever she did, she'd have to do fast. She rushed out without bothering to tell anyone that she was leaving.

The hot air slapped her in the face like a wet towel as she stepped out of the elevator and rushed toward her car. Once inside it, she started the engine, cranked the air conditioner to high and tried to think with a little more clarity than she'd been doing.

She punched in Logan's cell-phone number. "I heard from Cathy Shepherd," she said the second Logan answered. He exhaled so sharply she could hear it over the phone, but he didn't interrupt until she'd finished repeating everything she could remember from Cathy's phone call.

"That's a load of bull. She knows who killed Tess. Whatever Tess was in, Cathy was probably in it right along with her."

"You don't know that."

"I know she blackmailed my father. I know she knew the boys were McCains for years and never came to me. Are you in your office?"

"No, in my car."

"Good. I'm in a meeting, but I'll bring it to a quick close. Get here as soon as you can, and we'll talk this out and decide exactly how to handle the situation."

"I need to call Detective Morrison. He'll have to have a say in whatever we do."

"I don't want him involved in this."

She'd expected him to react like this, but she had to hold firm. "We can't bypass the authorities."

"I sure as hell can. If Morrison had put out an APB the minute we knew Danny and Davy were missing instead of days later, we might have located them while they were still in the area."

"I understand how you feel, but I have to call him. It's the ethical and legal thing to do."

"Ethical? We're dealing with murder and kidnapping and a woman we know was guilty of blackmail, and you're worried about being ethical."

"That's them. This is me. I have to call Detective Morrison. At least try to understand."

"If that's your decision, I don't guess it matters whether I understand or not."

That hurt, as did the disappointment in his voice. "I'll call you after I talk to Detective Morrison."

"I'd appreciate that. Morrison probably won't."

Her heart felt heavy when she broke the connection with Logan. She pulled into one of those rare available parking spaces on Canal Street, folded her arms over the steering wheel and buried her head while she fought off a wave of anxiety. How had this ever fallen into her hands?

The answer was easy. Both Tess and Logan had pulled her in, and now Cathy Shepherd was doing the same thing, making their problems hers. Making boys she had no actual physical connection with her responsibility.

Right now she felt like a traitor to all of them. Still, she punched in the detective's number. She'd done the appropriate thing all her life. Followed her aunt's rules: *Be a good girl. Obey the law. Study hard. Make your parents proud.* It was the only way she knew. It had never been enough to dissolve the nebulous emptiness that haunted her nor to stop the monsters that marched through the tormenting nightmares. This probably wouldn't, either, but at least she was doing something.

"What you got?"

"Is this Detective Morrison?"

"Yeah. I'm sorry. I was expecting someone else. Who is this?"

"Rachel Powers."

"Good to hear from you. Are you okay?"

"Yes, but I had a phone call from Cathy Shepherd about a half hour ago."

"She called you. That's a shocker."

She repeated the conversation again, this time pulling out her notes to make sure she wasn't leaving anything out.

"Three o'clock, huh? That doesn't leave us a lot of time."

"I also called Logan McCain. He's very concerned about getting his boys back safely. He'd like to be in on whatever decision is made."

"I'd rather not have him in the middle of this, but we may need him to come up with the funds, unless you have fifty thousand to play with."

Rachel's suspicion level rose a notch. Maybe Logan was right about not trusting the police. "Are you suggesting we just send the money without strings?"

"No way. I'm not even sure we'll need to arrange a wire at all. Tell you what, I'm working a murder scene downtown, unrelated to the Shepherd case. There's a restaurant near here. I know the owner. He'll let us sit in the back room where we can talk. Do you think you and Logan can meet me there in a half hour?"

"I'm sure we can."

She scribbled down the address. She'd be there with Logan. The decision would be made by him and the detective as it should be and all she'd have to do is follow instructions. Even that made her nervous

This had to be pulled off without a hitch or it could cost the lives of two four-year-old boys who liked dinosaurs. Even Aunt Gladys had never put this kind of pressure on her.

LOGAN LEANED BACK in the uncomfortable chair and looked the detective in the eye. "I don't like it. Too many things can go wrong."

"It's our best shot," Morrison said, apparently having already made up his mind how he wanted to proceed. "We find out where Cathy Shepherd plans to pick up the money, then stall the transfer until the local cops can get there and apprehend her."

Logan frowned. "Suppose she's not alone. Suppose she has some goon with her who starts shooting and the boys get hurt in the fray."

"She didn't say anyone was with her," Rachel replied.

"She blackmails people," Logan retorted. "I'd say there's a 99.9 percent chance she also lies."

Rachel tapped the end of her pen on her notepad. "Do you think she could have planned this all along, that she kidnapped the boys for a fifty-thousand-dollar ransom?"

Morrison refilled his coffee cup from the chrome thermos the owner had sat on the table. "If this were a ransom payment, I'd expect the amount to be a lot higher seeing as how the McCain family is one of the richest in the state. I think she's just after some quick money so that she can stay on the run, just like she says."

"And fifty thousand could let her run right out of the country." Logan didn't like anything about this setup. It was too risky. "How do you know the local cops will cooperate when we don't even know what state she's in?"

"Kids are involved. That's the surest way to get any cop fired up and ready to do battle."

"Will we actually transfer funds?" Rachel asked, "or just pretend to?"

Morrison emptied two full packages of artificial sweetener into his coffee and stirred as if he were whipping cream. "We can go either way. Sometimes it's safer to make an actual transfer. That way you don't have to worry about the tellers fouling up and giving the setup away."

"The money's not the problem," Logan said, still not convinced this would work. "My concern is that we wire the money, she gets it before the cops arrive and takes off with the boys. I want something foolproof. I want to know that when this is over, the boys are in the hands of the police. Then I'll fly wherever they are and pick them up."

"Nothing's foolproof, Mr. McCain. You know that as well as I do, but this is damn close. We'll arrange everything with your bank so that the money is not actually released until I have confirmation that the officers are in place to apprehend Cathy Shepherd."

"But if we stall, she may get suspicious and walk away," Rachel said.

"She won't walk if she thinks fifty thousand is arriving any minute. And minutes are all we're talking about."

Logan glanced at his watch. It was close to three. Rachel's phone would be ringing any second. If this worked, he could have the boys in his custody before bedtime.

"Okay. Let's go with it. I'll call my bank and alert them."

Rachel reached across the table and squeezed his hand. Hers were cold as ice.

When her cell phone rang, they all three froze in place. Finally she answered and they sat in dead silence, listening as she firmed up the deal.

"She'll be in place to receive the money at four o'clock," Rachel said, as soon as she'd finished her brief conversation with Cathy Shepherd. "She'll call on my cell phone then and let us know where to send it. That's all the information she'd give me for now."

"I was hoping she'd give us more notice," Morrison said. "But we'll make this work. We'll just have to move fast once we get her next phone call."

The tension that had been building in Logan's mind for the last hour finally broke. The decision had been made. He was ready to rumble. Taking action was what he did best.

CHAPTER FOURTEEN

BY THREE FORTY-FIVE, everything was a go. Rachel was sitting with Logan and the detective in a windowless office along with one of the bank's vice presidents. Logan and his family were obviously important customers. Though the VP wasn't told all the facts surrounding the transfer, she was being very accommodating and doing what she could to make certain there were no glitches on the bank's part.

At three fifty-five, Rachel checked her phone to make sure it was still turned on. It was, and the signal was strong. Now it was just a matter of waiting. Even the occasional attempts at polite conversation ceased as the minute hand approached twelve.

A week of panic, worrying and fear had come down to this—a cell phone and a clock.

The minute hand slipped past the twelve. Everyone had noticed. Their gazes were glued to the clock. No one said a word. Rachel tried to think back to her last conversation with Cathy Shepherd. Could she possibly have said something that tipped her off that this was a setup?

Ten after four. Logan stood and paced the room. "If she were going to call, she'd have done it by now."

Morrison stretched the muscles in his neck, turning from side to side. "Don't give up on her yet. She might be tied up in traffic."

"Or the first bank she tried might have been closed," Rachel said, trying to reassure him. It didn't work. Defeat and despair were written in every line of his face, and she was growing increasingly disheartened herself.

Her phone rang. She sucked in her breath and answered it. "Hello."

"You sound terrible. Are you catching a cold?"

"Karen."

"Excuse me, make that terrible and disappointed."

"Sorry. I've been waiting on an important business call. I thought this was it." And stupidly, she hadn't checked the caller ID before she answered. If she had, she'd have let it ring and not tied up the phone. "Can I call you back later?"

"Are you sure you're okay?"

"I'm good. Just tied up in something right now."

"I'm getting very bad vibes, Rachel. Tell me this has nothing to do with Logan McCain or Tess Shepherd."

"I'll call you later."

"I take that avoidance as a yes. I don't understand why you're letting that man pull you into this. This is so unlike you."

"Later." Rachel broke the connection before Karen could ask anything else or continue the lecture. "I'm sorry," she said. "That was a friend."

"Don't fret it," Morrison said, waving the apology off. "For fifty thousand, Cathy Shepherd will call back if she gets a busy signal."

But she didn't call. Not by four-thirty. Not by four forty-five. By five o'clock, Logan was cracking his knuckles and glaring at the clock as if it had taken on demonic properties.

At five after, he stood and punched his right fist into his left palm with such ferocity that Rachel cringed in empathetic pain.

"She's not going to call," he said. "All this, and she's not going through with it."

"I hate it, but I gotta agree with you," Morrison said. "For some reason she's changed her mind, but that doesn't mean she won't call later and try to set up payment again."

Logan paced the small room. "What kind of sick game would that be?"

"There's no way to know what's going on in her mind. But even if she doesn't call, it's just a matter of time. Photos of her and the kids and her license-plate number and description of her car are in every police station in the southeast and there's an APB out that says apprehend her on sight."

"And still she's out there doing her thing. So much for the efficiency of Southern police."

Logan didn't mention that he had his own man out there as well, supposedly the best in the business, and he hadn't located the boys, either.

But Logan was hurting. He was afraid for his boys, and he knew the way Rachel did that something far worse than traffic or a change of mind could have stopped Cathy from calling back at four.

Morrison and Logan thanked the bank representative for working with them while Rachel excused herself to go to the ladies' room. When she came out, Logan was waiting by the door. "Let's get out of here."

The bank was officially closed, but the guard was at the front door, dangling a loaded key ring, waiting to let them out. Logan took her arm as they went through the door and headed to his car. "I hope you don't have to go back to work."

"I'd planned to, but I suppose I could get out of it. I'm not sure I'd accomplish anything even if I went back."

"Then go with me," Logan said.

"Where?"

"The lake. We can take the boat out. I need the wind in my face."

The boat. Of course, the McCains would have a boat. Probably a yacht. Logan never flaunted his wealth. It was just there, part of him. It affected the way he thought, acted, dressed and talked. It gave him the freedom to be a lot more spontaneous than she'd ever been.

"I have on high heels and a suit. I'm not dressed for boating."

"There are some extra swimsuits at the boathouse. I'm sure you can find one that will work."

"Swimsuits are not one size fits all."

"Then we'll stop at your place and you can change clothes. There's still plenty of daylight left."

As far as he was concerned the decision to go boating was a done deal, but there was no indication that this was for pleasure. It was more an escape from a situation he could no longer deal with.

He was quiet now and walking so fast she had to jog a few steps every now and then to keep up with him. But when they reached the car, he opened her door and held it for her, always the gentleman. She started to back out of the boating trip, thinking that they both probably needed some time alone. But when she looked up, she saw the glisten of moisture in his eyes. It turned her insides to mush, and her own eyes teared up.

Instead of sliding into the car, she stepped closer to him and rested her head on his shoulder. He took her in his arms and held on tight.

The aftereffects of the hug stayed with her as she crawled into the car and fastened her seat belt. It had been brief but intense, and she knew she was falling hard.

CRAIG GRAVES sat in his darkened office and watched the performance again, all captured live on one of the hidden cameras he'd had built into all of the private rooms. Cheri and Logan McCain.

She'd been most accommodating, turning to face him, grinding her shapely little ass into him while she entertained him with a lot more than her body. Unfortunately, the focus wasn't quite sharp enough for Craig to read her lips. The fool. Did she honestly think she could get by with pulling a stunt like this right under his nose?

He'd suspected that day at the funeral that they weren't total strangers. Logan had ignored all the other dancers and gone chasing after Cheri. She'd purposefully ignored him that day, but then she'd known that Craig was watching.

If word ever leaked about what the Fruits of Passion was really about, they'd all go down. The bigger they are, the harder they fall. If that were true, reverberations would be felt all the way to the West Coast.

Craig had announced that there would be no Elite parties in the red room for a while, but he'd have to modify that rule. There would be one more party. The guest of honor would be Cheri Trosclair.

The verdict was still out on Rachel Powers.

THE BOAT wasn't a yacht. At least the boat Logan chose from the three moored at the McCain boathouse wasn't. It was a racing boat, slender and sleek, and polished so that the late-afternoon sun rays sparkled like diamonds when they ricocheted off the bright-red paint. Logan had motored slowly as he'd steered past the line of boathouses and the marina, but once he'd reached open water in Lake Pontchartrain, he opened it up.

The wind stole Rachel's breath and whipped her hair, slapping it across her face and into her mouth. She held on to the side of the boat with one hand and held her sunglasses in place with the other, exhilarated and frightened all at the same time.

Logan stared straight ahead, his full attention seemingly focused on pushing the boat to its limits. She understood now why he'd wanted to come to the lake. The control over a speeding boat was a potent antidote for the situation he was in with his sons.

He never slowed except when he turned the boat, and even then they went so fast she expected the boat to capsize and toss them into the lake. They rode until the sun sank near enough to the horizon that bands of gold and orange spread across the sky, and Rachel's bottom seemed permanently attached to the cushioned seat of the boat.

When Logan finally slowed the boat, they were in the middle of the vast lake, serenaded by water lapping against the hull and the echo of the motor that still roared in her brain.

She brushed her hair from her face with her fingers and pulled off her sunglasses to find it wasn't quite as dark as she'd thought. "That was quite a ride."

"I would have gone faster, but I thought I should break you in before going all-out."

"My body and heart thank you. Do you race in competition?"

"Not since... Not in the last two years."

"You must have won a few races."

"More than a few." He raked a clump of hair from his forehead and stretched his legs. "My brother and I raced together. He had no fear. Faster, higher, deeper. Always to the limits. That was Josh."

"Where is he now?"

Logan turned away from her, and stared into the distance. "He's dead."

Leave it to her to ask. "I'm sorry, Logan."

"That's okay, just not the best day to get into that. Let's talk about you instead."

This time she was determined to keep the conversation light. They'd been through enough emotional upheaval for one day. "There's not much to say. I'm an attorney. I live alone. Don't even have a cat. I like show tunes and old Beatles music. I'm a lousy cook, except that I make great chocolate chip cookies. And I'm pretty much a neat freak, a habit I was forced to develop in order to be tolerated by my Aunt Gladys."

"Were you ever married?"

"No, never even came close."

"Just haven't found the right man?"

"I've seen a few I'd like to have."

"Like who?"

"I'd mud-wrestle for Brad Pitt in a heartbeat. George Clooney's appeared in a few fantasies and Johnny Depp could probably start my motor in a crunch. What about you? Have you ever been married?"

"You're supposed to be our topic of conversation."

"You've heard it all. So were you? Married, that is?"

"Yeah. Once. For about five months."

"What happened?"

"I was living in Paris at the time, working in one of my father's foreign offices. She was French and incredibly sexy. We spent the first four months making love. The fifth month we realized we had nothing else in common. It was all downhill after that."

"So you just got a divorce without trying to make it work?"

"She met someone else and moved in with him. That didn't inspire a lot of motivation for marriage counseling. So I moved back to the States, and that was that."

"How old were you then?"

"Twenty-five. That was seven years ago. Fortunately, I've matured a bit since then." He reached behind him and opened the cooler he'd packed with beer and ice from the marina where they'd bought gas for the boat. "Racing's over. Time for refreshments. What'll it be?"

"I'll take one of the Abitas."

"You got it." He wiped the moisture from the ice off the bottle, opened it and handed it to her. He chose a Heineken for himself and took a long swig before sitting the bottle between his feet.

"Is this Aunt Gladys you talked about the one who raised you after your parents died?"

"That would be her."

"What's she like?"

"She's difficult to describe. A kind of Southern lady meets Joan of Arc. At least she was. She had a stroke a little over a year ago that left her with some damage to her short-term memory. Sometimes she knows who I am. At other times, she confuses me with people she knew years ago."

"That's got to be tough on her."

"I'm not sure she realizes it. She's just wherever she is at any given time, kind of like time travel except that she always has the modern conveniences."

"I'd like to meet her someday."

"Sure." When this was over. But if he thought he and the French woman who'd had hot sex for four months had nothing in common, how long could she and Logan possibly last? He lived in a world of fast boats, old mansions and million-dollar business deals. She lived in a world of twelve-hour workdays, dancing to whatever tune Williams, Williams and Castile decided to fiddle on any given day. And for fun, she went to dinner with Karen or caught up on her reading.

Besides, from all indications, Logan had no idea how his life would change once he was a full-time father of children who'd lost their mother so suddenly. In some ways it would even be worse on his sons then it had been for her. They were older, and their mother had been murdered. That would be frightening for a child of any age.

"I know just having the boys with me won't solve everything," he said as if reading her mind, or more likely her change in facial expression. "I'll never talk Tess down to them. Whatever she was or whatever she did, she was their mother. But I won't let them be touched by the fear."

He had it all figured out in his mind. She hoped it worked out that way for his sake and the boys. Hoped he got them back alive and well. If he didn't, and he had to face the worst, it just might destroy him.

She reached across the space between them and slipped her hands into his. "You'll make a terrific dad."

He leaned over so far that their heads almost touched. His nearness went to her head like strong whiskey, making her dizzy.

And then he kissed her. All the pent-up emotion of the day exploded in the kiss and she could feel the thrill of it zinging through every nerve in her body.

When he finally pulled away, she was too weak to speak…and burning with desire. She wanted more, so much more. But did she have the courage to take it?

CATHY WAS a wreck, partly from the fear, partly from exasperation that she'd been so close to getting her hands on fifty thousand dollars and a chance to start over somewhere down in the Caribbean.

Elton Pierce had been waiting at three-thirty when she'd herded the kids out the door of that stinking little motel room where they'd wound up last night. He'd just stood there, scowling, a cigar dangling from his mouth and a can of beer in hand.

She'd tried to get away from him, but Davy and Danny had run up to him like he was some long-lost uncle instead of a man here to kill them all. They had no more sense about men than their mother'd had. But then Cathy hadn't done too great in that department herself, at least not until she'd hooked up with Tess's dad.

Cathy glanced back again. The kids were sound asleep, each hugging a stupid stuffed alligator Elton had probably picked up at a convenience store where he'd stopped to pee.

She muttered a few curse words, just to get them out of her system now that the kids were asleep and it was safe to talk. "How'd you find us?"

"You're predictable."

"What's that supposed to mean?"

"You always buy gas at the cheapest spot around. And you ain't never been no place. I knew you wouldn't go far."

"I was clear up to Birmingham."

"That's nowhere. You didn't even change cars. And that mud you caked on it drew my attention right to it."

"I may not have fooled you, but you fooled me, Elton. I never thought you'd sink this low."

"Now isn't that just the call girl calling the prostitute a whore. You're the one who grabbed up the boys and ran out of town so fast you didn't even show for your own stepdaughter's funeral."

"To protect the boys."

"Don't play that goody-goody grandma game with me. I

know you too well." He twisted the knob on the radio, lowering the volume on the annoying sports talk show he'd had on for the last two hours. "You were looking for a ticket out."

"And what are you looking for?"

"Same thing."

"You son of a bitch. You kill my stepdaughter and then expect to cash in on her kids."

"You got a dirty mouth for a grandmother. If anyone's to blame for Tess's death, it's probably you. You got her mixed up with Craig Graves in the first place. And she damn sure learned about greed from you."

He was wrong about that. Tess put her to shame when it came to unquenchable greed. "Where does Craig Graves think you are?"

"Tracking you down."

"So you're double-crossing him, too?"

"It's called survival."

And that had always been Elton's strong suit. "You didn't happen to bring the things we left in the motel back in Fort Walton, did you?"

"Yeah. They're in the trunk. How'd you know I was in that room, anyway."

"You're so smart. You figure it out."

"So what were you thinking. A million? Two?"

"As ransom for the boys?"

"Of course as ransom. What did you think I meant? Sell on the black market? Their father's loaded. We should probably go for more."

"And if you collect, you'll deliver the boys to Logan and not kill them?"

"Sure. Why not? You know me. I never liked violence."

She stretched her legs in front of her. It was probably going to be a long ride. She might as well use her ticket. "Two million's a nice round number."

LOGAN DOCKED the boat at a popular seafood island on the Metairie side of the lake. A deck with picnic-style tables and chairs extended out over the water, and families and couples crowded the area to eat and watch the final plunge of the sun into the waters of Lake Pontchartrain.

But Logan had obviously done this before. He'd called ahead from the middle of the lake and put in their order so that it would be ready and waiting when they arrived. "I say we eat on the boat," he said, as he finished securing them to the dock. "It will be a lot quieter."

"Good idea. Do you want me to go pick up the order?"

"No, you just relax and have another beer. I'll be right back."

As soon as he left, Rachel reluctantly placed a call to Karen. She hadn't wanted to chat with her in the confines of the boat, not when she knew Karen was going to grill her about what was going on between her and Logan and why Rachel had been so secretive earlier.

After enduring a ten-minute exchange in which Karen tried to convince her to steer clear of Logan McCain, Rachel was relieved to end the call.

Deep down, she appreciated Karen's concern, but she had no intention of following her advice.

Rachel didn't know what the night might bring, but for once in her life, she planned to go for the gusto without any regard for what the consequences for her actions might be.

Sorry, Karen. I have to do this for me.

CHAPTER FIFTEEN

"I DON'T HAVE any old Beatles music," Logan said as he perused a stack of CDs. "How about some Harry Connick, Jr.?"

"Can't go wrong with a local legend," Rachel replied.

They were in the boathouse, upstairs over the three Mc-Cain-family boats. Besides the racing boat, there was a three-bedroom motor yacht and a sailboat. Logan had given her a quick tour of the yacht when they'd come in. She suspected it had cost more than the gross national income of several small countries.

The boathouse itself was roomy, but more comfortable than lavish. The main room was a large open area with windows on three sides, all overlooking the lake. The kitchen was along the east wall. The appliances were modern, but the table was old-farmhouse style, rectangular and made of solid pine. The chairs were also of pine as was a long bench that served as seating for the back of the table.

There were two sofas in the living area, both with lots of pillows and separated by a giant ottoman. The only other room she'd checked out had been the half bath just off the entrance, but she guessed that the small hall behind the sofas led to at least one bedroom and a full bath.

She ran her index finger over a row of books on the shelves that flanked the TV. Old classics like *Huckleberry Finn* and

Tom Sawyer rested alongside current bestsellers. The shelf above that held picture albums, all neatly labeled by year.

"Do you mind if I look at this?" she asked, pulling out an album with pictures from twenty years ago.

"You'll be bored silly, but go ahead if you want."

She took it with her and settled on one of the sofas, slipping out of her shoes and curling her feet under her.

"Can I get you something to drink? The bar is usually well stocked."

"Ice water would be nice."

"Sparkling or plain?"

"Sparkling." Since he'd asked. At her house the offer would have been over ice or straight from the tap. She opened the album. Each photo had a short sentence or two beneath it identifying the subjects and giving other pertinent information.

Harris McCain receiving the Man of the Year award at the Chamber of Commerce banquet.

"You look like your father."

"That's what everyone says."

"Did you only have one sibling?"

"Yes. There was just me and Josh."

"Whoever put the albums together did a very professional job of it."

"Mother did them. She'd been a newspaper photographer before she and Dad married, and she was seldom without a camera in hand when we were growing up."

"So you were constantly saying cheese?"

"Never. She hated posed pictures. We were constantly hiding behind locked doors to make sure we weren't caught in candid, compromising positions."

"'Joshua and Logan on the west lawn.'" She read the caption out loud as she studied the picture. One brother was being tackled by the other as he ran with the football. "You and your brother look almost exactly alike. You weren't twins, were you?"

"No, but lots of people thought so. He was fourteen months older than me. Needless to say, I was unplanned. Also a month premature."

"So you're the one doing the tackling?"

"No. He was shorter than I was, and he always hated that. He made up for his lack of height in other ways, though."

She skimmed a few more pages. Almost all the photos were of Logan and Josh. She stopped on one that had the two of them going at it, fists flying.

"That looks like a serious fight."

"It was. Most mothers would have broken it up. Ours grabbed a camera. She loved action shots."

"No wonder. She's got talent. Did she ever think about going back to work?"

He shook his head, and suddenly he looked tired, as if the despair that had hit him so hard this afternoon had returned. "She used to talk about it, but not anymore. After Josh was killed, she…" He walked to the window and stared at the lights in the distance. "You don't want to hear all the jaded family history."

"Not if you don't want to talk about it."

"It's pointless. Going over things you can't change gets you nowhere."

He stayed at the window while she skimmed the rest of the book, not commenting until she got to the next-to-last page. "You killed a deer? How could you?"

He stood behind her and looked over her shoulder. "Hey, that was my first buck. I killed one before Josh. First time I'd ever accomplished anything before he did. That was a big moment."

"And I can tell there wasn't a bit of sibling rivalry between you," she teased.

"Only constant. But it was no contest. He bested me at everything—well, except academics. That was never his bag."

He circled the couch and sat down beside her. "Must have been tough on you growing up as an only child. Who'd you fight with?"

"No fights. Aunt Gladys would never have allowed it. I was the model child. Studied hard, made good grades, obeyed the curfew and kept my room spotlessly clean. I was the basic dud."

"C'mon, fess up. You must have gotten into at least one cat fight growing up."

"No cat fights. I was too big a coward for that. I did sneak out of the house one night and go to a party Aunt Gladys had forbidden me to go to. I smoked my first cigarette that night. Big mistake. She found out I'd gone and grounded me for a month."

"Your aunt was a tough cookie."

"She was, but in a way I understood it. She was a lot older than my mother, and having a small child dumped on her when she was used to living alone was a big adjustment. Plus, she wanted me to be the wonderful person my mother had been. She wanted her and my dad to be proud of me. I think I heard that every day of my life. I know I still hear it in my sleep."

He slipped an arm around her shoulder. "You must have gotten your toughness from your aunt. I don't know how I'd get through this without you."

"You'd find a way."

"Still, not many women would stick their neck out like you have for someone else's problems."

"I'm not a hero, Logan."

He ran his thumb up and down the tendons in her neck. "Can't prove that by me."

"Then you're reading too much into my actions."

"You underestimate yourself."

She snuggled closer. He thought she was doing this for him and for the boys. He was right in a way, but there was more to it. She was practically obsessed with the murder and the disappearance of the boys. Even though she'd been ordered to stay out of it by a deranged psychopath who'd planted a bloodstained shirt on her car, she couldn't comply.

Logan tangled his fingers in her hair. "I didn't get a chance to tell you before now, but I stopped at the Fruits of Passion on the way home from the airport last night. I finally got a chance to talk to the dark-haired dancer."

Rachel listened while he explained that his conversation with the woman named Cheri had taken place during a lap dance. He didn't indicate in any way that the experience had been more than a vehicle to gather information, but the image of the beautiful woman in his lap disturbed her.

Everything about Fruits of Passion disturbed her. "Did you tell Detective Morrison what Cheri told you?"

"I'm sure he's questioned her himself. He's questioned all the dancers."

"But she might not have told him the same things she told you."

"And she likely didn't tell either of us the full truth." He pulled her closer. "I've told you everything I learned, so let's drop the subject of Tess and Cheri."

"We seem to be dropping a lot of subjects tonight."

"It's been a rough day."

Too rough, and now the evening had grown awkward. "I

think that's my cue to head home," she said, glad that she'd picked up her own car when they'd stopped for her to change. "It's been a trying and exhausting day for both of us."

"Did I say something that upset you?"

"All of this upsets me. Murder. Children in danger. Mysteries that can't be solved."

"It upsets both of us." He kept his arm around her. "I'd hoped you wouldn't want to go home tonight."

She hadn't wanted to, but now it seemed the only sensible thing to do. "This won't work, Logan. Things are too unsettled to start a romantic relationship."

"So what is it you're saying? That we should be miserable alone? That I should pretend I don't worry about you constantly? That I should lie about wanting to be with you? That the kiss on the boat meant nothing?"

His eyes were dark and compelling, intense, the way the kiss had been. "I don't mean to push you away, Logan."

"Then don't. Stay here with me tonight. If you don't want to make love, then just let me hold you. We'll do whatever you want, even separate bedrooms, but stay."

"If I stay, we both know what will happen."

"But only one of us is fighting it." He trailed tiny kisses from her forehead to her chin, and then his mouth found hers and she forgot all the reasons why she should leave. She lost herself in the thrill of him, and all she wanted was more.

"I'll stay, Logan, but I don't want to talk any more about Tess or the boys or Fruits of Passion… I don't want to talk at all."

"No talking. I think I can do that." His hands pressed into her back as he pulled her closer. "I want you, Rachel. I want to hold and kiss you and make love to you, but I won't, not unless you want it, too."

"I do." Her answer was a whisper, hoarse from the desire that was burning inside her. "Make love with me, Logan."

He swallowed hard. "Are you sure?"

"I'm sure. I'm very sure. No talk. No problems. No promises. Just make love to me."

He kissed her again, then lifted her in his arms and carried her down the hall to the bedroom. There was no turning back now. The fears and dangers would still be there when the sun came up tomorrow morning, but tonight she'd sleep in Logan's arms.

CAREFUL NOT to wake Rachel, Logan eased his arm from under her shoulder and slid his legs over the side of the bed. In spite of all the fears that plagued his mind, or maybe because of them, making love with Rachel had been as perfect as anything he'd ever known.

Having sex for him had always been more physical than anything else, mostly about exploring bodies and finding sexual satisfaction.

But not this time. This time it been consumed with Rachel. He'd loved trailing his fingers across her abdomen, fitting his lips over her nipples and feeling them grow hard against his tongue. He'd loved the moist heat that had dripped to his fingers when he'd put his hand between her naked thighs. Most of all he'd loved that she'd responded to every move of his fingers, lips or tongue.

Before tonight he'd only had sex.

Tonight he'd made love.

He tiptoed across the floor and stood in front of the window. He could see the lights of the causeway and little else except the endless black water tied in a ribbon of silver moonlight.

He was glad that the first time they'd made love, it had been here in the boathouse. It had always been a special place to him. Even after Josh had quit coming around their parents' house, he'd meet Logan out here and they'd take the racing boat out. Logan had thought that Josh was going through a phase, that he'd kick the bad habits and get it together.

It hadn't happened that way.

His death had been the hardest thing Logan had ever had to face, the hardest thing he'd ever expected to be hit with. But now there was Danny and Davy and he was feeling the pain all over again.

And there was Rachel, the one good thing that had come from all of this. He should have told her the truth from the very beginning. He would have if he'd known how things would develop between them. Now it would be more difficult.

But he had to do it—before they made love again. And he hoped that would be very, very soon.

RACHEL RUSHED into the office at seven-fifty on Tuesday morning, still ahead of the office staff and partners in the firm, but late for her. She'd wakened at five this morning, managed to sneak out of the bedroom without waking Logan and made the trip from the lakefront to her downtown condo in record time.

Not that she'd wanted to rush away from Logan. She'd have loved to crawl right back into his arms, meld against his naked body and kiss him awake. But then she'd have never made it across town before the morning traffic turned I-10 into a parking lot.

He'd called her at her condo, upset that she'd left without saying goodbye. Only she sensed he was more worried than upset, especially since he'd called her again when she'd reached the office.

"You must have found a new place to sleep."

Rachel felt the burn in her cheeks as Ted stepped out of his office and followed her into hers. "I don't know what you're talking about."

"I believed you when you said you slept here," he teased. "But this morning I beat you in."

But obviously not to work, since he was standing in her doorway chatting about nothing. "Guess there really is a first time for everything." She sat down to her desk and the file she'd left open when she'd rushed out yesterday.

"If you'd been this late the day Tess Shepherd came in, you'd have missed talking to her altogether. You know they still haven't made an arrest in her murder case?"

"I haven't been keeping up with the coverage," she lied, hoping that would put a stop to this conversation.

"I read in the paper this morning that no one's seen her kids since she was murdered."

"I'm sure they'll find them soon."

"I doubt it. I'll bet you anything they'll find them dead."

The words gave her chills. "I really have to get to work."

"All work and no play…"

"Gets my work done and keeps Phillip Castile off my ass. You should try it." She gave him a wave of dismissal, which he ignored. She wondered if the whole office knew that Tess had been in the office the day she was murdered. Her guess was that they did.

"Mr. Castile's no problem," Ted said. "You just have to know how to handle him."

"You mean how to suck up?"

"That, too. You know I went down to that gentleman's club the other night where Tess Shepherd worked. They have got some real classy dames in that place."

"Classy dames. Wouldn't that be an oxymoron?"

"You mean like honest lawyers?"

"I'm honest. And hardworking, so if you'll excuse me."

"You'll never guess who I saw in that club."

She looked up from the file she'd been trying to review. "So don't tax my brain. Just tell me."

"Stone Littleton. I mean he was close enough I could have reached over and touched him."

"What a thrill."

"You are hard to impress. Anyway, that's not all."

"I was afraid of that."

There were footsteps in the hallway. Ted shut the door behind him and walked over to Rachel's desk. "I went over and talked to him, told him I was with the firm of WW&C. He clapped me on the back and invited me to have a drink with him and his buddies. What do you think about that?"

"I think he may cast you in a movie and make you a star."

"Make fun, but still I met him, which is more than anyone else around here can say. Castile never introduces him when he comes to the office. Anyway, that's my big story for the week. Your turn."

"You know me. I'm a dud. I have no story." Except that she was thoroughly entangled in a murder case and sleeping with one of the suspects.

Ted left, but now her mind was stuck on Tess Shepherd and the Fruits of Passion. She opened the bottom desk drawer where she kept her handbag, unzipped the side pocket and pulled out the mystery key. It had to fit something. But what?

She tried to force her mind back to the task at hand, but instead her thoughts turned to Logan. And to think that a week ago, work was all she'd thought of.

CHERI GROANED as the piercing ring of her phone woke her from a sound sleep. Who'd be cruel enough to call a working girl before noon?

She stretched between the satin sheets and glanced at the clock. Okay, before one. She rubbed the dregs of sleep from her eyes with one hand and reached for the phone with the other.

She woke the rest of the way at the sound of the voice on the other end of the line. Craig Graves.

"Sorry to wake you, Cheri."

He didn't sound mad. That was a good sign. "It's okay. What's up?"

"I have a little something I'd like you to look at."

"New dance outfits?"

"More personal. I'd rather not discuss it over the phone."

"When do you want me to come in?"

"Now would be good. Just come straight back to my office. I'll be waiting for you."

"It will take me a few minutes. I'll have to shower and dress."

"Take all the time you need, as long as you're here within the hour."

Okay, so maybe he *was* mad. If he'd found out she'd talked to Logan McCain Sunday night, she'd have a devil of a time talking herself out of this one. But she could do it. It wasn't as if she'd double-crossed him the way Tess had. She'd just done a little creative lap dancing to get rid of an annoying guy.

Basically, she'd done it for Craig. She'd just have to make him see that.

"I'll be there," she said, already staggering to the bathroom.

After showering Cheri dressed in a pair of white slacks and a blue cotton blouse, one too thick to see through. And this time she put on panties. She would have worn a bra, if she'd had one. Being covered gave her a sense of protection, even though she knew it was false bravado.

She went through the alley behind the club so she could take the back door and, she hoped, avoid seeing any of the other dancers. The door was locked, but she had a key. All the dancers chosen for the Elites had a key so that they could sneak into the red room unnoticed by the other employees.

Not even the other dancers were ever to know about the Elite. That was spelled out in the code.

She knocked once at the door to Craig's office. One step inside the door and she knew she was in big, big trouble.

CHAPTER SIXTEEN

LOGAN'S OBSESSION with finding the boys was more consuming than ever since the botched attempt to track down Cathy Shepherd. He still came to the office every day, but he'd canceled all non-urgent appointments and luncheon engagements and spent his days in frustrating efforts to move off dead center.

He'd hired a third private investigator to see what he could find out about Tess. The net result as far as discovering anything useful in locating the boys was zero. He'd also tried unsuccessfully to get an appointment with Craig Graves. The jerk wouldn't even return his phone calls.

Logan checked his watch. A quarter past five. There was no use in hanging around here any longer. He could worry at home and in lots better company. He picked up the phone and punched in Rachel's cell-phone number. Busy.

She'd been on his mind all day, tiptoeing around the aggravation and soothing his troubled spirit. Everything about her amazed him. If he wasn't in the middle of a crisis, feelings this strong for a woman would probably scare him to death. Now, they held him together.

He tried her number again, and this time it rang.

"Hi, Logan."

"You sound perky for a woman buried in corporate legalities."

"That's because I'm in the process of straightening my desk and getting ready to call it a day."

"Good. Me, too. Why don't I pick you up? I'll take you by your place to pick up some things so you don't have to leave at the crack of dawn tomorrow."

"I'm sorry, Logan. I already have plans for tonight."

The rejection hit harder than it should have. One night of making love didn't give him a claim on her life, especially when all he had to offer her at this point was trouble. "Guess I was taking too much for granted."

"It's not that. I'd love to come, but it's Karen's birthday and we've celebrated all our birthdays together since freshman year at Tulane."

That eased the disappointment, but not much. "I understand. Can't break tradition."

"I'm sorry. I would have said something earlier if I'd known you were expecting us to get together tonight."

"My fault," he said.

"Have there been any new developments in the search?"

"None." He filled her in on what he'd been up to all day. "The investigator collected a file of information on Tess. There are some suspicious hikes in spending over the last few months and a couple of solo trips to the Cayman Islands when she'd never done anything like that before, but there's nothing to link her to criminal activity."

"I'd like to see the file sometime."

"How about after dinner?"

"Tonight?"

"Just a thought."

"It would have to be late. We're stopping by the nursing home to visit my Aunt Gladys after dinner and then I know Karen will want to stop in somewhere for a margarita."

"More tradition?"

"Yeah. We won't be terribly late since it's a work night, but I'm sure it will be close to ten."

"Ten's fine. Be as late as you like. Just so you show up. I don't want to sleep upstairs in that creepy old monstrosity of a house by myself."

"Okay, wise guy."

That was taken care of, but there were other worries creeping into his mind now. "Let me send a driver for you. He can chauffeur you and Karen around tonight, then bring you here when you finish toasting her birthday in style. That way you can have several margaritas."

"That's very thoughtful, but I can't— You're talking body-guard service, aren't you?"

So she'd seen right through him. "There's no use in taking risks."

"I haven't had a threat in days."

But the killer was still out there, and in spite of his sick threats, Rachel was more involved than ever. "It's no big deal, Rachel. The company frequently uses a driver for social events."

"We peons don't, and I'm not sure how I'd explain that to Karen."

"We can make it a limo, and you can say it's a surprise for her birthday."

"Better not. Then she'd really think I've been sniffing the whiteout."

"Then we'll make it a Mercedes. I'll have the driver call and he can pick you up in the lobby."

"Do you really think this is necessary?"

"No. Just a precaution. I'm paranoid these days. Humor me."

"This feels creepy."

"It's supposed to make you feel safe—and pampered."

He should say more, tell her she'd been on his mind all day along with his fears and total frustration; say that last night had been nothing less than fantastic.

But even thinking it sounded cheesy. "Have fun, and I'll see you later."

She thanked him again, and the minute he'd said his good-bye, he put in a call to Protection, Inc. He wanted the best man they had available. This was one thing he could make sure was done right.

"I hoped I'd catch you before you left."

Logan looked up. His father was standing in the doorway. He put his hand over the receiver, though the phone was still ringing. "I'll be with you in a minute. Important call here."

His father gave a wave and backed out the door. With any luck, he'd leave before Logan finished making arrangements for the bodyguard.

To increase that possibility, he took his time talking to Protection, Inc. It was fifteen minutes later before the details were ironed out to Logan's satisfaction. When they were, he stuck his head out of his office. His father was still there, sitting at Logan's secretary's desk and reading the evening news via the Internet. He stood and followed Logan back into his office.

"I don't guess you've had any luck locating the boys."

"Not yet."

"You still think they might be in some kind of danger?"

"They're not here," Logan said, stating the obvious. "That's all I know." He was being too short with his father, but the whole pseudo-concern bit galled him.

"Artie says you shut him out of the situation."

"It's not a legal matter at this point."

"It will be if you're arrested for murder."

"If I'm arrested, I'll need a defense attorney, not one of your yes-men."

"You don't have to be so smug with all of this, Logan. I know you're upset over the money I paid to Cathy Shepherd, but I did what I thought was best, the same way you are."

"What you thought was best was denying your own grandsons because their mother wasn't blue-blooded enough for you. It's the same way you forced Josh out of the family because you didn't approve of the way he wanted to live his life."

"The way he wanted to live his life got him killed."

Logan let it drop. There was too much at stake to waste time arguing with his father when it wouldn't change a thing.

Harris picked up a solid onyx paperweight from Logan's desk and moved it from one hand to another, a nervous movement, and he seldom saw his father nervous.

He set the paperweight down and shoved his hands into his pockets. "You're right. I should have handled things with Josh differently."

The words hung in suspension while Logan convinced himself that his father had actually uttered them. Even at the funeral when Logan had hurt so badly he wasn't sure he could go on breathing, even when his mother had collapsed and had had to be carried back to the car, his father had never once admitted any kind of guilt in Josh's death.

It would have meant a lot then. Now it just stuck in his gut and ground around with all the dread about Danny and Davy.

"I was probably wrong in not telling you about the boys," his father said, "but I never thought they were yours, not after the way that slut said you forced her to have sex. I couldn't believe that of you. I still don't, Logan. Whatever else, I know she was lying about that."

Logan walked behind his desk and wrapped his hands

around the back of his chair. His dad figured he'd made his atonement and was waiting for some kind of expression of forgiveness, but Logan didn't have it in him right now.

His dad walked to the door, then stopped and turned back to Logan. "Keep me posted, and if I can do anything to help, let me know."

Logan nodded. It was the best he could manage.

HOAGIE FLIPPED the hunk of onion that had fallen onto the lab report from the burger he was eating and kept reading. The stain on the child's shirt left on Rachel Powers's car *was* blood—chicken blood. That was the first good bit of news he'd gotten on the Shepherd case.

They were unable to pick up any prints from the shirt. The only prints on the note matched the ones he'd taken from Rachel Powers. The shirt was a J. C. Penney brand, purchased this year. That was the extent of information they could gather from it.

Hell, why was it that in those crime shows on TV the lab reports always came back with something that led them right to the perp? But then they always had the lab working full-time on their case, and they had all the resources of the FBI at their fingertips. In a city like New Orleans with more murders a year than there were days, it didn't work like that, not unless you had a high-profile case.

This one could be. All Hoagie had to do was release Logan's name to the press as being the father of Tess's children and a suspect in her murder, and the case would go prime-time, might even go national with those news channels all trying to out-scandal the other one.

But once Logan's name was leaked to the press, the murder investigation would become a sideshow. Reporters would get in the way, manufacture news where none existed by blowing everything out of proportion, and people who didn't remember what they'd had for breakfast that morning would suddenly remember details to tie the suspect to the crime—details with no basis in reality.

Better to do this his way: low-key, thorough. Besides, after what he'd learned today, he was almost positive that Logan had nothing to do with the murders.

He let the lab report fall to his desk and picked up his own findings. He'd found out more chasing down old records today than he'd picked up in a week of questioning suspects. Elton Pierce and Cathy Shepherd had been married in Texarkana, Arkansas, when both were seventeen years old. Elton had already had a juvenile record at the time.

Elton had a steady string of arrests for the next fifteen years, mostly for one con game or another, including robbing an elderly couple in Uncertain, Texas, of their life savings of $25,000. He'd done jail time on several occasions, none in the last ten years. He'd never been arrested for any type of violent crime.

His marriage to Cathy had only lasted three years, but during those three years, he'd obviously taught her the ropes. She had a record a mile long, no offenses that ever netted her more than eighteen months at a time in the clinker. Tess's father had been her fifth husband.

Cathy and Elton, together again. You had to wonder if this whole thing was the murderous result of some con game gone berserk. If so, the record of no violence had been broken. And now that it had, who knew where it would stop?

But surely a grandmother, even a step-grandmother, wouldn't do anything to put her own grandchildren in harm's way. Yeah, right. Like that man in Mississippi hadn't killed his wife and all three kids just last month.

He finished his sandwich, chugged down the last of a cup of lukewarm coffee and grabbed his keys. He'd call Logan from the car and give him the update on the bloodstained shirt. And then he'd pay a visit to Cheri Trosclair.

She knew something. He'd bet a winning lottery ticket on it. Hoagie just had to find a way to get her to talk.

HOAGIE TRIED the Fruits of Passion first. When he didn't see Cheri, he asked one of the other dancers. From the look on the woman's face, you'd have thought he'd asked her to give up one of her jiggling titties. She'd left him hanging while she supposedly went to find out if Cheri was working. She'd returned a few minutes later with the word that Cheri was out of town on a family emergency and they weren't sure when she'd return.

Hoagie was certain that that had come right from the mouth of her boss. He trusted Craig Graves even less than he did Elton Pierce. So when he left the club he made the ten-minute drive to Cheri's apartment.

She lived well for an exotic dancer. Her abode was a luxury apartment in a complex a block off the river. Security was tight, unless you had the code to get in. Hoagie did, one of the benefits of being in homicide—and of having dated one of the female security guards a few months back. The romance had been short-lived. Her gun was bigger than his, and her legs were hairier. He hoped he didn't run into her tonight.

He rang the bell and waited. No one answered, but someone was in there. He heard people talking—or else the TV was on. He rang the doorbell again. The noise stopped, but no one came to the door. This time he hammered against the wood with his knuckles.

Finally the knob twisted and the door opened an inch or

so, but all he saw were fingers wrapped around the edge of the door. The security chain stayed in place. "Detective Hoagie Morrison."

"I'm sorry. I'm not feeling well. You'll have to come back another time."

The voice was hoarse and shaky.

"I just need to ask a couple of questions."

"Not tonight."

Something was wrong. Cop's intuition, but it was strong. Could be that someone was in there with her—someone she was afraid of. "I have to insist that you open the door, Ms. Trosclair."

"No. Not tonight."

"We can do this nicely or I can come back with a warrant. It will only take a second." Major lie.

She loosed the chain, then moved away from the door. He stepped inside. She'd moved away from the door and was standing with her back to him. A lemon-colored silk robe grazed the contours of her hips, but her long black hair that was usually sleek and satiny was tangled and wild.

He rested his hand on the butt of his pistol, standard procedure when entering a room where he couldn't see the person's hands and didn't know if there were other people on the premises.

"Ask me the question, and then…"

She swayed, and before he could reach her she sank to the floor in a puddle of yellow silk.

He knelt beside her and checked for a pulse with one hand as he slipped his arm under her shoulders. It was then he got the first look at her face.

A string of curses flew from his mouth and his stomach turned inside out. Her face was so swollen she didn't look human, and when she opened her eyes, they rolled around in her head for a second before focusing on him.

"Who did this?"

She shook her head. A tear rolled from her right eye and off to the side.

He picked her up as gently as he could and carried her to the sofa, knocking away a half dozen throw pillows to make room for her. She felt even smaller in his arms than she looked; couldn't have weighed a hundred pounds, robe and all.

"Who assaulted you?"

"No one." Her voice was barely a whisper.

"I'm calling an ambulance. Do you have a preference which hospital you want them to take you to?"

"No. No ambulance." She tried to get up, but fell back and groaned. "No ambulance. No hospital."

"I don't have a choice, Cheri. I can't leave you in this condition."

"No. Please. No hospital."

He shuddered, hating even to imagine what she'd been through. "Tell me who did it. I won't let him hurt you again. I promise you that."

"I fell down the stairs. I was…running…and I fell."

"You have to tell me who hurt you, Cheri. If you don't he'll just keep on doing it."

She closed her eyes. For a second he thought she was dead, but she still had a pulse. Weak, but it was there. He took out his phone and called for an ambulance.

Probably a good thing she hadn't given him the name of her attacker, because the way he was feeling right now he could have shot the dirty woman-beating bastard and never batted an eye.

But he would find out who did this. And the son of a bitch was going to prison where, if there was any justice, he'd get worked over by his cell mates every day for the rest of his miserable life.

THE BIRTHDAY CELEBRATION was a bomb. It took Karen about two seconds to figure out the car-and-driver situation, and she went off on a verbal tangent about Logan using fear to push his way into Rachel's life and manipulate her to do whatever he wanted.

So the subject of Logan was off the table from the opening minutes. It was the first time in all their years of friendship that any subject had been taboo, especially a man.

Too bad, because Rachel would have loved to talk about her feelings for Logan. Only she wanted someone to be excited for her and tell her how lucky she was, not someone to warn her that she was jumping into a black hole that might or might not have a landing spot.

Her phone calls from Cathy Shepherd were also off-limits. Detective Morrison had warned both her and Logan to say nothing to anyone. Rachel understood the necessity of keeping the calls under wraps, but she hated lying to Karen. As a result, the conversation had fizzled after about ten minutes of shop talk and the rest of the evening had been strained and uncomfortable, a far cry from birthday celebrations of the past.

They'd decided against a visit to Aunt Gladys. There was no way of predicting her aunt's mood or mental state and Rachel wasn't sure she could handle another downer.

Visiting one of the downtown clubs for drinks didn't have a lot of appeal either, and Rachel had been glad when Karen said she had a big day planned tomorrow and was ready to call it a night right after dinner.

Her pulse jumped a notch when the driver turned into Logan's driveway, partly from anticipation, but there was a shred of nervousness jumping around inside her, as well. She wished they were back at the lake house instead of the aging St. Charles Avenue mansion.

The lake house had been cozy. The house on the Avenue was massive, filled with rooms that had been closed off from life for too many years. She imagined ghosts of McCains past roaming the rambling structure and wondering why a no-clout attorney was invading their fusty territory.

The creepy feeling evaporated the second she caught sight of Logan hurrying down the wide back steps to meet them. He greeted her with a hug, but when their eyes met, the contact was as intimate as a kiss.

He dismissed the driver and put a hand to the small of her back as they walked the stone pathway to the house. Moonlight filtered through the leafy branches of the giant oaks that canopied the house, and the sweet smell of honeysuckle and night-blooming jasmine drifted up from the garden.

Logan let his hand slip from her back and clasp with hers, and for a second she almost forgot the evil that had insinuated itself into their lives. But the magic only lasted until they reached the top of the steps, and the porch light illuminated the taut line of his lips and the frustration embedded in his face.

"I'm glad you're here," he said, squeezing her hand.

"Me, too."

"I was having a glass of red wine. Can I get you one, or are you saturated with margaritas?"

"Wine would be good. We never made it to Margaritaville tonight."

He raised his eyebrows questioningly but didn't push, and she didn't explain. He had enough on his mind. He picked up a wineglass and the rest of a bottle of cabernet and followed her to the den. She dropped onto the sofa while he poured her wine.

"I hoped all day that Cathy would call," she said.

"Me, too." He handed her the glass of wine and touched his glass to hers. "To happy endings."

"To happy endings." She couldn't help wondering if the toast extended beyond finding the boys to her relations with Logan.

"I know you must have been disappointed not to learn anything about Tess that helps in locating the boys," she said.

He nodded. "It's frustrating as hell." He put his feet atop the ottoman and pulled her into the crook of his arm. "You fit nicely there," he said.

She snuggled all the closer. She'd been wrong about the lake house. It was being in Logan's arms that made the intimacy work.

For a long time he just held her, the only sounds the creaking and moaning of the old house. In most new relationships, the silence would have been awkward, but with Logan it felt totally right. When he finally kissed her, she was already so into him that the kiss was like an extension of perfection.

She melted into it, needing it to push away all the ugliness, dread and fear she'd lived with for the last week. The present was frightening. The future was unpredictable. The only thing right was Logan's touch. Logan's kiss.

Her cell phone vibrated at her waist. She started to toss it across the room, but caught a glimpse of the number of the nursing home on the caller-ID screen.

She murmured a passion-groggy hello.

"I hate to call you this late, Rachel, but your aunt had one of her anxiety attacks again tonight, only it was much more severe than the ones she's had in the past. She was throwing things and trying to punch anyone who came near her."

"What did you do?"

"We called her doctor, but we had to use restraints on her until the medication he prescribed had time to settle her down. I thought you should know."

"What's she doing now?"

"Resting fitfully and calling for you. I think maybe if she heard your voice, she'd relax and get some rest."

"I'll be there in half an hour, and I sincerely appreciate your calling."

"We thought you'd want to know."

She dropped her phone to her lap and kissed Logan one more time. When she came up for air, she wiggled from his arms. "I have to go to the nursing home for a while. Can you call me a taxi?"

"I'll go with you."

"You don't have to."

"Good. I hate to do things because I have to." He stood and helped her to her feet. "Besides, I'm great with little old ladies."

"Prepare to meet your match."

CHAPTER SEVENTEEN

RACHEL FELT a new surge of panic when she reached the door of Aunt Gladys's usually impeccable room. A table was over-turned. Framed prints of pastoral scenes had been yanked from the wall and hurled to the other side of the room. The shawl Gladys wore every waking moment fluttered from the blade of the slowly moving ceiling fan. And a box of old black-and-white photos were scattered over the floor.

Aunt Gladys was sleeping, oblivious to the chaos.

Rachel walked to the bed and pulled the pale-blue sheet over her aunt's thin shoulders. The old woman made a small grunting noise, but didn't open her eyes.

A nurse walked to the door, her cap slightly askew, her white pants puckered at her plump waist. "For a quiet South-ern belle, your aunt can go on a wham-bang of a tangent. She sure caught us by surprise."

"Was someone with her when she lost control?"

"I was the first one to get here when I heard her scream-ing. She was throwing things and cussin' some guy named Melvin up one side and down the other. If old Melvin had been around, Gladys would have made chopped liver of him."

"Melvin." Rachel repeated the name aloud as she tried to think if she'd ever heard her aunt mention anyone by that name. If she had, she didn't remember it, and it certainly hadn't accompanied this kind of action. "Did she say why she was mad at him?"

"Nothing that made sense. He'd done something bad. That was all I could get out of what she was saying."

"Is there anyone on the staff named Melvin who might have upset her?"

"No one with a name even close to that. We've got a Jake, a Herman, Grady, Bill. No Melvins. We don't even have a patient here named Melvin."

"I wonder if she could have had another stroke?"

"I don't think so. One of the aides was in here about fifteen minutes before Gladys went berserk. She said Gladys was sitting in her chair there, wearing the shawl that's hanging from the fan and calmly looking through the snapshots." She glanced at the photos scattered over the floor. "Merlee said Gladys was so absorbed in the pictures, she only shook her head when she asked her if she wanted some juice."

Rachel finger-brushed flyaway strands of gray hair from her aunt's forehead. "Did Dr. Lane say when he planned to see Aunt Gladys?"

"He's going to stop in tomorrow. He said to tell you he'll give you a call once he's seen her."

"I just can't imagine what set her off, unless it was some traumatic experience from her past that got tangled up with the present."

"It could be a reaction from some of the medicine she's on. Dr. Lane will have to make that call."

"I hope he finds an explanation. The thought of her being restrained is really distressing."

"I'm sure. That's why we left the room like this, so you could see why we had to restrain her. I'll get someone down here in the next few minutes to straighten it."

"No need. I plan to stay with her awhile and putting her things away will give me something to do."

The nurse lingered, watching Logan pull the shawl from the fan and fold it into a neat square. He did have a way of grabbing female attention. Rachel introduced him as a friend, aware when she said it how misleading the term was.

They'd gone from acquaintances to lovers, but they'd never really been friends. She didn't know the little things about him that most women knew of the men they slept with. Did he like his eggs scrambled or sunny-side up? Did he keep the newspaper neat when he read it or scatter the sections all over the place? Did he like his steaks rare? His oysters raw? His movies action-packed?

They'd been thrown together by violence and held together by their concern for two small boys. Maybe that was the attraction—that Logan could care so much for sons he didn't really know. Only there was a lot more between them than just attraction, at least, on her part there was.

Logan took a handkerchief from his pocket and wiped a pool of spilled water from the bedside table. One of the richest and most powerful men in the city, yet he seemed perfectly at ease cleaning her aunt's room. He really was amazing.

"Have you actually never heard of this Melvin guy?" he asked.

"Never. Last time I was in here, Aunt Gladys went on and on about someone named Estelle. I'd never heard of her, either."

Logan got a towel from the adjoining bathroom and wiped off the framed prints while Rachel gathered the black-and-white photos.

"The frame's broken on this picture," he said, "but the others look all right. Want to tell me where to rehang them?"

"The one of the two children in the tree swing goes to the

right of the window. The hanger's still in place." She dropped the photos onto the bedside table, then went to help Logan with the prints.

In under thirty minutes they had the room presentable if not as nice as before her aunt had gone on her rampage. She was sleeping a lot more peacefully now, and the sounds of her deep breathing and sporadic low snores permeated the confined space.

Rachel started stacking the photos. "I wish I could keep her at home. Then maybe I could help her stay grounded in the present instead of sliding back into what must have been a troubled past."

"What kind of childhood did she and your mother have?"

"Their parents died of some kind of flulike virus when my mother was ten. There weren't any relatives to take them. Gladys was seventeen. She was allowed to live on her own, but Mother was put into a home for girls here in New Orleans. When mother was sixteen she left the home and moved in with Aunt Gladys. That's really all I know of their youth. Aunt Gladys never liked to talk about it."

"What about your parents?"

"Them, she loved to talk about. I don't remember them at all. I was only three when they were killed in a car wreck. According to Aunt Gladys, my mother was smart, beautiful, warm, loving and any other marvelous adjectives you can think of. My father was ambitious and handsome and both of them doted on me. So said Aunt Gladys on several million occasions."

"You exaggerate."

"Not much. My aunt's goal in life was raising a daughter my superhuman parents would be proud of."

"It must have worked. You are pretty terrific."

"I'm glad you think so."

He stepped behind her and put his hands on her shoulders, massaging the tight muscles in her neck. "I don't think it, I know it. You've handled me, Detective Morrison, threatening notes and phone calls, Cathy Shepherd and now your aunt without doing one 'oh, poor me.'"

"Lucky I didn't have to deal with a Melvin." She opened the door to the cabinet over the small refrigerator. "I can offer you a cup of hot tea or a bit of sherry."

"I'll take sherry."

She took two small glasses from the shelf and poured Logan a glassful and herself a taste. Sherry was not her favorite, but it was the one liquor her aunt always had around.

Setting her glass on the bedside table, she sat next to the bed and kissed her aunt's cheek. Her skin was wrinkled, but still soft from her years of coating it nightly with cold cream. She smelled of lilac, the way she always did.

Logan picked up one of the black-and-white photos. "This must be your mother. She looks just like you." He passed the picture to Rachel.

"No. I don't know who that is. I don't think I've ever seen this picture. She does resemble me, though." She turned it over and read the name printed on the back in pencil. The writing was so light, she could barely make it out. "Estelle Clark. That's Aunt Gladys's last name."

"Must be a cousin then."

"I don't have any cousins. My father was an only child. My mother's only sibling was Aunt Gladys."

Logan handed her another picture, this one of Estelle and Gladys, or so said the writing on the back. Estelle was younger in this picture, probably in high school. Aunt Gladys looked to be in her midtwenties, really cute in a full skirt, white blouse and a pair of sexy strapped sandals with nosebleed heels.

"Estelle could be your double," Logan said. "She's got to be a blood relative."

"If she is, I can't imagine why I never heard of her."

"Speak of the devil," Logan said, reading the print on the back of another photo before passing it to her. "Looks like Melvin and Estelle had a thing going on."

Rachel studied the snapshot, then turned it over. The notation on the back did indeed say Melvin and Estelle. Melvin was quite a hunk and he had his arm around Estelle. "Maybe Aunt Gladys was jealous because Melvin was hot for Estelle instead of her."

Aunt Gladys mumbled as if the reference to Melvin had seeped through the thick curtain of sleep. Rachel laid the snapshot on the table, suddenly uneasy at looking through the photos without her aunt's permission.

For some reason, Aunt Gladys had never shown these to Rachel, yet they'd been important enough to her that she'd brought them with her to the nursing home. Strange, since Rachel had done most of the packing for her.

"Estelle and Melvin must have gotten married," Logan said. "Here they are with a little girl." He passed the picture to Rachel.

The little girl was skinny and freckled with short reddish-brown hair pulled into dog ears. She was holding a curly-haired doll in one hand and hanging on to Estelle with the other. The picture began to fade, and Rachel closed her eyes tightly to fight off a wave of dizziness.

But even with her eyes closed, the picture was there in her mind. Melvin was growing bigger. His eyes had a glazed look. His hands were knotted into fists. Estelle put her hands over her face.

Rachel jumped from the chair and clapped her hands over

her ears. The monsters were stamping through her mind, so loud it seemed as if her head would explode from the noise.

"Rachel, what's wrong?"

She heard Logan's voice. It was coming from somewhere far away. It was the monsters that were near. Yelling. Horrible words. And her mother was crying.

"One, two, buckle my shoe."

LOGAN STOOD and pulled Rachel's trembling body into his arms. "What is it, baby? What's wrong?"

"The picture…"

"What about the picture?"

"That's me…and my…mother."

She bit her bottom lip and tried to look away, but he cupped her face in his hands and forced her to meet his gaze. "Are you saying that Estelle is your mother?"

"Yes. And Melvin was my father." She winced at the words, as if it physically hurt to say them. "He killed her." The words were a hoarse whisper.

She was breaking under the stress. It was no wonder after all she'd been through over the last few days. "Let me take you home, Rachel. Your aunt is resting, and you need to get some sleep."

"No. I'm not stressed. He killed her. My father killed my mother."

She started sobbing softly and her tears tore Logan apart. He didn't have a clue what to do for her, but he couldn't bear to see her like this.

"Don't let this get to you this way. It's Tess who was murdered. Only Tess. "

"No. He killed her, Logan. I know he killed her. I know it because…I was there."

She'd quit sobbing, but she was still trembling, and her voice and tone seemed far too resigned for this to be just an anxiety attack. Logan pulled away enough so that he could look into her eyes. "You're serious, aren't you?"

"I was there. I remember the room. I remember the doll."

"You were so young."

"Not that young. It's not uncommon for people to have memories that trace back to the time they were three or four."

"Are you sure?"

"I am. I wish I wasn't, but I am." She pulled away from him and walked back to her aunt's bed. "I'd repressed the memories all these years. That's why the nightmares wouldn't go away. I couldn't make myself remember. I couldn't let myself forget."

She laid her hand on her aunt's shoulder. "Years of lies. Even the picture she gave me of my parents was of someone else."

"She did it to protect you," Logan said, still wondering if Rachel's memories could possibly be accurate.

"It explains a lot of things. Like why I missed having a mother so badly. I frequently said I missed having parents, but that was never true. I never wished I had a father. Not once in all my life."

"And then a photo brought it all back."

"The photo and the experience with Tess and your sons. I couldn't think of them without feeling the old fears that had tormented me half my life."

"What else do you remember?"

"Nothing clearly except being in that room and being so afraid. And the noises, but I've heard them in hundreds of nightmares." She massaged her temples, as if that would bring her muddled thoughts into focus. "A policeman opened the door. I remember him. And my mother. So still. They wouldn't let me touch her. I remember they wouldn't let me touch her."

"No wonder you repressed the memories. They were terrifying."

"Your sons may have seen that same kind of terror, Logan. They may have seen their mother beaten. They may have seen her killed."

He'd known that, yet the reality of it seemed a lot more frightening now. The responsibility of parenting would be overwhelming. He was man enough to do whatever it took to get them back, but could he get them through the pain?

She bent over and kissed her aunt on the cheek. "She loves me. I don't know if she made all the right decisions, but she loves me like my mother would have, and I'll always be thankful for that."

It was 2:00 a.m. when Rachel and Logan got back to his house on the Avenue. Rachel was fatigued—mentally, emotionally and physically. She felt almost numb, as if the truth had split her open like a surgeon's scalpel but then deadened the nerves so she'd feel no pain.

"You can collapse anytime now," Logan said, leading her back into the house. "I'll carry you upstairs and put you to bed."

The numbness wore off in a heartbeat. "You're not leaving me upstairs in this monstrosity of a house all alone. There's probably ghosts under every bed."

"No way. The ghosts all live in the secret passages, and my grandmother would roll over in her grave at that description of her house." He smiled and tried to lighten the mood. "But I'm definitely not leaving you alone. And while the rest of the furniture in my bedroom dates back to some infamous French emperor, the king-size bed is from this century and actually comfortable."

"May I collapse in the bathtub first?"

"Absolutely. You can make yourself totally at home."

"Okay, but don't expect much of me tonight."

"All I expect is that you'll snore like your aunt."

He swooped her up in his arms and carried her up the wide curving staircase. She fell asleep before they reached the top.

LOGAN HAD COOKED breakfast for Rachel and tried to talk her into taking the morning off, but as tired and emotionally drained as she'd been last night, she'd been up and ready to go by 7:00 a.m. Had to get in those billable hours, after all. So he'd driven her to the office and then come home to get showered and dressed himself.

They were going to have to take a serious look at their schedules once the boys were in his care permanently. Not that he expected her to take on any responsibility for them, but...

Hell, he didn't know what he expected or why he was even thinking like this. He was crazy about Rachel, but the future was—the future. He had to find the boys and make sure they were safe before he could deal with anything else.

The phone rang. He raced to it, his bare feet slapping the worn Persian rug, hoping it was Pete Pellegrin with good news.

"Hello."

"Mr. McCain, do you have a statement to make about your missing boys or the fact that you are the prime suspect in the Shepherd murder case?"

"Who is this?"

"Maurrey Bruno, a freelance reporter with..."

Logan slammed down the receiver. It started ringing again, this time in unharmonious union with the doorbell. He traipsed the long hallway, pushed back the thick drape in the drawing room and stared at the Channel 12 news van parked in his drive. And the Channel 3 van pulling in right behind it.

The honeymoon was over. He went back to the kitchen and turned on the morning show just in time to hear the headline news.

"Logan McCain, prominent New Orleans businessman, has been named as a suspect in the recent murder of an exotic dancer he claims was the mother of his twin sons. His arrest is considered imminent."

Both phones were ringing now, and the doorbell was as constant as the bell on the ice cream man's truck. It was going to be one hell of a day.

He checked the caller ID on his cell phone. Dear old Dad. Logan picked up the phone. "I heard the news. Guess I'm a celebrity."

"Don't take this lightly, Logan. I just talked to S. R. Touissant. He's the best defense attorney in the city. Best in the South for that matter. He's agreed to take you on."

"I'll talk to him, but I'll make the decision on which attorney to go with."

"I'm trying to help."

"Or course. Has Mother heard the news?"

"Not yet. She's still asleep. I've put in a call to her psychiatrist. He's on his way over."

"Tell her I love her, and assure her that this will blow over quickly."

"Just don't do anything foolish, Logan. Don't admit to a thing. This could turn into a dogfight."

HOAGIE STOOD in the middle of the den floor in his boxers, dripping jelly from his piece of cold toast and muttering every foul word he knew. That took a good five minutes.

He'd given orders that nothing about the Fruits of Passion murders, especially the name of Logan McCain, was to be leaked outside his office. The chief had agreed with him on the strategy and backed him a hundred percent.

But someone had gotten diarrhea of the mouth. The mayor would expect a news conference and the chief would kowtow like he always did.

Hoagie would spend his time dodging cameras and pushy reporters and answering stupid questions like "Do you have firm evidence against Logan McCain and are the boys in danger?"

If he had firm evidence against anybody, he'd be getting an arrest warrant not blabbing about it to the media. And yeah, if you have two boys that have disappeared with their ex-con step-grandma, you gotta figure they haven't gone on a damn picnic.

He went back to the kitchen and tossed what was left of the toast down the disposal. Coffee. That's all he needed, with lots of sugar. Caffeine and sugar and more caffeine and sugar would be the only things that would ward off the headaches today.

He showered and shaved in record time and didn't remember that he hadn't brushed his teeth until he was already out of the drive. He rummaged in the compartment between the front seats, found a piece of mint-flavored gum and stuck it in his shirt pocket. He'd pop it in his mouth after he finished his coffee and before he talked to the chief.

He hoped the chief would be in. Not that they could do a lot about the situation now, but he wanted the chief and everyone else concerned to know he was pissed.

SOMETHING WASN'T RIGHT. Hoagie knew it the second he walked into the chief's office. He should be as mad as Hoagie was. The knot in his tie should already be pulled loose and he should have several half-smoked cigarettes poking out of that old green ashtray on his desk.

"I guess you heard the news this morning and saw the front page of the *Times Picayune*," Hoagie barked.

"I saw it."

"I never gave the word for that information to be leaked to the media. I don't have a case against Logan McCain. I don't have a case against anybody, but I had started to make some headway."

"The case is a week old, Hoagie. You knew the press would get hold of the Logan McCain angle eventually."

"I'm not worried about Logan McCain. I'm worried about a couple of four-year-old boys who haven't been located." And he was worried about Cheri Trosclair and any other dancer who might be about to get the shit beaten out of her by some dirty, sadistic coward.

"I know how you hate dealing with the media, but the scope of this case has changed now. Logan McCain's name is going to be a household word in this town before dinnertime."

"Logan's not the killer."

"You got proof of that?"

"No, but I damn sure don't have any real evidence that says he is."

"But he's still a legitimate suspect, isn't he? I mean he was in a custody battle with the murdered stripper."

Hoagie exhaled sharply. He hated being backed into a corner on nitpicking details. "The evidence points to something bigger than a custody battle. My hunch is the Shepherd and the Matthews murders have their roots in something that's going on at the Fruits of Passion."

"The club's been clean since the day they opened."

"Just because you don't see the dirt on the hands don't mean it's not hiding under the nails."

The chief nodded, leaned back in his big leather desk chair and worried the silver lighter that was always on his desk. "How many murder cases are you working now, Hoagie? Eight, isn't it?"

"Sounds right."

The chief nodded as if they'd come to some kind of major agreement. "I'm going to take you off the Shepherd and Matthews cases and give them to someone who's not so loaded down."

Hoagie felt a tightening in his chest and knew he was on the verge of exploding and saying things he had no business saying. He tried to count to ten under his breath and made it to five.

"I don't want off this case. I'm close to having some answers, real close."

"But you don't have any concrete evidence yet?"

"Not yet."

The chief smacked his lips as if he were finishing off a steak. "I'm sorry, Hoagie. I have to make this call. The case has moved to high priority, and I need a man on it full-time."

"Then take me off the other cases. Leave me with this one."

He was wasting his time. The chief had made up his mind. And it wasn't about Hoagie's caseload. He'd been here before. The chief was taking heat from somebody. He never took heat well.

"Who is it that's got friends in high places, Chief? Who wants me off this case?"

"I'm calling the shots, Hoagie. Me. That's it. And I've taken you off the case. Best just to let it go."

And that was that. Or maybe it wasn't. Craig Graves might

own somebody's sweet ass, but he didn't own Hoagie's. And if Craig was the one who'd put Cheri in the hospital, if he was the one who'd killed Tess and Hank or had them killed, he was going to pay.

One way or the other he was going to pay.

CHAPTER EIGHTEEN

RACHEL'S LEFT CONTACT LENS was protesting her lack of sleep the previous night by watering like mad. She walked to the filing cabinet where she kept her handbag, reached into the side pocket and retrieved her compact so she could check and see if her mascara was dripping down her cheek.

Not bad. The dark circles under her eyes didn't do a lot for her looks, though. Her fingers brushed Tess's key as she dropped the compact back into her purse. She pulled out the key and carried it back to the desk.

The mystery key, number 182. One hundred and eighty-two what?

Her intercom buzzed. She punched the button to take the message. "Mr. Castile would like to see you in his office."

"I'll be right there."

Phillip Castile. Just what she needed this morning. She took one last sip of her coffee, then opened the desk drawer and dropped the key into the compartment with the paper clips for safekeeping until she got back.

"You can go right in, Rachel. Mr. Castile is waiting on you."

Rachel smiled at her boss's secretary as if that were good news and walked into his office. It was a corner spot, with huge glass windows that overlooked the crescent of the river. Mr. Castile was standing at the window, staring out at the gray mist that hung over the city this morning.

"You made the morning paper, Rachel. Page one."

"I haven't seen the paper."

"I have it here. Let me read it to you. You're in the article headlined 'Local Businessman's Arrest Imminent in Murder of Stripper.'"

She sank onto one of the overstuffed chairs without waiting to be asked. She'd never seen Phillip Castile as openly agitated as he was right now. He ran a finger under the collar of his shirt, probably an attempt to loosen it and make room for his bulging veins.

She should be quaking in her stylish black pumps. She was, but it had little to do with the antics of her boss. Logan was all she could think of. She'd never expected it to go this far.

"'Rachel Powers, an attorney with Williams, Williams and Castile, spoke with Tess Shepherd on the day the woman was killed and agreed to represent her in a custody hearing to keep Logan McCain from taking the boys she'd raised since birth.'"

"I didn't agree to take her case."

"But you saw the woman here in our offices and let yourself get drawn into a sordid murder case."

"She didn't have an appointment. She just walked in. I talked to her a few minutes and that was it."

"Not according to this article. It says that you have been seen with Logan McCain in the Bourbon Street Club where the murdered woman worked as a dancer."

She groaned and squeezed her temples between the palms of her hands. She needed to talk to Logan. Or maybe it was too late. He might already be in jail.

"I'm sorry, Mr. Castile. I didn't start out to get involved in this situation, but I'm in it. Now I have to see it through."

"At the risk of losing your job?"

Make your parents proud.

The words echoed in her mind, but the effect was different now. Her mother had died at the hands of a brutal husband. It was years too late to make him pay, but Tess's killer was still on the loose, and it wasn't too late for him to be punished to the full extent of the law.

And somewhere out there two boys needed the love of their wonderful father to help them have the kind of safe, happy childhood they deserved.

"Yes, sir. At the risk of losing my job."

"You're making a big mistake."

"I don't think so, Mr. Castile."

He spread his hands, palms up, and shrugged his shoulders. "You have the potential to become a senior-level attorney with the firm, but it's your choice."

Her choice. A top position with Williams, Willams and Castile could offer her financial security and social standing. Standing by her principles would only offer the opportunity to look in the mirror every morning and like the person looking back at her.

And if she was really lucky, it might offer her the chance to wake up beside Logan McCain every morning for the rest of her life.

"I appreciate everything you've done for me, and I hope you'll convey that to Mr. Williams, Senior, and Mr. Williams, Junior, as well. But as of right now, I'll have to tender my resignation with the firm."

"In that case, I'd like you to clear out your desk and be out of here by noon."

She'd do a lot better than that. It wouldn't take her half an hour. She had a very large trash can and the first thing to go would be the picture of the handsome unidentified couple in the silver frame.

"LOOKS LIKE you finally hit pay dirt."

Hoagie grunted and motioned Griffin Paulson into his cluttered office. Paulson removed a stack of computer-generated statistics from a chair and straddled it with his long legs. "Are you going to make the arrest or let McCain's lawyer walk him in?"

"You'll have to ask the imbecile who leaked the story to the press. Apparently he knows something I don't."

"Oh, c'mon, the *Times* doesn't print stuff they can't verify."

"It wasn't verified with me. That's all I know. And if I find out who leaked those lies, I plan to wring his damned neck." He studied Paulson's expression. He could have leaked it. But then so could a half dozen other people.

"So what's the story on Logan?" Paulson asked.

"He didn't kill Tess Shepherd any more than you did."

"So who did?"

"Maybe Elton Pierce. Maybe Craig Graves. Maybe some guy with a really mean jealousy streak."

"Then what you're saying is you're nowhere?"

"West of nowhere. I'm off the case."

Paulson let out a low whistle. "When did that happen?"

"About ten minutes ago."

"I hadn't heard. The gossipers must all be on coffee break. So how'd it come down?"

"From the top. The chief called me in and said he was relieving me of the Shepherd and Matthews cases and giving them to someone who had less on their plate."

"That can't be all bad."

"I don't like having a case ripped out of my hands. If I ask to drop it, that's one thing, but having it stolen burns my buns."

"Who's taking over?"

"I don't know if he's been named yet, but if you hear anything that you think I might be interested in, give me a call."

"Even though you're off the case?"

"Yeah. Even though."

"You got it."

Paulson gave a two-finger wave and left. Hoagie gathered his notes. He'd had enough of headquarters. He planned to stop at the hospital to check on Cheri Trosclair. Just maybe she was ready to talk today. But first he had to do a little more investigating into the death of Joshua McCain.

He gulped the last of his coffee, spilling a few drops on his white shirt. Not even nine o'clock and the day was already in the pits. And he had a very strong hunch that it was going to get worse.

RACHEL BOLTED out the door, thankful she'd left her car here last night instead of dropping it off at her condo. Later she'd probably feel some regret at leaving WW&C and plunging into the ranks of the unemployed, but right now she was too worried about Logan to deal with regrets. She punched in his number on her cell phone.

"Logan. I heard the news. What's going on?"

"I'm not in cuffs yet."

"This is nothing to joke about."

"No, but I've exhausted all the curse words I know."

"Where are you?"

"Standing at my drawing-room window watching reporters jockey for position in my front yard."

"I'm on my way there."

"Don't. It's an ugly mess, and there's nothing you can do. If I get arrested, I get arrested."

"Have you heard from Detective Morrison?"

"Not since we were all at the bank on Monday."

"What about Pete Pellegrin?"

"I heard from him. The trail has totally dried up."

"They won't arrest you. They can't. You didn't do it."

"Atta girl. You want to be my defense attorney?"

"No, but you have to get one. Someone's beeping in. It could be Dr. Lane, so I'd better get it. I'll see you in a few minutes."

Rachel pushed the button on her cell and was greeted with, "Did you see the morning paper?"

Karen. Ugg. She wasn't ready for this. "I saw it, and I know what you're thinking, but you're wrong. Logan didn't kill Tess."

"The police wouldn't be planning to arrest him without some kind of evidence."

"It's a mix-up."

"What is it that guy does for you that has you eating out of his hands?"

"He's innocent."

"So where are you, anyway? I called your office. They said you wouldn't be in today."

At least they weren't announcing to the world that she was unemployed. "I'm in the car, driving down Poydras."

"Tell me you're not with Logan McCain."

"I'm alone…but I'm on my way to his house." It was just too hard to keep lying. "I'll be fine, Karen."

"All these years, I kept trying to push you into a relationship, and you fall for the one guy I try to steer you away from. You have fallen, haven't you?"

No use to lie about that, either. "I've fallen."

"Then nothing I say about him is going to matter. Just take care, Rachel. And don't take chances. Logan may be innocent, but there's still a killer out there who knows your name."

The words were chilling, but all too true.

"I'll be careful. I'll be very, very careful." She would be. She was nowhere near ready to die.

"I WANNA go home, Gramma."

"I know you do, Danny. Soon."

Davy pushed a toy car across the floor of the condo Elton had rented; one on the third floor that only opened with a key even from the inside. A key that he kept in his possession at all times. "I don't wanna go back. I don't like that man."

Cathy squatted on the floor next to Davy, keeping her voice low so it wouldn't carry over the sound of Elton's shower. "What man?"

"The one that beats up Momma. He's mean."

"Yeah, he's mean," Danny said. "I'm scared of him."

"Isn't Elton the man who was mean to your mother?"

"No," Danny said. "He's not mean. He bought me a toy alligator."

"He fusses at us," Davy said, "but he don't hit us and he don't hit Momma."

The wheels began spinning in Cathy's head. All this time, she'd thought it was Elton who'd beat up Tess, thought he was the one who'd killed her. He was Craig Graves's hit man. He did the dirty work. But if it wasn't Elton, then who was it?

"What does the mean man look like?"

"He's big," Davy said.

"And he told Momma to get rid of us. She made us go outside and play on those old dark stairs, but we sneaked back in."

Danny climbed over the back of the sofa and slid to the floor. "Yeah, I don't like him, and I don't wanna go back to Momma's, anyway. She's mean, too. She whips me and I didn't do nothing."

"Don't worry. You won't have to go back to your momma's again."

Elton strode out of the bathroom with only a towel wrapped around his waist. He motioned her into the bedroom, grinning like some stupid clown. She knew what he wanted. She hated the thought of touching him, but no use to start a fight in front of the boys. Not when she'd had sex with Elton plenty of times before.

But first she wanted an answer. She followed him into the bedroom.

"Who was Tess having sex with?"

"Be easier if you'd rephrase that to who wasn't the slut having sex with."

"Who beat her up?"

Elton dropped the towel and plopped across the bed, letting everything he had hang out. "You really don't know what was going on, do you?"

"Would I be asking if I knew? Who killed her? I have to know."

"Why? You planning to go after him?"

"No, I just don't want him coming after the boys."

"Don't worry. He's not coming near the boys."

"But he will. He knows they can identify him as the man who knocked her around. He'll kill them."

"Not a chance."

"How can you be so sure?"

"'Cause he paid me to do it for him."

"But you said you were only going to ask for a ransom, and then give them to Logan McCain."

"Since when do you believe anything I say?"

THE LAWN in front of Logan's house was much more like a jungle than a zoo. Rachel had parked around the corner in the closest spot she could find, then pushed her way through at least a dozen reporters, all sticking mikes in her face and asking ridiculous questions while the bright beams from one of the news vans all but blinded her.

The front door opened just as she got there, and Logan pulled her inside. He kicked the door shut with his foot and took her in his arms. Neither of them said anything. They just held on.

"They're like vultures," she said.

"You can't blame them. It's a story. That's their job."

"Then I blame Hoagie Morrison. How can he think you're guilty when he was with you the other day while you were doing everything you could to make sure your boys are safe and cared for?"

"It'll work out, Rachel. That's what you've been telling me for days. Don't go negative on me now."

"Do you have a defense attorney yet?"

"I'm talking to S. R. Touissant. He's trying to get in touch with the police and see if a warrant has been issued for my arrest. We'll talk after that. He did say he'd like to have the tape of your conversation with Tess."

She threw up her hands in frustration. "I left it in the tape player at WW&C."

"No problem. You can pick it up when you go back to the office."

"I won't be going back to the office. I quit—just before being fired."

"Fired? On what grounds?"

"Hanging out with the local criminal element. They don't like my name linked with yours or with Fruits of Passion."

"Those self-righteous, pious hypocrites. They'd screw their

own mother out of her retirement money if they thought it was good for their bottom line."

She filled him in on the details of her meeting with Phillip Castile while they walked to the kitchen and he poured them both mugs of very strong coffee.

She took hers to the table and pushed over a stack of photos to make room to set her cup. Unlike the ones in the albums at the lake house, these were a hodgepodge of loose photos.

She sipped her coffee, then picked up a photo of Logan and Josh standing next to the racing boat and holding a huge trophy.

"That's the last race we were in together," Logan said. "It was only a month before Josh was gunned down."

"Gunned down! By whom?"

"An officer of the NOPD."

That bit of news bounced around in her head, then settled in her stomach like a loaf of week-old French bread. "Why did the police shoot him?"

"It's a long story."

Which meant Logan didn't want to explain, but not only was she was up to her eyeballs in this investigation with him, she'd slept with him. That should make her part of the in crowd. "I'd like to hear it, Logan."

He paced the kitchen, back and forth a half dozen times before falling into the chair next to her. "I'll have to go back a few years for it to make sense."

"Go back as far as you need to."

He stretched his legs under the table and stared at his coffee cup. "Josh and my father clashed constantly, more so the older Josh got. Dad wanted Josh to go into the business the way every McCain for the last three generations had. Josh had other ideas."

"Like what?"

"He'd wanted to be a cop from the time he was ten years old and caught his first Dirty Harry movie on a friend's VCR. He never veered from that."

"Was he a cop when he was shot?"

"No. He didn't pass the physical. He raced the boat, collected speeding tickets like baseball cards and finally got mixed-up in drugs. Strange thing was, I never saw him high."

"Was he on drugs when he was shot?"

"Yeah. According to the autopsy, he had significant amounts of heroin in his bloodstream. There was a drug bust in a crack house over in old Algiers. According to the narc who shot him, Josh pulled a gun, and he shot him in self defense."

"You don't sound as if you believe that."

"I'd never known Josh to carry a gun. Wasn't any reason for him to. He didn't have any enemies. Everybody liked him."

"I don't remember reading or hearing anything about that."

"No. My father and the police department saw that it never came out in the paper. My father told everyone Josh died of a heart condition. He just failed to mention that a bullet from a cop's gun caused the condition."

"No wonder his death was so hard on you and your mother." And no wonder Logan had no use for the NOPD.

"Josh was Mother's favorite. I always knew that. She had a complete mental and nervous breakdown right after he was killed and hasn't been the same since. Mostly she sits in her chair and watches television all day long, every day."

The noise outside grew louder. Rachel followed Logan to the front of the house to see what had prompted the commotion. He pushed back the drape and the flashing lights of a squad car swept over the room.

Rachel started to shake. "What if they're here to arrest you?"

The muscles in his arms flexed, and he held her so tightly, she thought he might literally crush her lungs. They heard heavy footsteps on the porch, but still Logan didn't release her.

"There's one more thing I have to tell you."

"About Josh?"

"About Josh and about me. Try to understand. I never meant to lie to you. It just all got out of hand."

CHAPTER NINETEEN

"I NEVER HAD sex with Tess Shepherd."

Rachel stared at Logan, sure she must have heard him wrong. "What did you say?"

"I'm not the father of Tess's sons. I never met her before the day I showed up at her house to tell her I wanted custody of the boys."

"But Tess said…"

"I haven't had a one-night stand since my sophomore year in college, Rachel, and that one was rare enough I remember it. I woke up with a friend's girlfriend after a frat party he couldn't make, and we were both too embarrassed after that even to make eye contact."

Rachel shook her head. "This makes no sense. If they're not your sons, why are you fighting for custody?"

"Because the boys are Josh's sons."

"Josh? Your brother Josh?"

"Yes."

This was growing more bizarre by the second. "Now I really don't understand this, Logan."

"Tess had me mixed up with Josh. I thought that might be the case when I saw the strong family resemblance in the boys. The DNA testing proved me right."

"You said there hadn't been any DNA testing."

"You surely know me better than that by now. I had DNA testing as soon as I could arrange it."

"How could you when you've never had the boys in your care?"

"Artie found out where they get their hair cut and paid the barber to save a few locks."

"How did you get Josh's DNA?"

"Some woman claimed he was the father of her son before he died. He had DNA testing to prove her wrong. Artie got a copy of the test results for me to compare."

"So Artie knew all along?"

"No. I told him the DNA came out positive for the boys being mine, the same way I told you and Detective Morrison and my own father that they were my sons."

She leaned against the fragile Louis IV sofa in the drawing room and took a deep and very shaky breath. He'd lied to her from the very beginning and then used her to try and get custody of children that weren't his.

He put his hands on her shoulders, but she pulled away. "Is anything you've told me the truth?"

"Of course. I had to do it this way, Rachel. Otherwise I had no rights as far as the boys are concerned."

"Because they're not yours, Logan."

"But they're Josh's. All that's left of him."

So he'd concocted this convoluted scheme and made her a part of it, just as Karen had said. "You came to me with your lies that very first morning after Tess had been killed, and you haven't let up. Not even when…not even when we made love."

"You're blowing this out of proportion, Rachel. If I'd told you the truth, you wouldn't have told Detective Morrison they were my sons. I wouldn't have gotten custody of them even if the police had found them. I was just doing what I had to do."

"So where does the manipulation quit? Was taking me to the boathouse and seducing me part of the scheme? Were the kisses a ruse to keep me on your side? Was making love…"

"Stop this. You know better." His muscles flexed and he fisted and unfisted his hands. "I made love with you because I couldn't help myself, because you get to me the way no woman ever has, because I care about you—a lot."

The doorbell rang again. Logan stood there, staring at her as if waiting for her to say something, but her emotions were so tangled, she didn't know what she felt except that she couldn't bear to think of him being taken to jail.

The doorbell rang again. This time it didn't let up. Logan exhaled slowly, then went to the door, while her heart felt as if it were being ripped apart, shred by shred.

"I GUESS you have a warrant."

Logan's tone was cool, but not nearly as antagonistic as Hoagie had expected.

"No warrant," Hoagie said. "I'm just here to talk."

"You came in a squad car with flashing lights to talk?"

"No. The squad car came to work a wreck caused by rubbernecking at the TV cameras set up in your yard. I'm in the same old Ford, parked in the next block. May I come inside?"

"You can come in, but I won't be answering any more questions without my attorney present."

Which meant he'd be doing very little talking at all unless Hoagie could convince him that cooperating was the best way to get his boys back. Truth was, it might be the only way, and Hoagie couldn't guarantee that would do it.

Logan moved out of the way, and Hoagie stepped inside. He looked around to see if they were alone. Rachel Powers was in the big room just to the left of the massive foyer.

"Good to see you again, Miss Powers."

She nodded, at least he thought she had. It was difficult to tell for sure since she was standing in shadows in a room that was twilight dark in the middle of the morning.

"You may be able to fabricate evidence against me," Logan said, "but don't try to tie Miss Powers into Tess's murder. You have nothing on her."

The guy was touchy. A good sign there was more going on between Logan and Rachel than talk about the missing boys. "I'm not trying to tie either of you into the murder," Hoagie said. "Matter of fact, I'm no longer assigned to the Shepherd or Matthews murder cases."

That announcement drew the kind of shocked expression he'd expected from Logan. Got Rachel Powers's attention, too. She left the shadows and joined Logan and him in the foyer.

"If you're not on the case," she asked, "why are you here?"

"I have a few loose ends I need to tie up." Like finding out who assaulted Cheri Trosclair and who Cathy Shepherd was running from—or who had already found her and the boys.

Rachel stepped in closer. "Does this mean Logan is not about to be arrested?"

"I can't say one way or another. That's all in the hands of the replacement homicide detective. Mind if we sit down?" he asked. "Talk goes easier that way."

"Why not?" Logan motioned toward the room where Rachel had been. There were sofas and chairs in there, antiques that Hoagie figured would collapse the second he sat down on one.

"I'd sit better in a real chair."

"We can talk in the kitchen," Rachel suggested.

Logan hurried ahead of them and was gathering photos off the kitchen table when Hoagie arrived. He shuffled the last of them into a plastic storage container and slammed the lid down on it before Hoagie had a chance to see who was in the pictures.

"I don't guess you've heard from Cathy Shepherd again?" Hoagie posed the question to Rachel as he took one of the chairs at the table. *She* didn't need an attorney to talk.

"No. I keep hoping she'll call, but so far, nothing." She took the chair opposite his. "What will happen with the search for the boys now that someone else is on the case?"

"It's always hard to say how a new detective will set priorities."

"I'd think missing preschoolers in danger would be anyone's priority."

"I'm not saying it won't be. I'm just saying I don't know."

"You didn't come here to chat," Logan said. "So why don't you get to the point."

"The point is I'm still concerned about the boys and would like to make sure they get back to New Orleans safely."

"But you're off the case," Logan reminded him.

Hoagie ran his tongue over his top teeth, a habit he couldn't break. "That's why I'd appreciate it if you wouldn't mention what I'm about to say to anyone else."

"Like the replacement detective?" Logan asked.

"Exactly." The guy did catch on fast. "What I'd like you to do is call me directly if you hear anything else from Cathy Shepherd."

"Sounds as if you don't much trust your co-workers, Detective."

"I never said that."

"Don't worry," Logan said. "I don't trust cops, either."

Hoagie didn't argue the point. He cleared his throat and waited until Logan was looking straight at him so he could read his reaction. "There's been a new development in the case. Another dancer from the Fruits of Passion was assaulted on Monday and beaten within inches of her life."

"Who?"

"Cheri Trosclair."

Logan turned away, but Hoagie didn't miss the way he'd flinched at the news, almost as if he'd been hit. When he turned back to face Hoagie, his eye were piercing and his face impossible to read.

"If I were you, Logan, I'd stay away from the Fruits of Passion until Miss Shepherd's murderer is caught."

"Is that all?"

"Pretty much. You should be careful, too, Miss Powers. Avoid being alone in any unprotected environment or with any person you aren't certain you can trust."

"You make this sound as if you think I'll be the next target."

"Just a precaution. Never hurts to be careful. And I'll be counting on you to let me know if you hear from Cathy Shepherd?"

Rachel looked to Logan as if she needed his okay to answer. He shrugged his shoulders, but still she hesitated. "I'll keep you in mind."

Not the assurance he wanted, but he wouldn't push it. Aggravate them, and they'd be less likely to cooperate.

"Guess that's it," he said. He'd probably made a big mistake in coming here, but after talking to Cheri, he figured things were about to blow sky high at Fruits of Passion, and when they did, those little boys' lives probably wouldn't be worth a broken string of Mardi Gras beads. That is, if they were still alive now.

As for him, he was going out there to find a woman-killer. If the chief didn't like it, that was too damn bad.

"I GUESS I should go, too," Rachel said, once Hoagie Morrison had left.

"If that's what you want." It wasn't what he wanted, not with things so unsettled between them. But he didn't want to argue with her, either. Besides, if she stayed away from him, she'd probably be a lot safer.

He was fairly sure his seeing Tess was what had gotten her in trouble, and she hadn't said a thing to him that incriminated anyone. Hard even to imagine what kind of sick maniac they were dealing with or what was feeding his penchant toward violence.

"I'll call Protection, Inc. They'll send a bodyguard over," he said.

"No. I need some time alone. I'll be fine. I'll go straight to the condo."

"Did you just hear any of what the detective said?"

"I heard. I'll be careful." She slung her handbag over her shoulder and walked to the front of the house, opening the door a crack and peeking outside.

She hesitated, and it was all he could do not to slip his arms around her. If he tried, she'd only pull away again, and that hurt too much to make a habit of it. But when she opened the door all the way and he heard the eager cries of the reporters, he stepped in front of her and closed it again.

"I'll drive you home."

"Then we'll both be swamped by reporters."

"We'll go the back way, through the old carriage house."

"How will that help?"

"There's an underground passage between this carriage house and the one next door. The owners of the two houses built it to store liquor during prohibition. At least that's the story on it."

"So you can just walk into your neighbor's carriage house anytime you want and they can walk into yours?"

"It's no big deal. There's nothing in the carriage houses but spiders and a few scorpions."

"That makes me feel a lot safer. What will your neighbors say when they see us trespassing through their yard?"

"Nothing. They're in Europe for the summer. With luck, we might even make it to your car without being accosted by reporters."

The hallway that led to the carriage house had been an open walkway until his grandmother had had it fully enclosed a few years back. Her housekeeper was getting old, and his grandmother hadn't wanted her to be out in the weather when she was traveling to and from the main house.

Not that she'd actually done any housework for the last few years she'd lived in the carriage house, but by then she and his grandmother had become fast friends. A thin, frail, white woman, a thin frail black woman, both with wire-rimmed spectacles and thinning hair. In the end, the hallway between their two living quarters had been the only line that separated employer from employee.

His cell phone rang just before they reached the carriage house. He pulled it out of its holster and checked the caller ID.

Number Unavailable. His heart beat like a drunken drummer's. "I need to get this," he said. Rachel stopped beside him, close, but not touching.

"Logan McCain. What can I do for you?"

"It's what I can do for you. I have two boys that I believe you're looking for."

"Who is this?"

"I think the proper term for me would be *kidnapper.*"

"You son of a bitch. If you hurt those boys…"

"Yada, yada, yada. Don't bore me with idle threats, Logan. I'm in control. You'll do as I say or the boys will be visiting their mother—permanently."

"What do you want?"

"Two million dollars in unmarked bills."

"I don't have that kind of money just lying around."

"But we both know you can get it."

"I'll need some time."

"You have twenty-four hours. I'll call you back and tell you where, when and how we'll make the exchange. Be ready."

"I'll need proof you have the boys."

"You'll get the proof when you tell me you have the cash."

"Fair enough, but we'll make the exchange when and where I say."

"I have the boys, Mr. McCain. I'll make the decisions."

"I have the money. It's my way or not at all."

"Twenty-four hours. We'll talk then. No cops. I'll know if you call them. Believe me, I'll hear about it before you're off the phone with them."

Logan felt as if someone had drilled a screw through his head and tightened it to the point that he might become completely unwound at any second. He almost did when Rachel put her hand on his arm.

"Was that Cathy?"

"No, it was a man."

"He has the boys, doesn't he?"

Her voice cracked and he could stand it no longer. He pulled her into his arms and this time she let him hold her. "He's asking for a ransom of two million dollars."

"Two million. We have to call Detective Morrison. He'll know how to handle this."

"No police."

"You can't do this alone, Logan. The man is dangerous. There's no telling what he'll do."

"He said no cops, that if I called them he'd know immediately."

"That was surely just a bluff."

"It's not a chance I'm willing to take."

He tangled his fingers in her hair, and put his lips to her ear. "Stay, Rachel. Please. I need your calm strength. I need you."

She didn't answer, just took his hand and started walking back toward the main house.

"THE TWO MILLION is practically in my hands."

"You mean *our* hands, don't you, Elton?"

"Sure, baby. That's what I meant. You and me, partners again after all these years."

"Partners talk."

"Yeah, well I was never much for talking."

"You? Not much for talking? You talked old women who couldn't see to read into buying the complete set of Shakespeare and young guys into buying car stereo systems for vehicles they only dreamed of owning."

"That was the good old days, before everyone did all their buying on the Internet."

Cathy peeked into the next room to check on the boys. They were sleeping. Danny had the alligator Elton had given him clutched in his hands and tucked under his chin. Davy was sprawled across the covers like an airplane.

She dropped onto the stained, uncomfortable sofa next to Elton and propped her feet on the rickety coffee table. "So exactly what do you do for Craig Graves?"

"Whatever he needs done."

"Does that include beating up dancers?"

"You ask a lot of questions, partner."

"What really goes on at the Fruits of Passion?"

"Dancing. Stripping. A little private entertainment in the back rooms. Same as at all strip clubs."

"There was more. There had to be. Tess had too much spending money those last few months. She had to be involved in more than routine activities."

"Didn't you ask her how she made her money?"

"*Hmmpf.* She didn't tell me anything. I was the babysitter. That was all."

"You slipped, honey. You would never have put up with that in the old days."

"I'm too old for doing jail time now. Besides, I had a little low-risk blackmail business going on the side. And free room and board. Plus, the boys needed me. They're good kids. I couldn't have kids of my own. Not after that time you pushed me down the steps of that hotel in Atlanta."

"The floor was slippery. You fell."

She hadn't, but he'd convinced the hotel management of that and won a hundred-thousand-dollar lawsuit. She'd left him by the time he collected, decided it was better to be alive. "Who killed Tess?"

"You really don't know what's going on at the club, do you?"

"No."

"Well, I guess it's time you found out just what your little stepdaughter was mixed up in. And good at it, too. Damn good. Too bad she got greedy."

Elton left the room. When he came back, he was holding a flowered journal that she'd seen Tess writing in before.

"How'd you get that?"

"I was in the right place at the right time." He tossed it to her.

It hit her hands and bounced to the floor. She picked it up, skipped to the last ten pages and started reading. Two paragraphs down, her blood ran cold.

CHAPTER TWENTY

THE NOON NEWS broadcast on all the local TV channels recanted the earlier announcement that Logan's arrest was imminent. However, they reiterated that Logan was a prime suspect in the murder of Tess Shepherd.

Logan showed little reaction to the latest news other than being relieved that he might not go to jail before he could see the kidnapping ordeal through. He was completely focused on what he had to do, leaving Rachel to agonize alone over the blitz of media coverage and to wallow in apprehension over his upcoming rendezvous with the kidnapper.

Finally, she turned the TV and radio off and started roaming the massive house, exploring the rooms and the priceless antique furnishings in an effort to keep from going nuts while Logan made plans to meet the ransom demands.

Short of winning the lottery, Rachel couldn't have come up with two million dollars in a lifetime, much less twenty-four hours. For Logan, it was a matter of selling stock and moving funds around to make them more liquid.

He'd told the bank the money was to purchase a vacation estate in the Caribbean. They recommended he wire the money to its destination rather than dealing in cash, but recommend was all they could do. The money and the risks were his.

The most difficult part of the operation might be picking up the money and meeting the kidnapper without being followed by an entourage of reporters and/or cops. But Logan had a plan brewing for that, as well.

They'd escape through the carriage house, sneak inside his neighbor's back door with a key they'd left him in case of emergency, then appropriate their SUV. With luck, and the neighbor's heavily tinted SUV windows, they might actually escape unnoticed. Once they picked up the money, they'd drive to the boathouse and wait for the kidnapper's call.

Rachel was convinced that it would be simpler and safer to call Hoagie Morrison and have him orchestrate this, but Logan was adamant that he wanted no police interference. Once the deed was done and the boys were in his hands, he'd turn the full information over to them, but not before. If there was a screw-up with this operation, it would be his.

Her feelings for him were still confused. The lies and the manipulation still bothered her, especially when he'd waited so long to tell her the truth.

But his commitment to the boys seemed even more remarkable now that she knew he wasn't their father. Not only was he willing to give up two million dollars, but by meeting the kidnapper without police protection, he was putting his life on the line for the sons of his late brother.

If she compared that to her own father, Logan came out a saint, not that she remembered much about Melvin. Even after the breakthrough the other night in her aunt's room, the memories were vague. Loud voices. Stomping monsters. Seeing her mother's dead body sprawled across the floor. The icy dread and nebulous emptiness that never fully disappeared.

And now the old dread had joined forces with the new.

She trembled and leaned against an inlaid pearl desk with

elaborate Chinese carvings. The desk was more a work of art than a piece of furniture; remarkable even in a house full of exquisite antiques.

She trailed her fingertips along the surface. A rough edge pricked her skin and brought a drop of blood. Even the furniture knew she didn't belong here.

Her world had collided with Logan's. So had her heart. And no matter what the future held for them, she knew that she would never be the same.

RACHEL RUMMAGED in the kitchen and found enough food to throw together a supper of pancakes, bacon and eggs. Neither she nor Logan had eaten all day and they'd need food to keep up their stamina for what lay ahead.

Once she had it on the table, she went to the study and found Logan bending over a Louisiana roadmap, yellow highlighter in hand. His face was drawn and even his stance showed signs of worry and mental fatigue. She walked over and stood beside him. "I prepared a light supper. It'll be better if you eat it while it's still hot."

He glanced at his watch. "Eight o'clock already? I'm sorry. I should have cooked for you. I forgot all about food."

"I needed something to do. You should eat even if you're not hungry. You'll need the energy."

He nodded, but it was clear the idea didn't inspire any enthusiasm. He folded the map and brought it with him to the kitchen, tossing it onto the countertop while he washed his hands at the kitchen sink.

She nuked their plates for a quick warm-up, then poured them both a glass of cold milk.

They ate in silence for the first few minutes, both picking

at their food as if they suspected it had sprinkles of arsenic hidden under every bite.

"I think I have it," Logan announced, smiling for the first time that day.

"Have what?"

"A foolproof way to make the exchange."

His optimism made her nervous. "I don't see how any dealing with a kidnapper can be foolproof."

"Maybe not foolproof, but close, and it should be agreeable to the kidnapper."

"What's the plan?"

"We'll use the lake."

"I'm not following you."

"There's a dock on the north side, in a secluded area but fairly easy to find. The house it went with was damaged in a hurricane a few years back and was never repaired. I've never seen anyone in the area. It's completely desolate, but I'm pretty sure I could locate it, even at night."

A deserted dock in a secluded area. A kidnapper who was possibly also a murderer. Two innocent boys. And Logan. The images crept through her mind and the fork she was holding slipped from her fingers and clattered about in her plate.

It had a totally different effect on Logan. He started eating as if he were starved, cleaned his plate in minutes and poured himself another glass of milk. "It'll work," he said, returning to the table with milk and map in hand. "I'll take the racing boat over. He'll be able to see me coming and know I'm the only one in the boat."

"And you'll be an easy target if he decides to shoot you and take the money."

"No. That's the beauty of using the boat. I'll contact him by cell phone as I approach. I'll demand that he's on the dock with his hands in the air and one of the boys by his side. Then I'll have him tie the boat to secure it to the dock, making sure his hands are busy and not on a gun."

"Where will the other boy be?"

"He can leave him in the car, his insurance that I'm not planning anything funny. I'll give him one case of money and show him the other. Once I have one of the boys safely in the boat, he can get the second twin. I'll hand over the second million as the second child climbs into the boat. Done deal."

"Why would the kidnapper agree to a spot of your choosing? You might have police staked out and waiting. And you should, Logan." She brightened a little. "That's exactly what you should do."

"And have them start shooting at the wrong time and blow everything?"

"You have to trust someone other than yourself."

"I do. I trust you."

"That's progress." She couldn't keep the sarcasm from her tone. Logan didn't notice. He was too into his plan. "You need the police, Logan."

"No, but your first point was valid." He opened the map, then refolded it so that Lake Pontchartrain was centered.

"I won't back down on the boat scenario, but I'll let the kidnapper pick the spot. He can have the option of meeting me anywhere I can reach by boat. Then, when it's over, I can speed away so fast that even if he shoots at us, he'll never hit us."

"You'll have to have life preservers for the boys," she said, already imagining them flying across the water and speeding back to the boathouse. There was a chance it could really work.

"Absolutely. Life preservers, a calm lake and lots of luck. That's all it will take for this to work. Now I just have to convince the kidnapper of that."

"Will you have the two million ready in time?"

"I'm picking it up at ten in the morning. Then all I have to do is wait for the call."

But they had waited once before for a call that had never come. She picked up the dishes and took them to the sink, tossing most of her food down the garbage disposal. "I wish I felt half as confident about all of this as you do."

Logan walked behind her and circled her waist, pulling her against him. It was the first time they'd touched since the hug after the phone call. The tension swelled between them and so did her fears.

"Call Detective Morrison, Logan. Please call him. He'll know how to handle this in the safest way possible."

"I can't, Rachel. I have to do this my way. If I don't, and something happens to the boys, I'll never forgive myself."

"But what if something happens to you?" Her voice broke and frustration took over. She turned and pounded her fists into his chest. "You are so stubborn. So darned stubborn. You don't need anyone or anything."

He grabbed her wrists and held them until she quit shaking and fell against him. He held her close, cuddling her in his arms while she buried her face in his chest.

"I need you, and when this is over, I'll prove to you how much."

"Just come back alive, Logan. That's all I ask. Just come back alive."

Thinking he might not was tearing her apart.

They finished cleaning the kitchen together, and when she went to take a quick shower, he followed her. He shed his clothes and stepped into the steaming water with her, running his hands all over her slick body and kissing her from the neck right down to the small of her back. She turned to face him and they clung to each other as the hot water cascaded over and between them.

Tomorrow might bring horrors too frightening to even think about. But tonight they'd have each other in a swirl of steamy passion and bittersweet release.

LOGAN JERKED AWAKE and sat up in bed, wide awake but not sure why. He tiptoed to the window of the upstairs bedroom, pushed back the curtain and peered outside. The chaos had calmed some, but there were still strange cars parked in his driveway, no doubt inhabited by sleeping or sleepy reporters.

He'd have been within his rights to call a towing service and have them all carried off to the pound, but that would only encourage the feeding frenzy. He was about to go back to bed when he distinctly heard a door close inside the house.

It couldn't be wind. There wasn't a leaf moving on the old oak trees that canopied the house.

Leaving the curtain pushed back so that he utilize the moon's illumination, he opened the secret compartment in the antique armoire and took out his .38 Smith & Wesson. After checking to make certain it was loaded, he tiptoed toward the open door. A loud clattering noise stopped him dead in his tracks.

"What was that?"

He spun around. Rachel was rubbing her eyes and swinging her feet over the edge of the high bed.

"I'm not sure," he admitted. "Probably an unscrupulous paparazzi hoping for a shot of me dyeing my hair and getting ready for a daredevil run for the Mexican border."

"You have a gun!"

"Just a precaution."

She slid to the floor and pulled on one of his shirts she'd confiscated as a robe. "Did you call 911?"

"No."

"Well, I am. There's probably a police officer or two sitting in front of your house."

She grabbed for the phone by the bed. A waste of time. The plug was missing on it and Logan had never bothered to replace it.

"It's under control, Rachel. Stay here and lock the bedroom door behind me. If I'm not back in five minutes, then call 911. My cell phone's next to my side of the bed."

"If you're going downstairs, I'm going with you."

"Don't even think about it."

"I'm sure not staying up here by myself."

"Shh." This time the noise was closer; creaking noises on the staircase. Whoever had come into the house was making their way to the second floor in the darkness. "Do not leave this room."

RACHEL'S HEART was jumping like crazy. She looked around for a weapon of her own and decided on an ornate silver letter opener that was lying on top of the mahogany dressing table.

She grasped it like an ice pick, ready to stab into someone's chest—or groin—then tiptoed out the door just in time to see Logan's gun hand fly into action.

"Stop right there or I'll shoot."

"I should have known not to talk you into buying that gun."

"No. No way."

There was no gunfire, but Logan stumbled backward as if he'd been shot. Impulsively Rachel raced to him. By the time she reached him, the hallway was aglow from the ornate wall lamps that ran the length of the long hall. Logan was as pale as a ghost, and his pistol hung from a limp hand.

She grabbed it and pointed it at the man standing not two

feet in front of them, his hand still on the light switch. A man who looked enough like Logan to be his...brother.

"You low-down rotten scoundrel. You're alive!"

"Alive and kicking."

"We buried you. We..." Logan's voice broke. "I scattered your ashes."

"I know. It was the only way."

"It better have been, because you almost killed Mom."

"Yeah. I missed her and you. God, how I missed you."

The two guys fell into a bear hug and started beating each other on the back like crazed boxers. Rachel tiptoed back to the bedroom for more clothes. She didn't bother going into shock this time. The incredibly bizarre was becoming plain vanilla.

THE LAKE HOUSE crackled with tension, the intensity growing with every passing hour that the kidnapper didn't call. Rachel felt like yesterday's French bread with Josh on the scene. Not that Logan and Josh didn't try to include her in their conversation, but they talked in some kind of brother shorthand, and there was no way she could keep up.

She had Josh cornered now in the small kitchen where he'd gone to start yet another pot of coffee.

"I didn't hear the full story last night. Exactly why did you decide to play dead?"

"To keep from being dead."

"That's what I don't understand. Did this have to do with your drug addiction?"

Josh filled the coffeemaker with cold water and the filter with grounds. Once he'd flicked it on, he leaned his backside against the counter and faced her. "I was never addicted to drugs. I did smoke a little pot from time to time. A big mistake, just like mothers always tell you. Anyway, I started hanging out with some real potheads, then got mixed up with some of their friends who went for the harder stuff, mostly crack cocaine, but they were into all kinds of uppers and downers, as well."

"I thought Logan said you wanted to be a cop."

"I did, but I failed my physical. Since then I've discovered that was bunk. More of my father's creative use of money. There was nothing wrong with my reflexes or my heart."

"So how did you go from hanging out with crackheads to being shot and playing dead?"

"I saw guys younger than me so addicted they'd never have a chance at normal lives. Then, when the pushers came after me, trying to get me hooked, I decided it was time to switch back to the side of the good guys.

"I went to a narc I knew from college, filled him in on what I knew and agreed to help him go after the pushers. Only thing was, we both knew that if they ever found out I was the one that fingered them, my ass would be grass."

"So they planned a fake shooting in which you played dead."

"That's pretty much the size of it. I told them where and when to strike, and they conducted a raid. By the next week, word was out that one of the dealers suspected me of being the pigeon. So the cops gave me a gun and faked a shooting, saying they'd tried to stop me for questioning and I'd pulled a weapon."

"Did you go into protective custody?"

"They suggested it, but they had more rules than Dad. They set me up with a fake identity. I drove up to Montana and got a job on a ranch."

"So that's what you do now, work on a ranch in Montana?"

"Close. Eventually I bought my own spread with some

money I had stashed. And I have a regular job as well, at least as regular as I can handle."

"It seems running a ranch would be enough."

"It is, but I still have that taste for law enforcement. So up in Montana I'm known as Sheriff Josh Morgan."

"What? You never told me you were a sheriff," Logan said, joining them in the kitchen area.

"Well, little brother, you didn't give me a lot of time to talk last night. You sent me on that well-deserved guilt trip about what I'd done to Mom and you had all this excitement planned for my homecoming."

"How did you find out that sons you didn't even know existed had been kidnapped?" Rachel asked, still finding this a little hard to buy.

"I didn't know they were my sons until Logan hit me with that news last night. Hate to say I don't remember a Tess Shepherd, but I was a good deal wilder back then than I am now. Not so wild that I didn't know what No meant, though. The story of forced sex was definitely a lie. Anyway, I got a call yesterday afternoon from a Detective Hoagie Morrison."

"Whoa. Are you saying that Detective Morrison knew all along that you were alive?"

"No, nothing like that. But evidently he started investigating me and called the narc who'd supposedly shot me. He and I are still buddies. He's living in Alaska now and not involved in law enforcement so he didn't know anything about Logan's arrest. So basically I owe being here now to Hoagie Morrison. Man's got to be a hell of a detective."

"Tell that to your brother."

"In case you haven't noticed, my brother is a very stubborn man."

"Believe me, I've noticed."

Logan's cell phone rang. Rachel jumped, then stiffened, almost choking on the dread that settled in her throat. For all Josh's easygoing manner, he stiffened as well, and the lines in his face grew granite-hard.

Logan answered, then shook his head, the sign that the caller was not the kidnapper. He got rid of the caller in two seconds flat, then stared at the phone as if he could will it to ring again.

Rachel walked back to the sofa, suddenly struck with an overwhelming premonition that this was going to turn out really badly.

It was an hour before Logan's cell phone rang again. She knew from the look on Logan's face that this was it. Her stomach knotted, and when she stood, her feet and legs felt like lead.

"That was him," Logan said. "He won't give me a meeting place yet, but he wants me to take the boat to the middle of the lake. He'll call and tell me where to go next."

"He's making sure you don't have cops on the scene," Josh said. "Expect him to give you a location, then change to somewhere else at the last minute. Somewhere you can get to easily by water but that would take a lot longer to reach by land. That way the cops can't make the adjustment in time."

"As long as he's got the boys, we can meet wherever he wants."

Rachel wanted to scream that Josh should go. They were his sons. He was a sheriff. He should face the danger. But on a deeper level, she knew Logan was right. The kidnapper had made the deal with him. He'd have to deliver.

The fate of Danny and Davy was in his hands.

She walked to the steps with Logan and Josh, but stopped

at the top. The parting would be tough enough without seeing Logan speed away in the boat.

Logan pulled her into his arms. "It's going to be okay, Rachel. I'll be back soon with the boys. We'll celebrate tonight. Count on it."

And then he kissed her goodbye.

TWO HOURS LATER, Rachel was pacing the floor in the boathouse and going out of her mind with worry. Josh had left soon after Logan, claiming he'd go stir-crazy if he hung around doing nothing all afternoon. He hadn't asked her to join him.

She checked her watch, the way she'd done every five minutes or less over the last two hours. Logan could be anywhere now, off to meet the kidnapper or sitting in the middle of the lake waiting for the kidnapper to contact him with a specific location.

That could take a while even in the speedboat. The lake was huge. It took thirty minutes to cross it by car on the causeway. She took a new bestseller from the shelf, read the first page three times without having a clue what she'd read, then tossed it onto the nearest table.

For at least the tenth time that afternoon, she picked up the phone and checked to make certain there was a dial tone. All clear and waiting for Logan's call. Waiting seemed to be all she did these days.

Her cell phone rang. Aunt Gladys's doctor. She sucked in a deep breath and a healthy helping of guilt. With all that was going on, she'd forgotten all about the tests.

"Hello."

"Miss Powers, this is Dr. Lane. Do you have a minute?"

"I do, but can I call you right back from another phone? I have to keep this line open."

"Sure."

She called him back on the boathouse phone. "I hope this is good news."

"I don't think there's been any further stroke activity. I want to get her in next week to run a few tests, but in the meantime, I'd like to modify her medications. I've prescribed a fairly new drug that's had really good results with the kind of sporadic anxiety attacks she's experiencing. Side effects with the new medication are minimal."

"Will the drug have any effect on her memory or mental functioning?"

"That's pretty much a wait-and-see situation, but if we control the anxiety, we may see fewer memory lapses, at least that's what we're going after."

Memory lapses that took her into a past she'd spent years trying to forget. "I hope we see improvement," Rachel said.

"I'll have the nursing home keep me informed of her progress, but you should keep an eye on her, too. And try to spend time with her. You're probably the best one to help keep her grounded in reality, since you were part of her daily life leading up to the stroke."

No problem there, since she was out of a job. Amazing, but with all that was going on, losing her job seemed extremely insignificant.

She finished the short conversation, then stepped onto the deck. The lake was calm. Karen would say that was a good omen. She was a firm believer in omens and amulets and the power of positive thoughts.

She didn't believe in Logan McCain, but even Karen wasn't always right. Nonetheless, she was always a friend, and Rachel had never needed one more than she did right now.

She went back inside and called Karen from the same phone she'd used to talk to the doctor.

"What are you up to?" Karen asked almost before Rachel got *hello* out of her mouth. "Or dare I ask?"

"I wouldn't if I were you."

"That bad, huh?"

"Worse."

"The continuing saga of Logan McCain?"

"Sort of."

"Okay, I'm not going there again. And I'm not going to lecture you, either."

"Great. What's up with you?"

"I'm thinking of writing a book on the problems that come with being a disorganized slob."

Rachel knew it was taking a lot of effort for Karen to keep this light, and she really appreciated it. "What did you lose now?"

"The key to my locker at the gym. I had the thing in my hand one minute, stopped to take care of an emergency and it disappears into thin air. Someone's put a gris-gris on me. That's the only explanation. They don't want me to lose weight and become a thin sex goddess. Which reminds me, I picked up some gossip last night on Tess Shepherd. You didn't give me time to tell you about it earlier."

"How did you hear something about Tess?"

"She was a member of the same torture chamber I go to."

"Crescent City Gym."

"Right. A couple of women in my aerobics class were talking about her while we were waiting for the instructor. They had nothing good to say about her."

"What did they say?"

"That she was a certified bitch. She got mad at one of the cleaning women one day because she dropped a dirty towel near Tess's locker and didn't stop right then to pick it up. The next day Tess dumped the whole basket of wet towels on the floor so that the cleaning lady had to pick them up."

"Sounds like a bitch to me." And a woman who could have made lots of enemies in her short life.

"Another time some woman accidentally swung her arm into her during jazzercize class and Tess snubbed the woman from then on. Talk about carrying a ridiculous grudge. But they said let a man come around and sugar dripped from her forked tongue.

"Ah, here's the key. In my coffee cup and coated with gunk. If I leave now I can make the four o'clock aerobics class and still have time to make my seven o'clock speaking engagement to plead for more funds. I'll call you back from the car."

"That's okay. We'll talk later. Go get 'em, sex goddess in training."

"Take care?" The concern slipped back into Karen's voice.

"I will. You, too, Karen. And thanks for being there."

"Hey, what are friends for?"

Rachel walked to the window and stared out at the lake while her mind grappled to fit what she knew of Tess with the new information. Sexy. Abused. Bitch. Organized to the point she kept two sets of all her written records. She'd never have lost her locker key.

The key. Oh, God. Tess's key was just the right size to fit a gym locker. Rachel ran to get her purse and slid her finger into the side pocket. Nothing.

Because she'd left it in the drawer of her desk at WW&C. Right there with the paper clips. The memory hurt right down to her toes. She could call one of the secretaries. But Castile had probably already told them to keep her out. And she didn't dare trust Ted with this.

She'd have to go back to the office and get it herself and

she'd have to get there before five. Security would never let her in after five.

She called for a taxi, then scribbled a note to tell Josh what she was up to, just in case he got back here before she heard from Logan.

It was a long shot to think that Tess had stored her notes in her gym locker, but it was a shot. A chance to find out what Tess had been involved in that had gotten her killed. A chance to keep Logan out of jail.

CHAPTER TWENTY-ONE

CATHY LISTENED to Elton's plans for the lifestyle he had planned for his million. But she knew that if he pulled this off, he'd be leaving the country with two million dollars in his possession. She would be dead. So would the boys.

He'd planned it that way all along. Otherwise, he'd have never let her read the diary. Never let her know just how deeply he was involved in the perversions that had taken place on the third floor of the Fruits of Passion.

She'd never be able to shake the images that had crawled into her mind while she'd read of the activities that took place in the red room. Sadism in its most depraved form. Drugs used to heighten the satisfaction of sick men. Sexual deviancy that would have shocked the people of Sodom and Gomorrah. All perpetrated by some of the richest and most influential men in the city.

Now that she knew the names, there was no way she'd be allowed to live.

And Tess had been a willing partner in all of it. Had even been excited when she'd been invited to be a member of the Elite. But the worst thing she'd done was to sign the death warrant for her own sons. She'd let them see the face of her killer the day he'd first beat her up.

JOSH TOOK the stolen boat to the limits. It wasn't as fast as the one Logan was in. There wasn't another boat that fast for miles. But this one would do.

He slowed and took the high-powered binoculars from their leather carrying case, thankful he'd brought them and the other surveillance paraphernalia with him. He didn't use this stuff much in his job as sheriff, but an FBI friend of his did, and he'd been nice enough to loan it with no questions asked.

The high-powered rifle under the seat was his. All he'd had to do was pull it out of the locked storage bunker at the boathouse.

Logan was as headstrong as ever. He'd made Josh promise to stay out of this. Josh had.

He wondered how long it would take for Logan to accept the fact that he didn't have the moral fortitude that Logan had. The bottom line was he simply could not be trusted to keep his promises. No way was he letting Logan fight this battle alone.

LOGAN SLOWED the twin motors to an idle while he waited for the next phone call from the kidnapper. He was on the north side of the lake, across from the boathouse. The kidnapper had taken him on a wild goose chase to get here and he had no guarantee this call wouldn't take him on more of the same.

The helicopter flying overhead earlier had probably spooked the guy. But the chopper was long gone, and it was getting close to five o'clock. Even if the guy was antsy, it was time to act.

Finally the phone rang.

"You got your map handy?"

"It's right here." Logan took out a detailed map of Lake Pontchartrain and its shoreline, listening and marking the map so that he could find the spot the kidnapper was describing. The man's voice was still disguised, but every now and then Logan had the distinct impression that he'd heard it before.

"Remember, one sign of a cop and I shoot the boys first. You, third."

"There will be no cops. Just have Danny and Davy there and safe. Try anything funny, and the money will go up in smoke. It's wired and ready to blow." The last part was a bluff, something Logan had seen in a movie once. It had worked great on the big screen.

"Ready when you are."

The connection clicked and went dead. There was so much adrenaline pumping through Logan's veins as he cranked up the motors for the ride back across the lake that he thought his head might just explode and send him into orbit. Enough adrenaline that he could barely feel the pockets of fear hiding in his gut.

RACHEL REACHED the wide double doors that opened to the offices of WW&C at ten minutes before five, just as Phillip Castile was coming out of them.

He stopped in front of her, blocking her entrance. "Former employees are not allowed free access to the office."

"I'm aware of that. I just need to get something that I left in my desk drawer."

"I'm afraid we've already reassigned that office to Ted Boyd."

"Then let me ask him if I can look in the drawer. I'm sure he won't mind."

"He's in a meeting off-site this afternoon. Perhaps you can call him in the morning."

"This really can't wait. You can go with me. All I need to do is get a key that I left with the paper clips."

"I'm sorry, but I can't let you rummage in a desk that belongs to someone else."

This was crazy. She considered dropping to her knees to beg, but Castile would probably kick her while she was down. She was too desperate to think of a lie and never could carry one off, anyway. She'd have to go with the truth.

"This is very important, Mr. Castile. The object I left was a key that belonged to Tess Shepherd. I think it may unlock information that could lead to the arrest of the person who murdered her."

"Oh, Rachel, how did you ever let yourself get drawn into such a sordid mess?"

He sounded truly sorry for her. That had to be good. "I don't know, sir, but I really need that key."

"Of course. I'll go with you to get it."

She opened the drawer, holding her breath and praying that Ted hadn't trashed the key. But there it was.

"It's a strange little key," Castile said as she picked it up. "What does it open?"

"A gym locker, I think."

She'd probably taken the honesty bit too far, but it didn't matter. She'd either find Tess's notes or she wouldn't. "I appreciate your help, but I'm in a big hurry."

"I understand. I have some urgent business to take care of myself."

Rachel's fingers trembled as she fitted the key into the lock at the Crescent City Gym. She held her breath a second then let it out slowly as she turned the key and the door to locker 182 swung open. She reached inside and started pulling out everything in her reach. A pair of tennis shoes. A hair dryer. A makeup kit. Leotards.

And a thick looseleaf notebook.

She pulled it out, opened it and read the first page.

Gentlemen of the Elite
A True Story of My Journey Into a Sexual Hell
by Tess Shepherd

No wonder she'd kept such great records. She'd been writing a book. Rachel stuffed the clothes back into the locker and slammed the door shut. The exposé was in her hands, but the apprehension that had been building all day was near detonation. Logan should have called by now.

She'd walked to the health club from her office, but she'd have to take a taxi back to the boathouse. She wanted to be there when Logan returned with the boys. She tried to find a cab to wave down, but the only ones that passed were occupied.

Giving up, she called for one on her cell phone, then leaned against the building and opened the notebook to page one.

The word *gentleman* can camouflage men more depraved than Lucifer himself.

"I need you to go with me, Miss Powers."

She slammed the notebook shut and stared at the young police officer. "It's Logan, isn't it? Something's happened to Logan."

"That's right. It's Logan McCain."

"He's not…dead?"

"No, but he's hurt, and he wants you with him."

"What about the boys?"

"I think it's better if he tells you about them."

Somehow she forced one foot in front of the other as the

officer led her to his squad car. Panic took over to the point that she barely felt it when the hypodermic needle pierced her arm.

THE MAN was there, just as he said he'd be. And one of the boys was there as well, sitting on the end of the remains of an old wharf that had once been part of a fishing camp. There was a car parked on an incline about fifteen yards behind them.

The man waved him in, then put his hands in the air. The boy jumped up to stand beside him.

Logan looked back at the two bags of money. Ready to go. And so was he. He steered the boat to the dock, one hand on the wheel, the other holding his .38. He hoped like hell he didn't have to use it. All he wanted was a swift and uneventful exchange. Two million bucks for Josh's sons.

He was almost to the wharf before he recognized the man. The self-proclaimed manager of Fruits of Passion. Why was he not surprised?

He let go of the steering wheel and grabbed the end of his rope, twirling it so that the man could see what he had. "I'm throwing this to you. Catch it and tie the boat to that stud at the end of the wharf."

"You got it, *Mr. Logan McCain.*" He spat out the name as if it were too vile to be uttered any other way. "Do you have the money?"

"It's all here."

Logan tossed him the rope, then reached for a bag of the money. His muscles strained under the weight as he lifted it for the kidnapper to see.

"Hand it to me, and Danny can get in the boat with you."

"No, I don't wanna get in the boat."

"It's okay, Danny," Logan said, keeping his voice as calm

as he could. "I'm going to take real good care of you. I won't let you get hurt. We'll just go for a ride."

"Can my brother come, too?"

He was worried about his brother. Danny couldn't have said anything that would have gotten to Logan more. He had the gun in his hand, but it didn't matter. At this point, he could have killed the brute on the dock with his bare hands if that's what it took to save the boys.

"Sure. Your brother can come, too."

Danny turned back to the kidnapper. "Can he, Mr. Elton? Can Davy go with us?"

"Sure thing, boy. Both of you can jump right in the man's boat, as soon as he gives me what I want."

"You got it." Logan handed Elton the first bag of money.

Elton set it down a few feet from the edge of the dock, peered inside, then led Danny to the edge of the dock. He picked him up and handed him to Logan. The kid seemed to weigh nothing.

"I'll take that other bag now."

"Not until I see Davy standing on the wharf."

"What are you so worried about? You don't think I want the whiny brat, do you?"

"Then get him down here."

Elton turned back to the car and waved. Nothing happened. He waved again. All four car doors stayed shut. Logan's muscles tightened. He should have known this was going too easily.

"Looks like we have a problem," Elton said. "I'll have to go back and get the boy."

"Fine. Leave the bag of money on the dock."

Elton started back to the car. As he did, the car started moving. It was rolling down the incline toward the lake, picking up speed. If Davy was in it...

Danny started to scream. Elton had turned back to face them, this time with a gun in his right hand.

The car plunged into the water, soaking them in the cold spray. A second before it disappeared beneath the surface, Logan saw Davy's frightened face pressed to the window of the sinking car and heard the deafening crack of gunfire.

Logan pushed Danny to the floor of the boat and ordered him not to move. Elton was lying on the wharf as if he'd been shot, but Logan hadn't shot him. He didn't know who had, and he couldn't waste time finding out now.

He grabbed the heavy flashlight from the front of the boat and dove into the water. The lake wasn't deep here, but even if it wasn't over the window level of the car at first, it would be when the car sank into the mud.

His feet hit bottom. The water was to his chin. He swam to the sinking car, expecting to feel the sting of a bullet at any time. The window would be hard to break under water, but he could do it. He had to do it. Fast. Every second counted.

He hammered against the window, hitting it three times before it finally shattered. He kicked out the glass with his boot and swam into the submerged car. It seemed like forever before he located Davy, maneuvered his body through the open window, then pushed him to the surface.

"I'll take him from here."

"Josh."

Logan had no idea where his brother had come from or how he'd gotten here. He'd betrayed them all before, let them believe he was dead, let them grieve and miss him so that their mother had all but stopped living.

But he'd come through for them this time, come through for his sons and for Logan. Logan released Davy to Josh, then sank below the surface of the water until he had to come up for air.

By the time he did Davy was laid out on the old wharf, coughing and spitting up water; Danny was jumping around yelling about the car that had sunk; the kidnapper was lying in a pool of blood and his cell phone was ringing.

"TIME TO WAKE UP, sweetheart. The party's waiting for you."

Rachel heard the voice, but had no idea who was talking or where she was. Her mind was trapped in a groggy stupor that wouldn't turn loose.

"Is she going to be all right?"

"Yeah. Drugs will wear off any minute now."

"Why did you give her so much?"

"I didn't know how long it would take you to get the Elite together."

The voices grew louder. She tried to rub her eyes, but she couldn't move her arms. Slowly the figures that had been floating around her like giant sea creatures coalesced into human forms. "Logan?"

"No one named Logan around here. It's just you and a few gentlemen ready to party."

"Where am I?"

"In the red room on the top floor of the Fruits of Passion."

She tried again to move her arms. They didn't budge. Neither did her legs. Finally the haze cleared from her eyes and she looked up and saw herself in the overhead mirror.

She was lying on a nest of pillows and red satin sheets. The top sheet was pulled back exposing her bare breasts. She had on a pair of black lacy panties that barely covered her most private area and a garter belt that held up a pair of black lacy hose.

Her wrists were handcuffed to the railings of the bed. Her ankles were tied to the bottom railings with lengths of black satin.

But hers was not the only bed in the room. There were others. All in use by women in various stages of undress. One was completely naked, most cuffed, all beautiful and surrounded by masked men in black silk kimono-type robes.

The only man not in a robe was the cop who'd been talking to Rachel. He backed away as one of the robed men approached her. He had a leather whip in one hand and a small open pocketknife in the other.

He laid the whip and the knife on the bed beside her, then slipped out of his robe. "I drew you first," he said. "But don't worry. I'll go easy on you. Your finish belongs to an old friend of yours."

"What friend?"

"He's with the girl in pink feathers. Surely you recognize him even in his mask."

She turned and searched for the pink feathers. The woman had flowing blond hair and long shapely legs. A man still in his black kimono was running a huge feather up and down her legs, stopping every few seconds to poke her breasts with the shaft of the feather until she cried out in pain.

There wasn't a doubt in Rachel's mind that the masked man was Phillip Castile. All his rules. All his pious lectures. And he was part of Tess's hell.

The man with her took his pocketknife and slit one of the straps of her garter belt, then slid the cold blade along the edge of the bikini panties. "Get ready, baby, 'cause here I come."

One, two, buckle my shoe.

Three, four, shut the door.

The monsters were no longer marching through her mind. They were here.

CHAPTER TWENTY-TWO

LOGAN DROVE like a maniac, darting in and around cars and driving on the shoulder when it took that to keep from slowing down. He threw on his brakes as a delivery truck stopped in front of him, then swerved around it and made the turn onto Canal Street.

Cheri Trosclair's phone call had thrown him into such a state of panic, he'd practically gone into shock. He was still panicked, but adrenaline was shooting through him at such a frenzied rate his heart felt as if it were going to bust through the walls of his chest.

If the car hadn't been there, he didn't know what he would have done. He still didn't understand why it *was* there unless the first car's plunging into the lake with Davy inside it had been part of Elton's plan.

He pulled onto Bourbon Street. Traffic was at a standstill, and this time there was no shoulder to travel around it. Logan jumped out of the car and left it in the traffic jam. He ran toward the alleyway where he was to meet Cheri, zigzagging in and out of the street and incidentally knocking down a man who stepped in front of him.

Cheri was there, just as she said she'd be. His breath was jerky, and his lungs were burning by the time he reached her.

"Did you bring a gun?" she asked.

285 JOANNA WAYNE 285

"Two. Where's the key?"

She pressed it into his hands. "This will get you in the back door of the club. There's a staircase about halfway down the hall. Take the stairs to the third floor. There'll be a guard there. A cop. He'll have a weapon on him, and he won't hesitate to use it."

"Where is Rachel?"

"In the room at the top of the stairs. The red room where the Elite always meet. Hurry. Hurry or she'll be dead."

Logan raced the half block to the back door of Fruits of Passion, slipped the key into the lock and entered the empty hallway. His .38 pistol was in his pocket. Elton's automatic was in his right hand. The cop might not hesitate to shoot, but neither would Logan.

He found the staircase easily and raced up the steps, taking them two at a time. He didn't know what he'd find when he reached the red room, but if they'd hurt Rachel, if they'd molested or raped her, he'd kill them. He'd kill them and never bat an eye.

He spotted the guard as he rounded the last landing. He was standing with his ear to the closed door, eavesdropping on whatever was going on inside.

"Touch the gun and you're dead," Logan said.

"You're making a mistake."

"This time they'll bury my mistakes. Take the gun out of the holster with two fingers and drop it to the floor in front of you."

"There are dozens of men in that room and enough weapons to fill you so full of holes your own mother won't recognize you."

"Then I may as well start shooting right now." The cop was probably wearing a vest, so Logan took bead on the center of his forehead.

"Okay, okay," the guard said. "It's your funeral." He took his weapon by two fingers, but instead of dropping it in front of him, he dropped it over the edge of the banister. Somehow it fell the three floors and landed without discharging.

"You're too late, anyway," the cop said. "Even if she's alive, you won't want her now. Not after all the men have screwed her every way to Sunday."

Logan slammed the butt of his gun across the cop's filthy mouth and busted his way into the red room.

He didn't see Rachel at first. By the time he did, two men were running toward him. He fired his gun, hitting one in the leg. The other stopped.

And then he saw Rachel. She was spread-eagled on ruby-red sheets. Stone Littleton was standing over her, stark-naked, fully erect, his face mask pulled down and hanging around his neck.

He'd met Stone on several occasions. He'd never liked him. Now he hated him. His hand tightened on the gun, and he ached to pull the trigger and blow the producer to kingdom come.

Stone started backing away, and somehow Logan managed to hold his finger still. "Take the handcuffs off Rachel. Now!"

"Leave the handcuffs as they are." Craig Graves stepped to the center of the room and cracked a huge leather whip to punctuate his order. No one moved.

Logan took a step toward Stone, but he kept his gaze locked with Craig's. "You have until I count to three for someone to start releasing Rachel's handcuffs and untying her ankles. After that I start killing the men in this room one at a time until you're all dead, starting with Stone Littleton. One."

"He's bluffing," Craig said. "He's never killed a man in his life, and he won't do it now. All we have to do is rush him."

"Two."

"We'll take him down and he can die with his girlfriend. It's as easy to drop two bodies in the lake as it is one."

"Three."

Stone had picked up his black kimono and was trying to cover himself with it, but he was shaking so hard, the kimono kept sliding from his fingers. Logan fired, and the bullet tore a gaping hole in the dangling section of the robe.

"I'll free her. Let me get the key. I'll free her." The producer fell to his knees groveling until he'd retrieved the key from the pocket of his mangled robe. He started to unlock the handcuff on Rachel's right wrist.

Craig started toward the producer, cracking his whip as he approached. "If we let Logan McCain and Rachel Powers leave this room alive, we will all go to jail for the rest of our lives."

Another man stepped forward. "We didn't do the killing, Craig. You did. You're the one who'll go to jail. We'll deny that we've ever been here before tonight and that we're shocked at what you'd planned."

"Shut up, Phillip. You're the cause of all of this. If you hadn't fallen for Tess and started taking her on those so-called business trips, she wouldn't have learned so much about the crooked way you do business. Instead of letting her blackmail you, you could have let me kill her before things got out of hand."

"I don't know about Phillip," Stone said, "but I've never been here before tonight. I didn't hurt anyone. I was just here researching what goes on behind closed doors of a gentleman's club for my next movie."

Craig cracked his whip again, this time slapping it across Stone's legs. "You pathetic wimps. How big a fool do you think I am? I have videos of all of you for the last ten months. You're the ones who asked for this and agreed to pay whatever it took to get it. I'm not taking the rap for you. If I'm arrested, I will take every one of you down with me."

The men started arguing among themselves. If they rushed him, Logan could kill a few, but he couldn't kill all of them before they jumped him and wrestled him to the floor. He'd take Craig out first. If the leader was gone, maybe he and Rachel would have a chance to escape.

Logan fired a shot over Stone's head. "I told you to release Rachel."

Stone unlocked the cuff and Rachel sat up in bed, rubbing her wrists. Another man stepped up to loose her ankles, but Craig cracked the whip across his back and the man went down yelling in pain. Then Craig turned toward Rachel and lifted the whip.

Logan aimed the gun and fired. Craig went down. Blood gushed from his stomach, but still he kept on mumbling orders interspersed with curses.

The rest of the men were nervous, and Logan would have to move fast if he was going to get out of here with Rachel before they panicked and took him out.

"Okay, guys. Against the back wall. Rachel and I are leaving. Try to stop me, and you're dead."

"Like hell you are." Stone ran at Logan, and the others followed. He shot once, but they kept coming. One landed a blow to his head, and two were on his back.

Craig screamed a warning, but too late. A gunshot rang out. Stone broke into a stream of curses.

"The party's over. See how fast you can spread your legs and get your hands on the wall."

Logan spun around. Hoagie Morrison was standing in the doorway along with a half dozen cops with their pistols drawn.

"Get Rachel out of here, Logan. I'll take over from here."

Relief burned in Logan's gut as he dropped to the bed beside Rachel. He wrapped her in the sheet and took her in his arms, weak with relief that she was alive.

"Where are the boys?" she whispered as he untied her ankles.

So like her to be living through hell and worried about someone else. Once she was loose, he held her close and buried his face in her sweet-smelling hair. "The boys are with their father. Safe."

"Thank God."

"How about you, baby? Are you okay?"

"Yeah. I'm okay, Logan. I didn't think I would be, but I'm just fine."

"Then let's go home."

He swooped her up in his arms and carried her to the door. Detective Morrison moved back to let them pass. "For a rich son of a bitch, you did a hell of a job, Logan. One hell of a job. Now take care of that woman the same way."

"I plan to. If she'll let me, I plan to do just that."

For as long as she would let him.

EPILOGUE

Two Weeks Later

"ARE YOU SURE this dress is all right? It's not too dressy, is it?"

"It's not too dressy."

"But it's dressy enough?"

Logan kept his left hand on the wheel, but reached across with the right, took Rachel's hand and squeezed it. He wasn't about to let her know that he was as nervous tonight as she was, although for a different reason.

"The dress is perfect. Your hair looks great. The shoes are terrific. The earrings are superb. You are beautiful. And this is only my parents and Josh and the boys, not the Queen of England."

He pulled up in his parents' driveway. "This is it."

"The McCain estate. And I thought your house was huge," she said. "This one takes up a city block."

"It's a short block."

"How many people live here?"

"Mom and Dad live in the main house and Ben and Elsie live in the little house out back."

"Who are Ben and Elsie?"

"Mom's chauffeur and head housekeeper. The rest of the servants live off the property."

"I'm surprised Josh didn't just move back here with the boys."

"Mother would love that, but Josh likes the Montana life. He's got a nanny already lined up."

"So he's actually leaving tomorrow?"

"Yeah. It's probably best. With all the trials coming up, the Fruits of Passion scandal will be on TV constantly over the next couple of years. Elton for murdering Hank Matthews. Craig Graves for murdering Tess and Sandra Valencia and for almost killing Cheri Trosclair. It's better the boys don't have to hear all of that. Even little kids as young as them would pick up on some of it."

"It's amazing how well they're adjusting."

"You've helped a lot with that. Josh says he's not sure he could have made the transition from bachelor to daddy without your help."

"I've loved getting to know them, and it's given me something to do over the past two weeks beside try to decide what kind of position I want to look for."

He killed the engine. "Tired of corporate law?"

"I've been tired of corporate law since the second week on the job. I think I'd like working with individuals, perhaps in family law. I'd love to do some pro bono work from time to time, as well."

"You could open your own firm and do it anytime you wanted."

"That takes money. Oh, there's Davy and Danny!"

She forgot the job worries and climbed out of the car as the boys rushed to her. In seconds they were all over her, wrinkling her perfect dress. She'd never looked better, well, except every morning when her hair was tousled and her head was lying on the pillow beside him.

They went into the house. His mother met them at the

door, more animated than he'd seen her since they'd buried what they thought was Josh's ashes. Not only did she have Josh back, but she had grandchildren, as well. She latched on to Rachel immediately, and started talking a mile a minute.

Logan joined Josh on the back veranda where he was perched on the railing drinking a beer. Logan poured himself a glass of cold lemonade from the pitcher his mother had left on the table next to the porch swing.

"You look bored," Logan said, joining Josh at the railing.

"Not bored, but I'm eager to get back to the ranch. It's gorgeous up there this time of year. Everything's green and a lot cooler than August in New Orleans."

"So what's with you and Dad? You must be talking again."

"Dad and I had a long talk. He's still Dad, but he's trying."

"Are you certain you're the real Josh McCain?"

"Fatherhood's probably mellowed me a bit. Besides, I'll be in Montana. In the case of Dad and I, distance actually does make the heart grow fonder. Too bad I can't take Rachel with me, though. She's terrific with the boys and they adore her."

"Don't even think about it."

"You're really serious about her, aren't you?"

Logan nodded. "I still can't bear to think of how close I came to losing her. If Griffin Paulson hadn't been at Cheri's when they called him to do guard duty... If Cheri hadn't overheard him use Rachel's name and called to tell me... If we hadn't found Elton's getaway car when we did... If you hadn't called Morrison, and he hadn't shown up when he did... So many things could have gone wrong that night."

"But they didn't," Josh said. "You got there in time, and Rachel was spared being defiled by those perverted monsters. Of course, there wasn't much chance we wouldn't find the getaway car once Cathy Shepherd had freed her feet from the ropes enough so she could try to kick her way out of the locked trunk. You could hear that racket a mile away."

"It's still hard to believe that Elton was heartless enough to show Davy how to release the brake on that car and tell him to do it when he gave him the sign. Kid had no idea what he was doing."

"All part of the plan. He'd shoot you when you jumped in to save Davy, then he'd kill Cathy and Danny and split with the two million."

"It would have worked too, if you hadn't shown up with all your surveillance tools. I didn't even think about your being able to track me with those high-powered binoculars. But then you always did like high-powered toys."

"Some things never change."

"Not even Cathy Shepherd, but in the end she didn't turn out near as bad as the rest of them," Logan said. "She knew Elton wasn't really going to share the ransom money with her, but she still drove the getaway car to the ransom point, just in case she could find a way to save the boys."

"That's also why the DA let her plea bargain. She's helped with the boys' transition from her care to mine, but she's eager to get away from here, too. She's using the money from Tess's very sizeable bank account to start a new life on a Caribbean beach."

Josh finished his beer, then set the bottle on the railing between them. "I don't guess you'll ever know why Tess chose Rachel out of all the attorneys in the city."

"We know exactly why," Logan said. "Not only was Tess writing the book, but she had a diary where she kept written records of everything she did. She chose Rachel when she learned that Castile had propositioned Hank Matthews to kill her."

"How did Tess find that out?"

"Hank told her. Apparently he was in love with Tess. Furious, she paid Griffin Paulson to kill Castile. Paulson told her he'd think about it, but before he gave her an answer, Castile found out where she lived and went over there and beat the crap out of her. Unfortunately, that was Cathy's gambling day, and when one of the boys threw up at school, Tess had picked them both up and brought them to the apartment."

"So Castile hired Elton to track them down and kill them?"

Logan nodded. "So many lives ruined or lost because of a bunch of grown men playing sick, perverted games of sadistic sex."

"There's always been sexual perversion, little brother. Always will be."

"Even in Montana."

"Even in Montana, though I hope nothing on this scale. I'm just thankful that Cheri Trosclair got worried about the boys and came to you. Otherwise who knows how this would have ended?"

"Cheri's already moved on. I didn't even get a chance to thank her. Detective Morrison said she told him where to get in touch with her if he needed her to testify, but other than that she just wanted to start over in a new town and try to put this all behind her. I hope she makes it."

"Me, too."

The boys came running into the backyard, squealing and tossing an old football. "Hey, that's my old football," Josh said. "Where'd you get it?"

"My grandfather gave it to me."

"Then I guess I better show you how to use it. That ball has history."

"Yea! Daddy's going to play."

"Throw it to me first, Daddy," Danny yelled.

Josh clapped Logan on the back. "Fatherhood calls."

"It looks good on you. And in case I haven't said it, it's damned good to have you back."

Rachel joined him on the veranda as Josh left. Logan's heart did the crazy kicking-around thing it did whenever she came into view. Only it was worse today. Maybe his courage would return when he took her to the spot where Josh had taught him about defying fear and going for the gusto.

He took her hand. "Let's take a walk."

"I think you mother wants me to go to the garden with her to see her prize roses."

"The roses can wait. I have a tree house to show you."

RACHEL KNEW something was up, but she didn't know what. Logan had seemed distracted for the last couple of days, and several times she'd caught him staring off into space, so deep in thought she'd had to touch him before he knew she was around.

He'd been terrific, loving and warm and understanding, had even gone with her to visit her aunt a couple of times. But maybe things were moving too fast for him.

She hadn't actually moved in with him, but they'd spent every night together since he'd rescued her from Tess's hell inside the Fruits of Passion. And now she was here at his parents' for a going-away dinner for Josh and his sons. It had taken him five months to realize he had nothing in common with his ex-wife. It might not have taken five weeks for him to realize that now that the danger was past, he had nothing in common with her.

She should make it easy for him. Tell him she needed time away from him, tell him she wasn't in love with him.

But then she'd never been good at lying.

"I don't guess you can shimmy up the tree in that dress," he said.

She looked up and saw the remains of what must be the tree house he'd told her about. "I don't think I could climb that high in jeans and carrying a support rope."

"It's not so high once you're up there, but I can say what I want to say from the ground beneath it."

He let go of her hand, and she cringed, dreading to hear what would come next. He took something from his pocket and got down on one knee. Her heart jumped to her throat and stayed there.

"I love you, Rachel Powers. I don't know the exact second it happened, but sometime between thinking you had the best laugh I'd ever heard in a beautiful woman and going through hell together, I have fallen totally and completely in love with you. Will you marry me?"

Tears welled in her eyes. All her life she'd lived with a nebulous emptiness in her heart. But it wasn't there now. Her heart was filled with Logan. "I love you, Logan. I love you so very, very much."

"Then you'll marry me?"

"Yes. Oh, yes."

He slipped a breathtakingly beautiful ring on her finger, then picked her up and swung her around until she was so dizzy she couldn't have stood up if he hadn't been holding her.

"Let's not wait," he said. "I want a houseful of kids. You do want kids, don't you?"

"A houseful—but do we have to raise them in your grandmother's monstrosity?"

"We can raise them anywhere you want."

"A house on the lake with lots of yard to play in and a little apartment on the side."

"For the servants?"

"For Aunt Gladys."

"We'll tell her tomorrow," he said. "But we could start working on the family tonight."

He kissed her and her heart sang. And as they walked back to the house hand in hand, she knew that love was here to stay and that the monsters who'd haunted her since she was three would never come calling again.

Everything you love about romance...
and more!

Please turn the page for Signature Select™
Bonus Features.

Bonus Features:

BONUS FEATURES

The Gentleman's Club

A conversation with
JOANNA WAYNE

Joanna Wayne is the bestselling, award-winning author of thirty-two novels. She is known for cutting-edge stories of romantic suspense. Recently we spoke to Joanna about her writing career, her family and her favorite pastime activities.

Tell us a bit about how you began your writing career.

I grew up reading everything I could get my hands on. I remember a time in the fifth grade when I read nothing but books about baseball players. Then there was the horse period, followed by books about pioneers in the American West, then anything gothic. Fortunately, I got into the classics in high school because college was devoted to textbooks. Later, after reading *Salem's Lot*, I got hooked on horror for a while before being lured into suspense novels. And all the time I was reading, I kept saying that one day I was going to write a book.

The one genre I never really got hooked on was romance. But, oddly enough, when I saw that a class in how to write a romance was being taught at the local university, I decided to sign up. The class was taught by Emilie Richards. I read a few of her marvelous books, and right then and there I knew that was what I wanted to write. But, believe me, I had a lot to learn.

Was there a particular person, place or thing that inspired you?
I guess I'd have to say Emilie Richards inspired me to write romance and romantic suspense, but a lot of credit has to go to my husband who never once doubted that I'd not only write, but get published. He thinks I'm wonderful. That's a terrific quality in a husband—don't you think?

What's your writing routine?
It's changed over the last few years. When I still had a day job, I wrote at night, frequently writing into the wee hours of the morning. Now I find that my most creative period is early morning before my mind becomes too cluttered with the problems of the day. I usually get up at five and take my laptop into the family room and make my "nest" on the sofa among pillows and warm throws. In the summer I keep the air conditioner purring away so I can comfortably cuddle in my nest. In the winter I light the fireplace.

I write until my hubby wakes up about eight and talks me into coming back to bed for a coffee break and to touch base before the rest of the day begins. After that, I exercise, do a little house work, check e-mail, etc. and try to be showered and back at the computer by 1:00 p.m., a latte within easy reach. I try to get at least three more hours of writing in. I do this approximately five days a week. But, when deadlines loom, I've been known to write seven days a week, all day, or at least until I become brain-dead.

How do you research your stories?
Oh, so glad you asked. I LOVE research that requires me to get personally involved. One of my most exciting research trips was to a ranch in south Texas. While I was there, I took advantage of every opportunity to see what the life of a rancher would be like. I even tried my hand at fixing fence. The highlight of that trip was a roundup by helicopter. I loved it when the pilot asked if I wanted the door on or off. Didn't have to think about that answer. I wanted it ON.

Other research high points have been adventures in all parts of the country. A rodeo in Montana. A deserted beach in the winter. Vampire tours in the French Quarter. Spending the night in a bed and breakfast said to be haunted. Visiting the Seattle Underground. Climbing mountains in northern Georgia. And soon, I've been promised the opportunity to observe brain surgery in progress. Who knows what might come after that?

How do you develop your characters?
And, sorry you asked that. I don't actually develop my characters. They pretty much take over and develop themselves. I write by the seat of my pants, which means I just start writing and have no real

idea what's waiting around the next corner until it jumps out and grabs me by the throat—or the typing fingers in this case. No one is as surprised as I am when the characters turn out to have such complex personalities. But I always fall in love with my hero. It sure makes writing those love scenes fun!

Could you tell us a bit about your family?
Hey, I'm a grandmother. I could talk about this for hours, but I'll make it a little shorter than that. Between us, my husband and I have five children (three for him, two for me) and nine grandchildren. That's enough to keep us very busy. They are scattered about the South, from Georgia to Texas. We've recently moved to Montgomery, Texas, and that puts us within an hour of my daughter and my son, his wife and their two sons. I visited my grandson's third-grade classroom last year to talk to them about writing. He was thrilled. The difficult part was finding a cover that I could actually show his class without prompting the wrong kind of questions. It turned out the cover for *Family Ties* with the kid and the horse was perfect.

How did you meet your husband?
I picked him up in a bar. Don't laugh. It was almost like that. I was out with girlfriends and we had stopped in the lounge at the Hilton in Bossier City for a drink (I'm mostly a Diet Coke fan) and to listen to a popular band that was appearing there that night. Wayne was in town attending a conference with coworkers. They stopped in to hear the band.

He asked me to dance, and I was hooked from the get-go. We dated long distance for a year and a half after that. I lived at one end of the state; he lived at the other. But we talked every day. That was twenty-one years ago and I'm still in love—and I still like to dance.

When you're not writing, what are your favorite activities?
My favorite activities involve time spent with family and friends, weeks at the beach, traveling to Disney World and wild times at water parks. Or something as simple as a family dinner or reading stories to the little ones is always great. I also love to travel. One of my favorite trips was the three weeks my daughter and I spent roaming the islands of Greece. Another was a trip my husband and I took to Australia. And I'll never forget our experiences on Mediterranean and Baltic cruises. I also enjoy golfing and LSU football. Geaux, Tigers.

What are your favorite kinds of vacations? Where do you like to travel?
I'm open to almost any kind of trip someone suggests. Some of my favorites—aside from the ones mentioned earlier—include trips to the Olympics in Atlanta and to the Olympic trials in Sacramento in 2004. I spent a fabulous week in Seattle exploring all the sites of the city while re-searching *Escape the Night* and will never forget three fabulous days spent with Amanda Stevens and B.J. Daniels in a cabin on Mount Baker in Washington State brainstorming the gothic *FERNHAVEN* se-

ries (coming from Intrigue in 2005). I usually spend the month of November on the beach in southern Alabama and I enjoy trips into the mountains anytime. Love New York at Christmas, New Orleans in the spring, Banff, Canada or Colorado in the winter and the northeast in the fall. In other words, I'm easy.

Do you have a favorite book or film?

I like so many movies and books that it would be impossible to pick one. Some of my favorite films are *The Sound of Music, My Fair Lady, The Silence of the Lambs, A Knight's Tale* and *Gone With the Wind*. I like them all for different reasons. A hundred more fly to mind, but I'll stop there. As for favorite books, I'd have to put some of my old favorites at the top of the list: *The Grapes of Wrath, Johnny Tremain, The Call of the Wild, The Prince of Tides, Thornbirds, The Shining* and *Rebecca*.

Any last words to your readers?

Yes, I hope you'll all take time to visit my Web site at joannawayne.com or my pages at eHarlequin.com. And please drop me a line at joannawayne@msn.com. Tell me what you liked about the book, and, if you didn't like it, you can tell me that, too. I won't cry long. I really do appreciate your support. You keep reading, and I'll keep writing.

Marsha Zinberg, Executive Editor, Signature Select program, spoke with Joanna Wayne....
Look for Joanna Wayne's Harlequin Intrigue, *Security Measures*, in September 2005.

Romance—New Orleans Style

by Joanna Wayne

I was born and raised in Shreveport, a city tucked away in the northwest corner of Louisiana very near the borders of Texas and Arkansas. Although I'd visited all parts of the state in my younger

10 *days, it wasn't until I married and moved to the famed party city that I truly discovered the Big Easy's magnificent verve and sensuality. And now, though I've traveled to Paris, Rome, Venice, St. Petersburg, London, Barcelona and the Greek Islands, and loved them all, I've never discovered a city any more romantic than New Orleans, Louisiana.*

And I must say it's a good thing that I've shared many special romantic moments here with my husband, since friends visiting the city just assume that a romance writer will know the secret hideaways as well as the more popular not-to-be-missed activities to spice up their own love lives. You, too? Great, because I'm going to share with you my list of the top-ten romantic things to do in New Orleans. 🐚

10 No trip to the bayou state would be complete without a visit to the swamps and a glimpse of alligators floating down a sleepy, cypress-studded bayou. It may seem strange to think of alligators and swampland as romantic, but once you've walked hand in hand with your guy along the paths at Jean Lafitte Park, observed the wildlife in its natural wetland habitat and reveled in the colors and smells of hundreds of lilies in bloom, I'm sure you'll understand why I added it to my list.

Jean Lafitte Park is about 30 minutes from town, but well worth the time it takes to get there. If you don't have a car at your disposal, there are many commercial excursions that pick up guests from local hotels. The park itself has a visitors' center with exhibits and an excellent film showing the lifestyle of the citizens in the disappearing Louisiana wetlands. There are also several hiking trails; one suitable for people with difficulty walking on uneven surfaces. Nearby there are swamp tours which will take you on guided motor- or air-boat trips down the bayou, or, if you're more adventuresome, you can rent your own canoe.

I have a friend who claims that taking his girlfriend on a canoe trip down the bayou was the way he got her to fall in love with him. He says she was so frightened of the alligators, she had to cling to him the whole time. I don't know if he's right, but I do know they're happily married now.

9 No romantic weekend in the city is complete without at least one visit to Café du Monde for beignets and café au lait. Beignets are square-shaped doughnuts served hot and coated in powdered sugar. They are absolutely delicious, but the setting is just as appetizing and sensual as the taste of warm sugar on the tongue.

Café du Monde is an open-air café just down from the Moonwalk and Jackson Square. For a romantic encounter, try to find a table in a back corner, but close enough that you can hear the music from one of the ever-present street performers. Though the common dress is shorts and sneakers, don't be surprised to see people show up in formal wear. Beignets and café au lait are a tradition after any big night in the city and it's rumored that tuxedo rental establishments have come to expect the suits to be returned coated with powdered sugar.

Don't hesitate to kiss the sugar from each other's lips as you nibble the warm doughnuts. But you don't want to just get the white stuff on your lips. Be sure to have some of the sugar sprinkle into your cleavage and hopefully lower for removal once you're back in the privacy of your hotel room. The sugar must always be kissed off. What a tradition!

And if you work up too much of an appetite making love during the night, you can always return to Café du Monde. They'll be open.

8 Some of my most romantic evenings in the city included dinner in a moonlit-drenched courtyard in the French Quarter. You don't have to go to an expensive place. There are many moderately priced and inexpensive spots that offer an intimate setting and the traditional New Orleans fare.

One of my favorite is the Napoleon House. It's an old restaurant, dimly lit and fairly inexpensive. The food is good—great gumbo and a nice selection of sandwiches as well as more substantial entrées. Desserts are rich and truly decadent.

But again it's not the food but the setting that makes it so romantic for me and many of the other locals who've made it somewhat of a bohemian hangout. It's said to have been built by French loyalists who hoped it would be frequented by Napoleon. Apparently that never happened as he was in exile at the time, but still the place reeks with an aura of history. The rumor that a ghost shares the upstairs dwelling only makes it more intriguing.

I always take a table in the courtyard beneath the stars and let the classical music that fills the air seep into my soul while I sip wine and slide my foot up and down my hubby's leg beneath the table. And spoon-feeding him bites of rich bread pudding drenched in whiskey sauce is lagniappe.

7 In my mind, no trip to New Orleans would be complete without a night spent perusing the French Quarter with no plan at all. Start by ducking into one of the spots that specialize in daiquiris to go. If you prefer nonalcoholic beverages, they have those, too. Then make your way down Bourbon Street, peeking into the clubs as you go by. If you find one you like, stop in for a bit to hear the jazz or blues or share a dance or two. If not, keep walking and just take in the sights. Music is everywhere and dancing in the streets is always in vogue.

Before you get too tired, be sure to stroll to the Moonwalk and spend some time sitting on the boardwalk, holding hands and watching moonlight shimmer on the surface of the Mississippi River. You'll be serenaded by local musicians. Some are hoping for a dollar or so to be dropped in their hats. Others are playing for their own enjoyment. Either way, you can't miss. Be sure to steal a kiss—or two—before you head back to the streets.

6 One of my favorite ways to lull away a sultry summer afternoon or a brisk fall or spring day is to spend a few hours with the man I love in City Park. I suggest you start with a visit to the Sculpture Garden, where you can meander paths that wind around lagoons and beneath 200-year-old live oaks laden with Spanish moss. Even without the fifty sculptures, it would be nature at its sensual best. With the fascinating sculptures, it is a pure delight.

After that, stop off at the park's Botanical Garden. It is touted as one of the few remaining examples of design from the WPA and Art Deco Period. For me, it's just a marvelous walk through tropical and subtropical plants, a mixture of fragrances and beauty that awakens all the senses.

After that, spread a blanket in one of the quiet and secluded public areas of the park for a picnic next to a lagoon, where you'll find ducks, geese and beautiful swans to add their magic to the setting. Open the picnic basket and hand-feed your guy a luscious strawberry or a juicy raspberry. Memories are made of this.

5 What's a trip to New Orleans without an adventure into the dark and mysterious world of the spirits? Whether the thought of vampires send chills up your spine or makes you yearn to be nibbled on the back of the neck, you shouldn't miss taking in at least one of the many ghost, vampire or voodoo tours available in the Vieux Carré. The tour guides usually have a theatrical bent, which makes for an entertaining as well as haunting experience. Who knows what you might find lurking in the shadows of the Cabildo? But you'll definitely want to stay close to your man while you wind through the dark streets. And when the evening's over, you'll be very glad to cuddle in his strong, safe arms.

4 Every season in New Orleans has its own special flavor, but nothing beats Christmas for romance. From singing carols by candlelight in Jackson Square to perambulating through the Angel Hair Lobby of the Fairmont Hotel or indulging in a Reveillon dinner at one of the city's famous restaurants, the holiday spirit is boundless. But I'm convinced that the absolutely most romantic holiday experience is a carriage ride through Celebration in the Oaks.

Celebration in the Oaks takes place under the ancient trees of City Park and features millions of lights in a dazzling display, including an Acadian village ringing with zydeco music. It's a true fairyland, and you can enjoy it all nestled beneath a blanket with your sweetie. And if his hands—or yours—wander while you're enjoying the sparkle, well, who's to know?

3 Music, moonlight, nostalgia, dancing cheek to cheek. Is there any wonder that a cruise down the Mississippi River on a paddle wheeler is near the top of my list. With stars overhead and New Orleans slowly fading into the distance, you'll find yourself slipping back into a time when virile and daring gamblers stole the hearts of fair ladies with just a wink and a smile. You have several choices in types and lengths of cruises, but no matter which you choose, it will be one of the highlights of your visit to the city.

2 New Orleans is famous all over the world for its food and restaurants. I have literally hundreds of favorite eating establishments, from hole-in-the-wall spots that serve mouth-watering oyster po-boys to elegant restaurants on the river, and from small family eateries in the suburbs to intimate uptown bistros. But my most memorable moments in any restaurant have come over long, lingering lunches in the beautiful Garden Room of Commander's Palace.

The restaurant is like something straight out of a romance novel. Established in 1880, the Victorian-styled structure is painted white and turquoise and has turrets, columns and gingerbread. It's located in the Garden District, an area of stately Greek Revival homes, old aboveground cemeteries and streets arched by the branches of century-old oak trees. It's said that the restaurant was once frequented by riverboat captains and sporting gentlemen who rendezvoused with their lady friends in private upstairs dining rooms. It's easy to visualize that while sipping a mint julep or dipping your spoon into the sinfully decadent bread pudding soufflé.

After lunch, you'll want to go back to your hotel room for a long afternoon of sensual lovemaking. I guarantee it!

1 Deciding what should be number one on my list of most romantic New Orleans experiences was no easy task, but I guess it all came down to this: a jug of wine, a loaf of bread and thou. But to make it totally perfect, I needed music, moonlight and a maestro. My choice for the number one most romantic way to spend an evening in New Orleans is to stretch out on a blanket beneath the stars and enjoy a beautiful concerto played by the Louisiana Philharmonic Orchestra.

These outdoor concerts, while infrequent, are always well attended and highly anticipated by locals. Our picnic fare is simple, usually consisting of cheese, crackers, fruit and a rich, fruity Cabernet. The music is both soothing yet invigorating, and never fails to send fantasies frolicking through my mind. And when we steal a kiss during the crescendo, I feel incredibly close to my husband and know that our love runs as deep as the passions inherent in the masterpieces. Take it from me. It's as good as it gets.

If you visit New Orleans, I hope you find that my suggestions bring you lots of sensual pleasures. But no matter where your adventures take you, always remember, romance is where you find it.

Happy hunting!

Family Fun at Mardi Gras

by Joanna Wayne

I know everyone has heard about the wild happenings in New Orleans during the Mardi Gras season. You've likely seen pictures on television of people baring certain body parts in exchange for some inexpensive colorful beads, or folks in extremely skimpy costumes parading through the French Quarter, drink in hand. But if you're thinking that's all there is to Mardi Gras or that it's simply for adults, you'd be mistaken. Mardi Gras in the Big Easy offers something for everyone.

First, I should tell you a bit about the holiday. No one is exactly certain of the exact origins of Mardi Gras or the traditions that surround it, but Carnival, as it's frequently called, has become known as a season of merriment that begins on Three Kings' Day or Twelfth Night, which is January 6. This is the day the Magi visited the baby Jesus. The season comes to a close at midnight before Ash Wednesday.

Since the day before Ash Wednesday was traditionally a day of feasting, the day became known as Fat Tuesday, or the day they killed the fatted bull or ox. Mardi Gras is French for Fat Tuesday. Mardi Gras falls somewhere between February 3 and March 9—which also happens to be my birthday. (Could that explain why I like to party?) The date differs from year to year because Ash Wednesday is tied to Easter which occurs on the first Sunday after the full moon that follows the Spring Equinox. Mardi Gras falls forty-seven days before Easter.

There is no exact date for the beginning of Mardi Gras in New Orleans, but the Krewe of Comus made its debut in 1857 with two floats and riders wearing costumes and masks. They were accompanied by brass bands. Their parade and tableau ball set the stage for the many krewes to follow. The most famous of all is Rex, known as the King of Carnival. Rex was established in 1872 and is credited with introducing the carnival colors of purple, green and gold, which came to signify justice, faith and power. Those are still the colors of Carnival today.

Krewes are the organizations that give Mardi Gras its flavor, providing the parades and balls that are so much a part of the celebration. Each krewe has its own traditions, and not all sponsor parades. For those who do, the custom is for masked participants to ride atop elaborately decorated floats and toss baubles, mostly beads, to the parade goers. In recent years, the variety of throws has broadened. If you're very lucky at a Zulu parade, you might catch one of their highly prized gold-colored coconuts.

For some New Orleanians, Carnival is a year-round activity. One of the first chores of the upcoming year is to decide on a theme. Each float in the parade will come up with some element of that theme and then have the float decorated and costumes designed accordingly. All riders wear uniforms and masks. And plans must be made for the Mardi Gras ball and to choose a king and queen. Krewes vary in how they do this, but most of the details are steeped in tradition.

As with the krewes, most familiy celebrations are also steeped in tradition. Many spend every Mardi Gras day in their own "staked" plot in the grassy area in the middle of St. Charles Avenue. Some camp out all night with their array of folding chairs, blankets, ladders and cooking paraphernalia to make certain they claim a prime location to watch parades and catch throws. The wooden ladders, popular on all the parade routes, have seats on top that hold up to three small children and have a safety bar in front. During the parade, the kids climb in and usually at least one adult stations himself, or herself, on the back of the ladder to help steady it and catch the vast amount of throws that come their way.

When they're not catching throws, most participate in another of New Orleans's favorite activities—eating. Some cook out. Others bring huge picnic baskets and coolers stuffed with spicy fried chicken and other favorites. Some even rent hotel rooms along the parade route so they have easy access to a bathroom and places to plug in their portable stoves and Crock-Pots to heat their hots dogs and chili, red beans and rice. And a few are lucky enough to have friends who live on the parade route.

But no matter what they eat or how they prepare it, most will surely have a king cake or two to satisfy their sweet tooth. The king cake is strands of braided cinnamon-flavored dough baked in the shape of a wreath, then topped with icing and sprinkled with purple, green and gold colored sugar. And tucked somewhere in the middle of the cake is a plastic baby. Tradition says the person who finds the baby will be blessed with good fortune. But then it also requires the person getting the baby to purchase the next king cake. I wouldn't swear to it, but almost every office in the city has a rumor that at least one of the workers has swallowed a baby rather than take on the task of providing the next cake.

And at the end of the day, family members, weighed down with plastic necklaces, gather up the leftovers and their bags brimming with colorful throws and head home, tired, but happy. And already with plans for next Mardi Gras.

So no matter what kind of entertainment you're looking for, risqué or family oriented, you can find it at Mardi Gras in New Orleans. Come on down and *laissez les bon temps rouler.* Let the good times roll.

24

DR. PROTECTOR
by Jessica Andersen

Originally published as an online read at
www.eHarlequin.com.

CHAPTER 1

"HELLO? DAVE? B.K.?" Kelsey Sparks leaned over the security desk at Boston General Hospital's Developmental Research Building and told herself she wasn't creeped out by the empty lobby. "Hey, you guys. Do you want me to sign in or what?"

Her voice echoed and she shivered even though she knew her discomfort was foolish. The late-night walk through Chinatown had her jumping at shadows; that was all. Nobody had followed her. The shadows were just shadows; the footsteps all in her mind.

"Get a grip, Kels," she muttered, tightening her grip on her handbag. "On Monday Dr. Fong will make the announcement, and all this secretive stuff will be over. It'll be time to pop the champagne."

And drink it alone. Damn it.

She raised her voice. "Hello? Guys?"

Finally, a dark head popped through a nearby door. A big grin lit B.K.'s narrow, twentysomething face. "Hey, Dr. Sparks! There's two out in the bottom of the seventh and runners at the corners. Want to join us?"

A low hum of male voices told her there was already a crowd in the security break room watching the game. She shook her head. "No thanks, B.K. I'm headed upstairs for a few minutes." She made a face. "I forgot to lock up the lab notebooks before I left for the night."

The security guard, who was working his way through premed at a nearby university, grinned as a cheer went up behind him. "And Dr. Fong will go ape if he comes in tomorrow and finds out."

"Dr. Fong is a brilliant clinical researcher," Kelsey replied loyally, though *ape* was a pretty good description of both Fong's reaction and his physical appearance. However, the brilliant researcher and his less-brilliant-but-hard-working second-in-command, namely her, stood to make a bloody fortune when the results of their new anti-aging drug went public and the deal with Pentium Pharmaceuticals was signed. Sure, Boston General would take a hefty cut of the money, but what was left over would put Kelsey well on her way to buying that sweet little house on Beacon Hill and let her make some much needed changes in her life.

Like getting one.

B.K. arched an eyebrow. "Yeah, Fong's smart. But admit it, the guy's a little kooky." He twirled a finger near one ear.

She laughed. "I take the Fifth." But the quick con-

26

versation had driven the shadows of Chinatown back where they belonged. In her imagination. She adjusted her purse where she wore it bandolier-style across her body. "See you in a few minutes." She headed for the elevators, calling over her shoulder, "And don't let Dr. Fong catch you watching baseball when you're supposed to be at your post. He'll go ape!"

B.K.'s chuckle followed her onto the elevator, but the light mood didn't last, because the moment Kelsey punched in her security code and stepped through the airtight doors of the fourth floor, she knew something was wrong in the lab.

Goose bumps prickled her arms. The very air seemed to ripple in warning. And in the dim lab corridor, lit only by the exit signs and the LED lights of an army of equipment, she saw a stealthy slide of motion.

Someone was in the lab!

She froze, hoping the intruder hadn't seen her. Hoping he couldn't hear her heartbeat, which was suddenly thundering in her ears. Go back downstairs, she thought. Get B.K. and Dave!

But she couldn't do that. The intruder might escape. She glanced at the red security button beside the door. The whole lab was wired with them—a testament to Dr. Fong's paranoia. Except this was no paranoia; this was real. But she couldn't push the panic button. Not until she was sure the lab notebooks were safe. She had left them out. It would be her head, and probably her job and her slice of Pentium Pharmaceuticals' money, if anything happened to those results. Damn it.

Taking a deep breath, Kelsey slid along the wall away from where she'd seen the shadow. The lab floor was an interconnecting maze of corridors and clean rooms, but if she could just get to—

A rush of air from the open door to her right was scant warning. She spun toward it, but too late. Strong male arms grabbed her from behind, clamping across her ribs and pinning her arms to her sides.

Panic! Kelsey screamed and thrashed against his hold. She kicked back hard and heard her attacker grunt when her sensible heel connected with his shin. Her flailing hand touched the wall and she slapped blindly for the red panic button, which would send a silent signal downstairs. *Dave, B.K., help!*

"Goddamn it, hold still!" The deep, familiar voice froze her fear in an instant, and then melted it away in the warm wash of his breath along the sensitive spot beneath her jaw.

Luke?

His hold gentled and she shoved away, turned and faced him, fists clenched. "Damn it, Luke. What are you doing here? You're supposed to be in Europe. And how the hell did you get past the coded lock?" Her heart clogged her throat, blocking the questions she really wanted to ask.

Why did you leave? Why are you back?

In the dim light she couldn't see the green of his

eyes. His expression was familiar, yet not. Harsher than she remembered, and edged with new lines. He tilted his head in a half shrug. "I guessed your code, Kels. You've always used the birthdays of the people you love."

Dawn. The name punched through her like pain. Kelsey held up her hand and backed away from Luke just as the elevators opened and the guards charged out, batons at the ready.

"Freeze! Hands where I can see them! Up against the wall...*now!*" Dave barked, his twenty-plus years as a beat cop lending strength to the commands. B.K. slapped on the lights, casting the situation into harsh, fluorescent reality.

But Luke didn't flinch. He stared straight at Kelsey, green eyes as hard as they'd been the day he'd left her nearly a year earlier. As uncompromising. "You're in danger, Kels. I came to warn you. Fong's wonder drug is a fake, and in three days you're going to be caught in the crossfire."

B.K. lifted an eyebrow. "You know this guy, Dr. Sparks?"

"He works for the competition," she answered, irritated when she had to force the words past a tightness in her throat. She hated that her heart beat double-time at the sight of Luke's familiar too-long brown hair and the strong, tanned forearms that showed beneath the rolled-up cuffs of a light plaid work shirt. His jeans were snug and worn, and it was hard to believe anything false could come from a man who was part Paul Bunyan, part college professor. She'd fallen for his oh-so-sincere act once before.

It wouldn't happen again. No matter that the aching hole in her gut didn't seem so empty now…it wouldn't happen again.

She lifted her chin and repeated, "He's the competition. He works for Cartier, and they're three months behind us in getting this drug to market. They'll do anything to slow us down."

B.K. scowled. "Do you want us to call Dr. Fong? Or the cops?"

It was tempting. Very tempting. But after a moment's hesitation, Kelsey sighed and shook her head. "No. Get him out of here, and don't let him in again. I'll tell Dr. Fong about this myself." She glared at Luke. "And I'm filing a complaint with your bosses."

His eyes darkened. "I'm not trying to scoop your discovery, Kels. I'm trying to protect you."

"Shut up and get moving." B.K. poked Luke in the ribs with his baton.

As the security guards pushed him out, Luke leaned back and pinned Kelsey with a glare. "You're making a big mistake, Kels."

He stepped into the elevator, leaving her alone in the lab with only an echo of energy to mark his presence. That, and a fine tremble that worked its way through her body when she said to the emptiness, "No, Luke. Marrying you was a big mistake. This—" she glanced around the lab and absorbed the hum of the waiting machines "—this can't be a mistake. This is my life."

It wasn't until she reached her lab bench that it all came into focus. Shock and a sense of terrible inevitability worked their way through her as she touched the empty surface of the desk. "Damn it, Luke."

Her lab notebooks were gone.

CHAPTER 2

👁️👁️

"DAMN IT, LUKE, open up! I know you're in there, and I know you stole my notebooks out of the lab, you scheming son of a—" The furious buzzing of the doorbell drowned out the rest of the words.

Luke paused at the door to the Boston town house he and Kelsey had once shared and blew out a breath. He was a doctor. A respected scientist with one of the leading drug companies in the world. He could handle an irate brunette, even if she *was* his ex-wife.

Marrying you was a big mistake, Kelsey had said when she'd had him kicked out of Dr. Fong's lab over at Boston General earlier that night. But that wasn't true. The mistake had been his. He'd left her alone when she needed him. Well, not this time.

"Luke, let me in right now, or I'll—"

He swung open the door, only half-prepared for the desperate kick of his heart when he saw her standing outside.

In the eleven months he'd been gone, he hadn't managed to forget the way she used to purr his name at the back of her throat when they'd made love or the joy in her voice when she'd told him she was pregnant. But by the same token, he also hadn't forgotten the way she'd turned away from him in the hospital bed. The way she'd told him to leave.

And the fact that he'd gone when he should have stayed.

Scowling, Luke stepped back and waved her into the town house, which he'd reopened just that day. "Kelsey. We need to talk."

"You bet we need to talk." Her brown eyes snapped with temper and her dark hair, shorter than he remembered it, flared around her head as she stormed into the main room with its high, airy arches and natural wood. "What the hell do you think you're doing, Luke? And why aren't you still in Europe on your precious fellowship with Cartier?"

Her voice might have broken on the last question, but Luke decided it was his imagination. He'd told himself a thousand times that if she missed him, she would've answered at least one of his letters.

He ignored her questions and waved her to the fat club chair they'd picked out together. "You're in danger, Kels. Fong's new drug is a dud."

She remained standing and clenched her fists at her sides. Her voice rose. "Are you accusing me of fudging my results? Because let me tell you—"

"Of course I'm not accusing you. I know you better than that." Luke raked a hand through his hair and walked over. He leaned close to her and felt a pang when she leaned away. "You're the most honest person I've ever known. No, the drug works fine in the lab experiments. But the clinical trials..." He shook his head. "There are some really, really ugly side effects."

"Bull! You're just saying that because your team is three months behind us in developing it. We've dealt with the problems and we're ready to go to the next phase!" She strode toward him until they were nose to nose, eye to eye. Close enough to fight. Close enough to kiss. Luke felt the realization race through his body even as he saw the knowledge dawn in her eyes.

Lust had always been easy for them. It was the other stuff, like trust and dependence, that had been hard. Knowing as much, Luke stepped away and held up both hands. "Rumor has it some of the study subjects are being paid off to not report their symptoms."

"Rumor, hah!" she spat, crossing her arms and glaring. "More like libel! Don't think I'm going to let you mess with our announcement. We're going to publish our findings, sign the deal with Pentium and voilà!" She snapped her fingers. "Our future is assured."

Her words were pure bravado, but Luke saw a shadow of suspicion in the back of her eyes, and he pressed forward. "Dr. Fong's future is assured, you mean. Fifteen minutes after the money's in the bank, Fong will be on a plane to somewhere far away, and you'll be stuck here facing the blame when it comes out that half the results with your name on them are false."

She paled and fell back a step. "That's baloney." Her tone wavered, then solidified. Her eyes narrowed suspiciously. "Dr. Fong wouldn't do any such thing. You're making this up to buy your team time."

"The hell I am!" Luke advanced on her, half tempted to grab her soft white blouse and shake some sense into her. "I don't give a fig about the company or the drug at this moment. It's you I'm worried about!"

She stared at him for a beat before she drew herself up and folded her arms tighter across her chest. "Don't worry about me, Luke. I'm fine. In fact, I'm better than fine. I'm wonderful, and I have been ever since you left me!"

"I didn't leave you!" he snapped. "As I remember it, *you* divorced *me*."

"Because you left me in the hospital and took an eighteen-month fellowship in another country."

"Damn it!" Luke scrubbed a hand through his hair. How had the conversation gotten so out of hand so quickly? "You told me to go."

"You should have stayed." The sudden sheen of tears in her eyes was a punch to his gut.

He turned away. "I know."

Surprise tinged her expression, but she said nothing. After a moment, Luke sighed. It was too little, too late. But if it was too late for him and Kelsey, it wasn't too late for him to save her from her boss's dishonest plans. Carefully staying half a room away from her, he spread his hands. "Kelsey, please—"

"Where are my notebooks?" she interrupted in a choked voice. "Give them to me, and then get the hell out of my life, Luke. I don't need you anymore."

The words sliced through him, leaving him raw and bleeding, but he tried not to let it show. Tried not to let it hurt. He took a step toward her. "I need five minutes in the lab to prove it to you, Kels. Surely you can give me that much?"

She held out a hand. "The notebooks…or I call the cops."

"You won't do that, Kels." When her set expression told him otherwise, Luke fell back a pace. "Your books are still in the lab. I hid them so you'd come looking for me. I wanted a chance to explain that—"

"Where in the lab?" She was already halfway to the door.

Luke took a breath. "I'll show you." When she turned on him with a snarl, he met it with one of his own. "I said I'll show you." He softened his tone. "Just give me five minutes in Fong's office, Kels. I'll prove that he's faking the test results. I swear it."

"I'm not interested in your oath or in your proof."

"Too bad, because I'm not telling you where the notebooks are without it."

Luke saw her weigh the options. She could call the cops on him, but history—and dare he hope old af-

36

fection?—wouldn't let her. She could return to the
lab and search for the notebooks herself, or—

"Fine. I'll give you five minutes." She stormed out
the door before he could open it for her. He followed
and locked up, then turned to find her at the curb
looking futilely for a taxi.

He walked up behind her. "It would be faster to
take the bike."

She stiffened and stepped away. Her eyes darted
to the overhang beneath the porch, where he'd
chained the motorcycle they'd once shared so many
rides on. The turquoise-and-white helmet he'd given
her on their six-month anniversary was neatly
strapped to the back.

"You take the bike." She spun away from him and
started walking into the night. "I'll find a cab."

Luke wasn't sure whether he was disappointed or
not. Two days ago, when he'd first learned of Fong's
deception and the danger to Kelsey, he'd been forced
to move up the plans he'd made to win her back.
He'd thought he was prepared to see her again.

He'd been wrong.

He caught up to her at the crossroads, flagged a
passing taxi and held the door open for her. She didn't
protest when he slid in beside her and told the driver
to take them to Boston General Hospital.

She merely sat back as far from him as she could
get in the small space and said, "You have five minutes, Luke. Not one minute more."

"Five minutes," he agreed, hoping it would be enough.

It *had* to be enough.

CHAPTER 3

THE CABBIE must have sensed the tension between his passengers, because he delivered Kelsey and Luke to Boston General Hospital in record time. She let Luke pay—the trip was his idea, after all—and headed straight for the elevators.

She didn't bother to wake B.K. The security guard was sleeping peacefully across one of his textbooks, and nobody needed to know that she and Luke were searching Dr. Fong's lab in the middle of the night. Kelsey couldn't even believe she had agreed to bring Luke with her—he was the competition, for heaven's sake.

But this was Luke, she acknowledged with a heavy heart. He'd always known how to talk her into doing things she didn't want to do—like trust him….

And look where that had gotten her.

Annoyed, she scowled at him across the elevator and reminded him, "Five minutes."

He had five minutes to prove that Dr. Fong was setting her up to take the fall when their miracle anti-aging drug failed.

He nodded. "Five minutes." He lifted his hand as though to run it through his already tousled brown hair, then hesitated and let his hand fall.

It was, Kelsey thought with surprise, the first truly nervous gesture she'd seen from him in all the time they'd known each other.

For some reason, the realization wasn't a comfort. Then again, she hadn't been comfortable since earlier that evening when she'd found Luke in Fong's lab. Luke, who was supposed to be in Europe, not Boston.

Luke, who hadn't come back for her, but had come back to interfere with the multimillion-dollar Pentium Pharmaceuticals deal that was set for Monday. Damn him. It wasn't enough that he'd broken her heart, now he had to come back just long enough to ruin her new life.

Then he'd be gone again, no doubt.

More on edge than she'd been earlier in the evening, Kelsey keyed them into the main-lab lobby and tried not to remember that her security code was the birthday of their daughter, Dawn.

The day the little girl had been born prematurely. The day she'd died.

Resolutely, Kelsey tried not to think that Luke had remembered the date and used it to break into the lab. He'd remembered. What did that mean?

Nothing, she told herself. It meant nothing.

Annoyed anew, she glared at her watch, seeing the

digits glow in the dimness of the unlit lab. "Your five minutes start now."

But instead of scrambling in search of his proof, Luke turned to face her and was suddenly too near to ignore. He was so close she could see the pulse beating at his throat, so close she could smell the achingly familiar scent that reached out to envelop her in memories and regret.

"Kels—" he said softly. He lifted a hand and touched her cheek gently. "I just want you to know that—"

"What in god's name is going on here?" There was a loud bang, and the lab lights blazed on.

Kelsey stumbled away from Luke and turned toward the voice, surprise and embarrassment bringing hot color to her face. "Dr. Fong, I can explain! I was—"

She broke off, shocked fear rooting her in place at the sight of the gun in her boss's hand.

Fong gestured with the gun. "Yes, Dr. Sparks? You were saying?"

Kelsey said nothing as she grappled with the sudden realization that everything Luke had told her was true. Fong didn't care about her, and he didn't care about the patients. She had trusted him, and now he was setting her up to take the fall.

Luke stepped up beside her. "Is this your boss, honey?" His voice was friendly, his eyes anything but. "We didn't mean to disturb you, sir, but I insisted on seeing where Kelsey works."

As an excuse it wasn't bad—except that it was close to one in the morning.

Fong sneered. "Nice try, Dr. Sparks." He laughed at the surprise on Kelsey's face. "What, you didn't think I knew your ex-husband worked for Cartier Drugs? Spare me, Kelsey. I am a thorough man. When I realized some of the study subjects had been talking to Cartier…well, let's just say I've been expecting you, Dr. Sparks."

Fong's gun never wavered. It remained pointed at Kelsey's heart. When she moved, it moved. She could feel Luke vibrate with fury at her side. Afraid that he would try something stupid, she fumbled for his hand and was surprised to find that it eased her own tremors when he squeezed back.

"Dr. Fong," she began, "there's no need for drama. Luke doesn't mean any harm, and Monday's press conference will go off without a hitch, just as we've planned."

"Yes, it will," Fong agreed. "Because you two won't be there." He jerked his chin toward an intersecting hallway. "Second door on the left, and no funny business. I don't want to hurt you. I just want to make sure you stay put until after the big announcement."

Second door on the left? Kelsey balked. The empty climate-controlled room was fitted with an iron-tight mechanical lock, as were most of Fong's doors. They would be trapped, with no hope of escape except…

Except for the fail-safe override codes that had been programmed to keep absentminded researchers from locking themselves in. Fong wasn't in the lab much. He might not remember the overrides.

Fong jabbed the gun toward her. "Go on. Move."

Kelsey kept a firm grip on Luke's hand, willing him not to try any stupid heroics. They could regroup in the cold room and make a plan. Fong could not be allowed to sign the Pentium deal and disappear.

"You're not going to get away with this, Fong," Luke grated as he followed her inside their temporary prison.

"I just did, Sparks." With a jaunty wave of the gun, Fong slammed the airtight door. A moment later, Kelsey heard the mechanical hum of the latches being engaged, and the overhead lights went out, leaving them in darkness, save for the illumination that came through the single window in the door.

Luke's voice came out of the dimness. "Damn it, we're trapped."

Kelsey felt him let go of her hand and was absurdly emptied by the lack of contact. She kept her attention focused on the window, watching for her boss. "I don't think so. We'll need to wait until Fong is gone, but then I think I can get us out of here. There's an override."

"Ah, good." Luke's approval warmed her, though Kelsey knew she shouldn't care what he thought anymore. "That's why you didn't struggle much."

"That, and because he had a gun." She still

couldn't believe it. In the space of a night her ex-husband had reappeared, her boss had turned out to be a villain, her slice of the Pentium Pharmaceuticals money had disappeared into thin air and now…

Now, she had nothing.

Kelsey heard Luke prowling the confines of the small, dim room and knew what he would find. Not much. There were a few boxes of petri dishes under the waist-high counter. A small ladder leaned against one corner for when she needed to store samples on the highest shelves. And a single wool blanket was folded below the ladder.

"What's with the blanket?" Luke asked, as though he'd followed her thought process exactly.

"We used this as a cold room."

He cursed. "How cold does it get?"

"Minus twenty, but…" Kelsey paused. "You don't think Dr. Fong would—"

As though summoned by the mention, the scientist's shadow moved past the window. A moment later, Kelsey's stomach dropped when she heard the familiar churning boom of the air ducts realigning themselves to begin refrigerating the room.

"He would," Luke confirmed unnecessarily. "Bastard."

Fong looked through the window for a moment, a hard, evil smile turning up the corners of his mouth, then he sketched a wave and was gone. The lights in the main lab went out.

The room already felt colder.

"I'd be really worried right now if I didn't know about the override," Kelsey said as she moved over to the interior lock keypad. "I don't think it's possible to jam the fail-safe codes." *Please don't let it be possible.* She tried not to let her fingers tremble.

Luke pressed his face to the window. "Then get us the hell out of here. When I get my hands on that bastard…"

"Yeah. Me, too." Kelsey keyed in her override code with fingers that were already feeling cold and numb, though she knew it was in her mind. The room was barely cool.

She punched in the last number. The lock buzzed but didn't open. The keypad glowed red. Code rejected. Kelsey's stomach knotted, then dropped to her toes. She glanced at Luke and saw the knowledge reflected in his eyes.

Fong had changed the codes. They were trapped.

CHAPTER 4

LUKE WRAPPED the thin wool blanket around Kelsey's shoulders and hugged her tight. She didn't push him away, their problems momentarily forgotten in the enormity of what had just happened.

They were trapped in an airtight cold room until Monday. They would be dead long before then.

The silence was broken only by the rattle of the huge commercial blowers. He tightened his arms around her and wished to hell he'd never had the bright idea of breaking into Fong's lab in the first place. Protecting Kelsey. Hell.

He might just have gotten them both killed.

"I don't suppose there's a weekend shift that will find us in here?" he wondered aloud, not having much hope of it.

Kelsey shook her head, and her thick dark hair tickled his chin like it had so many times before— back when they'd been married. "No. Dr. Fong and I are the only ones who work in this lab. He's obsessed with security..." she trailed off into the clanking silence, then sighed. "I'm sorry I didn't believe

46

you, Luke. It's my fault we came back here tonight. My fault we're trapped in the lab's cold room. My fault that…"

She trailed off again, and this time he half turned her in his arms and tipped her chin up until their eyes met. "Hey," he said softly, "we wouldn't have needed to be here if I hadn't broken into your lab in the first place. It's my fault."

A sad, private smile touched her lips. "It's both our faults, then. Mine for not trusting you, and yours for…"

He filled in the blank. "My fault for not giving you a better reason to trust me." He lifted a hand and touched her cheek. "I'm sorry."

And they both knew he wasn't apologizing for what had happened in the lab.

Her eyes clouded and she pushed away from him. She walked to the far side of the cold room, trailing the blanket like a lost child. "Why did you come back here, Luke? It wasn't just because of the drug, was it?"

"Yes." He stood. "Well, no. I came back now because of the rumors, but I'd planned on coming back all along."

He took a step toward her, and was surprised when she held her ground in an obvious challenge. "Why?"

It seemed he wasn't the only one who'd gotten tougher over the past year.

He looked down and was caught in her too-familiar, not-familiar-enough brown eyes, in the sorrow at the back of them and the go-to-hell in the front. The cold air swirling around them felt like loneliness. "Because I was wrong to take that fellowship overseas after you miscarried our daughter. I shouldn't have left you."

She tore her eyes from his and turned away. "I told you to go." And from her grudging admission, he knew that she'd done some soul-searching, as well.

"True, but I shouldn't have listened. I should have stayed and toughed it out instead of running off to Europe where I could be alone. And miserable." He risked reaching out to cup her shoulders with his hands. "I missed you every goddamn day, Kels. I'm so sorry."

She didn't pull away, but she didn't turn into his arms, either. She stood staring at the dim, blank wall of the lab cold room, and he wondered whether she was seeing the simple headstone she'd picked out for their daughter. He'd visited it for the first time the day before, and he was surprised to find not tears, but rather a simple peace. A knowledge that he was doing the right thing.

Finally, she asked, "Why didn't you come back sooner?"

The easy answer was his fellowship and the professional responsibilities that had gone with it. But that was cheap, and they both knew it. Luke sighed. "I wasn't ready to, at first. Then, when I was… You didn't answer any of my letters."

She stiffened beneath his hands and her breath

puffed out on a cloud of icy vapor. The room was edging toward minus twenty, where it would stay for the rest of the weekend until Fong returned, expecting to find their cold, stiff corpses.

"So you're here because of the drug," she finished flatly. She turned to face him. "You wouldn't have come back if you hadn't heard that Dr. Fong—"

"Damn it, I would have come back!" Luke interrupted fiercely. "I want my life back. I want *our* life back. Don't you get it?" He advanced on her, crowding her into a dark corner of the frigid room. "I want *this* back."

Even as he bent and caught her lips with his, Luke cursed himself. This had always been the easy part for them. The flash and the fire were cheap, the emotions wary and tricky. But then her lips opened, almost involuntarily, beneath his—

And suddenly, nothing was simple or easy at all.

Luke flinched as the heat whiplashed through him, mocking the cold of the room. Her fingers clenched in his shirt, though he couldn't tell whether she intended to pull him close or push him away. Then that thought was gone. Their tongues touched, hesitantly at first, and Kelsey's flavor, rich and uniquely feminine, exploded in Luke's brain.

This is what he'd come back for. Kelsey. His Kelsey.

Wrong, his brain reminded him from the back of a lust-fogged corner. He'd come back to protect her. To, hopefully, work things out with her.

Lust was easy. Communication was not.

He framed her face with his hands and eased his mouth away, feathering the lightest of kisses across her lips and feeling the power punch through him and leave him weak. "Kels. We shouldn't. We can't. I didn't mean—"

He saw the moment she realized what they were doing. Her eyes darkened and she ducked under his arm to stand alone. She crossed her arms protectively over her chest. "You're right." Her voice was as unsteady as his legs felt. "I'm sorry. You're here for Fong, not me."

He cursed. "That's not what I said." But he was speaking to her stiff spine. "I'm here for you, Kelsey, but not to pick up where we left off in bed. That part was too easy for us. But Dawn's death…" He had to force the little girl's name out between clenched teeth. "Dawn's death and what happened after showed us that we need more than just sex, Kels. We need to talk more. Communicate." He spread his hands and waited for her answer, heart pounding both in fear and anticipation of her answer.

It came out of the darkness on a puff of freezing air. "Then I guess you already have your answer, Lucas. If I'd wanted to communicate, I would've answered your letters."

Disappointment was an icy knife in his chest, but he wouldn't let the slice be a fatal one. A year ago he might have cursed and walked away. Now he merely strengthened his resolve. They were going to hash this out one way or the other.

He bent and scooped the blanket off the floor. "Here, you'd better stay warm. I don't think the vents are going to quit anytime soon."

But she wasn't paying attention to him. She was staring up at the gaping grill in the center of the ceiling. Subzero air gushed from it, the humidity adding an eerie layer of sticky, sterile fog.

Luke draped the wool over her shoulders. "Kels? You okay?"

"The vents!" She grabbed his wrist. "Luke, the vents are big enough for the maintenance crew. *We can use them to escape.*"

His first jolt of excitement was quickly followed by an image of Kelsey crawling into a giant, churning fan. He caught her by the waist when she dove for the ladder in the far corner.

"Whoa! Slow down. Let's think this through. Those ducts lead from here to the blowers, right? It's a straight shot, Kels. No detours." But it got him thinking. Could they escape? Was there still a chance that they might defeat Fong and live to work out their problems?

Kelsey shook him off and dragged the flimsy ladder to the center of the room. "Everything here is interconnected, Luke, and the rooms are flexible. I've used this room as an incubator and as a cold room. There are hot and cold ducts going to this room and to the room next door where I have an experiment going. If we can get from here to there…"

"Freedom!" Luke grabbed her by the waist, lifted her up and planted a triumphant kiss on her lips.

She stilled. He froze. Realizing that he'd done just what he'd sworn not to do, he let her slide down his body until her feet were safely on the floor. He stepped away. "Sorry about that."

Her eyes darkened. "Yeah. Me, too. Come on." She turned away and bent down for the ladder. "Let's get out of here."

They tore strips from the wool blanket to protect their hands and faces from the freezing metal. But as Luke led the way into the ducts, hoping his body would protect Kelsey from the worst of the arctic blast, he wasn't feeling the full effects of the chill. His body retained the warmth from her touch, and his heart carried the knowledge that at the very least, they still had lust, the easy thing, between them.

Now he needed to convince her to believe in it long enough to figure out the rest.

That is, if they survived the weekend.

CHAPTER 5

THE AIR DUCTS echoed hollowly. THE freezing metal bit into Kelsey's hands through the thin strips of wool blanket, and her knees were numb from the cold that seeped through her jeans. Up ahead of her in the vent shaft, she could just make out Luke's silhouette as he inched forward to the junction where it seemed the hot and cold shafts interconnected.

If they could just get into the hot vent, they could drop down into the unlocked warm room where she'd set up an experiment the day before. They could escape Dr. Fong's imprisonment and alert the authorities to the clinical data he had falsified to make the new drug seem foolproof....

And then what?

Luke had come for Fong, not for her. A few kisses didn't change the fact that he hadn't come for her before. And it certainly didn't ease the sting that he'd found it so easy to push her away. Perhaps he was right that the sex had always been easy between them—maybe too easy.

But it didn't mean that talking about Dawn's death was the way to solve anything.

"I think I'm there." His words echoed back to her, distorted by the refrigerated gale being pumped past them and by the tight metal shaft they were scrambling through. The cold room was set to minus twenty, the air in the duct probably colder. Kelsey was almost numb. Luke, who was taking the brunt of the blast, had to be hypothermic.

"Can you break through?" He'd better be able to, or they were both dead, which was exactly what Fong wanted.

"I think so." Luke's words were followed by several loud bangs as he struggled for leverage. "Damn it, I— Ah!"

Suddenly, the cold air didn't seem quite so cold, as though warm was mixing in.

"Did you get it?" Kelsey called, already crawling toward him, knowing he had. "Are we in?"

"We're in. Follow me!"

The edges of the access hatch were sharp, but Kelsey didn't care. The shock of the warm air flowing over her cold body was worth the pain.

Moments later, Luke reached the vent hatch that opened out into the warm room. He kicked it open and dropped through, leaving Kelsey suddenly alone.

She closed her eyes and reveled in the hot air that scalded the backs of her legs and her scalp. Never had heat been more welcome. And when they escaped from the lab, she was going to take a very long, very thorough bath, and then she and Luke would—

She and Luke would do nothing. He would return to his work in Europe, and she'd look for another job. Maybe even another line of work. With Fong's dishonesty exposed, her own credibility would be shot. Nobody in the scientific community would believe that she had known nothing of his false clinical results.

She'd be unemployed, discredited and alone.

But she'd learned once before that alone was sometimes better. Sometimes being with someone was harder than being alone.

Luke's voice hailed her from below. "Kels? It's okay. You can come down now." When she didn't answer right away, his tone took on a note of worry. "Kelsey? Can you make it out, sweetheart?"

Sweetheart. She closed her eyes against the pain of the careless, meaningless endearment and forced herself to answer, "I'm fine, Luke. I'll be right down."

She'd drop down into the warm room; they would let themselves out into the lab, gather what evidence they could and set about destroying Fong's career.

And with it, her own.

Gritting her teeth, knowing she couldn't stay up in the air vents forever, Kelsey wormed her way forward and slid headfirst through the open vent.

Straight into Luke's waiting arms.

Where before, in the cold room chilled to minus twenty, their embrace had been a contrast of warm sizzles and cool skin, now the contact blazed through Kelsey with reckless, fiery abandon. She looped her arms around Luke's neck to brace herself and felt the heat battle with the cold, chilled core of her body. Of her heart. She stared down at his lips and at the fine sheen of perspiration that already covered his face, and she licked her lips.

"Kelsey." Her name on his lips was almost a groan. "We can't do this. We need to talk. We need to—"

She pushed away from him and dropped her feet to the floor. "We need to get the hell out of here and do what needs to be done."

She strode to the warm room door, pulling the tattered wool off her hands as she went. There was no way she wanted to enter into any deep, meaningful discussions with her ex-husband. When they'd tried such things before, she'd always ended up feeling soul-naked, while he kept all his barriers, all his distance.

Why would she think this time would be any different?

She reached for the door handle and the heat broke over her in a wave, and the last of the cold room's chill was melted by the relentless wash of hot air. The warm room was set to 98.6°F—body temperature. She knew, because she'd set it herself nearly eleven hours earlier.

"Kelsey—"

She didn't turn at Luke's quiet entreaty, no matter how hard the plea in his voice tugged at her. She stared out the single thick window set in the warm room door and shook her head. "It's no good, Luke. It never was." She grabbed the lever that would open the warm room door and tugged.

Nothing happened.

"Oh, God." She yanked again. The lock didn't budge.

Luke was at her side in an instant. "What's wrong? I thought you said this room wasn't locked?"

Through the glass of the small window, Kelsey saw the room's digital timer blink 1:14. "Oh, hell. My experiment."

Luke glanced over at the neat row of labeled petri dishes on the waist-high counter circling the room. "What about it?"

"Fong, in all his paranoid wisdom," Kelsey answered in a tone laced with sarcasm, "installed timed locks on the climate-controlled rooms so we wouldn't accidentally open one during an experiment and alter the ambient temperature even a fraction of a degree." She shook her head in disgust. "I can't believe I didn't think of that."

Luke touched her shoulder, leaving a hot, itchy imprint. "It's okay. We've both got a lot on our minds." He glanced through the small window, where the digital display had changed to 1:12. "Will the lock disengage when the time's up?"

She nodded and felt a trickle of sweat dance off her brow and slide down the side of her face to her throat. She dashed it away impatiently. "Yes, damn it. But that leaves us stuck here for another hour in this sauna." She glanced back up at the vent. "God, it's hot in here." Another dribble of sweat slid down to join the first.

"And it's going to get hotter," Luke agreed with a soft growl in his voice.

Or maybe it wasn't the actual physical temperature that was rising. Kelsey slid a glance over to Luke and saw him watching her with fierce intent. A pulse throbbed at the side of his throat, and he swallowed convulsively when their eyes met and held.

"We should—" she licked her lips "—take off a few layers. There's no sense in collapsing from heat exhaustion while we wait for the door to unlock."

He nodded. "You're right. We should undress."

But neither of them moved. Kelsey swore she could hear her heart skip a beat in her ears. Finally, she wet her dry-feeling lips with her tongue. "This is silly. We used to be married."

"*Used to be* being the operative term here, I think," Luke agreed wryly. He looked away, stretched his arms over his head and twisted, trying to unkink his back, or maybe because he was feeling the same restless energy Kelsey was, the urge to do something. Anything. He lowered his hands and glanced back at her. "We could talk about it."

Talk. Part of her yearned to try it, while the larger, smarter part of her insisted that, once again, she would be the one talking, not him. But still…

They had an hour to kill, and the temperature was rising rapidly.

Kelsey felt her lips curve. "Okay. We'll talk. But you go first. I get to ask you a question, and if I don't think you've answered honestly enough, I don't have to answer a question from you. Fair enough?"

He held her gaze for a moment, green eyes probing as though looking for a trick. Then they lit with wicked amusement. He tugged at his shirt and opened the top two buttons. "Fair enough, but I have a condition to add. For every question that one of us answers fairly, the other one has to remove an item of clothing." His grin broke out full-fledged. "It's only sensible, given the heat."

"Only sensible," Kelsey agreed feebly, her attention focused on the now loosened buttons of his shirt, which exposed a few inches of tanned, taut flesh.

"Okay, then." He dropped to sit on the floor, cross-legged. "Ask away."

Kelsey remained standing and the question popped out of her mouth before she was even conscious of having wondered about the answer.

"Why did you marry me?"

CHAPTER 6

OF ALL THE QUESTIONS LUKE had expected from Kelsey to lead off their impromptu game of strip-twenty-questions, *Why did you marry me?* was the last to come to mind.

Then again, the entire situation was bizarre. Trapped by her boss, Dr. Fong, while they'd been searching for evidence to prove that Fong was intent on selling a worthless anti-aging drug in a multimillion-dollar deal, they had escaped into this warm space only to find that the timed lock wouldn't open for another hour. Ergo, their decision to pass the time in conversation—something their previous sex-and-more-sex relationship hadn't relied heavily on.

Add in Luke's brilliant idea to up the stakes by losing a few articles of clothing—something they desperately needed to do, or risk heatstroke—and, bang! There you had it….

A really awkward situation.

Why had he married her? Of all the things Luke had processed in the eleven months they'd been apart, since she'd miscarried their daughter and he'd taken that fellowship in Europe, that was one question he hadn't answered.

In fact, it was a question he hadn't even asked.

"Because I loved you?"

Her eyes hardened at the uncertainty in his tone. "That's the easy answer, Luke. The sort you used to get away with before. Well, not this time. Try again, or it's not worth even trying this stupid—"

"Okay, okay." He held up a hand and felt a bead of sweat run down his back. God, it was hot. "I'm sorry. You're right." He paused. "But it's hard to think back to that time, you know? I'm not that same person anymore, so it's difficult to remember what I was thinking and feeling back then."

Her eyes softened, and Luke felt a kick of triumph. He chose his next words carefully. "We were finishing grad school and everything was going our way, remember? Post-docs at the same university all lined up, great careers all planned out and things were…wonderful between us." And suddenly he *could* remember what he'd been feeling; that sense of awe that such a smart, beautiful woman wanted *him*, loved *him*. "Not just the sex, but going jogging together and shopping and just…well, just talking."

He trailed off, realizing that they had talked to each other in the beginning. What had happened to that?

Without a word, Kelsey lifted trembling fingers to her damp, flushed throat and unbuttoned her white blouse inch by torturous inch. She drew it off her shoulders to pool on the floor behind her. The simple camisole she wore beneath was a pale peach satin that cast her erect nipples into dusky relief. "Okay. What's your question for me?"

Outside the little room, the digital timer counted down past the hour mark, and as much as Luke wanted to escape and bring Fong to justice—both for the falsified clinical data and for leaving him and Kelsey to freeze to death—he also wanted the clock to slow. He needed more time with Kelsey because something told him that what was said in the warm room would determine the fate of their relationship.

Because of it, he chose his question carefully. "Why did you tell me to take the fellowship in Europe?"

She'd been hospitalized following the late-term miscarriage. Miserable, guilty and unsure how to help her, Luke hadn't been prepared for Kelsey to turn her back on him and tell him to go. Maybe he should have fought harder, insisted on staying, but at the time he'd been hurt by her words.

And in a way, relieved to go.

She tangled her fingers together and stared at the floor. "Seeing you made it worse," she finally answered in a low, reluctant voice. "When you were around, all I could think about was the excitement of being pregnant and all the plans we'd made for our family…." When she turned her eyes up to his, they were dry. It seemed she had been doing some thinking in the past year, as well. "I wanted you to go away. Then I hated you when you went."

He nodded. "Yeah, that's pretty much how I felt, too." He pulled the tails of his shirt out of his waistband and saw her eyes follow his every move. Possessed by the devil, and by the memory of eleven months of lonely, restless nights, he took it slowly, unbuttoning his shirt and shrugging it off. The air burned his chest like fire.

Or maybe that was the touch of Kelsey's eyes after so long. Caught up in a sensual spell of his own making, Luke reminded himself that this wasn't about sex. It was about communicating. About asking the questions that had gone too long unanswered. He swallowed hard. "Your turn."

Kelsey stood, as though sitting cross-legged facing each other was too vulnerable a position. Or maybe because she was as unnerved by the sight of his bare torso as he was to be sitting there half-dressed.

He wore more than he might on a beach amongst strangers, yet here he felt twice as naked.

"Why did…" Her voice faltered and she tried again. "Why did you come back?"

She'd asked him the question before, and he'd told her a half-truth about Dr. Fong. Now he gave her the rest. "I came back for you, Kels. No more, no less. I'd been doing a ton of thinking and I realized I shouldn't have left you when I did, and I shouldn't have left it alone when you didn't answer my letters.

I should've camped out on your doorstep until you talked to me. I should've wooed you all over again." He stood as well, and ran a frustrated hand through his warm, staticky hair. "I should've done whatever it took to get you to talk to me." He blew out a breath. "And now look at us. Trapped in Fong's lab, almost dead of frostbite and now sweating our butts off while we wait for the door to open or Fong to come back— whichever happens first."

He started to pace, but Kelsey blocked him by stepping into his path. Eyes dark, she caught his hand and lifted it to her camisole. "We're both to blame. For all of it."

Blood rushed to his head, to his heart, to places lower down, and he slipped his hands beneath the peach satin. Her skin was smooth and hotter than the steamy air that billowed around them. She lifted her arms and let him ease the camisole over her head and off.

Bare chests only a whisper apart, he stopped. Lust was easy. Talking wasn't. "My turn," he murmured, catching hold of her hands when she would have lifted them to his face. "Why didn't you answer any of my letters?"

"Later," she murmured, and stood on her toes to close the distance between them. When their lips touched, he was lost. He'd spent too many nights remembering this, wishing she was there beside him, catching her scent on the night air and imagining he heard her sigh.

Later, he thought as he sank into the kiss and slid his hands down to cup her lower back and bring her closer. They would talk about it later.

Except there had never been a later for him and Kelsey. There was now or nothing.

The hot, steamy air slicked moisture on both their skins and made it difficult to tell where one of them left off and the other began. It was all warm, wet flesh and throaty sighs as he sampled the soft, sensitive spot behind her ear and heard her breath catch on his name.

The lust was as easy as always—and so much more complicated. He pulled away. "Kelsey—"

"Shh…" Desire made her brown eyes into deep, mysterious pools full of excitement, and maybe resignation. "It's okay. I understand."

And before his tangled tongue could ask what it was she understood and whether she could explain it to him, she had unzipped her jeans to puddle on the warm floor, then moved to do the same for him. Naked together now after so long, Luke was helpless against the fire raging between them.

He caught her by the waist, boosted her up to the edge of the counter, and stepped between her thighs to lose himself in the taste and the feel of Kelsey. His wife. The woman he loved.

When she moved to guide him home, he held back. "Kels, I don't have—"

She silenced him with a kiss. "It's okay."

To Luke, those two words were a promise, a new

beginning. It was okay for them to make love un-protected. They were married. They could try again to start a family.

It was going to be okay.

And then, in an instant it was better than okay, for she drew him inside of her and Luke heard the rush and the roar of blood in his head and the pounding of his heart like a runaway train and over it all, Kelsey's cries as they brought each other home, to the place they'd belonged all along. Together.

Spent, though not drained, Luke pressed his damp, sweaty cheek to hers. Over the noise of the hot-air blowers, he thought he heard a faint beeping outside the room. On the fifth beep, the door clicked.

66   Kelsey pushed at his shoulders and avoided his eyes as she slid off the counter. "Come on, let's get dressed, find some hard evidence to take to the au-thorities and get the hell out of here before Fong thinks to check up on us."

He held out a hand to stop her, to bring her back. "Kelsey."

She shook her head without turning around. "No, Luke. This changes nothing. All it proves is that we're still good in bed." She glanced over and colored slightly. "Or on a lab counter." She finished dressing and tossed his clothes to him. "Let's go."

Damn it. Luke dragged his clothes on while curs-ing his ex-wife in his head. Halfway through button-ing his shirt, he shifted to cursing himself.

When would he learn that sex didn't solve a damn

thing? They'd been talking, communicating for the first time since before she'd gotten pregnant with Dawn, and then...

Then it had all gone to hell in a handbasket, all because he couldn't keep his hands off her. Damn it.

"You coming?" Face impassive, though still tinged with high color, Kelsey stood at the warm room door. She peered through the single window. "Seems deserted. It's near dawn on Saturday, after all. Who would be in the lab?"

They both knew who. Fong.

She popped the lock on the door, but before she could open it, Luke caught her arm. "This isn't over, Kelsey."

Finally she looked up into his eyes, and he saw a poignant blend of old love and new resignation. "Yes, it is, Luke. I'm sorry."

And she was gone, leaving him in the warm room. Alone.

CHAPTER 7

THE AIR IN THE MAIN LAB was a cold slap after the hot, steamy atmosphere of the incubator room. And that was just what Kelsey needed, a cold slap of reality.

She couldn't believe she'd made love with her ex-husband in the warm room. That they'd been trapped in there together by her deranged boss was no excuse. That Luke admitted he'd made a mistake when he'd left her for a fellowship in Europe right after she'd miscarried their daughter was no excuse.

That he was still, hands down, the sexiest man she'd ever met—and the only lover she'd ever taken—was absolutely, positively no excuse.

She had no excuse. It had been a mistake. Period.

"Kelsey, wait!"

She shrugged off his hand, angry with him for coming back and stirring up all the emotions she'd managed to store away over the past eleven months, angry with herself for letting him get to her with that last question he'd asked her.

Why didn't you answer any of my letters?

The honest truth was that she'd answered every

damn one of them. They were in a box in the lowest drawer of her desk, not fifty feet down the next corridor. But she couldn't tell him that. It was her weakness. Her vulnerability.

And she didn't want to be vulnerable to him ever again.

So she squared her shoulders and tried to shake off the sudden surge of melancholy. They would find the evidence they needed to prove that her boss, Dr. Fong, had falsified his clinical trial results. They would use the evidence to foil his plans to sell the bogus anti-aging drug to Pentium Pharmaceuticals. Kelsey's career would be ruined by association, but it was better than the icy death Fong had consigned them to in the lab's cold room.

And once it was over? Luke could go back to his fancy European lab, and Kelsey would go back to…

Well, she'd find something. Maybe she'd adopt a dog. They were less disappointing than husbands, and when they strayed, it wasn't usually across an ocean.

Annoyed more with herself than with Luke now, she jerked her head toward the front of the lab. "Come on, my office is this way."

He followed on her heels, close enough that she could feel his breath on the back of her neck. It made her want to snarl.

They reached the small, neat office and Luke glanced around without any real interest. "We won't find anything here. We both know you didn't falsify the data."

For some reason, his confidence in her sent a warm glow through Kelsey. She immediately squashed it. "True, but I don't know how we could break into Fong's office. If you think the locks on the climate-controlled rooms are extreme, you should see the keypad he has on his door." She sat down at her computer and flicked on the monitor. "However—" she tapped a few keys and brought up the Boston General intranet "—he *is* something of a dinosaur when it comes to computer technology. It's possible that I can access his records from here."

Luke glanced at his watch, then at the sky outside, which was lightening to a slick, oily pink as the sun rose. "Fine. You work the computer and I'll see whether I have any luck with Fong's office lock."

Absurdly relieved she wouldn't have to share air with Luke while she hacked her way into Fong's account, Kelsey called after him, "Don't mess with the keypad, though. Two wrong codes and everything locks down and an alarm rings down at the security desk. Just like with the panic button."

She glanced up at the red button just inside her office door. It made no sense to summon B.K. or Dave, the two overnight security guards on duty. But it was a comfort to know the button was there if she needed it. If *they* needed it.

Them. It had been a long time since she'd thought of herself as part of a "them." Frankly there was no use in getting accustomed to it now. Luke would be gone as soon as his company's toehold on the new drug was assured.

Wouldn't he?

"It doesn't matter. Find the data and get the hell out," she told herself sternly and began to work.

Five minutes later, just as she hit the last key and sent her findings to the printer, Kelsey heard an ungodly crash from out in the hallway.

Luke! Her heart stuttered in her chest and she raced out into the lab lobby, expecting to find him hurt, or worse, especially when a second crash followed the first.

He wasn't in the lobby. He was in Fong's office. The wooden door leaned drunkenly on its hinges. The high-tech keypad was intact, still locked to the doorframe, surrounded by a few inches of splintered wood where Luke had hacked his way around it.

Cautiously, Kelsey stepped inside. "Where'd you find an ax?"

Luke looked up from a filing cabinet and grinned like the boy she'd first met so long ago. "In the fire cabinet above the emergency hose. You said not to mess with the keypad, so…"

She nodded. "Works for me. Let's search the office quickly and get the hell out of here."

"Your wish is my command," he intoned with a small smile, and Kelsey's throat tightened. In the warm room, he'd reminded her that there had been a time that they had talked about everything and nothing, and done so for hours. When had they lost that? Why had she blocked those memories from her mind and convinced herself that he had never shared himself with her?

Maybe, she acknowledged, because blaming him for leaving had been easier than remembering the pain she'd been feeling after Dawn's death. Remembering that he'd gone because she'd told him to go.

What if she had tried to share the pain rather than shutting him out?

"Kels? You okay?"

Shaken from her fugue, Kelsey glanced at Luke and saw little that had changed on the outside. His hair was still a little too long, his eyes still a striking green. He still wore lumberjack plaid shirts tucked into faded jeans. But something about him seemed different.

Or maybe it was something in her?

She nodded. "I'm okay." Maybe. Unwilling to analyze their relationship—or their past—any further, she crouched down beside him. "Have you found anything? Because when I was in his computer network, I found—"

Out in the lobby, the mechanical door clicked open. Luke hissed "Get down!" and shoved her beneath Fong's desk. He stood and moved away slowly. Kelsey could see his bare ankles and loafers in the eight-inch gap between the desk and the floor. Moments later another pair of feet moved into view.

"Hands where I can see them, Dr. Sparks. Nice

and easy. We wouldn't want you hurt, now, would we?"

Kelsey froze as hope rattled through her. It wasn't Fong's voice. It was B.K. from the security desk. She could explain everything to him and he would help them escape before Dr. Fong—

"Don't even think about it!" B.K.'s voice cracked on the words. "Dr. Fong left me his gun just in case you came back. Don't think I'm afraid to use it."

Oh, God. Kelsey's heart stuttered. B.K.?

"Does it even matter to you that Fong's new drug is going to kill people?" Luke asked. Kelsey saw his feet slide a half step back. B.K.'s feet followed.

"I don't know about his research and I don't care," the young guard answered, following Luke another step across the room. "He pays me good money to look after his lab."

"And Kelsey?"

"She'll be fine. He promised." But B.K.'s voice sounded less sure. He took one last step toward Luke.

And he was in range. Kelsey lunged forward beneath the desk and grabbed B.K.'s ankles. Luke leaped in a flying tackle and caught the young guard in the midriff. A shot went wild and the weapon flew out of B.K.'s hand and sailed toward the outer lobby.

Luke's fist hammered into B.K.'s face once. Twice. And the young man went limp. Luke hunched over his fallen enemy, breathing hard. When Kelsey stood and touched a hand to his shoulder, Luke reached up, grabbed her and held on tight. "Damn it," he said. "Just damn it."

"I couldn't agree with you more, Dr. Sparks."

Kelsey whirled toward the familiar voice, barely hearing Luke's curse. Her boss stood in the doorway, holding the gun with practiced, deadly ease.

Luke spat a vicious curse. "Fong."

"It seems that I was too easy on you earlier this evening," the scientist replied calmly, though madness lurked at the back of his eyes. "I should have shot you and been done with it." He shrugged. "Well, no matter. That is an oversight that can be quickly rectified."

He lifted the gun, aimed it directly at Kelsey and fired.

CHAPTER 8

LUKE THREW HIMSELF at Kelsey when Dr. Fong fired. He crashed against her and brought them both down, rolling to cushion the impact and dragging her behind Fong's desk for what pitiful protection it might afford.

The gunshot still echoed in the room, but Luke wasn't hit. Wide-eyed, Kelsey shook her head at Luke's unspoken question. She wasn't hit, either.

"Damn it, let go of me!" Fong's outraged shout brought Luke back around the desk in time to see the young security guard, B.K., struggling with the mad scientist.

Luke had thought he'd knocked the guard out cold. Fong had thought B.K. was on his side. Apparently they'd both been wrong.

"You said you wouldn't hurt Kelsey!" the young guard shouted.

Fong smiled evilly and brought his gun up. "I lied."

Without conscious thought, Luke grabbed the heavy fire ax he'd used to bash in the office door. He leapt out from behind the desk and swung the flat of the blade in a glittering arc that slapped the gun out of Fong's hand. Not waiting to give Fong another opportunity on Kelsey's life, Luke reversed the swing and hit Fong in the temple.

The thud of metal on flesh was sickening. Without a sound, Fong collapsed across the security guard.

B.K. looked up at Luke with young, tortured eyes. "I'm sorry I called him, man. He said he wasn't hurting anyone. He said he'd protect Kelsey."

"We all make mistakes," Luke answered, offering the man a hand up. He tried not to let the words echo in his head, tried not to remember Kelsey's comment when she'd discovered him in the lab the night before.

76

Marrying you was a big mistake.

No, getting married hadn't been Luke's mistake. His mistake had been leaving Kelsey alone rather than staying with her after she'd miscarried their daughter. And since then, he'd made another misjudgment. He'd made love to Kelsey instead of talking their problems through.

He risked a look at her as she emerged from behind the desk. Was that the last mistake, then? Was it really too late for them?

She joined him in the center of the room, and he had to force himself not to reach for her hand. He'd done his best. Now the decision was hers.

B.K. levered himself to his feet, black-eyed and bloodied from Luke's fists. "I'll call the cops." He blinked as the first ray of sunshine glanced through the window. "Hell of a Saturday."

When he had gone to make his call, Luke and Kelsey stared down at Fong's unconscious body. Finally she said, "Should we tie him up or something? It could take a while for the police to show up and I'm not looking forward to another scuffle. Or…" Her face lit with a faint grin. "We could lock him somewhere."

They dragged Fong to the cold room and removed the ladder they'd used to escape their prison. After they dumped him inside and locked the door, Kelsey took pity on her former boss and turned the thermostat to four degrees rather than minus twenty.

"Cold enough to make him uncomfortable," she said, "but not enough to kill him."

And then there didn't seem to be anything left for them to say to each other. Afraid if he stayed any longer he'd break down and beg, Luke turned away. "I'll wait for the cops downstairs, okay?"

He was halfway across the lobby when he heard her call, "Luke?"

He didn't turn back. "Yeah?"

Her pause seemed to last a century. Then finally she exhaled a breath. "Before…you asked me why I never answered your letters."

He willed his heartbeat to continue. "Yes?"

There was a rustle of denim as she turned away. "Come into my office. I have something to show you."

He followed her and watched her pull a fat cardboard box out of the lowest drawer of her desk. "What is this?"

"See for yourself while I go wait for the police," she instructed, and waved him to the desk chair that smelled of her.

Luke sat and opened the box. Pulled the first sheet of folded paper from the file. And began to read a letter dated ten months earlier.

Dear Luke…

KELSEY DEALT with the detectives Peters and Sturgeon who arrived rumpled and hard-faced, having been called from a brutal attack over at the Genetic Research Building. The victim, Genie Watson, was a young researcher Kelsey knew only as brilliant and somewhat shy. The E.R. doctors weren't sure whether she would live.

The brutality was a grim reminder of what could have happened to Kelsey if Luke hadn't been there to save her. She shivered at the thought, and she wondered how many of the letters he had read by now. What he thought of them.

"This is unbelievable," Detective Peters muttered, scrubbing a hand across his handsome face as a pair of uniformed officers wrestled a still-unconscious Fong out of the cold room and carried him to the elevators. "Two attempted murders in the same day and they're not related? That doesn't make sense."

"Sure it does," replied his partner. Detective Sturgeon's cheeks worked as he sucked on a peppermint. "Medical research is big business. Big money. There's no better motive than that."

"True enough." Peters flipped to a fresh page in his notebook. "Let's get a few details from Dr. Sparks—" he flicked a glance at Kelsey and amended "—the other Dr. Sparks, and be on our way."

But Luke wasn't where she'd left him. The box of letters sat atop her desk, neatly closed. The room was empty.

B.K. stuck his head in the door and addressed the detectives. "Luke said he'd come down to the station tomorrow to give you a report. He had something he needed to do."

The detectives grumbled but agreed that would be fine. They asked a few more questions, took copies of the falsified records Kelsey had found in Fong's online database and departed. B.K. escorted them downstairs, still trying to make amends for his lapse in judgment. That left Kelsey upstairs in the ruined lab.

Alone.

Damn. Had the letters been too little, too late? Probably. She should have sent them long ago. It seemed she and Luke had both been guilty of hiding behind old patterns.

Well, no longer. Kelsey gritted her teeth and stared at her reflection in the window. Her hair was a mess, she was wearing yesterday's clothes and she had a hickey that rode low on her collarbone. But she didn't care that she looked a fright.

She was going to get her man, as she should have done months ago.

Angry and invigorated, she punched the elevator button and rode down to the lobby, planning. She had no job and no reputation, so she could follow him to Europe, if necessary.

She would do whatever it took.

She gained the curb and lifted a hand for a cab.

The familiar, beloved voice was a welcome intrusion. "Hey, pretty lady. Want a ride?"

And there he was, astride the sleek black motorcycle they'd ridden so many times together, holding out the turquoise-and-white helmet he'd given her.

"I love you," she said clearly before her nerve could fail her. "I'm sorry I told you to go, and I'm sorry I didn't follow. I'm sorry I didn't mail the letters."

He caught her hand and eased her onto the seat behind him, twisting around so he could tug the helmet over her messy hair. "You kept them. That was enough." He touched his lips to hers, and she absorbed the burn of contact, so much hotter than the warm room had been. "I love you, too. And I'm sorry I left. I'm sorry I didn't come back sooner." His lips tipped up in that old, beloved grin. "So I guess we're both sorry specimens, eh?" He turned back around and revved the bike. "Want to go for a ride?"

Her heart tripped at the question, then settled into

a new, happier rhythm. "Where are we going?" she asked, not caring what he answered. To bed. To Europe. It didn't matter, as long as they were together.

He eased out into the snarled Chinatown traffic and called back over his shoulder. "I was thinking we could go sit by the swan boats and talk."

Kelsey wrapped her arms around his waist and tangled her fingers in the soft, light lumberjack plaid she would always associate with him. "Talk about what?"

He laughed, a young, carefree sound, as he swerved the bike between a pair of double-parked yellow cabs. "About us, of course. About why we should get married again. About where we're going to live and how many children we want. About anchovies and baseball teams and all those things we used to talk about. Do you remember?"

He revved up the bike, and Kelsey felt the surge of the engine between her legs and the warmth of the man in front of her. She tossed her head back as they sped away, and she laughed out loud. "I remember!"

And this time as she traveled the crooked streets of Chinatown there were no eyes following her, no stealthy footsteps in the shadows.

There was only Kelsey. And her protector.

THE END

Coming this July from NEXT™

JENNIFER ARCHER

A novel for those who enjoy the *good things in life...even in meltdown mode!*

Sandwiched

When her teenaged daughter and her eighty-year-old mother both started sneaking out at night, what was a forty-something woman to do?

SANDWICHED by Jennifer Archer

From Jennifer Archer, a humorous tale of the woman in between.

www.TheNextNovel.com

Four new titles available each month wherever Harlequin books are sold.

HNS

If you enjoyed what you just read,
then we've got an offer you can't resist!

Take 2 bestselling
love stories FREE!
Plus get a FREE surprise gift!

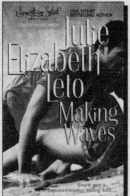

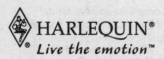

Signature Select™

COMING NEXT MONTH

Signature Select Collection
SMOKESCREEN by Doranna Durgin, Meredith Fletcher
and Vicki Hinze
Three women with remarkable abilities. Three explosive situations
that only they can defuse.... Nothing is what it seems in this
action-packed collection starring three sexy, savvy women who use
their unique abilities to save the day.

Signature Select Saga
SEASON OF SHADOWS by Muriel Jensen
Convinced someone is trying to keep his wife's "accidental"
death quiet, former soldier Jack Keaton arrives in Maple Hill,
Massachusetts, determined to uncover the truth. But local reporter
Kay Florio suspects Jack is in town on a mission of revenge...and
decides to "get close" to the sexy widower to find out!

Signature Select Miniseries
THE GUARDIANS by Kay David
An exciting volume containing two full-length novels from
Kay David's bestselling series, *The Guardians*. Join highly skilled
SWAT team members Beck Winters and Lena McKinney as they
find love while serving and protecting Florida's Emerald Coast!

Signature Select Spotlight
THE GENTLEMAN'S CLUB by Joanna Wayne
A murder in New Orleans's French Quarter has attorney
Rachel Powers obsessed with finding the killer. As she probes
deeper, she is shocked to discover that some of the Big Easy's
most respected gentlemen will go to any lengths to satisfy their
darkest sexual desires. Even murder.